JAN 0 4 2020

D1095967

JAN 0 1 2020

PRAISE FOR SARA WOLF'S
BRING ME THEIR HEARTS

A Goodreads YA Best Book of the Month
An Amazon Best Book of the Month:
Science Fiction & Fantasy

"A zesty treat for YA and new-adult fantasists."
—*Kirkus Reviews*

"Captivating and unique! Sara Wolf has created a world quite
unlike one I've ever read in *Bring Me Their Hearts*. Readers
will fall in love with Zera, the girl with no heart who
somehow has the biggest heart of all."
—**Pintip Dunn, *New York Times* bestselling author**
of the Forget Tomorrow series

"Thrilling, hilarious, addictive, and awesome!
I absolutely loved it!"
—**Sarah Beth Durst, award-winning author**
of The Queens of Renthia series

"Everything I need from a story. A standout
among fantasies!"
—**Wendy Higgins, *New York Times* bestselling**
author of *Sweet Evil*

"Sara Wolf is a fresh voice in YA, and her characters never
fail to make me laugh and think."
—**Rachel Harris, *New York Times* bestselling author**
of *My Super Sweet Sixteenth Century*

"From the start, this book completely stole my heart!
Sara Wolf has woven a mesmerizing tale in
Bring Me Their Hearts that had me glued to each
page, unable to put it down until the end."
**—Brenda Drake, *New York Times* bestselling author
of the Library Jumpers series**

"The battle between good and evil bleeds over the
pages of this exquisite fantasy."
**—Olivia Wildenstein, *USA TODAY* bestselling author
of The Lost Clan series**

"Original, authentic, and enchanting! Sara Wolf creates a
vivid fantasy world like no other. *Bring Me Their Hearts* is a
breath of fresh air in YA fantasy!"
**—D.D. Miers, *USA TODAY* bestselling author
of the Relic Keeper series**

"This was an absolute delightful bucket of sass,
witches, and stabbing."
—PaperFury

"Absolutely blown away by this world, with its
harsh realities and amazing characters."
—Pop Reads Box

SEND ME THEIR SOULS

Also by Sara Wolf

Bring Me Their Hearts Series

Bring Me Their Hearts
Find Me Their Bones
Send Me Their Souls

NYT bestselling Lovely Vicious series

Love Me Never
Forget Me Always
Remember Me Forever

SEND ME THEIR SOULS

NEW YORK TIMES BESTSELLING AUTHOR

SARA WOLF

This book is a work of fiction. Names, characters, places, and incidents are the product of the author's imagination or are used fictitiously. Any resemblance to actual events, locales, or persons, living or dead, is coincidental.

Copyright © 2020 by Sara Wolf. All rights reserved, including the right to reproduce, distribute, or transmit in any form or by any means. For information regarding subsidiary rights, please contact the Publisher.

Entangled Publishing, LLC
10940 S Parker Road
Suite 327
Parker, CO 80134
rights@entangledpublishing.com

Entangled Teen is an imprint of Entangled Publishing, LLC.

Visit our website at www.entangledpublishing.com.

Edited by Stacy Cantor Abrams
Cover illustration and design by Elizabeth Turner Stokes
Interior design by Toni Kerr

ISBN 978-1-68281-507-6
Ebook ISBN 978-1-68281-508-3

Manufactured in the United States of America
First Edition November 2020

10 9 8 7 6 5 4 3 2 1

entangled teen
an imprint of Entangled Publishing LLC

For S. It's been so long, hasn't it? We're here, at last.

Once, there was a tree in the middle of a hilltop graveyard. A traveler passed through, taking shelter from the rain under its branches.
"Have you seen many go?" the traveler asked.
The tree nodded its branches with the wind. "Yes."
The traveler thought for a moment and then, "Have you seen many arrive?"
The tree nodded again. "Yes."
"Well," the traveler surmised. "That's all right, then."

1

THE FALLING TOWER

Prince Lucien d'Malvane looks at me with the steady gaze of a wolf across a meadow. Waiting. Waiting for the others of his pack to join him. For me to join him.

And I look back at him, with six eyes Weeping blood.

His sister, Varia d'Malvane, waits for me, too. They're mirror images of each other—sheaves of midnight hair, skin like the summer sun when it sets. Profiles of marble, of hawk and owl. She stands poised and triumphant while her brother, the only boy I've ever loved, barely stands at all. He pants, haggard. He protected us from the Bone Tree's explosion with all his fledgling magic, with witchfire that melted every bit of snow off this half-demolished mountain peak. He's a witch.

But Varia's one, too.

She's so still, it's as if she isn't breathing. Perhaps she doesn't need to any longer, what with the valkerax-tooth choker around her neck—and all the Bone Tree's power it holds as hers to command.

To her, that choker means power. She'd faked her death, leaving behind her parents and brother. When she returned, she had me train Evlorasin—one of the massive valkerax—to suppress its hunger by Weeping. She bribed, killed, threatened for this moment. For her, that choker means *everything*. It means the culmination of five years of striving. Of blood. Of mercilessness and hope and everything in between. But to me, it looks like little more than a fancy shackle.

Malachite and Fione stare up at the Bone Tree swaying behind the crown princess. It's the only noise that dares to break the air—the rattling of the strung valkerax bones that form its bleached branches, its white roots, and its smooth trunk.

And from behind the tree, they rise.

The massive, twisting pillar of alive things, of bright white gargantuan wyrms in the hundreds, sways beyond the mountain peak Varia stands on. Just behind her, like a throne. A support beam. A terrible spine reaching all the way from the depths of the Dark Below and into the sky.

They're soundless. Or, at least, they're so far away you can't hear anything, not the scratch of scales I'm used to from Evlorasin, not the hungry shrieks and growls I know well. No, these valkerax are completely given over to the song. The hunger. The madness.

They're frothing, screaming, their fanged maws snapping with rage as they scrabble over one another, desperate to obey the Bone Tree's commands. Varia's commands. But on the mountain, we hear nothing. There's only the four of us, only one of us still human, all of us puffing exhausted clouds into the bitterly cold air as we watch the pillar extend. Grow. From raging hundreds to feverish thousands. Curling around one another, making a tower of their bodies through sheer frenzy. Utter silence.

None of us knows what to do, to say, in the face of thousands of starving valkerax clawing for the clouds. It's the sort of silence that echoes, trilling bells of terror in my hollow chest.

Varia has what she wants. But where's my heart? What *I* want?

I can feel it. I can feel her power surging through me like booze poured down a throat on a cold winter's night, like a flame burning up a line of oil and snaking through dry grass. The emptiness in my chest burns with her magic, every inch of void set aflame. It's beyond me. It's beyond anything I've ever felt—and I'm *Weeping*. I'm supposed to be in the center of stillness, untouchable by my witch. By her. But she can touch me. She is, *right now*. Her magic, her influence...it's reaching me. More than that—it's lying on me with its full weight, making it hard to breathe, to move a muscle.

She could.

Those two words echo shrilly in my skull. A static shot of fear runs down my spine, and I realize *she could*. With the sheer brute power of the Bone Tree behind her, she might be able to command me through the Weeping. My one ace, gone.

My one scrap of control, of independence.

Gone.

As always, I'm the first to do the most foolish thing.

"Varia!" I step forward, the mud and slush from the melted snow seeping into my boots. "My heart! Give it to me!"

Every word rings out easily in the empty air. Varia's onyx-shine eyes narrow imperceptibly, her smile eternal. She oozes around the Bone Tree's trunk, sliding her hand along it as she goes. Like she has all the time in the world. Like the world can wait for *her*.

"We *did* have a deal, didn't we?" She laughs softly. "And you've been so very loyal. Which is more than can be said for who you used to be. Or for most."

Her eyes slide over to Fione, who flinches back violently, palms hitting mud to stabilize.

It's selfish; I know it is. Fione's hurt, inside and out, and Malachite's bleeding from the claw wounds on his face. Wounds I gave him. Lucien's exhausted—even now, he struggles to stand, boots squelching hopelessly as he tries to get purchase in the mud. But Varia's fresh. Varia's new. Her face practically glows, her raven hair sleeker and shinier than ever before, as if she's eaten and slept well for a compounded million years. She cares for Fione and Lucien, I know that, but the hard glint in her eyes as she looks between her brother and her lover is new and strange and I don't like it. A wildcat's look. Every instinct in me screams of danger.

She may love them.

But the Bone Tree inside her—around her neck—might not.

The pillar of valkerax doesn't stop moving—a tornado of wyrm flesh climbing ever higher. Why are they going so high up?

"Zera!" Lucien barks suddenly.

Heat. My Weeping senses feel a spot of heat behind me. My head snaps back just in time to see black hair and then an arm lacing around my neck from behind. Casually. Leisurely. Varia holding me, as if she's embracing a friend.

I can't move. Every inch of muscle is suddenly granite in tar. It's her magic. It has to be.

"Zera." Varia's voice is calm, her breath on my ear. "You've done so well."

"Get—" Lucien scrambles in the mud, managing to rise to his knees. "Get away from her!"

Who does he mean? She from me or me from her? I can't turn my head, but I can feel it. I can feel her eyes burning out at him. Malachite gets it first. He always does—faster instincts than me. He moves for Lucien, pulling Fione along by the hand, the two of them sliding in front of the prince. Fione's shaking too badly to hold her crossbow cane up, but Malachite raises his broadsword in front of him, in front of all of them. Defensive, waiting, even as his milk-white fingers tremble around the handle. I've seen him stare down a fully grown valkerax charging at him, but now is when his ruby-red eyes hint fear.

"Give me—" I move my numb lips. "My heart."

"Is that all you want?" Varia asks innocently. "You could have anything, Zera. I'm the most powerful witch in the world now. Those High Witch fools, their eclipseguard, even my father, his entire army, every army on the Mist Continent—no one can stop me. Not anymore. With your Weeping and my power—we could carve the world anew. We could lay the foundation for what no king or empress or council in all of history could: peace. *Real*, lasting peace."

"My...heart..." I grit out.

"Just *think*, Zera," she implores harder. "Think beyond yourself. No war means no more Heartless. No more Heartless like you would have to be made. No one else would suffer as you have. Wouldn't that be worth it? Isn't that what you want—to stop the hunger? What if you could do it for *everyone*, forever? Make it go away once and for all, eternally?"

Forever? For *everyone*?

My eyes unsplit—six points of vision condensing suddenly into two. Pain and anger flood into me, the stillness of the Weeping draining away like a stabbed waterskin. The hunger comes crawling back, too, pulling itself out of the peaceful abyss claw by claw.

you can never be rid of me. you and I—one and the same. never one without the other. we grew you. we shelter you. we make you whole.

"Zera—" Lucien starts, making it to his feet shakily with the help of Malachite's shoulders. "Varia, let her go—"

"I'll give you what no witch has ever truly given you, Zera. A choice," Varia says patiently, stroking a strand of my hair idly. "Come with me now and change the world. Or stay here while I move on, and spend the rest of your unlife screaming into oblivion at the top of this mountain."

She means to leave me. To leave me here, while the radius between us that's required for me to function as a Heartless breaks. A Heartless can't exist outside of their witch's radius. It's only a mile and a half, but thanks to my locket, that length is extended. But she could still go far beyond it. I'd be stuck here forever, screaming soundlessly in mind-bending pain, no consciousness or feelings or senses at all.

"Zera, say her name." Lucien staggers toward us, fingertips going pitch-black as he conjures up magic. "Say her witch name, and I can free you—"

"Why would you want that?" Varia laughs in my ear. "Why would you want her, Lucien? She betrayed you over and over again. She's loyal only to her heart. Even now, she begs for it. A girl like her, selfish to the last, would never be loyal to you."

"Loyalty," Lucien grits out, black eyes searing, "is not a requirement to protect someone."

My chest swells. This is him. That *is* him, in one proud sentence. Selfless. Willing to stand for me, at the end of all things. I feel the thick blood tears on my face cut by something thinner, watery.

Real tears. Human tears.

My mouth moves, but magic surges through me faster than I can think.

"**Don't**," Varia commands, her voice dark. "**Don't speak.**"

The words almost bring me to my knees. Sledgehammers, beating on me over and over, forcing my lips into a single closed seam. It's so powerful I'm dazed, blinking in the bright light of the mountain, the shadow of the valkerax pillar swaying over me.

Us. Him. Lucien. My head *rings*.

My tongue's still, my lips obeying and unmoving. But my teeth—I don't use my teeth to speak, and they care not for the command. I bite until I taste blood, sharp pain.

"Lau—"

"**Don't!**" Varia snarls harder. The sledgehammers turn to boulders, a landslide, to a cascade waterfalling down and pulverizing me to nothing more than bruised lumps of flesh. And in the bloody wake, the creeping fear settles in—if Lucien becomes my witch, it's just another person who will use my heart against me. Another witch commanding me. Chained to another, to be used for his ends, his goals.

My own heart and own memories and own life still beyond my reach.

He reaches his hand out, all his fingers dark with magic now, the effort of standing quaking his knees. But still, he stands. Still, he waits. I look up at his soft face, the shadow of the valkerax swaying over him. Light, dark, light, dark.

"Whatever happens, Zera," he murmurs through cold-ravaged lips, "whatever you choose, I'll always be here for you."

will you? The hunger laughs. *or are you only brave and good now to get what you want, little prince?*

If I become his Heartless, he could command me. He could do anything he wanted to me, and I wouldn't be able to do a thing about it.

he could hurt you.

He could hurt me.

he could use you.

He could use me.

he could destroy you.

He could destroy me.

"Don't be naive." Varia laughs in my ear. "You know best of all that love is worth nothing. No one stays. Look at my brother—he's turned on me. His own flesh and blood he loves so much. Look at Fione—she betrayed me, and we were meant to be married. Love never stays. But power, Zera—power does. Changing the world permanently, enduringly, means more than love ever will."

The Weeping's fading so fast, her magic flooding back in to fill the gaps. Lucien stands there, eyes silk—strong and steady—and waits. Just waits. He looks ready. He looks…at *peace*.

Whatever I choose, he'll be here for me.

The valkerax pillar sways closer over his face, and I look up in dawning horror. Not up. They're not going *up*.

They're going *across*.

The pillar of valkerax bends at the midpoint, falling through the air and toward us, toward the mountain, with screaming velocity. A bridge. It's going to form a bridge—right at Varia's feet. I feel Varia's blazing magic stutter for a split second, a streak of panic in her as it flares out of her control, and she unhands me, her fingers going dark as she tries desperately to rein it back in.

"No!" she snarls up at the falling pillar. "Not yet!"

But the valkerax don't care. They're coming, plummeting to earth like fallen birds, growing bigger and bigger. My Weeping is almost gone, the peaceful void growing smaller and smaller.

It's now or never.

she is safer. The hunger tries one last, desperate, honest attempt. *you know what she'll do to you. but him...you have no idea. unsafe, chaos, a gamble, a danger—*

I've been afraid. I've fought a valkerax, I've lived among a human court who'd love nothing more than to burn me alive. I've fought off the first mercenary from Nightsinger's woods, shaking and clutching my sword. Fear never means nothing—not even when you're immortal. There's always the fear of pain. Without death, the fear of pain is the only thing you have left. The only thing that anchors you to the world, to the cycle of life and death like everyone else. One foot in agony, the other in the never-grave.

Fear means everything.

Fear is all I have.

I've never, in my entire life, been more afraid than the moment the words tumble from my lips.

"Laughing Daughter!"

2

HEARTS
BENEATH SNOW

If there's one thing I've learned in this wide world, it's that time is the rebellious child. Like yours truly. It doesn't act like you want it to, especially in crisis. Short moments feel long, long moments go by quickly, everything fragments and spins and comes in as feelings, scents, sounds when it should just be clear, concise thought.

The moment I say Varia's witch name, the rebellious child tears apart the world.

I know for certain that two things happen: her incredibly dense magic tries to clench down on me one last time and then instantly lets go. Freefall. An iron hand, choking me one second and gone the next. I hear her scream, frantic in a way the crown princess of Cavanos has never once been.

"No, no *no*—Lucien, give her back!" she yells. "She'll be your undoing! I know it! I can protect you from her—"

A tendril of her power shoots through my heart like an arrow, grasping. Searching. I gasp, choking on the feeling, but it's short-lived. Something not-me pushes the tendril out instantly, resistant and insistent and hard in its decision. Final.

Lucien's smirk is nearly too exhausted to exist, but he tries. A tinge of sadness there, almost.

"Even the mighty Bone Tree can't go against the rules, Varia," he says. "You should know that better than I. Much better. You had five years of formal training, after all."

"Lucien!" Varia's snarl turns keening. "Don't do this!"

The falling line of valkerax comes closer and closer, the ground trembling and roars crescendoing. A line of writhing white cuts the high blue sky in two. The impact's going to kill us all. I can see them now, their whiskers and their scales and their eyes—every valkerax with six ghost-white eyes and no pupils, and fear crystallizes into horror as I realize every single one of them is looking right at Varia. No matter which way their body is twisted, no matter *how* twisted or how fast they writhe, every massive wolf-maw head is focused dead on her. Like they're going to eat her whole rather than obey her.

There are so many. So many more than I ever thought.

Time behaves badly again—someone pulls me away by the hand, and even through the clamminess of their skin I know the feel of those fingers, those calluses. Lucien. A flash of white hair as Malachite pulls us both away from Varia, and Fione's broken sob as she raises her crossbow higher. Toward Varia.

The valkerax are close enough for me to smell their collective rotting breath.

Time slows. Impossibly slow, for all of one quick second. I turn my head over my shoulder, my neck bobbing at the force of Malachite's simultaneous yank, but my eyes strain to stay on Varia. A Varia standing alone in a muddy wasteland, looking at us. Betrayal, anger—all the burning emotions on her face melt away to something quieter. Lonelier as we flee from her. From it. White feathers and scales from the valkerax rain down like animal snow.

A lonely princess stands there and stares as the world falls down on her. A single white feather lands delicately in her outstretched palm.

The shadow of the valkerax eclipses her.

Impact.

The first bodies to hit the ground break instantly under the others, flesh and bone and valkerax screams. Blood vaporized by sheer speed explodes out, a fine, hazy red mist hanging in the air for a split second. And then the earth *heaves*, force rippling the mud like waves, and all four of us are flung off our feet like rag dolls.

Someone reaches for me in the air, gripping frantically and curling around me. We hit mud, not hard ground, going skidding for what feels like miles. Malachite to my side, Fione on top of me, Lucien around me, and then the ground gives way, and we fall into nothing. Fione's scream, Malachite's beneather swear, and Lucien's hand around my waist, his golden fingers turning black at the tips, up the knuckle, to the palm.

I know, deep down, that he can't protect me. I'm the immortal one.

It has to be the other way around.

I twist my weightless body in the air, clutching him close, covering his skull, his chest, his abdomen with all of me. The vulnerable parts. If we hit ground, I'll be first. I have to be first.

Bone and blood exploding, like the valkerax.

I have to protect him. I'm his Heartless.

No.

I'm *his*.

The wind whistles cold. Malachite shouts something. And then everything goes dark, the image of Varia standing alone with the white feather in her palm burned like an emblem on the back of my eyelids.

I t's not a dream. Not really. Not the way it's supposed to be, floaty and out of place and certain. There's the smell of blood everywhere. Darkness everywhere. Too real to be a dream but not real enough to be my reality.

I'm looking through someone else's eyes—two eyes, and in my heart there's an unshakable strangeness in seeing through only two. It's supposed to be more than two. Far more. I'm being crushed—no, not me, the person I'm seeing this through. Weight everywhere. We have to escape. A hand in my vision—not mine—reaches out into the weight, gripping, summoning, and a hot blast of fire explodes from their palm.

Light.

Light pierces through the flesh-dangling hole, and we crawl out, inch by inch, until we flop into freedom, the sunlight. The crushing weight moves from our outside to the inside. To our chest, where our heart should be.

A heart.

I can feel it beating. This is definitely not me. A mortal. They look down at their hands, golden hands with midnight fingertips shrinking, the animate darkness retreating to smaller and smaller bits until it's gone entirely. Human nails. Human skin. Half the fingers human, the other half wood.

Varia.

And the *screaming*.

Gods above and below, the *screaming*. Like broken bells, like metal on metal, like things dying and being born and dying all over again, an endless cycle of noise. We can barely hear, barely think. We fight vomit, collapsing to our feet and staring at the mud. Dirty. Unpleasant. Pointless. The world is spinning, and screaming, and sickening.

DESTROY.

The hunger? Here, in her, too? Witches don't have the hunger.

DESTROY.

Not the hunger. Not *my* hunger. This is clear, not tamed by magic or freshly consumed flesh. This will never be tamed, never be lessened. This isn't a hunger.

It's a *wound*.

DESTROY.

It's a command. An imperative. Our head floods with flashes of burning forests, of burning houses, of burning people. Flashes of lightning splitting the earth, of seas demolishing mountains, of broken bones and yellow fat and gray organ sacs spilled, burning wood and stone, rubble. All of it rubble, the flesh-kind and not-flesh-kind. And it never stops. Never pauses. Like a million chain link of memories that aren't mine or even Varia's. Ruin.

This thing in us wants ruin.

But we invited it in, didn't we? We're going to use it, aren't we?

It is *our* tool, not the other way around.

We get to our feet, the snarling and snapping of a thousand valkerax behind us, and we hold close the only thing we have left. A face. A sweet, apple-cheeked face with a mass of mousy curls, standing strong even as the images of death and ruin flash behind it.

We look over at the Bone Tree, no longer swaying in an invisible wind. It's perfectly still. And beside it, faintly and like a ghost, is another tree. One I know but Varia doesn't. One that I can see but Varia might not.

Like a trick of light on water, this tree wavers in the air. It's a mirage made of glass branches, glass roots, glass leaves, moving gently in some unknowable breeze.

The Glass Tree.

TOGETHER AT LAST.

In a stunning turn of events, my body wakes up before my brain does. And my mouth wakes up before the both of them.

"Old God's great hairy shit in a bush—"

"Whoa." A voice, and a hand instantly trying to press me down. "Whoa there, Six-Eyes. Calm down. You're safe."

I blink, and from the offending swathe of bright light carves shadow and color. Deep ruby-red eyes, ears so long and pointed they droop a little, a mouth that always looks slightly entertained. And three new, angry red claw wounds across a nose, ripping the corner of a mouth up. No pain in my body. I'm not hurt. But he is.

"Malachite!" I inhale. "What are you—" The room's strange, too much stone and blue velvet. I'm in a too-soft bed. "Where are we?"

"Some city. We're taking a break after all that horseshit, that's all I know. Hold on." He lifts one finger, rummaging around in his chainmail back pocket and pulling out a hastily scrawled piece of parchment. He clears his throat excessively and reads: "'Zera, I wrote this for you because Malachite likes to twist my words to his liking.'"

"Lucien." I exhale a half laugh, leaning back on my pillows. Malachite trundles on with all the emotion of a carriage wheel.

"'We're in Breych. It's a small Helkyrisian city just on the border.'" Malachite pauses, making his own addendum. "And is full of boring things like *books*. 'Varia's alive,'" he continues. "'I'm sure of it. Fione and I are fine—I've gone to speak with the sage, and she's conferencing with the local polymaths. We'll be back soon with a plan. In the meantime, please rest. Yours, Lucien.'"

"Is he really fine?" I press, zooming my face into the parchment. "Is Fione—"

"Don't ask me how." Malachite grunts as he crumples up the parchment and lobs it smoothly out the thin stone-cut window. "But he managed to cushion our fall with whatever scrap of magic he unbelievably had left. And by some stroke of rune-crusted luck, we ended up hitting one of Breych's many safety nets."

"Safety...nets?"

He sighs. "Knowing you, you won't get it until you see it for yourself."

He stands from the chair at my bedside and heads for the window, and my perfectly healed body follows him, the holes and tears in my clothes funneling cold air onto my skin. It's *so* bitterly cold—far colder than Cavanos ever gets, even in the dead of winter. The beneather motions with one long hand to the window, and I stick my head out.

"*Vachi-godsdamn-ayis.*" I breathe a white-cloud swear.

It's the city of towers I saw on my hike up to the Bone Tree, but real and eye level. It looked so small when I had Varia on my back, like a toy set for a child, and now it's looming all around me, on every side. Towers. Dozens upon dozens of towers, built straight off the stone of three mountain ridges, stately and yet placed in chaotic, half-baked rows. Some towers are grand and huge, with gargoyles carved in bone-moth likenesses and steeples of gold and lapis lazuli, while others barely look sturdy at all, their wooden supports rickety and their stone sills sagging with thick beards of moss, the roofs gabled simply in green and purple tile. Between the three close ridges runs a dizzying spate of rope bridges back and forth, some wide, some thin, but all of them connecting the towers. Sunset peeks out from between two towers, catching the diamond glass of their roofs.

And between the ridges? Between the towers? Nothing at all. Darkness. Hundreds of miles of drop, an abyss, yawning all around the city. I squint—not quite right. Threaded over the shadows of the crevasse I can see tawny strands. Woven. *Purposefully.* Huge beams of wood jut out from beneath the towers every which way, planted all along the stone ridges and supporting an intricate web of nets that spans the whole city, like a last halo of salvation, as if a massive spider's carefully woven a web around it. The wind whistles viciously, and I pull my head back in to avoid the shards of ice.

"The people here felt the explosion," Malachite says. "And the quake from the falling valkerax."

"Were any of them hurt?" I blurt.

He sighs. "Do you two have to do that?"

"Do what?" I blink.

"Ask the same question right in the exact same spot. You're either the same person or meant for each other."

He means Lucien. Heat tries to tickle my cheeks, but I won't let it.

"No one in Breych got hurt," he finishes wearily.

"Fantastic. How long have I been out?"

"Seven halves."

"Good!" I throw my hands up. "Not enough time to miss anything important. Where can I get clothes?"

"Here." Malachite walks over to a dresser, throwing me a drab-yet-functional mustard dress and a heavy black wolf-fur covering.

"Ugh." I wince. "The *colors*."

"Bright, clashing shit seems to be the order of the day around here." He opens his own leather covering to reveal a pink tunic with a mess of magenta ruffles. We both burst out laughing, the sound quickly swallowed up by the dour stone. The silence isn't oppressive, but it's there, echoing shards of reality back at us. A reality that's changed so quickly, so brutally.

Varia's gone. She has the Bone Tree. The valkerax.

I'm Lucien's Heartless.

Fione is...

Malachite and I—

"I hurt you," I say, reaching out to touch the edge of his face. Not the ointment-smeared wounds that must be agony but the skin still whole.

His red eyes soften, and his smirk crooks high. "You *wish* you managed to hurt me."

"Mal—"

"It's over, Zera." He cuts me off. Not hard. Easily. Gently. "You made your choice. And for once, I happen to agree with it."

I step behind the wooden divider, pulling the rags of my clothes over my head. It's not all forgiveness from Malachite. It can't be. His wounds are too fresh for that. My betrayal up until that moment on the mountain peak is too fresh for that. It's not forgiveness, but it's the start of it. Better than nothing. Kinder than nothing. He's so *kind* to me, even after everything.

I'm going to cry. I'm going to cry behind this godsdamned ugly divider. Ugh, no. I'm not. He wouldn't want that. I know that.

I know him.

I'm so glad I know him.

Quiet at last. A moment, behind the ugly divider, where I can be alone after everything. Well, not all alone.

never alone.

The hunger is so faint, I have to strain to hear it. That's a first. And possibly a last. Lucien's trying hard to suppress it with his magic. Devoting way too much to it, probably, more than Nightsinger and Varia ever did. It doesn't feel sustainable.

Me as his Heartless. Him as my witch. Is *that* sustainable? Is it even *right*?

What do we do after losing everything? We lost. Varia has the Bone Tree. We *lost*. I wasn't supposed to lose, but I did. I was supposed to get my heart, and now...

Now I have my friends again.

And maybe, some small part of me whispers, *that's a fair trade.*

"Well." I step out in the mustard dress and try the coyest of smiles. "I suppose we should consider ourselves lucky to still be alive to complain at all."

"Yeah." Malachite's mouth twitches as he offers his arm and a dripping noble accent. "My clashing lady? Shall we venture out into the city and hunt our lovable quarry down?"

"Verily," I agree, taking his arm with a terribly overacted haughtiness.

...

My room is a tower room, I learn, about as quickly as it takes me to descend the seemingly endless spiral staircase. But it's not the only room by far—this entire tower is an inn of some sort, with numbered doors all along the descent and a main room at the bottom serving drinks at a small wooden bar. The farther we go down, the colder it gets. Malachite opens the door and icicles ooze off the doorway, cracking and sliding soundlessly into the banks of snow below like blades into scabbards.

"It's even colder outside!" I whine. "How do people live like this?"

"Warmly," he drawls, motioning around at the rope bridges nearby, a throng of people walking back and forth about their daily business in heavy, eye-searingly colored wool. The beneather leads me over one bridge, then another, and I'm surprised at how sturdy the structures are compared to how fragile they looked from far up. No slots open in the lacquered slats, and not a single sway in the bridge, not even when it's full to bursting with momentum and wind.

Every step I take over a bridge slat is another step of worry. Of fear.

What do we even *do* now? Varia is the most powerful witch in the world, isn't she? And then there's us—my thief instincts muse over survival first, always. A beneather, a very smart girl with a crossbow aim, a witch, and a single Heartless. I know we have our strengths. But realism bites down on me hard—we have strengths, but none strong enough to face the Bone Tree power I felt in Varia.

She touched me even through my Weeping. Weeping, my last safety. A safety that's supposed to be *impenetrable*.

I'm so lost in thought, Malachite has to suddenly jerk me to one side to avoid a townsperson. "Hey, you feelin' all right?" He peers into my face.

"Y-Yeah." I smile. "I'm fine. Let's keep going."

The air is so crisp and thin up here, I feel dizzy and frozen on the inside all at once. The only sources of warmth are the occasional cracked-open tower doors as we pass, roaring hearths inside. Tower chimneys puff banners of velvet smoke up into the sky, rivaled in motion only by the multitude of spinning brass crosses on the roofs.

"Weather vanes," Malachite says, pointing to one fashioned in the shape of a spinning valkerax. "For wind speed, direction. That sort of thing. Apparently they predict future temperatures, too."

"How?" I marvel.

He shrugs and says simply, "Polymaths. Helkyris is crowded with them."

"Hard to pick them out," I muse. "When I'm so used to them wearing those hideous brown robes."

"Didn't you wear one once?"

"And I hated every minute of it." I smirk up at him. It's true, though—unlike Cavanos, the polymaths in Breych don't adhere to a strict dress code. Or any dress code at all. I can't see a single brown thing—just color after woolen color, like flowers crowded together or overexcited butterflies.

"I think I get it," I say finally as we cross a far wider bridge, this one carved with wolf heads on either end.

"Took you that long, hmm?" Malachite drawls.

"It's all rock and snow here." I ignore him. "Gray, white, gray, and more white. What else do you do when you're living in a monochromatic world, other than dress up to the explosively hued nines?"

Malachite smirks and I go quiet, watching my boots cross the bridge, the wind whipping my hair around my neck. I put one hand on my chest. It's so strange—I was so convinced a day ago that, if I walked up that mountain, I'd come back down human. Remembering. Whole. But my chest is still empty. Life hasn't worked out the way I planned for, schemed for, sacrificed for.

Betrayed for.

Lucien's my witch. My heart is missing still, but it's never been fuller. I've never felt it more than this moment, swelling with something I can't even name. Pride? Relief? Fear. All of it mixed together in a murky whirlpool, and me holding on to whatever pieces of the shipwreck that float by. Right now, it's the idea of seeing Lucien again. My feet get quicker, my thoughts slower.

He's my witch.

There's a contract between us, magical and invisible, and I might still not know all the rules. I know more of them now, to be sure—more than I did three years ago when I first became Heartless. But not all of them. I don't want to have to know all of them. I'm happy to be alive, that we're all alive, but a nagging worm gnaws at the base of my skull—I should have my heart back. I'm meant to be human.

I want to be human.

With Varia, I wanted to be human.

What do I want now? With Lucien? With myself? A witch who cares about me is still a witch, and—historically—they haven't been all that generous with me.

I try to smile at a little girl passing with her father, her wool covering dyed bright orange and pink. She just stares and stares. But not at me.

"They've never seen a beneather before." Malachite answers my unasked question.

"Can't imagine many beneathers make the journey from the deepest depths to the highest peaks very often," I tease.

He smirks back. "I'm the special-est of cases."

The cold bites at us, propelling us forward. It's supposed to be summer, for Old God's sake! It's incredible what the people of

Helkyris have done with such a small space—barely any ground to walk on, and they've built an entire *city*! Terraces are their ingenious solution, carved into the sides of the three ridges to make more space for people to sit on stone benches, to take in the view of all-green Cavanos from low iron fencing, to linger around market stalls propped up here and there selling hot spice drinks and warm baked treats. It's a city of levels, of steps, and by the time Malachite leads me to a massive dominating tower of quartz-flecked brick, I'm puffing my lungs out.

"This is the sage tower," he says. "One for each Helkyrisian city. Center of local politics and social news. Fills the same sort of role a New God's temple does for Cavanos villages."

I stare at him. "Did you get smart while I was knocked out?"

"No." He laughs. "Lucien. His whole prince-encyclopedia-brain thing."

"Ah." I open the heavy wooden door for him, and he ducks inside. This tower is cavernous, open, lined with benches and tables and the staircase tucked neatly in a corner, spiraling up into an endless column of misty, incense-choked air. The tower's so high, you can barely see the roof, the top of it, darkness all the way up until a pinprick of glass lets light in. The walls are lined with doors, with alcoves of packed bookshelves built into the stone. I'm used to oil lamps, expecting them, but instead there are white mercury lamps.

Or what I *think* are mercury lamps. These are burning far too brightly and too purely to be the ones I've seen in Cavanos. Just one or two are needed to light an entire area. It's possible the polymaths here perfected them—possible and absolutely jaw-dropping. If Cavanos had this sort of technology, it wouldn't need all the white mercury it ships in from Avel and goes through like water.

"This way." Malachite points at a far room. Our footsteps echo on the cold stone floor until we reach the door, and he knocks in that pattern he always does for Lucien. Three raps, then two.

"Come in."

At the sound of Lucien's voice, all the little hairs on my arms stand up and start to burn. My witch. My prince. *Mine?* No. My witch, but not my prince. The people's prince. He's only ever belonged to his people.

My unheart spasms with the realization he's lost his sister. Again. This time to power, not faked death. This time she chose to leave instead of being driven out. He must be devastated.

Malachite pushes the door open, and the smell of cinnamon and clove bulls us down. Rich tapestries frame a round meeting table at which stands a half-bent elderly walnut of a man dressed head to toe in emerald green and gold, and Lucien, dressed in light blue and the softest smile when he sees me.

"Zera."

He makes a polite half bow, excusing himself to the old sage man, and walks over.

It's just one word. It shouldn't make me so happy. It should take more than just one. It should take books, endless epic poems, a bard's monologue to make me feel this hot, this strong, this quickly. It's not fair. It's not fair he can do this to me.

it's not fair we're still the monster.

The room is dim, but my eyes catch every fold of cloth on him, every freckle, every inch he crosses in his boots to reach me. My witch. Their prince. His eyes—I'm so used to seeing his eyes as hard onyx shards. Betrayed onyx shards. Bitter onyx shards. But now, *right now*, they're spills of ink. Liquid, gentle, reflecting the scarce light of the room and my own nerves back at me.

He stops right before the danger. Right at the border of my space and his. He knows. He can sense it, just like I can—the two white-hot rings that radiate out from us, pressing, waiting, watching each other's every move.

"Are you feeling all right?" he asks. "You were out for so long—"

"Fine." I smile, tense. "Perfectly fine, Your Highness."

"You—" Lucien's eyes flicker. "That's—you don't have to call me that anymore."

"You insisted."

"And now I insist on taking it back."

There's a buzz that starts in my veins, and I can't tell if it's the smell of his skin I know so well by now or his magic that keeps me alive.

the only thing that keeps us alive. he's our one tether to life; he holds our life in the palm of his—

A bag. It's shoved at me so quickly, I don't understand what it is until I see the stitching. Haphazard, poor needlework in fine gold thread that reads: Heart.

It's so close and tantalizing, it almost distracts me from my first thought: *a bit unoriginal, isn't he?* Varia, at least, wrote Traitor on mine. But his is just a label for what's inside. Plain. Simple. Maybe that suits him. Maybe he's the sort of witch who values simplicity.

"Here." Lucien holds my heart out to me, the bag faintly beating, faintly lumpy.

My brain throbs. Echoes no one else can hear emanate from the heart bag—echoes of memory, like imprints of a body in the snow I can't remember the face of. Who was here? Someone. My parents, maybe. My past, certainly. I can almost hear words, laughter, the smell of cinnamon.

I don't dare to dream. To believe. I want to—I want more than anything to believe he's the sort of person, the sort of witch, to give me my heart back instantly. But I've met too many witches to fall for it again.

"You're letting me hold it?" I tease. "Awfully nice of you."

"It's yours," the prince insists. Iron shavings eke their way into his ink eyes, hard and sleek. "If you want it."

It's too good to be true. He's too good to be true. Nobody

moves in the room—not the old sage man, not Malachite, not Lucien, not the thousand-year-old stones of the walls. So I decide to, walking a slow perimeter of the round table and running my fingers along its surface.

"Hmm." I hum idly. "Are you sure? I'm very useful, you know. Immortal at all times, unaging at all times. I can't promise I'll be quiet or polite at all times, but I can give it a good try."

I near the old sage man, all his creases and crinkles watching me.

"Heartless?" he asks, his voice low and croaky with pipe smoke.

"Just one of many." I smile at him and curtsy. "Pleasure."

"You've been through enough—" Lucien doesn't let me get away. He strides after me, rounding the table and cutting off my circuit. "For this damnable thing. I'll put it back right now."

I see his fingertips blacken, golden twilight turning to deep night.

It's here. Finally, after so long. He's going to—

if you lose us, how will you protect him?

My eager thoughts snap-freeze.

without us, you have only your sword. we keep you from true death. If you lose us, you are weaker. weak enough someone may kill him before your very eyes.

Weakness. I've felt weak for so long, for three years, but feelings are rarely reality. The witchfire in Vetris where he almost died, the night of the Hunt where he was very nearly murdered by Archduke Gavik. If I wasn't immortal—I couldn't have helped him. He would have *died*. And now, with Varia on the loose, leading a thousand-thousand valkerax into battle against the world—death is never far off. For anyone. Him most of all.

if you lose us, you might lose him.

I know he'll try to stop her; I can see it in his eyes. I saw it the moment I walked in—sadness, yes, but tempered by a horrifically strong will. He has a plan.

If I'm human, I can't protect him.

you could run. take it and run.

I could.

you won't.

I won't. Not anymore.

Not when I've found him again.

He holds out the bag so innocently, so convinced of his own conviction. Of course I want it. I betrayed him for it. I lied for it. I sided with Varia for it. His fingers deepen with night, determined to give me what he thinks is what I want.

What I thought I wanted.

I know better now. Varia taught me better. Wherever she is, I'm faintly thankful to her for the trials, the errors, the pain. The realization.

"It's never been my heart," I say.

The darkness on his fingers stops growing, his face going still, and his black eyes confused. "What do you mean?"

I laugh and round the table past him, coming back to where I started next to Malachite. "It was never my heart I wanted. What I wanted, always, was to feel human again."

"Then..." He starts forward. "Here."

"It took me a while to learn. It's a hard thing to learn."

"Zera, please, just—"

"That little beating thing in your hand, Your Highness," I interrupt him, "doesn't make someone human. It makes their chest a little heavier, their body a little louder. It gives them a drumbeat to march to, a compass to navigate by when the sun goes down. But it's not the thing that makes one human."

His fist holding my heart wilts, his brows knitting. "Then... what does?"

My smile breaks in two. I know what I have to do now. No— I've always known, since that night at the Hunt, when my body reacted before I did. Something in me has always known.

"What makes us human is a feeling," I start. "A feeling I get when I'm with you."

Lucien's eyes widen and then catch fire.

"If," the old sage man croaks, "I may interject."

Grateful for the spotlight off me, wanting Lucien's burning eyes off me, I wave my hand at him. "Please."

"There are a great many polymaths here in Breych. They study night and day the secrets of life, of nature, of the sky and the void beyond it."

"And?" Lucien impatiently leads. Our proper prince, interrupting his elders? Since when?

"Recently, a very interesting theory has been put forth by Miralin's sect, hypothesizing that some kind of energy is given off upon death. Mercurial energy, kinetic energy, heat energy— they aren't quite sure what it is. But it seems to be there, for all species, across all ages. Perhaps—" He pauses, looking up at me. "Perhaps this is what you would call the 'soul.' Perhaps that is what makes us human. No..." He glances at Malachite thoughtfully and corrects himself. "Perhaps this is what makes us exist, here, in this moment on Arathess, feeling and thinking both sweet and terrible things."

For a moment, nobody speaks. It's a big thing, too big to shoulder. We share it all, in this room, the weight of it near-crushing on its own and only manageable together in silence. Until Malachite gives off a snort—the pleased kind. Lucien won't stop staring at me. And I at him.

"Forgive me." The sage taps his cane on the ground. "In my old age, I've become the rambling sort. Let us adjourn the meeting for now, Your Highness. We can resume in the morning when you've had rest."

"Thank you, sir," Lucien says, never once looking away from my face. "Until then, the way guide you."

"And you as well." The old sage nods with a wry grin.

Time behaves badly, again and again. Lucien's steps over to me are so slow, so stretched out, and then the heat of his hand on mine is fast and all at once, and I'm walking, no—*running*, both of us running out the door and the tower's main room and past the snow and ice and onto an empty bridge where no one walks, no one looks, and then warmth, all of it. Warmth blazing against the freezing cold, on one side of my face, around my waist, against my chest and lips.

Him. A kiss, a clasp, fire burning in my mouth and in my stomach and in my face and he's *everywhere* and *I want* him to be *everywhere*. The hunger evaporates in the heat, there one moment and gone the next, not even ash left.

Ah, some faint part of my disconnected brain thinks, *so a kiss can be like this. Not like the world ending. But like the world beginning, too.*

It has to end. Everything has to end sometime, and time stops behaving badly when I least want it to—cold air lashing my skin as we pull apart.

"Every day." He cups my face in his hands, his gloves doing nothing to stop the warmth radiating from his palms. "Every day you weren't at my side dragged on like slow torture."

"I'm sorry." I laugh. "It was my duty, wasn't it? To keep you entertained. And I vanished on you."

"This is not entertainment—" His lips meet mine, mumble half buried in my skin. "This is a promise. You and I, for as long as Arathess exists with us on it. And after that. And after *that*."

It's silly. It's sweet. Can I have this? Do I deserve this? Maybe. Maybe not.

Maybe what I deserve is not for me to decide.

I can't even think about the past. It's blown away, like strong wind over dandelions. Every mistake, every hurt, every betrayal, everything we did to each other in Vetris, said to each other—

these kisses heal it all shut. Heal it all closed. They will scar—of course they will. But they've stopped bleeding.

And I'm so deliriously *glad* to stop bleeding.

My laugh this time is water, running unsteadily and recklessly. "I'll have you know, eternity is unbearable."

He leans his forehead on mine, our breath mixing white in the freezing air and his dark eyes gleaming with sun. "But with me?"

"But with *you*, Lucien d'Malvane." I kiss his proud nose, making a pressed line down to his lips. "Far less so."

3

THE HARDEST PROMISE

Love is, of course, a tad bit different for me than it is for everyone else.

Lucien is still very much my witch. But it's hard to remember that when we spend the rest of the afternoon wandering Breych's hundred bridges, taking in every angle of the view, and talking about nothing at all—jokes about the nobles back home, about my time in the woods, his childhood memories. He says Fione's all right, as all right as anyone can be after losing their loved one. Varia threatens at the surface of it all, his parents and his people, too. But he pulls it back—for me or for himself, I can't tell.

The hours soar by on easy wings made of his smile and his laugh. We make it easy on each other, because we both know: after this walk, after this time together, the real battle begins.

The one to stop his sister.

The one to, maybe, save the world from her. And her from herself.

But where do we even begin? Who even has the answers for us?

Sunset marks the end. Malachite finally comes to fetch us, but knowing him, he was watching all along. Politely, of course, he insists. With his back turned every time we decided to touch mouths. Lucien is fifteen different shades of red, helpless against the onslaught of Malachite and me teasing him together.

"You had no right to watch, Mal," Lucien insists.

"Luc, I spent nine years watching you be *boring*. The least you could do is let me watch when you decide to be *interesting*."

"You can't lurk forever." I slap Malachite's shoulder playfully.

"Watch me," he shoots back. "Just kidding. You can't. Because I'm very good at hiding."

"You're going to get very good at jail shortly," Lucien mutters.

"Throw me in if you have to." Malachite sighs. "But know I can expertly digest most forms of substratum stone."

"Sky jail," Lucien adds. "Where you can't eat your way out."

"Well," Malachite faux huffs. "*That* seems a little excessive."

My laugh scares nightdoves off a nearby tower, all of them flooding into the sky on indigo wings, their white breasts flashing in the first starlight. A real laugh. *Gods*, how long has it been since I laughed without a weight on my chest? Years, it feels like.

Dinner is, of course, also a tad bit different for me than it is for everyone else.

My plate on the long oakwood table of the old sage's house-tower dining room is piled high with the fattiest livers I've ever seen, garnished with a gooey pool of grapefruit-red pig blood. Everyone else has perfectly seared pheasant with gleaming sugar-roasted yams and vivid green wyrmfruit compote. Absolutely *grotesque*.

Helkyris and Cavanos share few things, but one of them is the stuffy meal seating tradition. Lucien sits at the first right, as is custom for the highest-ranking guest, and Malachite tries to lean on the wall, but the sage won't have any of it, guiding him to sit next to Lucien and offering him a beneather spirit of some sort. I smirk and take a seat across from the prince, but one seat down. The chair next to mine is Fione's. The old sage finally sits at the head of the table. Y'shennria's teachings whisper I'm supposed to refer to him as "Elder." And here I thought her lessons on Helkyrisian titles were utterly pointless. I'll have to apologize, next I see her.

if we ever see her alive again.

I put my napkin in my lap. No ifs. Only whens.

Fione is the last to join us, nose and apple-cheeks red from the cold as she rushes in, shaking snow off her velvet covering and her mouse-colored curls. Her eyes catch mine, and for a second it's hard to breathe. The pain on her face is so raw. It bleeds out from the corners of her pursed lips, her cornflower-blue eyes. Eyes that should be happy. Smiling. Not weary, and certainly not dusted with the thick, dull fallout of loss.

She looks away first. I stand up quickly and intercept her cane as she hands it over to the guard.

"I've been awful lately." I smile, setting the cane gingerly against the wall. She bites down on a wince, keeping her neck Duchess-Himintell-long.

"You're here now," she says woodenly. "That's all that matters."

"Please, ladies." The sage motions to our chairs. "Sit and partake. You must be starving."

"Some of us more than others." Malachite nods to me. I'd make a playfully rude gesture, but I have the sneaking suspicion that it might send the ancient sage into heart failure, so I settle on a winsome smile instead. But it doesn't last long, Fione's human scent pulling me back. Lilacs and skin.

I pivot and gulp down whatever's left of my reservation.

"I'm sorry—"

"You didn't make her choose the Bone Tree." She cuts me off smoothly.

"Fione—"

"It's not like you could've chosen otherwise. You were her Heartless. Lucien's explained to me how that all works."

"Fione, let me apologize properly. Please?"

Her eyes rivet to the floor, and the dining room goes silent, the sputter of white mercury lamps and distant clang of the kitchen the only sounds. I reach slowly, oh so slowly, for her hand—her small, elegant hand with all her perfect fingers. Fingers that made her crossbow cane, that made the jeweled dagger of her and Varia's relationship into a white-mercury bladed thing, capable of giving me back the ability to Weep.

She sacrificed that dagger, their dagger, for me.

Her skin is so cold, frail as porcelain, and there's a heartbeat where I think she's going to pull away, but she doesn't.

"I'm so sorry," I whisper. "For everything. For not trusting you. For turning my back on you and giving her the Tree. You deserve a better friend."

I squeeze softly, trying to work some warmth back into her. She has every right to be blazingly furious. To walk away, right now, and ignore me like I don't exist. I didn't make Varia choose the Bone Tree over her, but I'm the whole reason Varia found it. The whole reason she left Fione and Lucien all over again.

"And you." Her voice comes out small, eyes on the floor, catching with the sparkle of tears. "You deserve to be free. Like everyone else."

I can't stop my own tears at the sight of hers. At her words that mean more than she'll ever know.

"I am." I laugh, moving to wipe her face for her. "Thanks to you."

"I didn't do anyth—"

"You made a white mercury blade. You made me Weep when I thought it was impossible. You're brilliant. You did what your uncle, what every single pus-headed polymath in Vetris couldn't do. *For decades.* You're incredible, Fione. You're the smartest person I know. And with your brain, and my balls, we're going to find her." I clasp both her hands in mine, trying to peer into her eyes. "Do you hear me? We're going to find her, and stop her, and bring her home. To you. I promise you."

She finally, *finally* looks up, eyes streaming. "Alive?"

I catch Lucien's stare, and Malachite just looks away. Neither of them knows. We don't even know *how* to stop her. We don't even have a plan yet. Or, at least, I don't. But I know the easiest way would be death. It's an unwritten rule, hanging in the air like a low white crow.

I look back at Fione. "Death stops someone forever," I say. "It's the simple way. The easy way."

Fione's eyes crack at the edges, the light dimming from them as she looks at the floor again.

"But you know me," I chirp. "I've never taken the easy way in my entire unlife. And I'm not about to start now."

Her head snaps up, pure, unfiltered hope blazing out of her gaze. Malachite leans back in his chair with a little smirk. Even the old sage looks faintly pleased. But Lucien's face doesn't change at all. Stony. Unconvinced.

Is he ready to kill Varia?

No.

I know firsthand no one's ever ready to kill—their own sister least of all.

Fione's expression is flush with hope. Hard with it. Making it armor when it doesn't need to be—or maybe it has to be. Maybe that's the only way she can hold on to it—not as a blade but as a shield. Her body's still, calculating. Always calculating with that immaculate mind of hers—to believe in me, in what I'm saying, or not? To believe in the more logical thing, the more likely thing—Varia's death, or to take an impossible gamble on believing in her life? A happy ending, even when the world inside her bleeds misery?

"I know promises aren't possible to keep for some people." I hold her gaze, steady. "But I'm not some people. I promise you,

Fione; I'll bring her back. Alive."

Fione's smile breaks her rigor, and before I know it, her arms are pressed around my waist, squeezing tight.

A hug.

From her, to a Heartless she was so afraid of.

"Thank you," she murmurs into my shoulder. "Thank you, Zera."

We part with shy smiles, and the two of us slide into our seats at the table, and dinner begins. I try to ignore Lucien's stony gaze as I cut pieces of the fatty pig livers off and eat—*slowly, behind your napkin,* Y'shennria's voice in my head insists. *And make sure you wipe the blood off your chin, for Old God's sake.* The sage asks me polite questions about Heartlessness, and it's strange to have someone asking these out of curiosity, not malice. Not suspicion or hatred. It almost makes me feel sort of...*accepted.* Or at the very least less *chased out of town with fire and sharp stones.*

Fione chimes in with her own observations. "It's remarkable the range-extending magic on your necklace has lasted this long," she says. "Most powerful relics like that are functional for only a few weeks, at most."

"Yes, well." I smile at her. "I'm *special.* And so is my jewelry."

My eyes flicker to Lucien, ready to play, and for a split second, his granite expression fractures, twin tugs at the corners of his broad lips. All right, so. It's not a whole smile. Not anywhere near as beautiful as the ones he was giving me during our walk this afternoon. But we'll get there eventually.

"There's no need to worry over the necklace." The prince stares at me. "She and I won't be parted again."

"You never know!" I tease him. "The gods might have something to say about that."

"The gods"—Lucien lifts his chin, onyx eyes catching light—"will have to wait their turn."

Suddenly, holding his gaze is like trying to hold on to water, to quicksand, to an ember cupped in my hands. I can't. I look anywhere but him, my face hotter than the fire in the hearth. Fione slyly pokes at her greens, and Malachite's smirk is so blatantly *knowing*, I get the overwhelming urge to fight him. Politely. With many knuckles.

It feels surreal to be able to sit down and eat a dinner at all. With friends. *Friends.* I thought I'd lost them forever. But nothing's lost forever, is it? That's not the nature of nature — absolutes aren't true or real. Absolutes are human inventions, because the tide isn't always high. The moons aren't always full. The grass isn't always green, and the sky isn't always blue. Even the sun isn't always in the sky. *Feelings don't change easily*, Lucien said once.

"But that doesn't mean they don't change at all," I whisper into my wine. A month ago, I wouldn't have dreamed of this moment, warm and content and laughing over food. I'd given them up in my mind; Fione and Malachite and Lucien most of all. I almost start to cry again, happily.

uselessly.

I swallow more liver to shut the hunger up. But, however faint and however irritating, it has a point. This isn't the time for tears. Not for me, anyway. There's work to be done.

I open my mouth to say something about Varia, asking the table to start formulating a plan for her, for our next move. But I catch Fione's smile as she talks and Lucien's scoff. Not tonight. Tonight, for one night, they should rest. I've been fighting the hunger, fighting for my heart for so long, that I almost forgot about rest, about the concept of it. Everyone needs a moment to breathe. Tonight's for mourning, for recuperating, before the fight begins all over again.

I rake my eyes over Lucien's face.

I could do with a rest, maybe. Just for one night.

After spiced cake and aged tea, the old sage offers us his

assistance tomorrow, and we agree to meet in the morning at his tower.

"To make plans," Lucien asserts, half of his words hanging unsaid. *To fight Varia.*

We walk back through the night and to the inn together, the Blue Giant above swollen and full with azure moonlight. It shades the pure banks of snow on the ridge a deep blue, everything radiating melancholy and a faint feeling of being underwater. Fione hurries into the inn first, Malachite lingering in the door.

"You two comin'?" he asks. Lucien looks over to me, and me up to him. It's the sort of look full of knowing, sore and heavy with it, and it makes my unheart curl at the edges like burning parchment.

"In a bit," Lucien assures him. Malachite makes a shrug.

"A walk it is. I'll get my sword, then."

"You won't be following," Lucien continues. Malachite pivots back with a quirked brow, the open doorway spilling fire heat and the smell of mulled mead.

"Oh?"

"Malachite, dearest." I reach up and softly yank on his long ear tip. "Don't make me duel you to get some peace and quiet."

"You already did." He motions at the three distinct scratches on his face. "And I'd say you won."

Guilt needles through my chest, but the beneather takes my falling hand in his long-fingered one. His skin is cooler—much cooler than a human's.

"You could ask Lucien to heal those," I say. "With magic."

"I'd do it, too." Lucien nods. "Or at least I'd try."

"S'not the beneather way." Malachite shrugs. "In the time it takes to heal a wound, you're supposed to train to defeat whoever gave it to you."

"Which means?" I ask.

He squeezes my fingers. "You and I *will* have to duel. A lot.

Whenever's best for your busy schedule, of course." His words are an easy joke, but his ruby eyes are the most serious I've ever seen them, almost clear violet in the blue moonlight. "It's not just me anymore, you know."

"What?" I blink.

"Caring about Lucien. We're in this together now. Right?"

He's asking if I'm staying. If I plan to stay, after every time I've run, shrugged Lucien off. He's asking if my feelings are true. If I'm not just a Heartless of Lucien's, obligated to protect him. He's asking if I'll leave again or if I'm here to stay. Forever.

The prince stares above our heads, leaving me to make my own decision. I swallow hard with my best determined face and nod.

"Yeah. Together."

Malachite studies me, my expression, and then lets go of my hand, a massive grin on his pale face.

"You're terrible at being serious," he says.

"You're nothing to quill home about yourself," I scoff.

He reaches out and ruffles my hair with a chuckle. "Good to have you on board, Six-Eyes."

And with that he turns, closing the inn door behind him. It's not just a turn. It's not just him leaving us alone. It's him trusting me with Lucien. Handing over the reins he's held tight for so long. A passing of a torch.

A warm tug at my hand. Lucien.

"It's a beautiful night," he says.

I make a wry smile as we start walking. "Underselling it a bit, aren't you? It's practically dreamy."

"Indeed," Lucien agrees, turning his long collar up against the wind. "Walking with you—it feels like a dream I've had countless times. I'm almost afraid I'll wake at any moment, and you'll…"

He trails off. The parchment curl of my unheart tightens, my fingers becoming hyperaware of his. The crunch of snow under our boots, the smell of coalsmoke from every tower chimney. The bridges we cross creak faintly in the frigid breeze but never shudder or sway. Sturdy, enduring. Predictable like I've never been. Reliable like I've never been. To him least of all.

I shiver, and the warmth is instant and all around me—Lucien draping his covering over my shoulders.

"Don't." I jump, shoving it off. "You're going to freeze—"

"Am I?" he lilts. "Or am I a witch, with enough magic to warm myself?"

"How—how much magic do you have left?" I blurt. "That witchfire barrier you made, slowing our fall—those aren't easy things."

"No," he agrees. "They aren't."

"If you use too much, doesn't it hurt you?"

I know that from Nightsinger, from watching her try to work magic when she was sick with winter congestions. It's dangerous, to go beyond your body's threshold. And there may be "no coming back," whatever that means. Nightsinger never did it, but she alluded to it.

Lucien stays quiet, the eeriness building nests in the void.

"Doesn't it?" I press. "Are you…did you get hurt?"

"That's none of your concern," he rumbles.

"You're my witch now," I insist. "It's very, *very* much my concern."

I lift my hand to touch his face, the right side, and he doesn't move. With slow unease, I watch as he shrinks away only when my hand cuts across his left side.

"You—" I swallow, resting my hand on his glass-cut right cheekbone. "What happened to your eye?"

It's the same dark shard of onyx. It moves with his gaze, but it's then I realize this whole time it hasn't *tracked* movement. Not once. I thought he was just recovering, reacting slowly from the exhaustion of everything that'd happened. But I was wrong. I walked on his right side, and he looked at me with his left.

His right eye isn't working. He just moves it to whatever his *left* eye sees.

But the emotion isn't gone from them. I can see the urge to pull away from me, to build his impenetrable walls and insist he's fine. The princely shell, coming up like a tide.

"Please," I say with as much softness as I can. *"Please."*

The shell suddenly stops, the bricks coming down. He puts his hand over mine on his cheek.

"It's gone," he whispers. "The right one. I can't see anything."

"But—but it'll get *better*. Right?"

He shakes his head. "I can feel it. I felt it…when it happened. The nerves are closed. Burned out. It's never coming back."

"You of all people have to be more careful—"

"I know. But I had to do it, to save us."

"Then save your magic now," I insist, thrusting the covering back at him. His laugh is light, even if his words are dark.

"I have to use it now. More than ever. Rather, practice is more important now than ever."

It goes unspoken. He means Varia. Preparing to fight her.

"She has years on me," he presses, lacing his warm fingers thoughtfully through mine one by one. "Once I awoke as a witch, I learned everything I know by watching her. Feeling her power around me, around the city, and how she wove it. She's so *incredibly* powerful. Was. Even before the Bone Tree. But now that she has it, she's ascended even further beyond me. Beyond any witch in this world."

"Your Highness—"

His reaction is instant, arcing his tall body around and into me, his lips burning hot against my mountain-cold ones. A gentle insistence of skin, and a sly sweet promise of things to come. When he finally pulls away, each bone in my body is limp, at a tender ease.

"Every time you call me that, I'm going to kiss you," he says. "Perhaps then you'll break the habit."

"Th-That's, that plan—" I start. "Considering how many of the best polymath tutors you've had, that plan's a scathing disappointment. It won't even work."

"I know." He smiles.

"I'm going to slip up on purpose," I threaten weakly.

He puts his forehead to mine, his murmur soft. "In all honesty, I'm hoping you will. Many times."

I've felt so many quiets in my life. So many silences that lingered, in different ways. Some crash, some burn. Some fall slowly, like snow, and others pelt heavily, like rain. But this one is strange and new.

This one *trembles*.

What comes next? I know what comes next. I know, as he leads me back to the inn tower, to the blazing of the hearth melting the snow on our eyelashes, both of us dripping water and laughter up the stairs.

Boots are awfully pointless, aren't they?

Your cheeks are so red, you look scrubbed raw.

I do not!

If you go any faster I won't be able to keep up.

Teleport a little, then, Sir Witch.

We barely make it past each torch before I pull him in to me, over and over, searingly desperate to make sure this is real and not some figment of my Heartless brain dying somewhere, on some forgotten plain. Some gift from the gods in my final moments.

Dreams can feel real. Dying dreams most of all.

And then I'm back, standing in the tower room I woke up in halves ago, a hand in mine and a smile mirroring my own. With slow movements, Lucien peels my snow-wet covering off, kissing a deliberate line down my neck. The near-dead embers in the hearth have nothing on the glowing blaze that starts to lick at my insides—

he could command you to do anything, and we would be powerless to resist.

—and then all at once, it vanishes.

"Lucien." My voice sounds small in the stone room. I try again. "Luc—"

He straightens in a blink, eyes roaming over my face. "You're pale. What's wrong?"

"I—" I swallow. "I don't think I can do this."

I watch his expression, ready for disappointment. But there's none, just a wry smile where it should be. He backs up, putting a slice of thoughtful space between us.

"All right."

"Aren't you—"

"No," he cuts me off. "What you want, you shall have. What you don't want, you won't have. It's that simple."

All the fear in me drains, and it feels like I've taken a physical step away from some unknowable cliff's edge. His warm hand moves, achingly, to tuck a strand of blond hair behind my ear.

"That's better." His smile widens (that sunrise smile, the beginning of it all). "Some color back in your cheeks."

"Being undead doesn't mean we should strive for unbeauty." I flip the rest of my hair over my shoulder, and Lucien's laugh echoes as he seats himself on the bed, pulling off his boots.

"You've never once been unbeautiful, Lady Zera, and you know it."

"Hey!" I bend to unlace my own boots. "If I can't call you Your Highness, you can't call me Lady Zera!"

"Says who?"

"Me! Your Heartless!"

"My Heartless," he repeats, and the words suspend in the air. I almost regret them, regret reminding us both of the power imbalance, until he says, "I never did ask—how long do you intend to stay my Heartless?"

I say it without thinking: "For however long you need me."

Dark hawk eyes cut over to me, his fingers undoing his shirt buttons freezing. "That's not an answer, Zera. What do *you* want?"

It hits me like a runaway carriage—silent road and then thundering all at once. No witch of mine has ever asked me that question. Not even Nightsinger, the most temperate of the past two. It was an implicit understanding with Nightsinger; she saved my life, and she didn't want to be anywhere but the Bone Road forest. With Crav, Peligli, me. She wanted us there with her. To protect us from the outside world that was so cruel to children most of all.

But I'm not a child anymore.

I'm Zera Y'shennria, first Heartless of the witch Black Rose, the Starving Wolf, Six-Eyes. I helped Laughing Daughter obtain the Bone Tree, and with it, the power to destroy everything. Wherever you're flying right now, Evlorasin, you were right. Even in madness. *Especially* in madness. The Starving Wolf's hunger for her heart opened the gates that held back the end of the world.

"I opened the gates," I say. "So I should close them."

"Not obligation, Zera. Not selfless sacrifice." Lucien's voice gets harder as he stands, shirt swaying open to reveal skin under firelight. "What do you *want*?"

Breathing's hard again. "The only thing I've ever wanted. To make up for what I've done."

"And how does one do that?"

"Protecting you," I say. "Stopping Varia."

"And?"

"And." My throat tightens. "Making graves."

"For who?"

My smile feels small, undeserving. "Will you help me tomorrow? Before we go to the sage's meeting? There's something… something I have to do."

He walks over, honey and spice, and puts a kiss to my forehead. "Always."

The bed is warmer tonight. Warmer than it's ever been and stranger. But easier, too. Lucien catches me looking at him on the pillows, and he smirks.

"You have my permission to stare at me all night."

"And why would I do that?" I fire off a half-downy mumble. "I've already memorized everything on you."

"Well." His smirk grows unmanageable. "Not everything."

Since when is *he* the one who seduces, instead of me? My face fills red.

"Princes aren't supposed to have roguish manners."

"And ladies aren't supposed to sleep in beds with unmarried men."

"Only married men, then."

He hefts up on one elbow, tracing my hand under the covers. "What are you implying, Lady Zera?"

"Go. To. Sleep." I pause. *"Your Highness."*

The kiss comes, as I knew it would, breathless and enmeshed in each other, and I'm the first one to pull away and the only one to roll over in faux grumpiness, Lucien's laugh rumbling the mattress.

I try to sleep—try so hard to play at being as human as he is—but I fade in and out, waking up in the odd hours to reach over and feel that he's still there. Still real.

Still with me, despite everything.

Despite how many mistakes I've made.

4

THE FIRST DREAM

The dream. Again. The one where I have a heavy, heart-beating chest.

The dream where I'm not myself but Varia. I see through her eyes, her dark bangs on the edges of my—our—vision.

But where my head is full of the hunger, full of the yawning void of hunger, hers is *screaming*. Again. Always.

<u>DESTROY.</u>

It burns against my mind, like sticking my hand into a pile of embers. Like the witchfire that killed me in Vetris—Lucien's. It sears, it melts, it obliterates. I can just barely hold on to my thoughts, and it's not even my body. I'm just a visitor.

How am I visiting? How am I having this dream again, seeing through her again?

I try not to think about that as Varia turns her head, unbelievably overcoming the mind-bending screaming with sheer willpower. Enough to blink, enough to move.

We're standing in grass, the flowing grasslands of central Cavanos. The night wind ripples through it, caressing it peacefully. The only peace we can see, can sense. Everything above the grass is fire—all we can see is fire. This place has been on fire before, many times. Innumerable people have died here. Will die here.

<u>DESTROY IT ALL.</u>

Varia looks up, holds out her night-hued wooden fingers. I

can't feel the spell, even though I'm in her body. But I can see what it does—shimmering the air just before her, a low, soundless hum, and then a violent popping noise as someone materializes from the wavering air. Someone with long white hair, with ice eyes once cruel, now hollow, and dressed in a gray robe that covers his head.

Gavik. Fione's uncle, Varia's first Heartless, and the man who tried to kill her so long ago. Who drove her out of Vetris because he feared her, feared the Bone Tree that called to her in her sleep. He's the man who tried to kill Lucien, too, and who succeeded in drowning hundreds, if not thousands, of witches. He was once the most powerful man in Vetris, in Cavanos, one of the most powerful people on perhaps the whole Mist Continent.

But now his expression crumbles to nothing more than dust when he sees Varia.

"Y-You? How did you— I was in Vetris. Did you... No." His ice eyes widen. "The Crimson Lady wouldn't let you spell me away—"

"No one *lets* me do anything anymore," Varia says softly. "Least of all a little tower stuffed with your precious white mercury."

His eyes dart to Varia's neck, our neck, to the Bone Tree choker that I know is there. Made of valkerax fangs. Made of pure magic, pure *power*. I recoil at the terror that flashes across the former archduke's face.

"New God above. You've done it. That foolish girl helped you, didn't she? You have it now, and now—" His throat bobs, and a strange calmness comes over him. "You're going to kill me, aren't you?"

She doesn't even grace him with a yes or a no.

A genocidal maniac. A religious fanatic. A fearful man, whose fear hurt and destroyed the lives of so many.

DESTROY.

Varia's hate burns cold. Burns like winter, like Breych in the dead of night, like putting a hand to a block of ice and leaving it for eternity. Our hand pulls out a velvet bag, embroidered with the word leech.

"No—I can help. You need me—"

He doesn't even get the chance to beg.

She denies him the chance, like he denied so many witches.

Her wooden fingers collapse, fisting around the bag. A second of resistance, of Gavik clutching his chest frantically, eyes bugging out of his skull, and then the give.

The squelch, the blood running down her fingers, the velvet soaking wet and dripping onto the waving grass.

I've never seen it. I've heard of it, feared it like a nebulous reaper far off, but I've never seen it happen in front of my eyes.

But it does.

Gavik's chest implodes—ribs and flesh exploding, painting the grass with viscera in every direction. Wet splatters on Varia's face—our face—but she never flinches. Not for a second. She watches every slow moment as Gavik's knees buckle and his corpse falls into the grass face first. Horrified face first. No grave marker. No pyre. Nothing.

And the screaming in our head lessens. The fire, the images of death—they start to fade. Like someone ushering the horrible orchestra into another room and closing the door. It's all muted. I—we—can think again, clearer.

We've destroyed.

We've obeyed.

And the screaming rewards us.

I feel Varia's face smile. A delighted grin as she wipes pieces of Gavik off her cheekbone with slow ease, as her fear of the screaming turns to calculation. As she realizes the rules of it, the requirements.

"We don't need anyone anymore," she murmurs. "Least of all a maggot like you."

She turns. Gavik's gone. I don't mourn him—he was no one

worthy of mourning. But Varia's words, the coldness and calmness in them, I mourn that. I feel it, deep down. I feel her sense of betrayal, her wounded trust, her aching love. All of it. All of it sadness like thorns, pointed out at the world.

And on the horizon of her mind, a roar. A roar, as the screaming comes back quickly, furiously, ravaging every thought in its path.

<u>DESTROY IT ALL.</u>

The morning breaks cold and snappish over Breych's three ridges. Lucien wakes me, and I mumble my surprise.

"You're still here."

"For as long as you'll have me." He laughs. "Come now. It's far past sunrise."

Past sunrise. How long was that dream? It *was* a dream, right? No—it was reality. I saw Gavik die. Just like I saw Varia crawl out of the valkerax pile, alive and whole.

Do I even tell Lucien? His wound over his sister is no doubt still raw. And how can I tell him when I don't even know why it's happening? How do I tell him of the pain his sister is feeling, the betrayal?

One thing at a time, Zera. We're in a warm bed now, with a warm boy.

enjoy this ease while it lasts, the hunger taunts. **for it will not last long.**

I push out the lingering dregs of the dream and sit up with a groan. "Why did you wake me?"

"Don't we have something to do?" he asks.

"Yes. But I'll have you know I've plucked out men's eyeballs for far lesser crimes than this."

Whichever romantic poet forgot to mention how exceedingly impossible it is to get out of a bed with your lover in it owes me, and I take my payments in gold and endless praise, thank you very much. I manage to dress as he does, our backs turned to each other.

"Is the prince of Cavanos trying to sneak a peek?" I tease. His fluster is immediate.

"Don't tempt me."

"Likewise," I chime.

When we make it outside, the pure, fresh snow crunches underfoot like particularly stiff glaze on a sweetround. It's my turn to lead—I pull Lucien gregariously around the early-morning stalls selling fabrics, beads, wire. A handful of little iron bells, in the Cavanos tradition. Red ribbon. White wood. It won't be the usual pyre and metal orb carved with an eye placed in the mouth. It's not the New God's way. But it can't be; I don't have the bodies to burn. Only the memories. Only their faces, pressed like flowers in the pages of my mind.

This is the old way to do things. The non-denominational way, the unfashionable way. The only way I know how, from reading the inscriptions on the mass graves near the Bone Road. The war graves. This is the only way left to me. I won't be Varia. I won't be Gavik.

I will make graves for those I've killed.

In a little teahouse, over steaming cups of chocolate, Lucien helps me, pulling the bundles of white wood sticks tight, wrapping them with red ribbon, and attaching a single bell to each silken strand. Fourteen bundles for fourteen men. Fourteen bundles for the years I didn't know any better. Fourteen mistakes. Fourteen ignorances. Fourteen things I've done and can't undo.

Life. Life as equally important as death.

And a Heartless, who took far too long to figure out that particular detail.

Someday, someone will see the fourteen bundles of white wood wrapped with red ribbon, adorned with iron bells, set deep and well into the snow on the top of a distant ridge, accessible only by teleportation magic or flight, and they will wonder. They won't see the girl setting them, one by one, but maybe, *just maybe*, they'll hear her tears, echoing beyond the stone and out over the world.

"What took you two so long?" Malachite looks up when Lucien and I enter the sage's tower. My steps feel the smallest bit lighter as I half skip over to a chair beside Fione and settle in.

"Icicles," I chirp. "All over our noses. You should've seen it—one sneeze and we were practically wielding swords on our upper lip."

Fione makes a catlike smile beside me, sipping her licorice tea. "Inventive as always."

"And this is *before* I've had my morning tea," I agree, and take a sip of my own drink. Sitting beside her feels right, still. The dream lingers, still. Gavik's dead. I know she had no love for her uncle, but I can't bring myself to tell her. In doing so, I'd have to tell her I can see things from Varia's eyes. And I know Fione would ask me to reason with Varia, to beg her to stop it all. I know she would.

It would be giving her false hope, after I've given her real hope.

"*Greshoir étta.*" The old sage croaks the Helkyrisian greeting as he enters, little arms full of books that Lucien instantly lunges to help him with. "Your Highness, I can—"

"Just Lucien, please," the prince insists, piling the books on the table.

The sage sighs. "Very well. I hope you all slept decently."

"As well as can be, Elder." I smile. "Any news?"

"Unfortunately." He nods, settling in an armchair by the fire and cupping his chocolate eagerly with knotty fingers. "I've contacted the Court of Five Violets with the news of Princess Varia's decision. They're moving to post the western armada along our shared border to monitor the situation. The rest of the fleet is mustering in Silvanitas, and every trade caravan from Braal to Trinito has been rerouted there."

"Translation?" Malachite looks to Fione and Lucien in turn.

"Helkyris's airship armada is the only one of its kind in the world," Fione says, voice even. "Limited by the fact their engines fail over seawater. The unrefined white mercury they run on doesn't react well to large amounts of salt vapor. But their intercontinental prowess is tremendous."

"Translation for the translation, anyone?" I ask.

"They're gearing up for war," Lucien says. "Consolidating their resources over the capital city. Pulling the armada in from all over the country communicates they aren't even considering being open to negotiations. And that they're viewing Cavanos as the only threat worth their attention." He frowns. "*All* of their attention."

"Which leaves the cities on the western coast almost completely defenseless to Qessen pirates," the sage mutters. "Not to mention the Feralstorm."

"All this for the valkerax—"

"This is the bare minimum preparation for the valkerax," the sage interrupts, waving his hand at the books. "I've pulled every Old Vetrisian tome on the subject I could find. There is, unsurprisingly, very little humans can do to prepare for a valkerax attack."

"You're not badly defended here in Breych," Malachite grunts. "Sheer mountain faces on all sides, no paths up. It's not like the valkerax can hitch a ride on the airships."

The sage traces a book cover. "The tomes say they can fly."

The room goes deathly quiet, the fire crackling as he looks up at us with his wrinkled eyes.

"Is this true? Have you seen it?"

"One of them can," I admit. "I know that for sure. Most of Vetris knows it, too. But that one isn't on Varia's side."

"If the princess has the Bone Tree, they are *all* on her side."

"How do you know that?" I narrow my eyes.

"Unlike Cavanos, Helkyris does not burn books it doesn't agree with." His eyes twinkle back at me. I raise my chin.

"Right. Regardless, this valkerax isn't on her side, Elder. I'd stake my immortal life on it."

"Why?"

"I taught it to Weep. It's free of the Bone Tree's command."

"Ah." He nods, chin in his hand. "Weeping. I've read of it in the rare Sunless War record. You are…capable of it?"

"I'd do a casual demonstration, but that's against the spirit of the thing."

"Can you teach any number of the other valkerax to do it, too?" he presses.

My laugh bursts out, and I just barely cover my mouth.

"S-Sorry. No. Not without a lot of drugging, underground dungeons, and dying on my part. It's a frankly awful time. And a lengthy one."

"Not feasible, then," Fione muses, pulling out a notebook and a quill. She scratches something out.

"You thought of that already?" I tilt my head.

"Obviously." She taps her quill on another sentence. "What about the Bone Tree? Can we go back to the mountaintop and destroy it, strip her of her source of power?"

She's the Duchess Himintell right now. Strong spine, unblinking periwinkle eyes. Apple-cheeked, blushing-in-love Fione is nowhere to be seen. Malachite and I share a look as

Lucien shakes his head.

"The Bone Tree's gone," Lucien muses. "That thing on top of the mountain is a shell—the entirety of its magic is inside her now."

"In that choker around her neck," I say. "Right?"

Lucien shrugs. "I can't say. But it's a physical symbol of her new power, certainly."

"It's feeding off her," Fione says. "Her magic. Which means we don't have much time to stop her."

"There is a time limit either way, Your Grace," the sage says. "When one takes into consideration the imminent loss of life from a valkerax invasion."

My stomach turns uneasily. The dream last night...Varia was close to Vetris; she was in the grasslands. But she wouldn't—her parents, the king and queen, are there. She wouldn't kill them. She's still Varia, and the Varia I know treasures the people she loves.

Even if they've betrayed her.

But her parents haven't. She loves them. Vetris is safe. I'm not sure about anywhere else, but I'm sure Vetris, at least, is safe.

"How do you stop someone with the most powerful weapon in the world?" Malachite muses.

"Calvary-General Rodituller proposes two theories in his *Recitations of Field Warfare*," Lucien says. "You either amass an equally powerful weapon of your own or you destroy theirs."

An idea comes to me. Not a great one, but at this point I'll take anything.

"It's like the hunger," I say. "The hunger binds me to Lucien. There's a voice—I think it's the same hunger—connecting the valkerax to the Bone Tree. If we could weaken that bond somehow, like white mercury does—not Weeping but a spell, or...*something*. I don't know."

"Yes," Fione agrees dryly. "If we could undo an immensely powerful Old Vetrisian artifact with a spell, it'd solve many problems."

"But there's gotta be something, right? There was the Hymn of the Forest, and the Elder here has read books about valkerax and their connection to the Bone Tree. It's *recorded*. Someone has to know *something*."

"Elder?" Lucien looks at the sage. "Any ideas?"

He shakes his old, wispy head. "The books I spoke of said nothing of weakening such a bond. That is knowledge the world of Arathess hasn't seen in a very long time—from the time of Old Vetris. I can think of only one entity who would know what you seek. The High Witches of Cavanos."

"You really think they'd help *us*?" Malachite scoffs.

"Three enemies means two of them are friends," the sage says. "Princess Varia is using magic against the world. Surely they'd want less of that."

"The High Witches haven't been seen in decades. Do you not have Helkyrisian witches who'd know something?" Lucien asks.

"As I'm sure you're aware, Your Highness, Cavanos has always been the seat of magic. Witches in the rest of the world have not perfected magic as they have, through regrettably constant strife. Ildolia on the Star Continent is perhaps the only rival to Cavanos, but even their magic falls short, and you would find the journey too long, too allowing of Princess Varia's destruction. Cavanos was the seat of Old Vetris, the very heart that beat outward the blood, and that legacy lingers in your witches."

The sage leans back, smacking his chocolaty lips with an air of certainty.

"Yes. Yes, I'm quite sure. There is no better place to learn of the magic binding the valkerax than Windonhigh."

"The last witch enclave in Cavanos?" Fione asks. "The one no human has ever found?"

"Precisely," the sage asserts.

"My sister's been there," Lucien says.

"Then surely," the sage leads, "you must hurry. If Windonhigh *does* know how to stop the valkerax, it will be the first place she destroys."

"Uh, hello?" Malachite frowns. "Breaking the valkeraxes' bond with the Bone Tree means they'd be let loose on the world. You know, the whole reason Old Vetris banded together in the first place?"

"We hold on to it, until we have a better plan," Lucien says.

Malachite shifts uncomfortably on the wall. Fione stares down at her notebook intensely, her still quill blotting an ever-expanding dot of ink in the center of the page. My dream bubbles up—the fevered one I had when I blacked out from the fall, the one this morning. I'd *been* Varia. I had her hands, her arms. Her body. I was in her body, seeing through her eyes. And the voice in my head, worse than the hunger, wanted to destroy everything. But it wasn't hers. They weren't *her* thoughts. Fione was superimposed on the destruction. Fione was the only thought she still had that was her own. And if the rest wasn't hers, then…

"The Bone Tree wants this." I break the quiet. "It's urging her to destroy."

"How would you know that?" Fione's voice is instant and biting. Understandably so. How dare I presume to know what Varia's thinking, feeling? I'm not the one in a relationship with her. It's time to tell them. No more secrets. Secrets are what drove us apart in Vetris.

"When we fell, I blacked out," I admit. "And I had this dream. I was with her. I saw through her eyes. And this morning, I had the same dream. She was—"

"She's alive," Lucien says, an assertion, not a question.

I nod. "The valkerax fell on her, but she cut through them. I could hear something screaming in her head, like the hunger screams in mine. But hers was louder. Untempered by witch magic. It wanted ruin indiscriminate. It was fury and fear and pain, all at once. And the only way she was keeping sane was by holding on to the idea of—"

My eyes skitter over to Fione, and I feel suddenly raw with the awareness of what wounds I'm testing the stitches of. I clear my throat.

"She killed Gavik."

Fione has the same reaction her love did—she doesn't flinch. Lucien exhales, just barely, and Malachite rolls his eyes.

"Fuckin' finally," Mal says. "Good riddance."

I inhale sharply. "The Bone Tree wants her to destroy. Anything. Everything. But she's fighting it. She's trying to keep it in check so she can accomplish her goals. It got softer when she killed Gavik, but it didn't go away. It's so godsdamn *powerful*, like nature itself—"

"She can," Fione interrupts me. "She will."

Lucien glances over at me, then her. "Of course she will."

Their faith in her is ironclad. Or maybe they just want it to be. Belief is sometimes the only thing you can hold on to. But I've felt it. By some arsed-up twist of dream-magic, some echo of Varia being my witch once, I've *felt* what she's feeling. What she's going through. And no mortal would be able to keep strong against something like that for long. Worry runs taut threads through the room, between Malachite and Fione, between Fione and Lucien most of all.

Windonhigh. If the sage is right, the High Witches have to know something. Some spell, some information to help us separate the valkerax from the Bone Tree. But no human's ever found Windonhigh—not even Nightsinger ever mentioned it to me.

And then it hits me: the letter. The one Y'shennria sent me while I was still Varia's Heartless. I scramble in my pockets, pulling it out from the little bag I keep the fragments of Father's sword in—blade and hilt, disassembled. The bag made for me by Lucien.

"Here," I chirp, flattening the letter on the table as everyone bends over it. "Y'shennria sent me this when I was in Vetris. She said to come to Ravenshaunt when I got my heart back."

"And?" The old sage wrinkles his nose. "How does this help you young ones find Windonhigh?"

"Y'shennria is an Old God family," Fione interjects. "She conspired with the witches to steal Prince Lucien's heart, but when she failed, she fled."

"She was confident she'd be safe," I say. "On the night of the Hunt, when she sent me off to take Lucien's heart, she assured me she'd be fine, that the witches would give her asylum."

"And the only place left that's safe for witches is..." Lucien murmurs, eyes sparking as he looks up at me.

"So." I clap my hands together, standing and dusting my garish skirt off. "How long should I book our vacation to Windonhigh for?"

5

TO VETRIS

When Varia first dragged me up here in a fit of excitement, she failed to mention the only way down off the Tollmount-Kilstead mountains involves very large and very unstable-looking hot air balloons. Or rather, hot air balloons attached to ships by copper lashing cable.

Which isn't a recipe for disaster at all.

"For the last time, Zera, it's not *air*. It's aergasel. It's lighter than air, and it provides support to the thrusters by lessening the velocity of the load required for takeoff—"

"Fione, you're beautiful," I start, wrapping the fur covering around me tighter as the crate-lugging, passenger-swarmed bustle of the chilly Breych airdocks hums around us. "And extremely smart, and incredibly good at explaining things, but alas, I have no heart and very little brain."

"It's not air, is all." She leans on her cane to avoid a man carrying what seems to be ten boxes crowded with furiously mating chickens on his shoulders.

"Then why call them *air*ships?" I ask.

"Because it's easier than calling them *aergasel*ships."

"Fair." I nod. "But still mystifying. I'd call them *tit*ships, personally." A pause. "Because that's what they look like."

"Yes." She giggles. "I got that."

"Hey, you two!" Malachite shouts, his pale, lanky frame

towering over the crowd. "This way!"

I pick up my bag and lug Fione's far fancier one over my shoulder for good measure. She pouts, a shard of before-duchess, before-heartbreak showing through.

"I'm perfectly capable of carrying my own things."

"I know. But do you *want* to?"

She glances at me sheepishly. "No?"

"That's what I thought." I muscle through the crowd, shoving as many people aside as will let me to make just a bit more room for her. Most of the crowd are armada soldiers, coming in from the sleek black airships sent to the Cavanos-Helkyris border. They don't look like titships in the slightest—all dark lacquer, their aergasel balloons streamlined and tipped with terrifying black iron warspikes. They fly flags of deep purple with four bronze wildcats centered around a moon—the seal of the sage-dukes of Silvanitas, Fione informs me. Breych is, apparently, one of the few cities nearest the border, and that means one of the few places the armada can refuel.

"They got here quick, huh?" I shout back at Fione over the engine drone.

"I told you, the Helkyrisian armada is one-of-a-kind. They fly at speeds of up to thirty miles a half and can pivot 180 degrees in a matter of seconds—"

"Ooooh, cannons!"

"Are you even listening, Zera?"

"All ears, Your Grace!" A passing carriage of birch branches thwacks me in the side of the head, roughly clipping my temple. "Make that just one ear, Your Grace!"

We finally reach the far end of the dock, where a chained gangplank hovers precariously over a very far drop down into the mountainous abyss. The merchant ship it's attached to is being loaded with barrel upon barrel of some sort of pickled good—the vinegar a strong perfume in the air. Fione gags a little, pulling her scarf over her mouth.

"It's like—like sour feet!"

"Could be worse!" I chime. "Could be actual feet!"

The weight on my back lifts, Fione's bag taken from me. I'm halfway through a whirl to grab whichever wharf rat thinks I'm an easy target when Lucien's voice lilts in my ear.

"Allow me to lighten your load."

He's dressed in his black leathers—not the same as his disguise as the altruistic thief Whisper, but close. The hooded cowl, the closer fit for mobility. It's an echo, but not the whole thing. He sees me staring and smiles over his cowl.

"Thought I ought to start blending in."

"So you chose a full black outfit in a place with nothing but snow," I drawl.

"Old habits die hard," he says simply.

"Or not at all, in my case." I tap my empty chest, and he laughs low in my ear, kissing my temple gingerly.

"Are you all right? I saw that load of branches hit you."

"Oh, psh." I wave him off and start up the gangplank toward Malachite. "Don't worry about me."

"What am I supposed to do, then?"

"Take up crocheting?" I throw a smile at Malachite. "Nice of you to commandeer the only ship smelling of pickled feet for us."

"Considering they're doing this for absolutely *free*"—Malachite's milk brows knit as he leans in and whispers—"maybe don't go around complaining about the smell."

"Complain louder about the smell. Got it. Fione, where do you want to sit?"

The duchess looks unsteady on her feet, and Lucien grabs her elbow to steady her when one of her gags wrenches her entire body to the left.

"Somewhere on the railing it is, then," Lucien says, grinning back at me and helping her toward the side of the ship. The flame-haired captain and her crew come aboard. She nods at us as she passes on her way to the helm.

"No drinking, no smoking, and for the love of mercury piss in the buckets, not on the deck."

"Yes, Cap'n," Malachite salutes, and the red-haired woman launches an eyeball-inquiry my way.

"You. You look like trouble."

"Astute *and* gorgeous," I say, making my best Y'shennria curtsy. She's buying none of it, her gaze narrowed.

"You're the other bodyguard, then?"

I know better than to flicker a look at Malachite. "Yes."

"No sword? No weapon?" She scoffs. "A bad one, then."

"Oh, it's all hand-to-hand combat from me. A bit of biting here and there."

"She's good for it," Malachite jumps in, and when the woman throws him a nasty look, he adds, "Cap'n."

The captain sizes me up one more time. The woman has the instincts of a wolf—she's every inch right about me. Trouble is all I know how to make.

"You work for what you eat." She grunts.

"Gladly." I smile. *And what I eat is you.*

Finally, she turns and starts barking orders into the frigid air, and the crew scatters to haul rope. "You—" She points to me. "On the anchor. And you, beneather—you're on winch release. The disc levers over there, the middle one. Get to it!"

"Aye-aye!" I salute, dashing over to the heavy iron clasp and the ten sailors attempting to haul it off the magnetic dock and wind it back into the airship. Malachite only breaks two levers before the captain realizes just how strong he is and has him hauling rope effortlessly instead.

By some combined miracle of our strength and the captain's precise maneuvering, the airship starts to move, drifting away from the Breych docks and floating with generous creaks out of the mountain's shadow and into the pale sunlight of Cavanos, the green of its grasslands beckoning us home.

I don't get any time to breathe, though, because the captain has me running water and rations to the crew. They're heading for Avel, passing over Cavanos to the south and only to the south, considering the news about the valkerax has quickly broken on Breych's shore. They're willing to stop for a bare few hours at a hilltop village in Cavanos called Trillmarc, and that's when we'll get off.

We agreed, in the sage's tower, that Y'shennria's letter was our best bet, and so we're heading to Ravenshaunt, where Y'shennria said to visit when I'm free. I'm free now, in a manner of speaking. Freer, at least, than when I was chained to the idea of my heart and the guilt of killing.

But guilt never really goes. I made the graves for the fourteen men, but they aren't gone. Just quieter. Maybe the guilt will never be gone, not completely. Maybe you just live with it, until it becomes as natural as part of your body, another limb you move through the world with.

Maybe guilt isn't about mourning people but about making them a part of you as you go forward.

As the ship cuts to the right, Cavanos grows closer. Y'shennria grows closer. I try and fail to tame the constant pangs of giddiness that run through me at the idea of meeting her again. The hum and whir of the thrusters gets stronger toward the back of the ship, a lullaby that, in the quiet moments, nearly puts me to sleep. Fione, on the other hand, is having a far less soothing time. Her retches are so loud, they echo among the mountain ridges like queasy thunder. At some point, Malachite takes over my job of watching her and rubbing her back supportively, and Lucien finds me staring out at the view on the deck, lacing his hands around my waist like a quiet assurance.

"Busy?" he asks.

"Not anymore," I say, leaning back into his chest. The wind

whips his dark hair around his eyes. I rub a strand of it between my fingers. "Not as short as I remember it."

"I'll cut it again, if you like."

"Absolutely not. Granted, the revolutionary gesture did make me fall for you harder, but your best look is long and shiny."

"It's a pain to wash," he admits.

"As if you washed it yourself," I scoff. "You had servants."

"I wouldn't let them touch my hair," he insists. "The nursemaids loved calling me difficult for it."

"I'll stop, then." I drop the midnight strand, but he takes my hand and presses it against his cheek.

"I'm willing to make an exception."

"How charitable of you." I laugh. The ship turns, the wind battering at our backs now, and the ridge falls away from us, revealing the rest of Cavanos.

And the smoke.

Lucien's body around me tenses hard as rock almost instantly, and both of us straighten.

"Is that..." I trail off, peering into the distance.

"Gods," he breathes. *"No."*

He lunges for the railing, gripping it with white knuckles.

Marring the perfect emerald roll of the grasslands is a blackened banner consumed by the edges of riotous flames. Smoke billows into the air, tall and wide as storm clouds, taking up nearly the whole eastern horizon. The Crimson Lady, the spires of the castle—Vetris, as big as it is, is *completely* obscured. King Sref had ordered his troops to burn the forests after his declaration of war on the witches, but not like this. This isn't one forest, burned by human hands. This is a whole third of central Cavanos up in flame and ash, the ground entirely blackened dead and cratered deep. Not a single tree left, not a stone, not a road or village remaining.

Everything. *Gone.*

She wouldn't. She— Her mother and father...

"She didn't!" I choke out.

The great wall of Vetris—breached. Gaped open by fire and black brimstone.

The shake starts in Lucien's shoulders and works its way to his whole body. Like fire. Like the fire just below him, eating his kingdom. His people. Vetris looks superficially intact, but it's hard to see details through the choking smoke. I walk up to his back, afraid of it and keening to comfort him all at once. What do I even do? All I can do is what I want to do—touch him. Lightly, gripping his elbow to root him here with me, moving up to his hand. Ice cold.

What can I even say? Nothing. Except exactly what I want to.

"I'm sorry. I'm so sorry."

His throat bobs, and then he whirls, black eyes ink and midnight and stuck like burrs to me. "I have to stop her."

"I know."

Our words are simple, said simply, and yet anything but. Scratch the surface and below are a thousand-thousand clockwork arms, spinning and whirring. History. Battering the two of us as we fall through it without a choice.

we made every choice to be right here, right now.

The hunger is right. I made the choice to do this. To go down this path. To stop Varia. Lucien's hands grip mine, tight.

"I'm going to use it for good." I pause. "I'm going to use the hunger in me to put things right this time."

He leans in, forehead to forehead, and gives a shuddering gasp. "I'll help you. My magic is yours. Whatever you need, it's yours."

"I need you—" It's my turn to swallow. "Just as you are, right now. Brave as you are. Scared as you are. Hopeful as you are. Just like this."

Before now, I never knew an embrace between two people could feel like one trembling body, one trembling heart, one person made from two, made from nothing, made from chance and choice and love.

6

SERPENT LIKE SALVATION

The news about Vetris spreads around the crew like the fire that's consumed it.

Lucien stays at the railing for hours until the wind changes, east-northeast to south, or so the captain says. The smoke then clears, and we can finally see it. Vetris, in flames.

Vetris, *ruined*.

I kick myself. I should've told him—I should've told him I saw her near the grasslands in my dreams. I didn't. I didn't, and now...

your mistrust will kill them all.

I push the hunger down and breathe. Nothing to be done. There's nothing to be done now. The fourteen men taught me this, and taught me it well. It's the past. Lesson learned. I have to learn from it.

Even if I told him I saw her near Vetris in my dream—what could we have done? She's so powerful. We can't weaken the bond between the valkerax and the Bone Tree, not yet. What would it have done, other than cause him great grief?

The exact grief he's feeling now.

Fione, with nothing left in her stomach and half recovered, pulls her weary self over by the railing and offers Lucien her brass seeing tube first. And then he offers it to me, his face stone and yet green on the edges.

The white walls rot gray with ash and smoke, the glistening

palace's spires are fragmented and broken, the body of two massive valkerax impaled on them and dripping blood down the palace's marble walls. The Crimson Lady is torn asunder, its two perfectly cleaved halves crushing scores of houses below it. Vetris's only hope against Varia's magic, the entire reason I was sent into Vetris instead of a witch—now nothing more than red rubble. Red, strewn with long white shapes. Valkerax, dead. Dozens of them. But not hundreds. The dense army camps ringing the city are scathed by fire and craters and broken horses, dogs feasting on the remains.

Crows—black ones—wing in heavy murders over what's left of the city.

Vetris lost.

Just like that. As easily as that. All the combined might of the polymaths, all of Cavanos's army, the thing the witches feared so dearly—defeated. Vetris won the Sunless War thirty years ago, against the might of the witches and their Heartless and their magic. But against the valkerax...

The seeing tube is strong, but not strong enough to see the individual details—whether or not the aquifers are intact, how many bodies there are.

"South Gate sustained the heaviest damage, looks like," Malachite says dully. "And the noble quarter is completely trashed. Judging by the valkerax corpses, it wasn't an instant attack—the royal family might have had time to evacuate."

It's a kind word, meant for Lucien. But the prince's expression doesn't so much as twitch. And the swirling in my gut says otherwise. The palace is rubble and sand. No one could've lived through that.

"There's not enough dead valkerax—which means she didn't even send her main force." Fione's voice is cold, compact. Only what's necessary. Her way of dealing. "An auxiliary would be enough to do this—twenty or thirty."

Just twenty, *just* thirty...did all this? I know how big the valkerax are, how powerful. I trained Evlorasin, for New God's sake! But still, I'm aghast. Lost for words, for thought. Lucien says nothing, seeing tube riveted to the city again. Malachite pats him once on the shoulder, then wisely steps back to give him room. The beneather makes his long-legged way over to me.

"I'm amazed they took down that many valkerax," he mutters at my side.

"Likewise," I say softly. "But I suppose the majority of the king's forces were gathered in the city at the time."

"Except that just means they have nothing left to fight back with. That's why Varia hit it first, probably: hamstring the bulk of their forces at once, and they lose all hope."

I watch Lucien's hawk profile. "He wants to be down there. With his people."

"Sure. But that's not gonna stop Varia. He knows that. We all know that. Our best bet's Windonhigh. Find what we need to know, get out, and use it against her."

"Fione's taking it too well."

"Nah. She's just hiding it."

"And you?" I ask. "You seem awfully calm."

"I'm used to losing a lot of people at once." He sighs, resigned. "Comes with the territory of hunting bloodthirsty giant wyrms, you know? Doesn't mean I don't feel it; I've just learned to deal with it. You've gotta deal with it, or it drags you down into despair. Big endless pit."

I nod. "Yeah. I know."

"'Course you know. But the nobles over there don't. They're different from us. I mean, they *do* know, but only in theory, in war tactics. Books. Concepts and tutoring. Not reality. So go easy on 'em."

"I'll try."

He pats me on the shoulder the exact same way he did Lucien, then heads over to the captain at the helm. The crew's whispering can't be contained, filtering in from behind me.

"Begods, *look at the state of it.*"

"*Spirits save us—*valkerax. *My grandpa'd be rollin' in his grave if he could see this.*"

"*There's none left to see. None but corpses in Vetris now, I reckon.*"

"*Ach, shhh! Don't ya know that black-clad one's the prince of Cavanos?*"

"*And I'm a sage-duke. A prince wouldn't be up here bumming with us. He'd be down there, fighting or fleeing or whatever it is royals do during war.*"

"*We've still got the whole armada, don't we?*"

"*The valkerax keep in Cavanos, there's nothing to worry about. Let 'em rampage, long as they stay away from my wee ones cross the mountains.*"

I feel it suddenly, like a latch clicking into place. My limbs go numb, zinging as if asleep, and Lucien seems suddenly...bigger. Taller at the railing. He's a vacuum pulling my eyes in, my body in.

Magic.

"Lucien!" I stagger as the airship gives a massive heave. The crew crows about turbulence, and I manage to scramble off my knees and toward the prince. "Lucien! What are you doing?"

He won't turn to face me, but his hands on the railing are already pitch-black up to the wrists. The wind whips his hair back and forth, erratic. I know that wind. The wind before teleportation.

"Don't!" I shout over the howling. "Lucien, it's too far away; you'll hurt yourself again—"

"*Again?*" Malachite catches my arm as the ship gives another heave.

"He's—" I gesture wildly at the prince's back. "His right eye, it's gone! Using magic beyond your physical limit is— He's going to teleport down there—"

Malachite snarls a beneather swear and launches himself forward, grabbing the railing and Lucien's shoulder all at once.

"Luc, look at me—"

And he does. He tilts his dark-haired head over to his bodyguard, his friend, and the hawk-eyes I know so well are eclipsed, no whites to be seen. Black and only black, deep and endless.

"There's no time." Lucien's voice comes out even, still as water. "We go."

"Mal!" I reach for his hand, grabbing Fione's and pulling her toward Lucien. Fione's moment of confusion, Malachite's tense brow of realization, and then the feeling of being pulled inexorably somewhere, in one arrow-direction by the guts, the sounds of the howling wind and the uneasy crew and the creaking airship evaporating into total silence. Blue sky, white sky, and then black. Nothing but black.

With the faintest pop, color flicks on again—crimson flames licking old wood buildings. Sound crashes down on my ears all at once: screaming, crying, hysterical shouting, and the crackly eating noises of fire. A village. We all stagger forward into a village on fire, Lucien clutching his left hand to his chest and panting.

"Luc!" Malachite turns to him. "What's wrong?"

"Help...them." He points with his right hand at the village. "Go."

"Lucien—" Fione starts forward.

"*Go!*" His roar is louder than the fire for a moment and his eyes, now normal again, flicker over to me, wordless and pleading.

go, the hunger echoes him faintly. But he's put no magic behind it. It's not a command. It's a wish. A desperate request.

"C'mon!" I snag Malachite by the chainmail. "We're pros at this by now, right? You check the buildings still standing, Sir Fireproof. Fione—let's gather the survivors and get them to a safe place."

Lucien's eyes soften in gratitude. Malachite tries to argue for one second, sees the look between the prince and me, and makes the decision to dash into the blazing walls of fire. I take off downwind, and Fione trots after me, keeping up surprisingly easily considering she just spent the last couple halves retching.

"Not a fan of the sky, huh?" I shout back, passing her my handkerchief to cover her nose and mouth.

"Certain parts of me aren't keen on the sky, apparently. The polymaths say every day we should try to learn something new about ourselves."

Her dry joke gets me, but only for as long as it takes for me to see a little crowd of huddled children by the remains of the town well, smeared with ash and fear. I gather them up with promises of their parents, and Fione offers a few of the more dazed-looking ones water from her skin.

"What happened?" Fione asks a child gently. They gulp water greedily, and lower the skin only to point wordlessly at the ground.

There, in the perfect ashen detail of the dirt, is a massive scratch mark. Four lacerations deep and long in the earth, punctuated by a titanic paw impression, white fur and scales scattered about.

Valkerax.

It might still be around. Lucien—I can't be worried about Lucien. Not now. He teleported us from an airship who knows how many miles in the air to the ground. To a village somewhere in Cavanos. All four of us. By himself. It took three witches to teleport just me from Nightsinger's house to the Bone Road. And after Varia teleported herself and me to the Tollmont-Kilstead mountains, she was so exhausted I had to carry her the rest of the way to the Bone Tree.

He's hurt himself. He had to, to do this.

I shake my head, gold hair sticking to sweat. I can't think about that now. He wants me here, doing this. Not worrying about him. But I can't help it. If he keeps going like this—if he keeps trying to help people with his magic without regard for himself, he'll...

The children follow behind Fione and me like exhausted ducklings, too scared to even cry or complain. The only thing that makes them jump is the occasional crack of wood as another village building collapses. The smoke's not thick enough to obscure vision—the southwardly wind mercifully wicking most of it away. Less casualties, then, at least by smoke inhalation. It's the little things in life.

Ingeniously, Fione uses her seeing tube to point me in the right directions—east, a pair of elderly men; northeast and between the burning market stalls, four teenagers trying to persuade a terrified cow to move. It finally decides moving's the better option when I lovingly bite its flank as hard as I can with all my Heartless teeth. The children don't follow me after that, preferring Fione and the more human adults, and I can hardly blame them; I wouldn't trust a lady with fresh cow blood on her mouth, either.

At last we catch up to the majority of the village, stripped down to near-nothing and forming a long chain of sweaty bodies between the secondary well and a burning building, passing buckets upon buckets of heavy water to each other. On the frontlines, another chain of humans frantically shovels as much dirt onto the fire as they can, swapping in another villager when one starts to buckle. It's an incredible display of human cooperation, but it's a futile one—the building looks to be on its last legs, and the rest of the village is faring no better.

"What is that building?" Fione asks.

"The main granary," one of the teenagers speaks up. "For winter."

"The most important building in the village," I muse.

"If we lose it..." An elderly man trails off at the look the children give him.

"You won't."

The new voice comes from behind us, and we whirl. In my heart I already know who it is—always. Lucien. He looks better than when we first arrived, his left hand no longer cradled by his right. Maybe…maybe he *didn't* hurt himself? No. He's just hiding it. For me. For all of us.

Because he's the prince of Cavanos, and he's been taught to show nothing but strength.

follow his example, you useless creature.

I step forward, the hunger and worry gnawing equally at me. At the determined look in his eyes. But Lucien cuts me off, catches me in it, and smiles. That real, true smile, cutting bright against the smoke and gloom.

"It'll be fine," he says, confident.

His body goes completely still as he bows his head ever so slightly on his chest. He holds both his hands up, and I'm only half relieved to see the left one rise. It shakes, his fingers trembling as they turn midnight to the knuckles. He's not up for this. He's going to hurt himself—

How can I stop him?

How can I stop him from doing what he wants to do? What he's always done? Protecting his people is what he lives for, I know that, and *still*—

Cries rise up as the chain of men scatter, all of them clutching their buckets and fleeing from the pure, transparent column of water rising from the well's mouth like a languid snake. Malachite rushes into the town square just then, covered in soot and carrying an unconscious little girl in his arms, a terrified woman trailing behind him. He shoots a look at me, red eyes in red flames, and all I can do is shake my head.

Let him.

All we can do is let him.

This is what he wants, more than anything.

The water column writhes, undulates, and then pauses at the very peak of its height, looming tall over the village. And then Lucien gnashes his teeth, eyes flying open and the whites crawling with tendrils of black. Like a signal, the water darts forward, languid no longer, and winds between the piles of dirt being shoveled, picking up more and more of it, the transparency turning thick and dark. Mud.

The men leap back, the children start to cry, and elders make Kavar-praying motions, fingers to their eyes, and for a moment, I'm reminded of Ania. Ania Tarroux, the pious, beautiful, kind Goldblood who taught me how to pray.

Ania Tarroux, the girl I tried to give Lucien to. The girl who died, torn apart by Heartless on the road fleeing with her family to Helkyris.

I raise my fingers to my eyes, too. But it's not the New God I pray to. It's her.

Because she feels more real.

Because she loved him too, once.

Please, Ania. Please shield him from his own magic.

The muddy column grows distinct—fangs, a frill, a snub-tipped nose, and a long, forked tongue. A real snake. A snake like on every banner of his father's, every seal of his letters, every emblem of his breastcoats. Surrounded by the d'Malvane snake, making it flesh. Maybe not on purpose. Maybe, deep in his mind, it's a symbol he's always wanted his people to know as one of safety. Not Vetrisian witch-persecution. Not Vetrisian noble excess. *Protection.*

The snake hovers, as long and wide and big as a valkerax, and then strikes. It lunges after the fire on the granary's roof, snapping its jaws as the muddy water surges over the building. The snake eats the fire, a trail of smoke hissing up wherever it touches, and the fearful cries of the villagers slowly, *slowly* turn to cheering. Malachite whoops, and Fione's tense face allows a single small smile, one of the children squeezing her hand. Even the cow seems to relax, drooping its head and picking at a tuft of spared grass.

Lucien remains taut, arcing his midnight fingers to the left, and the snake moves with it, scattering over the village and shedding itself as it goes—sheafs of water like scales being dropped, all the fire sputtering out on contact. One by one, the village houses stop burning, smoldering down to mere hissing embers. Lucien raises his arms, and what's left of the snake ascends, higher and higher, before bursting out of its shape, muddy water raining down on the last of the buildings.

The cheering grows thunderous, and Lucien is swarmed by his people. Sweat and mud slicks his brow, but his face—his *expression*. Gods, it's like nothing I've ever seen. I thought I knew him happy. I thought I knew what that looked like. But I had no clue. I had no idea he could smile this big, laugh this purely and without care, the arms of his people reaching for him and embracing him tight. Like a savior. Like a brother.

Like a friend.

If there's one thing I've learned to admire about humans, it's that when there's nothing left, they become strongest.

The village is a blackened mess. The graves have been dug, and the bodies of loved ones buried. Not many.

not enough.

Even one is enough, I argue with the hunger.

The little girl Malachite saved is now an orphan.

The village gathers around her, around the campfire they've made—with some hesitation—to roast sweet tubers and saltpork. Women thread thoughtful fingers through the girl's messy hair, coo over her brilliant, sharp dark eyes. Her name is Dewen. She's five—almost Peligli's age—and she refuses to leave Malachite's side, shadowing him like an overly attached ferret and demanding to be picked up every few seconds. Malachite obliges insomuch as his patience allows, which is to say, instant deference every single time.

"You're awful light for a human," he grunts, circling the fire with her.

Dewen kicks her feet against his chainmail. "No."

"Yes," Malachite argues sagely.

"No!" She pouts.

The beneather looks over to where I'm sitting on a pile of mostly clean debris and grins. "Is it just me, or does she sound like someone you know, Six-Eyes?"

I stick my lip out exaggeratedly. "No."

He laughs and saunters off to show Dewen the Red Twins— two blood-red crescents high in the sky. I surreptitiously shove more of my dinner into my mouth—depressingly, fresh organs very suddenly became a non-rarity in this village. Most of the cows burned to cinder, but a few of their corpses were intact enough to feed from. Fione cut me out a liver herself, which I thought awfully nice of her.

As I wash my bloody hands in a nearby bucket, a sigh slips out. I didn't expect Lucien to wait on me hand and foot with soggy organs when I became his Heartless, but I didn't expect him to not speak to me for two whole halves, either. Granted, he's been surrounded by a thick ring of villagers since the moment he saved them—busy organizing the recovery efforts, turning down what gifts they could salvage from the fire and what village girls suddenly think him overwhelmingly attractive. And I mean, I've been busy also. Staring. And dressing what wounded would allow me near them with Fione. But mostly staring.

I suppose a busy prince is better than one who gazes off into the distance, toward the smoke column of Vetris, with eyes like the end of the world. But even so, I catch him doing it in quiet flickers between the bustle. Mourning.

I can feel Fione's gaze on me as she nears, wiping bloody hands on her apron. We both thoroughly inspect the crowd of villagers from afar.

"Aren't they supposed to hate witches?" I blow air out.

"It's difficult to hate someone who saves you," she muses. "Or someone who looks like, well. *That*."

She motions to Lucien's muddy everything. Even exhausted and covered in dirt, he's all sharp points and dark brows.

"They do share the same parents, don't they?" I lean back against the debris, wood digging into my back. There's a stillness, and then Fione heaves a sigh too, thumping me on the side of the boot with her cane.

"Come on. Let me show you how it's done."

"How what—"

She grabs my hand in her tiny one and pulls me to my feet with surprising strength. Haphazardly—but together—we march over to the thronging crowd around the prince.

"I learned very quickly that when one is in love with royalty," Fione says, words clear over the food-fire's gentle crackle, "they will always be busy. Always be in demand. One has to insert oneself into their lives, or you'll become just another subject. You'll fade away into the tapestries, and then they'll ask you where you were the whole time, and when you try to explain, it all becomes a massive load of irritation. Excuse me, *excuse me*, behind you—"

She shoulders through the crowd, parting them with the force of her stride and the height of her chin alone.

"But you're an archduchess!" I protest. "There's no way you—"

"Nobility is nobility," Fione says, weaving around a block of men. "Royalty is royalty. It's another world entirely, and all we can do is look in from the outside. And occasionally yell, when appropriate." She turns and barks shrilly over the crowd, "Lucien!"

I see his head pivot, his eyes widen, and he starts excusing himself and making his way over to us. Fione turns to me, the cold-tempered mask she's worn since Varia left the slightest bit softer.

"You're part of his life now. You get to take up space. You get to be greedy too, Zera. Never forget that."

Coming from her, after she's lost Varia...the words are as bittersweet as the sentiment. I try a smile and clutch her hand tighter. "Thank you."

A call from the medical tent draws her periwinkle eye, and she releases me. "I should get back. Good luck."

"Don't work yourself too hard."

"Impossible. Have you seen these hands?" She smooths her palms over each other. "I've barely worked a day in my life."

"You've worked quite a lot! With your brain."

"Brains are not hands."

"They're basically the same thing."

"If they were, perhaps we'd have an easier time holding on to our thoughts." She pauses, her grin miniscule. "This conversation is complete nonsense. You're rubbing off on me."

I grin back. "Unfortunately."

Her mouse-curls fade into the night, vanishing as she steps inside the medical tent. A voice warms the air behind me.

"Zera."

I turn to see Lucien standing there, all the villagers' eyes on him. Some try to hide it better than others, but most don't bother. He's their prince, after all, and a witch. I glare up at him.

"I'm still trying to figure it out," I say.

"Figure what out?" His black eyes gleam curious.

"Whatever it is about you they find so fascinating."

His scoff is soft. "I'm sure you have at least some idea."

"None at all, I'm afraid." I turn on my heel and start walking away from the throng of onlookers, into the near forest. "Except the part where you saved a lot of them from certain death. But that's not typically a quality I look for in a man."

"And why would you?" he agrees lightly, following after me. "You're immortal."

"True." I wave a finger. "But even immortals appreciate being saved from pain from time to time."

A blazing heat streaks into my palm, fitting there against my skin. He pulls, the momentum whirling me around and into the crook of his arm, pressed against his chest.

"Were you?" His brows knit down at me. "In pain?"

His mouth is so close, his cheekbone smeared with mud, his hair disheveled in a way it never got in the palace. Breathless. Sincere.

"N-No." The shameful truth squeezes out of me. "I—I just wanted your attention."

He tilts his head, outline near-fitting like a hovering puzzlelock before my nose and mouth. "You have it."

Warm ribbons wind down my throat, through my chest, pulling me closer to him. Enmeshed. When did it become so easy to touch him, so perfect? When did it become so easy to imagine him against my skin, over and over—

He swipes one finger along the bridge of my nose suddenly, then holds it up for me to see the gray smear.

"Ash." He chuckles. "You're covered in it."

"Don't bother forgiving my impertinence, but you're no bastion of cleanliness yourself, Your Highness—" I dodge out of his retaliatory kiss, putting a young tree between us.

"Then..." He peers around the trunk. "Should we rectify our sullied states?"

"Common Vetrisian if you please," I request, sidestepping his hand as he reaches for me. His dark eyes catch red moonlight.

"There's a creek not far from here—the headman told me it's where the well's source begins."

"And muck up what little water these poor people have left with our sheddings? I counted you better than that, my prince."

"There's a pool downstream. It'll be fine. More than fine—clean. Possibly even romantic."

"You are exceedingly good at precisely two things, Your Highness." I rest my chin in a branch and smirk up at him. "The color black, and wooing a woman with the idea of basic hygiene."

His gaze is a carefully kept smolder. "You're not going to let me kiss you right now, are you?"

"No."

"Very well." He rounds the tree. "Onward to basic hygiene, then."

With the most unsuitably giddy smile on my face, I follow him over the forest floor, the two of us picking through roots and around mossy boulders in wordless rhythm until the sound of the creek welcomes us. The pool is deep and small, the creek's waterfall a gentle patter as it empties in and then back out. Summer graces the little oasis with hanging strands of moss threaded with ground violets and white starflowers, the scent like melted sugar and the best parts of an apothecary. The tendrils float in the water, white and purple petals skating over the surface in a gentle, effervescent swirl with the current.

"Far more beautiful than I thought," Lucien breathes. "He made it sound like a mud hole."

He turns, and I hear him turn around again when he realizes I'm halfway through pulling my shift over my head. All I can see is gauzy white, and then freedom, my clothes pooled around me and the night air caressing my bare skin and the prince's back to me.

"Lucien," I start. "Aren't you coming?"

"In…" I hear him swallow. "In a moment."

If my smile gets any bigger, I'm fairly certain my head will split in two. And not in a way that can be healed back up with magic. Triumphant even in nakedness, I hover at the pool's edge and then slip in.

"Oh! It's perfect. A little cool, but that's never stopped me before."

"I remember it stopping you once," Lucien counters, unbuttoning his shirt. "When we first met."

"You were awfully cold, weren't you?" I laugh, wetting my hair. "Blackmailing me every chance you got."

"A precaution," he argues with zero bite to it.

"A way to test me, more like." I swim over to the side of the pool. "Well? Did I pass?"

I watch him shrug his shirt off, sword-muscles and thief-muscles and prince-muscles rippling beneath skin. His shoulder blades are as wicked sharp as I remember them—his spine a beautiful curve into the hem of his pants.

Pants.

Oh gods.

I look away just in time, the sound of a belt hitting the ground. My skin prickles red-hot under the water, goose bumps and tightness and...I can't let him see me like this. Cool. Composed. Zera Y'shennria is always cool and composed and ready with some quip. Worldly. Experienced. Never shy. It's one thing to see myself naked, but seeing him—

"I thought you said the water was cold?" His voice filters out from somewhere to my left, the water rippling as he slides in. "But your face is bright red."

"It—it is! Cold!" I start, my throat suddenly sand and gravel. "I was just—"

And then he's there, in front of me, standing chest deep in water and close enough to feel his body heat radiating through it. Droplets gleam on his collarbone as he leans in, putting one broad hand to my forehead.

"Do you have a fever?" He pauses. "Is it foolish of me to even ask if Heartless get sick?"

I can feel the outline of him, the barest skimming of skin against skin—my thighs, his wrist, his ribs, my fingers. Touching me. Just the lightest touch—

he used that against you, the hunger faintly calls from the depths. *touch.*

My eyes dart up to his face, points crystallizing in the mush he's made my brain into. I start, my laugh fragmented.

"I was so happy to be with you again, I almost forgot. You— Varia said you're a skinreader. All those times in Vetris, that kiss—"

Lucien's hawk eyes close for a moment, then open with renewed determination.

"I'm sorry," he says. "For all of that. The first time was a mistake—I didn't know I could do it. It just...happened."

"All your powers?" I press. "Just like that?"

"It was a dream." He nods. "Varia used to tell me witchbloods became true witches in dreams, but I never understood it. Until it happened. That night I called you to the West Tower, with Malachite and Fione, I dreamed of a tree."

I slide my fingers through the black-silk water uneasily. "The Bone Tree?"

"No. Just a tree. One of many, in a barren forest of red. It glowed faintly pearl, faintly rainbow, but it was just a tree. I dreamed of it, and it—it didn't *speak*, per se. But it stood there, and I watched it, and it made things happen in my head, feelings that weren't mine. Places I'd never been to. Moments I'd never see."

"It wasn't...it wasn't covered in stained glass, was it?"

"Like from the Hall of Time?" he muses. "No. Though I suppose even that's gone, too."

He stares into the water, the perfect dark reflecting his own face back at him. I can see the destruction in his head, playing out in the iron memorization of his home, his city. He knew every street, every street urchin. He knows what Vetris looks like destroyed without even having to try.

"I'm sorry," I say. "About Vetris."

"You shouldn't be."

"I got her the Bone Tree. I—"

"You know my sister by now. You know how determined she is. She would've gotten it one way or another. And my father—" His next inhale comes sharp. "Vetris has no idea how to fight against valkerax. No one does. No one but the Old Vetrisians, and they're long dead and gone."

"The beneathers," I try.

He thinks about it, then nods. "If we could get their aid—if I could speak to the ancestor council, I might persuade them. But—"

His shoulders faintly shake. Gingerly, I raise my hand to him, warm skin on warm skin.

"But what?" I press.

"It takes twelve beneathers to take down just one valkerax. And a majority of them die in the process. They're strong, immune to fire. The *human* death toll to kill just one...it's not feasible. The sheer amount of valkerax we saw with Varia that day on the mountain— there's too many of them. Even *with* the beneathers' help."

"But we can try," I say. "Maybe—when we explain to the High Witches what's going on, they'll want to help. And then we get the beneathers, and what's left of the Cavanosian army, and maybe the Helkyrisian armada, and together—"

"It's just the four of us." He sighs. "We can't remake the old concordats. That was a thousand years ago—and it took decades of valkerax violence before the Mist Continent caved and made them."

"But we can *try*," I stress.

My hand slides down, and he captures it with his, bringing it to his lips. Featherlight, still, molten beneath the satin sheen of water.

"Just for a night," he murmurs against my palm. "Just for one night, I don't want to think about it. Is that...selfish of me?"

My laugh is half breath, all nerves. "You're allowed to be

selfish once in a while, Your Highness."

His eyes dart up to mine, the unspoken future written out, chosen by my word choice. Choices, made one by one, to bring me standing here, in a starlit pool with the most beautiful person I've ever known.

I reach my free hand out to his left one, wanting so badly to interlace our fingers. He's looking at me with so much softness, but his hand doesn't. Doesn't give. It just hangs there, my fingers working into his clumsily. Doesn't he feel it?

He glances down, and I see his eyes widen. But still, his fingers don't move.

"Is...is something wrong?" I ask.

"No." He pulls his hand out of mine. "I'm just tired."

Cold, slow horror crawls into my lungs. The teleportation of the four of us from the airship all the way into the village. And then the water snake, winding and enormous.

"Lucien, your magic—"

Suddenly, he pulls his whole body away from mine, and his hawk eyes harden. "It's not that."

"Then what is it?" I step in, the water feeling like tar. "What else makes you lose function in your body? Surely you weren't poisoned when I wasn't looking?"

Lucien turns, bracing his hands on the rock wall like he's going to pull himself out of the pool. But he just hovers there, clutching on to the harsh, wet rock, to the cracks and crevices of it, one hand limper than the other.

"You can't keep doing this to yourself." A plead tinges my voice, and it's so strange. Uncomfortable and pinching like a brand-new pair of shoes.

"It's *my* magic," he asserts softly.

"You're *my* witch," I fire back. "I'm your Heartless. It's my magic, too."

He falls silent at that, and I watch the water ripple around the small of his torso with a helplessness bubbling in my veins.

"You said," I start, "that whatever I choose, you'd still love me. So I'm telling you now: whatever you choose, I'll still love you. But I won't stand by and watch you hurt yourself over and over. You've done that enough for the both of us."

He's quiet, and then he tilts his head barely over his shoulder, nose and mouth strong. "There's no other way to stop her."

"There might be. You don't know that for sure."

"I know that when the time comes, I'll have to fight her," he says. "Witch to witch. And the thought terrifies me."

"She—she won't kill you—"

"No. But I might kill her."

A thousand weights settle on my chest in an instant. His own sister. The sister he looked up to so fervently, the sister he missed so dearly. The sister who grew up with him, who looked after him. Family. If I could remember what family meant…would I fight them? Knowing I might have to kill them?

No. Not in a million years.

From somewhere completely unknown, I fish up the courage to speak. "It'd be different, I suppose, if you hated her."

His laugh is the bitter, quiet kind. "Yes. It would be."

I wade over, ungraceful and uncaring and desperate to touch him. To make things right. Or even just a little right*er*. I wrap my arms around him, pressing all of me into his back to let him know I'm here. Always.

"I'm sorry." I say the only thing I can say. His voice this time is hoarse, and on the verge. Of what, I have no idea. I might never know. But I don't need to know.

All I need to do is be here.

"As am I."

7

THE IRON LADY AND THE STARVING WOLF

A dream again.

I'm— *No.*

Not me, *her.*

Varia's standing on a beach, me inside her body and looking out. I've never seen the ocean, or if I have in my past human life, I can't remember it. Those memories are sealed in my heart. It's water, *so much water*, but it's wide and wild and pulsing like living steel edged white.

She stands on a gray-sand beach and looks out at the ocean. She can feel it calling, a faint bell with only one word, getting louder.

destroy.

destroy.

<u>**destroy.**</u>

This world must be destroyed.

She looks down at her hands, at her wood fingers and fine nails. She hates the world, and it should all be destroyed. Every last unfair bit of it. No! *She doesn't.* She loves it. She loves…a girl. But which girl? Mousy hair, blue eyes, but her features are lost. Lost in the sea of burning and ravaging and breaking.

destroy.

The voice is the hunger, and it is not. It's the inverse, the opposite, the void where there is presence. It is a voice without sound, thought without intention. It's a hunger stranger than mine. Different than mine and yet the same. It wants us to be the worst we can be, always.

Our black hair whips around our face, the sea breeze brutal, and we watch it be brutal to the water. To the world.

Beneath the torrid waves, white manes rise like shark fins.

I wake up with a headache and a looming sense of dread. Varia. No mistaking it this time. That was Varia, what she was seeing. But *why* can I see through her? Why only in dreams? And why is she standing on a beach, staring?

Staring at *what*?

I think about telling Lucien and Fione and Mal. But then I get a horrifying thought—if I can see through her, can she see through *me*? Am I endangering everyone? *Again?* But I have to stop her. I have to stay with them and stop her.

All I can do is put my boots on, one lace at a time.

The village is sorry to see us go.

They stand at the edge of the ruin that was once their home, a nauseating mixture of mud and blackened char squelching beneath so many pairs of boots. The mosquitos are out in full force, the air heavy and muggy with a looming thunderstorm, but they couldn't care less, gathered as they are, waving their prince off down the road.

"We could've taken *more* cheese," Malachite drawls, his arms packed full of paper-wrapped wheels of the stuff.

"You look ridiculous," I tease. "Like you're about to tip over."

"Into a bed, hopefully, where I will stay for the rest of the season."

"Nonsense," Fione says as she passes us, cane thumping more

easily in the drier mud of the road. "You have work to do. We all do."

"Ravenshaunt is twenty-five miles northeast," Lucien asserts, looking at a half-burned map the headman palmed to him before we left.

"Should we commandeer a horse? Or four?" Malachite asks, adjusting cheeses so his hand can twitch back toward the blade strapped to his spine.

"No," Lucien says. "When we get closer, I can teleport us."

"No, you will not," I start. "Save your energy."

Lucien's eyes grow tired and thin as he looks over at me. "My magic is a tool, Zera. It should be used."

"Yes," I agree lightly. "But not for every little thing. We have legs, Lucien. We can walk."

"It would be faster to—"

"I'm not going to have you lose another hand just because—"

I bite my tongue too late, and not hard enough. Malachite and Fione go still, the birds in the trees go still, and Lucien makes a clicking sound.

Malachite starts toward him, cheeses spilling. "Luc, you can't do this horseshit so lightly—"

"It's not horseshit," Fione says evenly. "It's magic." She fixes her gaze on the prince, periwinkle-blue turning icy on the edges. "Which means it's dangerous. You have to treat it with respect."

"You don't understand—"

"No, *you* don't understand," I interrupt Lucien. "You're important to us. You're the one who ties us together—ties the whole fucking *country* together. Sacrificing parts of yourself to stop Varia faster is not how we do this."

"Then, pray tell." He snarls. "How *do* we do this? You obviously know better than I."

of course we know better. The hunger grows louder, as if it's echoing his anger. *silly young thing, we've been fighting before you, shedding blood before you—*

"I *don't* know any better," I fire back. "But this can't keep going on. You need to get a handle on your magic. You need to understand—watching you throw pieces of yourself away just to stop Varia—"

"I will do whatever it takes." His voice turns stony, with none of the vulnerability from the pool last night. "Alone, if I have to."

"Don't be ridiculous," Malachite scoffs. "I thought we've learned our lesson about 'doing things alone'—"

"If the four of us are going to stop my sister," the prince interrupts, "if we're going to stop who knows how many thousands of raging valkerax, all of us have to be ready. Ready to do *anything*."

He's made some decision between last night and this morning. I watched his back as he slept, rising and falling in his bedroll in the woods, and I knew his mind was churning. But not in this direction. Our direction.

"Lucien—" I start.

"You're just as bad as she is!"

It's a loud, clear voice, burning in the muggy air. Fione, her hair undone, sweat beading her brow and anger flushing her whole face the brightest red. Since the moment Varia touched the Bone Tree, she's been subdued, tempering herself to keep back the pain. But now it radiates off her like heat waves.

"If you think sacrificing yourself to stop her is the right thing, then you're just as bad as she is. Just as fanatic. Just as foolish. Just as short-godsdamn-sighted!"

Her shrill notes ring. Malachite's chest deflates, and I can't look anywhere but at my hands.

"I don't want to lose her!" Fione shouts. "I don't want to lose you, either. I don't want to lose *anyone* anymore!"

I look away with a wince. Fione's voice fractures, the shards of her anger falling by the wayside as her fists unclench and her eyes water.

"If the only way to win is by losing, then I don't want to win at all."

human fools, the hunger sneers, burning quieter now. *nothing can be gained without something being lost. that is the nature of nature. it is futile to fight it.*

Lucien looks utterly thunderstruck. Malachite's frozen, Fione panting. Above us, the storm clouds roll out a too-perfect rumble of thunder. The graves. I look up, to the white peaks of the distant Tollmont-Kilstead mountains. All I can think about are the graves, sitting in the snow. Fourteen red ribbons, fourteen iron bells. My steps are tender as I walk up to Lucien's side. Not touching, but close enough.

"Is death really a victory?" I ask him softly. "Is sacrifice really something to celebrate? Or something to mourn?"

Lucien's head inclines ever so slightly over his shoulder, hawk eyes slicing just the barest part of my neck. Malachite is the first to start walking again, gathering the spilled cheeses up in his arms.

"Arguing's better when you walk," he says. "Gets all the angst out through the legs."

Fione finally breaks her gaze from Lucien's face, and she starts walking after the beneather, cane stabbing the ground with remnant simmering fury. I reach out two fingers to touch Lucien's hand—the left one. The unmoving one.

"You—" I swallow. "You're important. To me."

He says nothing, mouth tight and faced away from me.

"I'm the Heartless," I say. "I grow back. Let me do the sacrificing, all right?"

There's a moment where he pivots, looking as if he's about to say something. But then his brow furrows. He thinks, tries to open his mouth again. The words are hard. They always are.

Sometimes, words aren't needed.

I squeeze his left hand in mine, and he switches me to his right hand, the one that can squeeze back, and together we walk down the storm-shadowed road.

Optimistically, I never thought I'd see the Bone Road again. Maybe in the afterlife, in the final fevered death-dream of mine, but not in the flesh. Or the dirt, as it were. The same long twin ruts in the road, the same rabbit dens and long grasses swaying, the same Sunless War mass graves in the distance—graves that will swell to capacity soon—between boggy pools and throngs of fireflies. It's the same, save for the minor fact that Nightsinger's forest is missing.

Though "missing" isn't the right word. When fire takes something, it takes violently and with scars—visible dark reminders. Swathes of black as far as the eye can see, crisped trunks of only the tallest trees all that's left. If I squint, I think I can see the stone foundation of Nightsinger's cabin, but it's more likely wishful projection. More likely a lump of decaying plant matter. This massive scar, all that's left of the place I spent three years of my life. Living. Dying. And living again. Fighting my first fight. Dueling my first duel. Learning to love Crav and Peligli, each in their own way. Learning to love Nightsinger, and hate her, and admire her all at once.

Learning how to live again, without a family. Without humanity. Without a heart.

Nightsinger and Peligli and Crav left before the fires. Y'shennria promised she'd warn them, and I trust that she did. They're alive still, somewhere. But the forest is very much dead. If I close my eyes, I can still hear the woodlarks calling to each other, the crackle of branches as animals move through their daily ritual. The breath of the forest.

Gone.

The smell is decay and burned things. This is what it feels like to be empty. To miss something you never thought you would.

Lucien catches my stride as we walk past it. "This...isn't this it? Varia told me—"

"Yeah," I agree quickly.

"I'm sorry," he says.

"Why? You didn't burn it down."

"No. But my father did."

"Don't start apologizing for awful parental figures." I force a smile at him. "Or we'll be here all day."

His snort is faint, but he stays with me every step of the way, until we peel off from the Bone Road entirely and onto a smaller path, and I'm secretly grateful for it.

As the Ravenshaunt name implies, one sees the ravens first, circling heavy in the sky. And then one sees the ruined parapets, thirty-year-old bleached banners caught between the holes in the mortar and rippling in the wind. Thunderclouds gather like steel wool over the skeleton of the fortress—castle? Keep? I'm not sure what to call it now. All I know is it was once a home. For Y'shennria, for her family.

Time changes things.

Even an immortal, magical thrall who never ages.

"She just said she'd be waiting here for you?" Fione asks.

"Yeah."

Her rosebud lips crinkle. *"Where?"*

"All right, yes," I start cheerily. "It's a pile of rocks. But maybe there's a door on it, somewhere."

"We should spread out and search," Lucien agrees. "Mal, take south. I'll take north. Fione, west, and Zera—"

"East. Got it."

His voice stops us before we can scatter. "Be careful. I think there's magic here."

"What kind?" Malachite quirks a white brow.

"The waiting kind."

It's ominous, but we have work to do. We peel off, Malachite and me walking the same direction. There's a beat, and then I smile.

"First one to find the magic probably perishes."

"Cheery thought," Malachite agrees, and I nudge him.

"Look on the bright side. There's a one in four chance I find it and that's fine. But, I mean, even if you die, Lucien can just make you a Heartless! With me."

He shoots me a withering ruby-eyed look. "You seriously don't know by now?"

I blink. "Know what?"

"Have you *ever* seen a witch with a nonhuman Heartless?"

"I've seen maybe four witches in my life."

He sighs. "Only humans can become Heartless."

"Oh." I blink. "Well. That explains a lot."

"Does it?" he drawls, pushing me gently away from him. I stumble to a stop in front of the east side, and he turns the corner around half a stone stairwell and is gone.

Y'shennria's home is even more ruined than I thought. Up close, you can see all the witchfire marks, black and deep, and the remnants of a battle. Massacre, really. Old, *old* bloodstains on scraps of rug and bookshelves, hidden from the elements by the ruined walls so well I wouldn't know the brown marks were blood at all if the hunger couldn't smell it. I shudder and try not to think of any of the bloodstains being Y'shennria's. Or worse—her family's. Her baby's.

This place is just a shell—barely any infrastructure left at all. Y'shennria's hiding *here*? Maybe there's a cellar sequestered away somewhere, because there sure as the afterlife isn't a single room left intact. There isn't even enough hall left to walk in, my shoes finding purchase in the titanic piles of stone bricks and wooden support beams bleached pale by the grassland sun.

The thunderstorm hits right when I reach the top of one such pile, crackling lightning across the sky. This pile is the tallest out of the ruins and gives me a perfect view of everyone else— Lucien with his eyes to the ground, Fione tapping semi-intact walls with her cane suspiciously, and Malachite on his hands and knees, listening with those blade-long ears of his. A banner flaps beneath my feet, and I squat, pulling it up by its loose threads and admiring the washed-out emblem I can finally see—a raven with four wings taking off from a single tree.

"Where are you?" I whisper to the emblem. "I miss you."

Something behind me crackles and I whip around, ready for the inevitable landslide of brick and wood I've created by disturbing the pile. But there's nothing. No movement, or rather, a movement so small I barely see it at all. There, in the center of the pile and on the very top, something pokes up green from the dust and debris. It grows, bigger and bigger, before my eyes and only when it sprouts a bud and many fine thorns do I realize it's magic.

A magic black rose that blooms right in front of me.

Y'shennria. The thickets of them in front of her manor in Vetris.

I can't contain my laugh as I walk over and peer down at it, half embarrassed. "You seriously weren't supposed to hear that."

"There you are." I jump at Lucien's voice so close all of a sudden. He's standing behind me on the rubble, eyes riveted to the rose. "Gods above—emotion magic."

"Is that…a big thing?" I ask.

"It's difficult," he asserts.

"Oh? And how would you know? Have you been trying to spell emotions lately?"

"For a while I thought I could get you to leave Varia using it," he admits. "But it turned out to be far beyond my capabilities. And my conscience."

I ignore the barest swelling of my chest. "Right. So. What does this little thing mean?"

"Someone who knows you made this spell," he muses. "They knew you'd come here, and you'd feel a specific emotion in this approximate area. It's tailored to you, and only you. Very delicate work—and a very powerful witch."

My heart hammers. "Nightsinger?"

He pauses for a moment. "No."

"How would you know?" I frown. "You've never met her."

"I've felt her," he says. "Through you. No, this is someone much more powerful. And with help from someone else, someone who knows you very well."

"Y'shennria," I breathe. "This is her sign to me. Can you do anything with it?" I pause and give him a knowing look. "Something that *won't* hurt you?"

"Perhaps," he agrees. "Go find Malachite and Fione, and I'll think of something."

I have the creeping urge to refuse, thinking it some ploy to get me away so he can do risky magic again. But he just stares at me, and I know I have to go. I have to trust him. If we don't have trust between us, we have nothing.

When I get back with Mal and Fione on my heels, Lucien is sitting by the rose, stock-still, his hands folded in his lap. He looks comfortable, but there's a sheen of sweat on his temple, and his grimace is one of pain.

"Is he all right?" Fione asks.

"He's not doing that overexerting thing again, is he?" Malachite reaches out to shake Lucien's shoulder when a voice cuts through the air.

"I wouldn't touch him if I were you."

All three of us whirl, Malachite's unsheathing blade ringing, the rapid clicks of Fione's crossbow cane unfolding, and my claws piercing out through my flesh instantly, bloodied and over-ready. I freeze at the figure standing on the pile with us, velvet purple cloak billowing around them. They lower their hood, and all it takes is seeing that gorgeous mass of fluffy hair pinned with amethysts to know.

My claws jerk back in, my eyes wide. "Y…Y'shennria?"

Her dark face with its high cheekbones lights up, softly and all at once. "Zera."

Her voice. It's the same. Cool, precise. It echoes even now in my head as it always has, teaching me, reminding me of the rules.

In Vetrisian court custom, one does not embrace. Unless one is family.

I run, unthinkingly—scrabbling over the pile, bricks and wood flying, my arms reaching for her through the swirling dust.

And she catches me, hands and all.

Scarred neck and all.

Smile and all.

"I must admit—you surprised me, Your Highness," Y'shennria says, her arm laced in mine as we walk the perimeter of Ravenshaunt. "The rose's spell was to bring me to Ravenshaunt should Zera return, but I didn't expect to find you here—casting your own spell of all things!"

"You find me just as surprised, Lady Y'shennria," Lucien admits. "With all due respect, Father and his ministers had you branded a traitor. I thought I'd never see you again."

"On the chopping block, maybe," Malachite offers.

"Malachite," Fione warns. "Manners."

Y'shennria smiles, her every step like air over water—all elegance and measured steps. "Oh, Your Grace, I hardly think that's of much concern now, considering the position we're all in."

Just having Y'shennria close, the ability to walk with her like this—it's everything I've been wanting. To have someone who knows what I've been through is a silent source of strength. It's strange to say, but even her lavender perfume relaxes me. Lucien, on the other hand, is the exact opposite. His posture's completely changed—from Whisper-relaxed to Prince-straight. Y'shennria clearly reminds him of the court, of his position. Of everything he left back in Vetris.

"Now then." Y'shennria's smile fades, her seriousness bringing the faintest of creases to her mouth. "I'd appreciate it greatly if you would tell me why you're all here, and with Zera still Heartless."

Catching Y'shennria up on all of what'd happened after she left is easier than I expected—a lot of it she'd heard from secondhand witch sources inside Vetris. She's already acutely aware of King Sref's movements thanks to Windonhigh's vigilance, so I don't need to tell her about his army gathering. Or being destroyed. Evlorasin escaping was another thing she didn't need to be told—the whole country knows a radiant, rainbow-sheathed valkerax had burst forth from under the city and flew away. Everything else is fair game—Varia, the Bone Tree, Evlorasin's training. She wants to know everything. And, unlike nearly everyone else I've encountered, her dark eyes hold not a scrap of judgment for my choices.

"You did what you thought was best for your own future. Albeit misguidedly." She looks at Lucien with a small smile. "It sounds as if she's given you enough headaches for a lifetime, Your Highness."

"Two lifetimes." He sighs, rubbing the bridge of his nose.

"And it sounds as if you wish for her to give you more. Why else would you make her your Heartless?"

"Necessity," I blurt before he can say anything. "Varia didn't seem keen on letting me go, even after our agreement."

"You *are* very useful." Y'shennria's lip-twist is so small, I'm guessing only I notice it. I give her a casual shrug and a full-blown smirk.

"And here I am, unable to admit to it because you taught me modesty above all things—"

"Forgive me, Lady Y'shennria," Fione interrupts. "But where

have you been?"

"The only place Old God families like me are safe anymore," she answers swiftly. "Windonhigh."

There's a beat as the four of us share a look. Y'shennria obviously notices it—she's a master of social cues, after all—but she pretends she doesn't.

"I was planning on bringing Zera up to Windonhigh, should she come," Y'shennria continues, glancing over at me. "Nightsinger's there. And Crav and Peligli haven't once stopped telling me how much they miss you."

A sharp pang runs through the center of my chest. "They're safe?"

"The safest place for them in Cavanos," Y'shennria agrees. "Yes."

It's hard to know when you've been holding on to something until you finally let it go, or it leaves of its own accord. You can't know how heavy it weighs on you until it vanishes, and all that weight is suddenly and wonderfully missing. I'd been carrying around so much worry for the three of them that only snowballed the more Vetris geared up for war, and now...

Now there's room to breathe.

"Sometimes, the gods aren't so bad after all." I exhale.

"We're searching for a way to destroy Varia's hold over the valkerax," Lucien starts. "Is there any way we could accompany you and Zera to Windonhigh?"

Y'shennria's lips knit in a tight line. I know that look. It's the "with conditions" look.

"A High Witch made this rose for me, as a favor. I was to bring back only Zera."

"Y'shennria...please." I turn to her. "I'll beg if I have to."

She thinks on this, the wind rustling through her high hair, and then she turns back to Lucien.

"You must understand, Your Highness. You may be a witch

now, but you are still the prince of Cavanos. The enemy."

"There *is* no enemy anymore," Malachite cuts. "Vetris is gone."

Fione and I both look to Lucien, but he's completely still, even his hands slack.

"Not entirely gone," Y'shennria starts softly.

"But debilitated enough they won't be an issue for the witches," the beneather presses. "Not for a long-arse time."

"You'd be surprised at the human ability to bounce back."

"And you'd be surprised, ma'am, at what little tolerance I have for pointless upworlder squabbling. The valkerax are here. And we have to stop them. Are your High Witches going to help or not?"

Y'shennria moves from one foot to the other, her lavender silk dress swaying uneasily with the movement. Malachite won't give an inch, chin high and eyes red spears.

"I promise you," he continues, hard, "that witch flesh and human flesh burn the same."

None of us says anything, Lucien not stepping in with a reprimand, nor Fione with an addendum. Just silence. Just Y'shennria's hazel eyes flickering over each of us in turn, and none of us blinking.

Finally, she exhales what sounds like a laugh. "I see you're all very serious about this."

"And I see you aren't as much," Lucien says. She turns her eyes on him slowly. Tension winds the air like a bard turning his lute, tight and absolute. I can't stand to see the two of them at odds, so I step in.

"Everyone's trying, okay?" I hold up my hands. "Y'shennria, just two days. Give us two days in Windonhigh, and we'll be gone."

"'Us?'" she leads. "So you'll leave with them?"

"I—"

"What about Crav, Peligli? Nightsinger? And..." She trails off, looking at her own hands. "You'd be *safe* with us."

"I know." I nod. "I know that. And I'm grateful for it. But I—"

I gulp. "I have to finish what I started. Varia has the Bone Tree partly because of—"

"Zera," Lucien exhales the word, like a reminder I'm not at fault.

"Because of me," I finish. "She has it sooner, now, because of *me*. I enabled her power. And I'm going to disable her power. I'm not going to run from guilt anymore. I'm going to fight, like Reginall said—every moment of every day."

Y'shennria's silent for a long moment, her brows tightening over her sharp eyes. I know she's tabbing me up, calculating hows and whys. Finally, she gives a quick nod.

"Very well. Two days."

"Let us go, then," Lucien says. "Immediately, so as to inconvenience you as little as possible."

"It's no inconvenience to me, Your Highness," Y'shennria says, motioning for us to follow her over the rubble and back to the rose sprouting there. "It is the High Witches who will have issue with it. They are not the most trusting sort."

"Understandably," Fione murmurs.

Y'shennria gathers us around the rose and looks to Lucien. "You may have to contribute to the teleportation spell, Your Highness. They are expecting only two to return."

Lucien nods. "Right."

"Don't overdo it," Malachite warns.

Lucien shoots him a tired smile. "Yes, *sir*."

Y'shennria has us clasp hands, the black rose centered in the middle of us. Lucien bows his head, his fingers holding mine going black. His left hand—it might not work, but the magic still eats at it whenever he casts. Maybe…just *maybe*, someone in Windonhigh can give him the witch wisdom he needs to temper his magic. To stop using it to destroy himself. That's all I can hope for, because he hasn't listened to me thus far.

I swallow imaginary glass.

if the boy you love destroys himself to stop his sister because you gave her the Bone Tree—

My brain brandishes a white mercury sword against the hunger, the gloom.

No.

We're fighting the guilt this time. To the teeth.

To the death.

The thunderclouds choose that moment to finally open up, a gentle pitter-patter pattering down harder until it's entire sheets of water dumping on us, completely drenching the bleached and thirsty ruins. We wait, and wait again, a string of sick-wet moments, until my ears pop with that familiar nothingness, the world dimming to rushing blackness, and light and sound coming back in all at once.

Thunder replaced by rushing wind. Not the sort I'm used to—through trees or bushes or the grasslands. Lighter than that. Freer than that. Wind without boundaries, unhindered, howling against and with itself. The light is the near-dying sort, the sun hanging low and silver on the horizon.

But I see it clearly.

Just the horizon. Just the sun, and stretched out before us are nothing but puffy white clouds. A quilt of them, as far as the eye can see. We're high, *so* high. We're standing and dripping water on a small platform of what looks like dirt and stone, overgrown with moss and grass. It looks like land, but it isn't. It can't be, because there are *clouds* simmering just inches away, the drop down hundreds of miles.

"Windonhigh," I hear Fione mutter next to me, and I turn to face her direction.

There, on top of the endless sea of cotton clouds, is green. Green land, rife with trees, and between them sandstone spires like lighthouses, like the *tallest* lighthouses in existence, stretching so high they seem impossible. Impossible too in the way they're twisted, smooth and hollow with hundreds of windows and yet bent around each other organically, like stone trees grown side-by-side. The stone spires end somewhere, the green trees end somewhere, sheer cliff-faces peeking from white fluff. The land looks like it's been lifted from the ground, torn out, dirt and stone and roots dangling down into sheer blue sky.

A city.

It's a city in the sky.

And the *crows*.

White crows everywhere—in the trees, in the spires, flying and nesting and chattering. White deer, eating from the little meadows dotting the city. Pure white bears, sunning themselves in the afternoon light filtered through the trees, fishing in little rivers that start somewhere I can't see and drip diamond water over the edge of the land and down into the sky.

White animals, this many—*witches*. Witches shapeshifted.

Hundreds of white crows streak by us, close enough to drop feathers, close enough to hear their cawing and see their black eyes watching. They tear through and by us, doing easy loops around my head, hairpin-turns over Lucien's shoulder, swirling between Fione and Malachite in dizzying spirals. The cacophony blasts my eardrums, ringing wingbeats and scratching caws, and as quickly as the horde comes, they're gone, only three crows hovering on the little shard of sky-land we stand on.

And then they're not crows at all. White feathers elongate, take on the color and texture of cloth, bird-legs turn to human-legs in a twisted flash, and three people stand in front of us, hair blown by the wind.

Witches.

A particular witch, with an awe-inspiring mane of tawny hair and the stature of a statue—thick arms, powerful waist, and a face like the roundest moon with the brightest smile.

"Zera." Her green eyes crinkle. "Welcome home."

8

WINDONHIGH

"Nightsinger!" I cry, the looming death-drop just beyond my feet forgotten as I launch myself at her. "I—I never thought—"

"As did I," she agrees softly, embracing me. Always soft, eyes evergreen. "I'm sorry. I'm sorry for sending you off on such a selfish mission—"

"It's okay. Really." I flash a smile. "We're here now, and I'm starting to learn that's all that matters."

Nightsinger's nod is small, her smile wry. "Crav and Peligli are very excited to see you. You must have so much to talk about." Her eyes slide over to Lucien as he steps to my side. "Ah."

"Greetings," he starts with a careful bow, eyes never leaving her.

"You—" One of the witches at Nightsinger's side narrows his gaze.

"We will allow them entry, Valeweaver," Nightsinger says instantly. "For he is witch."

"It is custom to entertain brethren in one's home," the other witch at her side murmurs, her stunningly embroidered mantle lifting in the wind.

"But—" Valeweaver's tail of braids whips with his indignation. "He looks exactly like Laughing Daughter. He feels just like her. Is she not—is *he* not—"

"He's the prince of Cavanos," Malachite suddenly cuts in,

standing in front of Lucien with what I know by now to be his lightly menacing aura. "And if you've got a problem with that, you can take it up with me and all four feet of my sword."

"What our beneather friend means to say," Fione jumps in, "is that we won't be here long."

"They've requested two days," Y'shennria says to Valeweaver.

"How do we know he's not on the Laughing Daughter's side?" he argues. "They're family! They're—"

Lucien muscles around Malachite, his expression all granite and ice. "My sister and I have parted ways. Forever."

To hear the words from his own mouth, in his own voice, is chilling. It stirs up some sick feeling in my gut. Guilt. Guilt and the hunger that preys on it.

because of you—

But we fight it. We fight it instead of give in to it. We cut it off, we don't even entertain it anymore. The wind brays at our wet clothes, and Fione starts to shiver. I walk over and offer her my arm, a body-heat embrace, and she takes it, leaning hard into me.

"It is not for us to decide whether they stay or go," Nightsinger says. "Guests of import are to be brought to the High Ones. Do you have objections?"

Valeweaver frowns but steps back. "No. None."

"Wonderful." Nightsinger turns to me and smiles. "Then let us depart. There are so many eager to meet you."

"Go where, exactly?" Malachite motions at the empty sky separating us and the major floating landmass in the distance.

"You, sir, speak far too much for a bodyguard," Y'shennria quips.

Malachite feigns utter flattery, fanning his face. "*Goodness.* Thank you."

"Can my friends and loved ones maybe try to get along, please?" I posit the question to the air, not really expecting a response.

"Prince of Cavanos, come, if you would," Nightsinger says over the squabble. Lucien walks to her, to the edge of the small plateau we stand on, and they face outward toward the sky together.

"What, pray tell, is your witch name?" Nightsinger asks. Lucien hesitates, and Nightsinger senses it, smiling gently. "No harm can be done to one witch with another's name. That is only a Heartless's caution. But it must be shared if you wish to spell with us."

I watch his dark eyes thinking, choosing to trust the other half of his bloodline, and then he says, "Black Rose."

"Black Rose." Nightsinger offers her hand. "Shall we?"

Something wordless passes between them, and he takes it. Their fingers grow instantly dark, too-quickly staining with midnight void at the same rate, like mirror images of each other. Lucien lets out a strangled choke and pulls away like he's been burned. The sound of Malachite's sword unsheathing is a half-second harbinger of his anger. And mine.

"What did you do to him—"

"Don't hurt—"

"It's fine," Lucien says suddenly, panting and holding his hand up to us. "Both of you. I'm *fine*."

"Apologies, Zera," Nightsinger says softly. "You must be so worried. What a tangled thing, to be both Heartless and lover."

I blink, not understanding at all. But Lucien does.

"You—" he starts. "You're a skinreader, too."

"You are?" I turn to her, agape. I never knew. Not for the three years I lived with her.

Nightsinger smiles patiently, fox-green eyes two content slits. "Together we could do great things, Black Rose," she says. "But for today, we will only make a path."

He's looking at her with a whole new expression—something like fear, like respect, like a student looks at a teacher, and then he nods.

"Together," he says.

"We could help—" Valeweaver offers.

"No." The other witch shakes her head. "Let our new brethren learn."

Nightsinger offers her hand again, and this time Lucien takes it without hesitation. The wind blares between the silence, between their fingers growing black at the tips and upward, and then it happens.

I've learned magic is silent, until suddenly it's not.

There's a persistent, quiet crackle like a sugar crust being broken, and then the empty space of cloud between our plateau and the main land springs to life, the clouds shifting and moving and reassembling into one flat white plane, wispy lattices growing around and up until they enmesh as one.

It's a tunnel. A beautiful, unreal tunnel spun out of clouds.

Nightsinger and Lucien let go, and she starts walking across, flanked by her two witches. Y'shennria follows, and I'm about to yelp for her to stop—she'll fall through. They're *clouds*. But her silk shoes land as if it's solid ground, the only clue it's not being the little puffs of white wisp eking from under her soles with every step. And the fact she's not plummeting to her demise.

"I suppose this would be a bad time to mention I'm afraid of heights," Malachite drawls.

"Close your eyes," I tease. "I'll lead you by the hand."

"If you wanted to hold my hand, Six-Eyes, all you had to do was ask."

I boop his nose. "You're delusional."

Lucien turns to us then and says, "Let's go."

"Do we have to?" Malachite asks. "It looks like death."

"Oh, please," Fione snorts. "It's just magic."

She's the first to walk past Lucien, to set foot on the cloudbridge and cross it with her head held fearlessly high.

"The polymathematical genius is right," I chirp, walking after her and stamping my boots hard on the cloud for effect. "It's. Just. Magic!"

Malachite follows, one toe at a time, swearing in beneather the whole way as I tug him along. Lucien catches up to me and slides his left hand in my free one. Even if he can't move it, it feels good. A reassurance.

"It was hard for you in that forest for three years," he murmurs. "Wasn't it?"

The question catches me off guard and digs far deeper than it should. Than I want it to. Did he—

"I saw it," he admits. "Through Nightsinger."

I want to get mad at this invasion of privacy, but I can't. My past is the one thing I don't mind him seeing, the one thing I never told him properly. Maybe it's better he saw it through Nightsinger— more accurate. More real. More true to why and how I came to Vetris to steal his heart.

"It was...it was dark," I start. "And lonely. But not always. Isn't that how everything is, though? How life is?"

"No," he says. "I think you had it differently than most. And harder than most."

I nudge an elbow in his ribs lightly. "So did you."

"I didn't ever lose my heart," he says. "Or watch my parents get killed. Or get killed myself. Or lose all those memories."

His insistence hits like a bell, echoing in my empty ribs. I want to argue, to insist he had it worse, but there's no use in comparing things, is there? It's all right to say I had it hard. It's all right to say I suffered and not put someone else before that. My pain is my pain, and it feels good—more than good—to have someone recognize it. To have *him* recognize it. My face crumbles with it all, and I lean into his shoulder as we walk, the piercingly blue sky surrounding us. Malachite stops groaning so much behind us, as if picking up on the feeling.

"I'm sorry," Lucien says. "That I was so hard on you—so

bitter—for wanting your heart back. If I had known what you'd been through up until that point—"

"It's okay," I say, half muffled by his shoulder. "You didn't know. But now you do."

"Now I do," he agrees softly, wiping the sudden tear off my cheek with his working hand.

When we all set foot on the mainland, the cloudbridge instantly vanishes, blown away by the wind until there are nothing but remnant wisps of structure left hanging in the sky. Y'shennria and the two witches separate from us, but not before Y'shennria gives me a perfect curtsy.

"You must come to my apartments for dinner, Zera. Maeve is making a venison roast, and Reginall has been polishing the silverware idly for many a day."

My chest inflates. "Wouldn't miss it for the world."

"You are invited too, Your Highness. And Your Grace. "

"I would be honored," Lucien agrees, and Fione nods.

"Then…" Y'shennria curtsies again, and I curtsy deeper back, our eyes meeting as we come up and the smallest smirk on her face obvious. "Try not to get into too much trouble."

"No guarantee!" I laugh, and as she walks away I'm struck by how glad my unheart is to know she's safe, and here, and that I'll eat dinner with her again. Small things. Important things. Direly important things, in the middle of a war.

For all its height way up in the sky, Windonhigh is surprisingly temperate. When we four finally catch up to Nightsinger, she explains it's because of magic. A dome of magic, to be precise, that keeps in the breathable air produced by the trees and siphons more from the sky. The dome maintains a constant temperature, meaning it's never not the most pleasant of springs in the city.

Because, despite the fact it's dripping with magic, it is still a *city*.

Sandstone paths carve inward to the city center, dividing the sky-land up into four quadrants—not entirely unlike Vetris. They're all named after the four animals witches can shift into—Crow, Bear, Deer, and Fox.

Fox is mercantile—stalls and shops tucked into sandstone corners and down little alleyways, brilliant banners of crimson and gold strung from every eave. The crowd is a mix of all ages, all skin colors, all hair types, but their clothes have a theme—flowing, robe-like things, cut in what Vetrisians would consider odd places to show skin and shoulders and knees.

Y'shennria trained me well—no piece of bone or brass jewelry escapes my eye. Piercings are very popular in Windonhigh, it seems, all manner of lavish studs lined over brows and jawlines and on collarbones. We get strange looks, the witches doing their daily shopping looking at Lucien most of all. It's like they can sense his magic, that he's one of them. They stare, whisper, trying to figure him out, and he has all their attention. Or, most of it. The rest of us are just his curious window dressing.

The only ones who don't openly stare are what my thief instincts assume are lawguard equivalents—witches in black armor, spiked all around the shoulders and collar and boots. As if they didn't look intimidating enough already, their mostly smooth, small-horned helmets encase their entire face—dark and reflective—and yet somehow they can see, tracking us as we walk. It's not a pleasant feeling, but it's one I'm used to.

The Deer quarter is the housing area, where the tall stone spires wind around one another seemingly into infinity. They loom up into the heavens, near touching the sun and ribbed with long curlicue lengths of stairways and dotted with proud balconies. Nightsinger explains they're mostly empty due to the Sunless War. There aren't nearly enough witches to fill them anymore, and suddenly the towers I thought looked grand now only look lonely.

But witches wash their clothes in the nearby river, fingers black as they spell the water to move in tight, cleansing whirlpools, and others lay out vegetables and salted meats to carefully dry on blankets in the sun, and a few older witches cradle babies to sleep with creak-voiced lullabies, and life indelibly goes on.

It goes on around glass, because deep in the riverbed, I catch the glint of it. Thick, clouded, and raw. Raw, jagged glass seemingly...*growing* from the riverbed. Embedded. Emerging. Not little pebbles or discarded shards. This is so thick it's like glacier ice, big enough to be boulders. Why would—why would glass just be sitting there? In the open?

I shake it off quickly. Magic is magic. Who knows what purpose it serves?

Crow is the quarter for farming and art, and by "art," I mean "extremely magical art." To be completely godsdamn honest, I had no idea magic could look anything like this; on the edges of small plots of farmland, there are incredible sculptures of glass—thin, refined glass—filled with living lights bouncing around inside, like trapped fireflies. When we get too close the sculptures *move*, and I let out the ugliest yelp of my life. Malachite almost beheads one with his sword, but Lucien pulls him back at the last second.

The glowing glass sculptures roam around Crow's grounds—prides of wildcats, snakes slithering underfoot, jellyfish floating in midair as though it were water. It's so surreal to see witch children running around, playing among and with the living sculptures, transforming in a blink into little fox kits, little bear cubs, and back again, their laughter ringing all the while as they chase one another.

"The sculptures look best at night." Nightsinger smiles placidly.

"What are *those*?" Fione points. I follow it to what looks like another clump of solid, raw glass, this time jutting out of the grass and looking decidedly out of place in the midst of so many refined glass sculptures. There are more of them, scattered about and stabbing up from the ground in variable heights and shapes. Obelisks, almost. The children don't go near them, giving them a wide berth as they play.

I watch Nightsinger's eyelashes flicker. "Nothing of import. Please, let us continue."

There are mushroom gardens, some of them as tall as trees and as little as sewing needles, a few oozing beads of fluorescent sap and others curling tendrils in and out like breathing, and some belching forth puffs of great glittering gas when footsteps approach. Fione and Malachite both lose their minds when we come across a human-tall mushroom that's clear and faceted and deep blue, like it's made of sapphire, and I can listen to their incoherent babbling for only a moment before I'm completely lost in the jargon. Something about *subterranean life cycles* and *spore rarity* and *volcanic conditions*.

"You have to present one of 'em to your partner," Malachite explains. "If you wanna get joined. Married, whatever. You gotta hunt one down but it's spiritsdamn hard. And they're never that big." He looks at my bewildered face and waves me off. "S'a whole beneather thing."

"You *never* see them aboveground!" Fione insists, and for this one moment the usual curious twinkle is back in her eye. "They require incredibly high levels of bessell acid to grow! And then there's the pressure, the small-worm growth, the light levels— whoever made this had to get every single aspect perfect. Has to! Continuously! Or this would wither in a second!"

"I'll pass your compliments on to the artist," Nightsinger smiles.

"Is it art?" Lucien asks quietly. "Or is it a show of magical strength?"

"Both," she says. "Feats of magic *are* our art, brethren. To make art is to be strong. To have precise control over your magic, to have the diligence to maintain it and see it through, to have the endurance to practice and not give up—all indicators of strength. Of worthiness in magic."

"Aha," I start. "So it's a competition."

"Somewhat," she agrees. "A competition, and a display, and a communication."

"Yeah, well, this one says, *'Don't fuck with me and my giant glintshroom.'*" Malachite waves his hands at the sapphire fungus's everything, and Lucien and I laugh.

The Bear quarter of Windonhigh is, unfortunately, no laughing matter.

It's the seat of war and politics—the High Witches have a stately sandstone tower in the very center, this one not curly or whimsical in the slightest. This building stands perfectly straight, perfectly conical, great banners of red and gold strung from a gleaming lapis orb on the very top, and descending long down the sides of the building, pulled taut at the ends to form a beautiful spiral that undulates in the wind and frames the massive staircase leading up to the dark, open archway of an entrance.

"The walls." Malachite points when we get closer. Sure enough, dozens of runes are carved into the imposing building. Familiar ones—ones I've seen on the stone gates of Vetris.

"Old Vetrisian." Fione marvels. "I've never seen so much of it before. And so *intact*."

"The witch-cities were constructed in the Old Vetrisian era," Nightsinger says. "And I'm afraid Windonhigh is one of only a handful left in the world. We are hardly capable of making such a large piece of land float anymore."

"How did you guys stay hidden for so long," Malachite muses, "if the Helkyrisians have airships? They'd see you up here, right?"

Fione shoots him an "obviously" stare. "If the Helkyrisians flew a ship into Cavanos territory, it would be an act of war."

"Ah." Malachite puts his fist in his palm. "Right you are."

"Do you know what keeps it floating?" Lucien asks.

Nightsinger flashes him a small smile. "Not entirely. Magic, perhaps. Technology, maybe. But an Old Vetrisian blending of the two is most likely. They were a decidedly advanced bunch, but we work to understand them—and what they've left behind—every day."

"Do you have polymath equivalents researching it?" Fione blurts.

"Something like that," Nightsinger agrees.

There are more of the spiky witch-lawguards here than anywhere else—whole platoons doing drills on the grass, throwing fireballs at distant stone targets.

"Eclipseguards," Nightsinger offers. "They are lawguards and soldiers all in one, and watch over Windonhigh with their life."

"Are they—" I pause.

"Some of them are witches," she says quickly, anticipating me. "But the majority are Heartless."

I watch them drill with intent eyes. All adults—or so it seems. But age is deceptive for a Heartless. Most of the eclipseguards look to be in their prime—middle twentyish—but Kavar knows how old they really are. Maybe the witches un-Heartless them, just so they can age to their primes. Who knows? It comforts me only a little to know very few of them have probably lived longer than the natural human lifespan—the Sunless War wiped out most of the Heartless and witches thirty years ago. These Heartless are fifty years old, at most. Maybe sixty. And here I was, thinking my nineteen years were ancient.

with any other witch, you'd be one of them.

At my side, Lucien starts glancing his thumb idly over mine. Reassuringly. Slowly. A satin metronome that ticks out *I'm here.*

"If you would, Black Rose." Nightsinger motions up the massive staircase that leads into the stalwart building. "The High Witches await."

Certainly, they wait. They wait for us to ask them for help, for a spell that could somehow weaken the Bone Tree's hold on the valkerax. They know best about thralldom, and about how it might be broken.

We have no leads but them.

Malachite sets his jaw, and Fione grips her cane harder. Lucien flashes me a smile—taut and nervous deep in its roots—and lets go of my hand, starting up the stairs lined with eclipseguards.

We follow our prince.

9
MADE WHOLE

The inside of the High Witch's building is unnaturally cool and dim compared to the bucolic magical springtime outside. Unlike the oil braziers and white mercury lights of Vetris, the witches use living flame—a massive hiss reverberates in the echoing hall, and Malachite unsheathes his sword and I drop my center, ready to fight. Fione's more willing to give it the benefit of the doubt, watching the streak of black witchfire arc over our heads as it moves between the mouths of two stone wolves.

"Ingenious," she murmurs, periwinkle eyes drinking in the long rows of stone wolves on either side of us and the streaks of witchfire that rhythmically jump between them, illuminating the hall in bursts. "They've staggered the release of the fire to ensure there's at least one light source at all times." She turns and looks at us. "You two are a bit jumpy, aren't you?"

I smother a laugh, and Malachite rolls his eyes.

"Excuse me for being 'a bit jumpy' around witches who may or may not wanna gut us," he says.

Fione sighs and shakes her head like she's instructing a child. "They have *magic*, Mal. If they wanted to gut us, they would've done it already, and there's nothing we could've done to stop it."

"A practical—if chilling—thought," I agree cheerily.

"I'm serious," Malachite insists, lowering his voice so just we can hear. "Luc's not really one of them. They could turn on him.

And if they do—"

"We'll use our words like grown-ups." Fione straightens. "Or rather, I will, because I can't trust you to string two civil words together when it comes to Lucien's safety."

"What about me?" I point at myself.

Fione's grin is barely there in the fire-washed gloom. "Unfortunately, Lady Zera Y'shennria, you make far too many jokes for your own good. Or for the good of political bargaining."

"Fair." I smirk.

The building is labyrinthine, and the farther we get from the entrance, the colder it becomes. Curls of mist hang on the ground, swirling into nothingness as they're displaced by our shoes. Windows start to appear, or what I think are windows. It's actually great jagged insertions of glass—not the thin sort, but the thick, unpolished, raw sort I saw outside. This time it grows into the sandstone walls—*from* the sandstone walls in irregular patches, almost like veins of ore. It's so thick it lets no light in at all, only captures it. Nothing can be seen beyond it. Not windows, then, and neither was the glass intentionally built—it looks far too...*organic*.

Nightsinger points Lucien down a series of twists and turns, eclipseguards watching silently as we pass. The glass veins become more common the deeper we go, and bigger—taking up whole walls, arcing over to replace entire sandstone tunnels with glittering black.

"Interesting design choice," Malachite murmurs in awe.

"It wasn't a choice," I mutter back. He doesn't press it, but he does start to narrow his ruby eyes at the glass with a newfound suspicion.

Suddenly, Nightsinger stops us before a seemingly innocuous wall. She nods at a nearby eclipseguard, and the guard nods back. They lift their spear, and next to me I feel Malachite tense, but the spearhead whips around to hit the wall instead. The impact should be short-lived, metal on solid stone, but it rings like a bell. Exactly like a bell, hollow and lingering. Lucien makes a step back as the wall begins to crumble, rubble spilling over the misty floor like an ancient, too-dried thing. No dust, which means we can see the door revealed in the wall clearly—stone. Pure stone, and far too heavy to open with manpower alone.

Which is why, when the doors part swiftly and easily peel apart, I know it's being done by magic.

Lucien tries to immediately march in, but Nightsinger stops him with a hand on his shoulder. "A moment, Your Highness."

He turns, eyeing Nightsinger as she steps in and whispers something to him. He nods, thanking her and then turning to us, his face set with all its princely cool.

"Let's go. Together."

"Together it is." Malachite strides in headfirst, disappearing into the darkness of the open door. Fione follows, and I lace my fingers in Lucien's hand again, smiling up at him.

"Together it is."

The darkness envelops us instantly, and I startle at how familiar the air suddenly feels—heavy, important, different. This is the same feeling I always had walking up the stairs of Nightsinger's cabin and to her sanctuary of a room.

This air is ripe with magic.

"What did she say to you?" I ask softly, the hall echoing my every noise.

"She warned me," he murmurs.

"Of...?" I lead, but he doesn't say anything more, and it puts me on edge. There are no lights in this hallway, none until the very end, where a cold gray light filters through.

We break into it, like surfacing above water.

Eclipseguards—I see them first. Lined up in the dozens against the room's circular wall. Malachite and Fione are frozen in front of us. The room itself is gigantic, cavernous in a way I've seen only once before—the arena beneath Vetris where I trained Evlorasin. It's almost as big as that, the floor entirely slate, and the walls entirely, *entirely* raw glass. A plateau high up forms from the glass, sleek and strangely polished compared to the rest of it, and from that plateau, the High Witches stare down at us.

They don't move. Just stare.

Because they can't move.

Because they're encased in glass.

Seven chunks of glass jut out from the wall situated atop the plateau, these chunks nearly human-sized and polished clear. The size of small boats, or maybe coffins. Coffins, I decide, because the seven pair of eyes staring down at us must be dead.

After all, people sawed in half are most certainly dead.

Seven witches are encased in glass, each of them missing body parts. One of them is nearly untouched, with only a leg missing. But another is just a head. An unblinking head, staring down at us. Most of them are missing their torsos, their arms, but nothing is torn. It's all clean, precise chunks taken, with no blood. No hanging organs or ligaments. Only smooth skin where the severances begin and end.

Lucien's hand grips mine harder for a moment, and then he lets go.

And then *they move.*

Seven pairs of eyes move with Lucien as he steps up and makes a bow.

"High Ones," he says, rich voice echoing in the cavernous room. "The Black Rose honors you."

Malachite's head turns woodenly to look back at me, and Fione's face tinges both curious and utterly terrified. I don't know what to say, what to do. Something tells me if I so much as twitch, I'll be watched, judged, and summarily taken care of. If not by the dozens of eclipseguards on the walls, then by the looming witch monoliths themselves.

They might look still, but something in me screams they are very alive. Can they even *use* magic? They have to—Y'shennria said the black rose that led her to me was made by a High Witch. One of these seven. Why are they missing their body parts? Magic? Is it like Lucien's eye or his hand—eaten up by the most powerful magic and then discarded because it's no longer of use?

How are they *alive* in there? Is it like my Heartlessness?

All I can do is listen. Watch. Wait for my witch's orders, just like the eclipseguard wait for theirs.

Suddenly, one of the glass monoliths blazes to life, red light illuminating the glass from the inside—showing exactly the witch inside, missing legs and an arm and half their skull, only one eye riveted to Lucien.

"What honor do you bring us, Prince of Cavanos?"

The voice is deep, booming in the high ceilings. The red light flickers with the cadence of the witch's voice, like lips moving, like sound becoming visible.

Lucien straightens from his bow, onyx eyes sharper now. "My sister Laughing Daughter has taken the Bone Tree."

"You bring us information we already know." Another monolith on the opposite end lights up, a witch with long hair and no arms and a voice like a blade. "Hardly honor at all."

"'Taken' is a generous term," a monolith of a witch with just their chest and head says, lighting up. "And implies conscious autonomy. The Bone Tree has chosen her. It chose her from birth. Laughing Daughter had no say in the matter."

I see Fione bristle, her fists clenching under her wool covering.

"The valkerax rise again," the first monolith says. "With much thanks to your Heartless."

The eyes move, all seven pairs of them at once, from Lucien to me. I swallow the urge to run, all the magic in the air crystallizing and prickling against my skin. A promise of needles. A promise of pain.

"There's no use in placing blame," Lucien starts instantly. "My sister would've gotten the tree eventually."

None of the monoliths speak. Lucien angles his body in front of me, between them and me, and my blood thrums.

"She's none of your—"

"She is precisely our business." A monolith flares to life, the voice furious.

"With all due respect to the High Ones, I'm telling you," Lucien insists, his own voice blooming anger. "My sister—"

Every other monolith lights up, sound and light gearing to explode in argument.

"Heartless," the middle monolith croaks—no booming, no blades. Just slow, ancient words from an old, old witch encased in glass only as a head. A head with frazzled white hair, whose mouth never moves. His speech silences the room, silences Lucien and makes the other six monoliths go dark again instantly. He's...talking to *me*? He must be, because he waits for me to acknowledge, and I start forward.

"Y-Yes?"

"You have taught a valkerax to Weep."

Not a question. A statement. I nod. "Yes. Sir."

"Has the valkerax told you your true name?"

"Yes." I try to hold my chin up, but the magic bristles heavy at me.

"Would you say it before us?"

A request. Not a gentle one—one made of old, old bone and old, *old* steel. I want to dart my eyes to Lucien, to ask with my eyes if it's all right to tell them. True names mean something. Witches seem to value them highly. But I can't move.

we are in danger. we can't disobey. The hunger slithers through me uneasily, around the cracks in the magic, around

Lucien's unbridled, uncontrolled feeling of worry. *say it.*

"Starving Wolf."

The silence that follows my true name reverberates in on itself—deep and long—and then the monoliths light up. Softly. Their whispers flicker crimson into Lucien's abyssal eyes, watching me wordlessly. And then they stop, suddenly, and the center one, the old witch with just a head, speaks again.

"At the end of the world, there will be wolves."

I'm utterly lost, so I croak, "Sir?"

"A saying," he continues. "Passed down many a generation. Long forgotten in origin but true in nature."

Evlorasin's words, mad as they were, stroke eerily at the back of my mind.

A wolf to end the world.

One of the monolith's whispers is too loud. "They cannot fly. They've lost the knowledge. Even if she's taught one, it is just one—"

Lucien squares his shoulders and braves speech.

"I came here, High Ones, to ask your aid. The Bone Tree is an Old Vetrisian invention. Surely you must know a spell that can interfere with it."

"Why would we interfere with that which keeps the valkerax in check?" A monolith flares to life.

For a fraction of a moment, Lucien looks like someone's hit him. Alarmed. Fione's eyes widen, and Malachite's narrow.

"They aren't in check anymore. My sister has it," Lucien argues. "My sister *controls* it!"

"You are presumptuous." Another monolith lights up, blade-voice snickering. "And very confident in your sister's abilities."

"This magic—the Bone Tree is half the witches' doing!" The prince's brows knit deep, anger edging his cheekbones. "You would take responsibility!"

One of the monoliths bleeds black from its base, the glass

turning from transparent to opaque as animate midnight slithers up the facets. It happens so fast—Lucien's whole body giving instantly, forced to his knees. He grunts and snarls as he fights the invisible weight, magic crushing in on him.

I lunge at him, and Malachite draws his weapon, and in the next second all I can hear is a ringing in my ears, my head on the slate floor and my body crumpled against a wall and dozens of feet away from Lucien. I taste blood on my lips. Malachite's fared no better—his broadsword spiraling up in the air and sinking deep into the slate floor. He runs over, trying to pull it out, but even with his beneather strength, it won't move an inch.

"Listen well, Black Rose, and carefully," one of the monoliths says. "The Bone Tree requires a powerful witch to feed once every century. Of this we are sure. It chooses this witch and consumes them. Of this we are sure. The Laughing Daughter fights it, but it will consume her as it has all the others. She uses it, but it will use her, in the end. And when it is over, the Bone Tree will be sated with magic enough to keep the valkerax in the Dark Below for a hundred years more. Of this we are sure."

"You're just going to—" Fione's throat bobs. "You're just going to *let* her die? *Let* her wreak havoc on the world? What if she comes for you?"

"We have ways and methods. We will be safe. We cannot speak for your kind, though, human."

My anger boils up, faster than the blood over my lip. Fione's hand around her cane goes slack, and it drops to the ground with a clatter.

"You're using this," Lucien manages, throat dry and cracking. "You're using my sister to—to wipe out the humans for you? *To wipe out my kingdom for you?*" He roars the last words, the echo harsh and burning.

None of the monoliths speak until the center one lights up, voice even despite everything.

"The scales have been, for a great time, tipped toward humanity. And now, with your sister, they will become balanced once more."

A cold nausea works into my stomach, and I can't tell if it's all me, or some of Lucien's feelings, or a dizzying combination of both. We thought they'd help us. It would make sense for them to want to stop Varia, stop the Laughing Daughter who took shelter with them five years ago, who learned from them, who took one of their magical artifacts and turned it against the world. It would make *sense* to want to help. But they're using this. They're using the crisis for their own benefit. And that's…

I wipe my split lip, swallow more blood, and rise.

"You realize the valkerax have fire, right?" I limp back over to the monoliths, Lucien's magic healing me rapidly. "No matter how many eclipseguard Heartless you have, the valkerax will burn through them like kindling, and you'll be left defenseless for the hours it takes for them to heal."

"There will be no more discussion, Starving Wolf," one of the monoliths echoes. "You have conspired with the valkerax. You have done nothing but risk everything. And for that you are held in contempt."

I can't stop my scoff. "Bit used to that."

There's a swell of black midnight on one of the monolith's facets, and I brace myself for retaliation. For pain. But it never comes. Instead, something small and brass appears in midair before Lucien—a medallion, embossed with a wolf and covered in tiny jet gems.

"You will take this sigil. It will allow you free passage within the city. On the morn of Watersday, you will be gone."

Lucien's disdain is clear on his face as he takes the thing, gripping it tight in long fingers and a longer frown.

"As you will, High Ones."

His bow, and our bows, feel forced. Fione picks up her cane

with trembling hands. The magic holding Malachite's sword finally gives, and he manages to pull it out of the stone and sheathe it again.

As we walk away, I'm the only one who looks back. I'm the only one who sees the slivered hole the blade left in the slate closing up—filling with raw, cloudy, rapidly solidifying glass, like a wound does with blood.

Strangely, the labyrinth we traversed to get to the High Witch's door is gone. When we walk out of the monolith room, there's only one hall, and it stretches long into darkness, the exit a glaring white light. We walk in silence, all of us mulling over what just happened. Some of us more politely than others.

"*Sarvetts*," Malachite snarls finally. "All of 'em."

"Conniving cave scorpion," I chime. "Right?"

He looks at me with the barest rub of irritation. "Is that all that sticks in your head? My beneather swears?"

"And, occasionally, hopes and dreams."

Nightsinger's waiting for us when we walk into the sunlight, her smile rose-tinted and sweet as ever.

"I can tell from your faces it didn't go very well," she says. Her eyes fall on my chin, to the bloodstain I know has to be there.

"Not well at all," I agree. Her smile curls apologetically at the corners.

"Come. Let's get you to the guest quarters, where you can clean up and rest."

The four of us follow her out of Bear quarter and back into Deer. My eyes catch on every eclipseguard, feeling half sorry for how much the High Witches rely on them. Unless...unless they have some other way I don't know about to defend from the valkerax. A spell, maybe? But the witches of *old* didn't even have spells like that. They had to join with the humans and make Old Vetris to survive, make the entire Bone Tree to survive. So why are the High Witches now so confident in their ability to drive the valkerax off?

"Lucien." Fione draws even with him. "There has to be—"

Lucien's eyes flicker to Nightsinger's back, her swaying mane of hair, and he cuts the archduchess off. "In a moment."

It's a Vetrisian noble court message—subtle, all in the eyes. He obviously doesn't trust Nightsinger. Fione has the same idea as me, maybe, but we can't talk about it with my old witch around. And that stings more than I thought it would.

The sun sets much later up here—or rather, with how high up we are, the sun takes a lot longer to dip below the horizon. We spiral up the spiral ramps of the residential buildings, catching whiffs of herbs and roasting potatoes and fish. Dinner. Dinner smells, like any dinner smells in Vetris. Through little windows above us, witch families tuck their children into bed, pulling wood-slat blinds shut for the night, sweeping away the day's leaves from their doorsteps. Some of them wave at Nightsinger, and she smiles and nods back. The stares are still a thing—always aimed at Lucien, like he glows or displays something different only other witches can see. Or maybe an outsider witch is that much of a rare curiosity.

Nightsinger finally stops in front of an empty apartment on the incline, pointing to the medallion in Lucien's hand.

"The sigil will allow you entry past the door. There are extra linens, and the woodbin refills automatically when it gets low. Just be careful to extinguish your witchfire before you leave."

"All right." Lucien nods. "Thank you."

"I'm sorry, Black Rose." She smiles at him, then me. "And to you, Zera. I'm sorry we couldn't help you more."

We. Her and the High Witches, together. Lucien wordlessly

waves the sigil over the door and walks in, Fione and Malachite following after him. Nightsinger's rueful smile widens at me.

"I suppose you don't want to hug me now, knowing what I am."

"Is it—" I swallow. "Does the skinreading always happen when you touch someone?"

"No. I've lived with it long enough—and there are teachers, here. I learned to control it. It's considered proper manners, after all, even among witches, to refrain from invading private memories."

"Yeah," I laugh a little. "Right."

"Your prince, however, does not know how. It runs quite wild in him."

"Can you teach him how to...you know."

She shakes her mane of tawny hair. "Unfortunately, it's something that requires years of practice. I could give him some basics, but I fear he doesn't like me very much."

"No, it's not—"

"Rather, he doesn't like the High Witches." She interrupts me smoothly, without a hint of judgment. Her eyes crinkle. "Few do. They are leaders, not friends."

"Why were they..." I swallow. "All that glass. Like it was growing. I saw it *growing*." Nightsinger's smile fades, and I press on. "What is that stuff? Magic? Why is it poking out of the ground all around the city—"

"I'm sorry, Zera," she says, whirling away. "I have to go. But Crav and Peligli are having dinner at Y'shennria's tonight. Her apartments are one level above you, facing south. Tell her I said hello, would you?"

"Nightsinger."

She looks back over her shoulder ever so slightly.

"I'm sorry, Zera. But you are no longer mine. This divides us in spirit, but you will always be in my heart."

She's in a human shape one moment, and the next her sleeves

elongate, her tawny mane wraps around and into her, covering her in white feathers as she shrinks, grows wings, and flies off into the night. I watch her until she's a faint speck of snow spiraling down into the trees of Fox quarter.

There are so many stars up here, so completely free from cloud cover that they radiate their own light. Packed tight and close, like diamonds on a queen's bodice, they glimmer among the silky darkness of the sky.

The queen. Queen Kolissa, Varia and Lucien's mother. She's dead, isn't she? Ash, like most of Vetris.

She killed her *mother.*

She said she would carve the world anew, not raze it. But how much of her is her, anymore, and how much is the Bone Tree? Who destroyed Vetris? Varia or the Bone Tree demanding destruction inside her?

I breathe in and try to focus on anything else. The Red Twins peek over the horizon, rising equally as slow as the sunset, their crimson craniums bare, shy, and waning new. The starlight catches on the ground, radiating into and out of the chunks of glass jutting from Windonhigh's grass, and the bad feeling in my stomach balloons like a child blowing a sheep's kidney full of air. I can't even pinpoint it—I can't tell whether it's fear or anger. All I know is this feeling is bad. Terrible. Something bad is here, around me. Or maybe in me. I don't know anymore. But it only gets louder when I stare at those chunks of raw glass growing up from the dirt.

Something wrong.

Something *terrible.*

And I recognize it, in that instant. The wind whips my hair and I remember where I've felt this before—my dream. That dream of two tree pendants, of that awful feeling of what would happen if I didn't bring them together. That dream of the Hall of Time and the stained glass shattering, that lonely tree wearing the shards like armor and then teeth, all pointed at me. *So incredibly lonely.*

But how can a tree be lonely? How can the same feeling appear in a dream and out of a dream? Varia showed me the glass shard inside my heart bag, and she told me it's what kept me alive.

Is it what keeps those High Witches alive, too?

Is it...the Glass Tree?

"Zera."

Lucien's voice. I turn to see him leaning against the doorway, a decided weariness in his eyes.

"Hey." I smile. But he doesn't.

"We should go," he says. "To Y'shennria's dinner she invited us to."

"Right." I calm the swell in my heart at seeing her again, at seeing Crav and Peligli. "Got anything nice to wear?"

"They left us some things." He motions inside the guest apartment. "Come choose, before Malachite steals all the pretty ones."

I pause. But we're thinking the same thing, because he says, "If they won't help us, Zera, we'll do it ourselves. No matter what." He grins. "Didn't you promise Fione? You'll get Varia back alive. No matter what."

I laugh, too small to even be a real one, and nod, following him inside.

The chaos of getting dressed is a welcome change from the somber mood. Fione has to help us all—clearly the inner workings of overlay back-clasps and double-thread-Avellish knots elude all but the archduchess.

"I thought you were supposed to be good at this stuff, Luc," Malachite grumbles, trying to force his paper-pale, slender leg through some fabric.

"That's a *tunic*, Malachite, not pants." Fione sighs, snatching it from him and righting it.

"Oh." Malachite pulls it over his head with a muffled "Cheers."

"Fione." Lucien motions hopelessly to a complex braiding pattern in vine-green silk down his chest. Fione looks up at me as she fixes my own braid pattern on my shirt.

"Just do what I did for him, would you? I have to help Mal before he rips everything in two."

"*Horseshit.*" Malachite's voice resounds over the sound of tearing seams, and I chuckle and make my way to Lucien. The guest apartment is entirely fueled in light and heat by his witchfire—the purple-black of the fire blazing in braziers glancing over his chest. I try not to look at him or acknowledge the fact he's totally bare beneath his complicated shirt.

"You've done this before, then." His voice rumbles as my fingers clumsily fix the first braid.

"Not especially." I bite my lip and force a braid under itself. "I think these were designed to be fastened with magic, actually."

"Sadistic," Lucien says, smirking smallish down at me.

"Or ingenious." I ignore the heat rushing like water through me. "Fairly easy to pick out the spies if they can't button their trousers like the rest of us."

"I managed that much, at least."

I swallow what feels like a quiver of arrows. "S-Sure. Good."

Warm hands suddenly envelop mine on his shirt, and he presses them to his bare chest. That blazing honey and pepper scent wafts from his neck as he leans down, nudging my chin up and up until finally, *finally* our lips meet. Streaks of fire tremble from me into him and back again, down to my belly, and Malachite's squawking and Fione's chiding fade into nothing, my blood rushing in my ears so much louder, harder, stronger—

Lucien pulls away at the last second of my sanity slipping, eyes clouded.

"I didn't mean to, so suddenly—"

"It's okay," I blurt. "It's...more than okay."

"You were just…are just." He swallows. "Beautiful. And seeing you so immersed, trying so hard." He pauses. "You stick out your tongue, you know."

"D-Do I?"

He nods, grinning lopsidedly. "When you're thinking hard about something."

"Strange," I lilt. "Because when you're thinking hard about something, you make no expression at all."

"Should I?"

"Maybe. How else will I know to spring a kiss on you out of nowhere?"

His laugh is soft and deep. "I'll keep that in mind."

Fione sighs at us. "The world includes more people than just you two, you know."

"Regrettably," Lucien says, never once looking away from my face as I finish the braid up his shirt with renewed vigor.

"First I guard him with my life for most of my life," Malachite huffs. "And now he's saying he wishes I was never born!"

I lay a hand on the prince's chest to indicate I'm done, and he immediately turns to Malachite and reaches for him, wrapping an arm around his neck and pulling him into a headlock.

"I heard that, Mal."

"Yeah!" The beneather squirms, clearly able to get out of the grip but allowing it. "Good! You ungrateful little bug!"

Lucien tries to yank him around, but Malachite ducks out of it, turning the tables on the prince and reaching for his collar when Fione taps her cane on the sandstone floor loudly.

"Enough! We can't keep Lady Y'shennria waiting."

"She hates tardiness," I agree lightly. "And clams. But mostly tardiness."

The beneather rolls his eyes and shoves Lucien away, and Lucien's laugh is nice to hear. It's nice, to see them playing around. To see Lucien being carefree, even when it's hardest for him to be. Even if his heart is heavy. It's nice, to walk beside him up the ramp, the stars gleaming down on us and Fione and Malachite walking with us, arguing over something small and probably etiquette related.

"You can't put your feet on the table." Fione sighs.

"Why not? We're not in Vetris anymore! No more stuffy rules—"

"There are still *rules*," Fione quips. "You're the prince of Cavanos's bodyguard. So start acting like it."

"Spirits. You're no fun anymore." Malachite sighs. "I liked you way better when Varia was—"

He stops himself. Fione's back goes straight, and Lucien and I exchange a glance.

"Sorry," the beneather says quickly. "I didn't mean—"

"Here we are." Fione strides ahead of us, stopping before the south-facing door and tapping on it with her cane.

"Fione," I start.

"No." The archduchess interrupts me, her every word laced with steel. "We're not here to dwell on the past, Zera. All of you. We're here to change the future."

"It's all right to talk about these things, though—" Lucien starts, but she slices him off at the knees with her gaze. The starlight glimmers off her mousy hair, the periwinkle in her eyes turning to ice as she reminds us of the sober reality.

"As long as Varia d'Malvane has the Bone Tree, I don't want to talk. I want to *do*."

10
THE REPRIÈVE

Y'shennria greets us at her door dressed in delicate black knit lace and a ruby-dotted net in her hair. If she notices the awkward atmosphere among the four of us, she doesn't remark on it, showing us elegantly into the larger apartments. It's lit up by witchfire—though by which witch, I'm not sure. More importantly, it's decorated with all her old furniture, or most of it anyway, and my heart perks up seeing the familiar loveseat, the embroidered chaise lounge, the black leather couch on which I spent so much time bleeding and training to become a lady. The amazing bookshelves are here, replete with her whole library and the iron and glass orbs of varying spikiness I used on my shoulders to agonizingly train my posture. Even the grandfather sandclock is here, ticking out the halves in slow seconds.

Even Reginall is here, dressed in a smart suit and his manicured mustache and offering us tangerine cordials on a tray.

"Regi—" His name gets stuck in my throat, but he's much calmer. He puts the tray down on the table and holds out his wrinkled hands to me. I dash to him, reaching, and he clasps me close, kind eyes twinkling.

"Milady Zera. How long it has felt, and how joyous it feels now. Are you well?"

"Well." I nod, my smile so big it feels like it'll split my face. "Better. I'm doing—" I look back at Lucien, at Fione and Malachite.

"So much better."

"I am very glad to hear it. I was muchly worried when we had to leave you behind in Vetris." He looks down at my chest, as if searching. "Lady Y'shennria told me you are still Heartless."

"Yeah. But I chose it this time." I smile. "Turns out, it's far easier to stop a valkerax incursion when you're immortal."

"And the hunger? It does not call to you?"

"It does still. But Lucien's doing everything he can to keep it quiet. And I've learned to—not *accept* it, per se. But work with it. A little."

Reginall looks at the prince and then back down at me, the crow's feet in his eyes crinkling. "I see."

"There's so much I have to tell you," I blurt. "I Wept! I did it, just like you taught me."

"Ah." He waves. "I hardly taught you anything. I merely told you snippets of rumor."

"But it worked!" I insist. "I did it. I can do it now. Well, not now, because I've changed witches again. I'd have to be cut by a white mercury blade, but Fione has one and—" I smile wider at the confused look on his face. "It's a good thing, I promise. I even taught a valkerax how to do it, too."

"A valkerax." Reginall breathes, eyes going wide. "Well. It seems we have much to talk of indeed. But first, a refresher for the lady."

He offers me a tangerine cordial with an overdone politeness, and I take it with equally overdone politeness, and the two of us chuckle uncontrollably at the stringency of it all.

I whip my head around. "Is Fisher here?"

Fisher, the man who drove me around in Y'shennria's carriage in the before times. Before I was exposed as a Heartless. He'd been my only companion, my only source of kindness some days.

Reginall shakes his head. "He went home, south. Back to the Empire."

I grin ruefully. "As long as he's safe, then."

Y'shennria's cook Maeve is in the kitchen, stoking the witchfire as she hobbles about and stirs varying pots of bubbling goodness. She squints up at me and pats my hand when she recognizes me, a missing-tooth mumble of *here again, the strange thing* as she turns back to the pots. Perriot—dressed in silk stockings and looking much cleaner than I saw him in Vetris—suddenly bursts into the kitchen trailing two other children.

Turquoise eyes. Deep skin. Crav. Blond hair, chubby fists. Peligli. A moment of silence where they stare and stare, their jaws open. They're all right. *Alive.* All my limbs feel like soft butter. I imagined them dead so many times.

I sink to my knees and hold my arms out.

"Zera!" Peligli's the first to shriek, launching herself into my arms with such force I'm almost bowled over.

"Peli." My laugh bubbles up as I clutch her close. "Oh *gods*, Peli. I'm so glad you're okay."

"Me fine!" She can't stop shrieking, but her puffy-cheeked face becomes very serious all of a sudden. "You fine?"

"I'm fine," I assure her, and she looks me over warily, picking at my dress like she's trying to make sure. I feel a familiar brooding presence to my left and look over to see Crav standing there. Still frowning. Still Crav, as ever, and it makes me laugh.

"Hello, Crav."

"Hello," he mumbles, and then, "You could've sent a letter."

"Yeah. My bad." My eyes well up, everything blurry as I reach for him. The words are simple between us, but I know he means so much more, and I know he doesn't want to hear it from me. Softness in words isn't his style—but the way he gives when I pull him in to me speaks volumes. The way he wraps his hands around my shoulders and clings speaks books and books, whole trilogies unfolding in his emotions. In mine. In all three of ours.

Lucien and Malachite and Fione leave me to cry and laugh

and everything in between. Peligli won't stop asking where I've been, and when I tell her the city, she frowns and says it's a bad place. Of course she'd say that—she spent all of her young human life there, on the streets. I'm surprised she even remembers it was bad; Heartless lose their memories the moment they lose their hearts. But maybe it really was that bad for her, leaving lingering scars. Scars that, one day, when this war is over, I hope she never remembers. I glance over at Lucien, talking with Fione. Lucien's made friends with so many of the urchins in Vetris. Urchins like Peligli used to be.

Urchins who might be dead now.

I clutch Peligli closer to me, and she lays her head on my neck.

"Is that your father's sword?" Crav points to the sheath on my belt. I uncurl and smile at him.

"No. Just the pieces of it. It broke, and Lucien was kind enough to reforge the blade for me."

"Hrmph." Crav sniffs. "A warrior should never journey without their sword."

"You're right." I nod. "As soon as I find a proper blacksmith, I'll have it remade. I promise."

"Make sure they're good," he asserts. "And make sure they use a threaded bi-fold method to attach it, or it'll come off the second someone tries to disarm you with a hilt twist."

"Noted. Thanks, Crav."

His blush is faint. "Whatever."

Suddenly Y'shennria calls for us to come to the table, and we do, all three of us hand in hand.

"Crav's teaching me sword stuff," Perriot pipes up, cheek smeared with a bit of pheasant gravy.

"Oh!" I swallow a bite of the seasoned livers Maeve made for us Heartless. "Is he? That's wonderful. He taught me to duel, you know."

"Literally everything she knows is because of me," Crav sniffs, pushing his liver around on his plate.

"Not bad, kid," Malachite marvels.

"I'm not a kid," Crav snaps. "I'm a Heartless."

"Wait...*really*? You really taught *her*?" Perriot's eyes go wide. I don't think I've ever seen him so expressive. He used to be so meek and quiet. He's really grown, a few months older and away from Vetris. Crav and Peligli, on the other hand, have hardly changed at all. A symptom of being Heartless.

Do I change? *Have* I changed?

It's the hardest question to ask oneself, and the hardest to answer.

"She's pretty good at dueling, too." Malachite smirks at me, his three mouth-scars I gave him stretching scabby-red. "Except when she faints."

"That was one time," I grumble. "And it was because of Lucien's white mercury sword! Hardly something I could control."

"I'm good at dool also!" Peligli announces, beating her legs back and forth under the table.

"More like drool," Crav rolls his eyes.

"Would you—" Perriot swallows. "Can you show me, Lady Zera? A real duel?"

Malachite raises a brow at me. "You heard the whelp, Six-Eyes. Do you wanna?"

"Absolutely." I smile. "Tomorrow you lose, then."

"I'll be referee," Crav asserts, and I grin at him with a twinkle in my eye.

"I heard"—Y'shennria leans in over her sardine fry—"that there was a record number of girls clamoring for blademaster lessons from their fathers after your and His Highness's duel."

"Kavar bless me, for I *have* sinned," I agree cheerily. "I've brought self-defense to the noblewomen."

Y'shennria's smile is short-lived, because she and I both realize it across the table. The whole of the dinner realizes it—

Lucien most of all. Vetris is gone. The nobility, the common people—who knows how many of them are still alive. If *any* lived through the attack. We could be talking about the dead, for all we know.

Even the kids recognize the tension and go quiet, Peligli's legs stilling. The atmosphere strains against itself until the prince breaks it.

"Lady Y'shennria," Lucien starts. "I'm going to destroy the Bone Tree. It's the only way to stop my sister."

My unheart clenches. *Destroy?* I thought—I thought we were only going to weaken it, its spell over the valkerax. But one look in Lucien's eyes and I know plans have changed—if the High Witches won't help us interfere with it, then…then there's only one thing we can do.

The scrape of silverware across dishes is the sole sound. Y'shennria's hazel eyes glint keenly through the witchfire candles on the table.

"Forgive the extreme disrespect my words are about to incur, Your Highness," she says. "But I know you value honesty. Would it not be easier to kill Her Highness? The Bone Tree is an Old Vetrisian artifact; there is no guarantee it can be destroyed, let alone—"

"No," Fione says. "We're destroying the tree."

t'would be so much easier to rip out the throat of the Laughing Daughter, the hunger sneers.

Y'shennria's knowing gaze flickers, and she looks at me as if for confirmation we're truly taking the most difficult way. I nod at her. *The only way.*

"The High Witches will not offer us aid," Lucien continues. "But we require knowledge. Of magic, of Old Vetris, of how precisely the Bone Tree works. They wouldn't give us the spell—if there is any—to weaken the valkerax's connection to the Bone Tree and subsequently turn them away from my sister. Which means only one path is left to us now. To destroy it."

He doesn't come out and say it. He doesn't say, *would you know where to find such knowledge in Windonhigh?* but it doesn't need to be said. Y'shennria thinks for a long moment and then looks up with a covering sort of smile. The kind she used to change subjects among nobles flawlessly back in the Vetrisian court.

"Reginall, I think we're ready for dessert."

She doesn't answer the prince's unspoken question. I expect Lucien to ask it again, or more clearly, but that's not how Vetrisian nobles work. So when Reginall comes out with a massive hazelnut delight—the little towers of cream in ceramic boats dotted with four ripe cherries—I don't know what I'm expecting. But I certainly didn't expect Y'shennria to take the warm pot of butter-syrup and stand, going around the table and pouring some on the delights herself. A task usually reserved for servants.

"There we are, Your Highness." Her voice is smooth. "I anticipated this dish just for you. I remember you being quite fond of it as a child."

"I was," he agrees, and for some reason his gaze won't leave his delight. He traces the fall of the syrup with his eyes with an intensity completely unwarranted for a simple dessert.

"He really loved sweet shit when he was little," Malachite agrees, shooting a glance over at the kids at the table. "Uh. Sweet *stuff.*"

Crav gives him a withering look. "I know what 'shit' is."

"Shid!" Peligli chimes happily, beating her fork against the table. "*Shid shid shid!*"

Perriot, perhaps the most polite of the three, panics and tries to distract her with a cherry, which Peligli joyfully accepts, her mouth staining deep fruit-red. She'll bleed it out from her eyes later, as Heartless do with all human food, but her temporary joy is worth it. And the temporary silence.

Y'shennria pours syrup only on Lucien's and then lets Reginall pour it for the rest of us, sitting back down in her emerald skirts elegantly. It's so bizarre, but Lucien and Y'shennria just go on to talk spiritedly about the precise height, in miles, of Windonhigh, and Fione joins in with equations eagerly. Malachite looks a little sick when they settle on a massive number, but I'm still stuck on the syrup. Have I lost my courtly edge? I know there's something to read between the lines in what Y'shennria did, but why would she—

I'm staring down at my own delight when it hits me. The spire of fluffy cream off-center, the four cherries situated around it evenly, as if demarcating quarters.

Quarters.

The spire in the center is the High Witch building in Bear. And the four cherries are the four quarters—Bear, Fox, Deer, and Crow.

I look over at Lucien's dessert, untouched.

The syrup Y'shennria poured pools on the edge of Crow.

If Y'shennria had to resort to visual representations in whipped cream instead of telling Lucien the information she wanted to out loud, it means several things, all of them troubling.

One, we might be being listened to.

Two, if we're being listened to, it means someone views us as a potential threat.

And three, whatever Y'shennria's pointing us to is likely heavily secret, and therefore, heavily guarded. Heavily important.

There's a fourth, of course. And it's that Y'shennria is giving us this information at great risk to herself. Once again, it's Vetris all over—Y'shennria putting her life and the lives of her household on the line to help me. Not the witches this time, but *me.*

I watch her smile at me through the candlelight over my teacup—cinnamon and dread wafting into my senses.

She's doing this for me.

And this time, if the witches catch wind of it, she has nowhere else to run. Windonhigh is the last sanctuary for an Old God family like hers. If they don't kill her, they'll chase her out to the ground, to Cavanos, to a Cavanos being ravaged by the valkerax. A Cavanos where no one is safe anymore.

Peligli passing out on the couch, drooling, is the first indication that the night's grown too long. The second is Crav succumbing, too, Peligli's little head on his lap and his book slipping from his fingers. I catch it just in time, moving to put it back on the shelf when Crav's stunning turquoise eyes flutter half open.

"You're not leaving again, are you?" he mumbles sleepily. I smile, but it's the sort of brittle effort that breaks my unheart in two.

"I might have to."

He thinks on this, eyelids too heavy to keep open for long. Emotional exhaustion is a more powerful narcoleptic for Heartless than anything, and the three of us reuniting was no easy thing.

"Will you come back?" he finally decides to ask, and I can't help my laugh. I drape a nearby sheepskin throw over him, the fluff obscuring his chin.

"You still don't pull any punches, do you?"

"Answer me." He frowns over the fluff.

"I don't know, Crav," I admit. "I have to go do something pretty dangerous. I might not come back."

"You're Heartless," he argues. "We always come back. Unless..." He swallows. "Unless your witch dies. That prince guy."

This punch is more of a slam directly to my solar plexus, nearly winding me. But I manage a soft "yeah."

"If he dies, you die together," Crav mumbles.

"Yeah."

A pause, the black fire crackling in the fireplace, and then, "He's like the High Witches, isn't he?"

I freeze. "What do you mean?"

"They're missing parts. He's missing an eye. And his hand."

"How do you—"

"I'm a prince, too. Of the Endless Bog. I notice things." Crav's scoff is almost swallowed up by the sheepskin. "Things about parts used for battle most of all—you either notice or you die. Nightsinger took us to the High Witches when we first came here. And that prince guy feels the same as them."

Lucien? The same as the High Witches? What does that even mean? Crav shifts under the sheepskin, getting more comfortable.

"They get eaten," he mutters, sounding more exhausted than ever.

"What?"

"That's what Nightsinger told Peligli and me," he continues. "When we asked why the High Witches look like that. She told us they're getting eaten, slowly."

"Eaten by who?"

Crav slumps, and I lean in and shake his shoulder softly.

"Crav, eaten by *who*?"

He jolts awake and then falls into tiredness all over again, mumbling as he goes.

"...Some tree."

All that raw glass, sprouting up from the ground, encasing the High Witches. The glass splinter in my heart bag Varia showed me. Archduke Gavik told me the witches made the Glass Tree to keep their loved ones alive. And thus the Heartless were born. The Bone Tree chose Varia to eat her power.

But that means...the Glass Tree has to eat, too.

11
THE GLASS TREE

Saying goodnight, tonight, is like saying goodbye.

I kiss sleeping Crav and Peligli on the foreheads and tuck the blanket around Perriot tighter. Reginall and I embrace, for what feels like the first and last time all over again. Maeve waves me off when I try to kiss her ancient cheek. Fione and Lucien give Y'shennria the proper bows, and even Malachite makes a motion of politeness, which Y'shennria raises her eyebrow at disbelievingly.

"Thanks, ma'am," the beneather says. "For looking after our Six-Eyes."

Lucien nods at his side. "You have my gratitude for it, Lady Y'shennria."

She makes a modest half bow, rubies glinting in her high hair. "I've done very little, Your Highness. She took care of herself, if anything."

"And you taught her how," Lucien presses. Y'shennria seems taken aback at this, and looks to me as if for confirmation. I give her a nod, and the brightest smile I can manage.

"It's true, you know. I am where I am because of you."

Y'shennria's scoff is light, and Lucien and Malachite back up to give us space as I move in to her. I reach out my hands, holding her ring-encrusted ones lightly.

"You still have no idea how to hold a fork," she starts, and I can hear the strain in her voice.

"Which is why I'll be coming back. For remedial lessons."

"Don't," she says. "Don't come back. You have no friends here."

"Except for you."

Her steady gaze quavers, hazel on my blue, sadness on my sadness.

"I am not a friend," she corrects. "I am a home." Her words are arrows, the warm sort, and I let them pierce me, one after the wonderful other. Her grip intensifies. "You will always have a home with me, Zera."

I start to cry but hold it back just on the edge. "Thank you. Thank you, for everything—"

"There is no need for such final gratitude. We *will* see each other again."

Her expression is solid, unwavering. I pull myself together as a noble lady might. As she taught me, and teaches me, always. It wouldn't do to be weak now. Not when things are just beginning, when the battle is just beginning. Head high, shoulders back, thoughts clear.

"We will."

Her edges dissolve at my agreement, and her hands move up to my face, cradling it with pride shining in her eyes.

"Alyserat," she says. Alyserat: her baby girl's name. She told me her baby girl's name, the night I left for the Hunt. And she's telling me it now, again. An Old Vetrisian name, and they liked to name their children after songs. Proverbs. Poems. Warnings.

Alyserat means *"Fear the past, not the future."* A reminder. A good luck charm. A blessing. *Her* blessing. And it means even more now. I won't fear my past ever again.

I won't repeat the past. Ever again.

"Alyserat." I smile back at her.

• • •

Tonight, walking away from a door feels like walking over the edge of a cliff.

Lucien feels it, too, somehow, and he laces our fingers together the whole way back to our guest apartments. Not saying anything, just holding. Just being here. Existing with me, beside me. And that's all I need. But it's not all I want.

I tell him what Crav said about the Glass Tree, the High Witches being eaten, and his face doesn't move for a long while. Malachite and Fione walk ahead of us, until his bodyguard looks back.

"Something went on, Luc. At the dinner. You gonna tell me what it is, or do I gotta guess?"

Lucien looks up, dark eyes pointed. "It's not safe to say."

"Ooookay," the beneather leads. "Then what's the plan?"

"We dress for easy movement," he says. "And you follow me."

"Tonight?" Fione asks. "It has to be tonight?"

"The sooner the better," the prince says. "Time is against us here."

"You mean the High Witches are against us," I say, and he nods.

"They're tightening defenses as we speak, closing ranks. Against the valkerax, against anyone. Us included."

"Infiltration it is." Malachite opens the door to the guest apartments, and we all shuffle in. "My favorite. Miles better than torturing."

"A night of rest sure would be nice," I mourn. "We've been on the go since the airship. And you mortals tend to need sleep."

I look pointedly at Lucien but he ignores me, packing a pouch full of medicinal herbs instead.

"And you immortal Heartless tend to underestimate us."

Fione's eyes flash determined. "We do what must be done. Tonight."

I know there's no talking her down. She's not going to budge—but I'm worried. Staying so strong must be taking a toll on her. She hasn't shed a tear, or shown much emotion at all, since the village on fire. And I'm worried. She was such a tender thing when I first met her. She had—and still has—that backbone of steel. I'm worried she's using it like armor against the world, *and* herself. But how can I even say that? How can I bring it up? Everyone has a different way of dealing with this, and who am I to tell her hers is wrong?

"Rations," Malachite says, tossing Lucien an armful of flatbread and seed tack. "Enough fuckin' cheese to last a lifetime, still."

"We'll take a quarter wheel," Lucien says. "Not much room else—we need to move light. Be sure to refill your waterskins, too."

"You gonna be okay to do magic, Luc?" Malachite asks.

"Fione, what do you know about the Glass Tree?" The prince ignores him.

"Glass..." Fione trails off, taking mental inventory. Gods know how many books she's read in her lifetime, and she must be scouring them all. "There's a mention of a Glass Tree in the Hymn of the Forest, of course, but we all know that. '*The tree of bone and the tree of glass will sit together as family at last.*'"

"And there's the stuff Varia told me," I add. "The glass splinters in the Heartless bags—those are from the Glass Tree. That's the key ingredient to making us Heartless."

Next to me, Lucien reaches into his covering and pulls out the small sack stitched with gold thread and the word Heart. "You mean like this?"

I suck a sharp breath in when I see the sack move. "My heart."

ours, the hunger oozes out of my ears. ***ours, ours ours. not his. take it. take it now.***

I fight every scrap of human memory that comes clawing back, faint and fuzzy and smelling of cinnamon and feeling of home and calling hard and fast to me, like a key to a keyhole, a polymath machine piece to another, begging to be made whole, to work again, to become what we were meant to be all along, our natural state, our true self—

Lucien reaches into the bag and presses out the tip of a sharp, long glass shard. Not raw, refined. Transparent, not cloudy. Thin, but real.

"How did you get that, Lucien?" Fione asks. "That particular shard?"

"I woke up with it in my hand," he says. "When I had that dream of the single dark tree, when it whispered my witch name to me. I woke up with magic in my veins and this glass shard clutched in my hand."

"So it was given to you," Fione muses. "By whom? The High Witches?"

"No. The tree gave me my witch name, and it gave me this shard. I'm sure of it."

"So it was the Glass Tree, then."

He shakes his head. "Neither glass nor bone. It was just a tree, glowing a little rainbow."

The room goes quiet, all of us thinking.

Malachite rubs his white hair frustratedly. "Thinking's my least favorite thing."

"Likewise," I say.

"I've heard it implied," Lucien starts, flickering eyes over to me, "that the Glass Tree needs to feed. Would that make any sense, Fione?"

She muses it over, slowly folding a pair of fresh trousers into her bag. "If the Bone Tree needs a strong witch to feed off once every century, as the High Witches said...and if the Glass Tree is a replica made of the Bone Tree by the witches, then—yes. It's not unlikely the Glass Tree needs to feed off magic, too. Witches, to be precise."

"Seven of them," Lucien says. "Encased in glass."

"Is that why the High Witches were missing parts?" I ask. "Did the Glass Tree...eat them?"

Malachite groans. "Being eaten slowly is my least *least* favorite thing, I just decided."

"They feed the Glass Tree seven powerful witches to keep it working," Lucien muses. "To keep the Heartless production line working. Without that Tree—"

"There are no Heartless," I finish for him. Our glances at each other are nothing if not grim.

"Is this Glass Tree thing here?" Malachite stresses. "Like, in Windonhigh? Or is it like the Bone Tree, and it moves around a lot?"

"Without access to the witch library, I have no clue," Fione says. She slowly looks to Lucien. "Is that—"

We all look to the prince, but he ignores us still, wrapping the flatbreads and putting them into his pouch with great care and a few clipped words.

"Refill your damned waterskins, for gods' sakes. It's going to be a walk."

We do as we're told, and we walk as we're told, down the spiral ramps of the living towers, then to the dewy grass and prettily kept road. Windonhigh at night is nothing compared to Vetris at night, with its many thousands of gemlike lights all stacked on one another. But it has its charms. The glass beasts in Crow quarter gleam even brighter against the darkness, traipsing through the grass like illuminated dreams. The glass birds flicker through the trees, flirting with shadow—there one moment and gone the next and back again—all pink and yellow and orange light bouncing off one another. Like captured stars, like captured *magic*. The wind rustles leaf against leaf, the whisper following us as we skirt the art installments, the massive sapphire mushroom radiating light doing us no concealing favors.

"Never there when I *want* to find you," Malachite mumbles at it. "And here when I absolutely *don't* want you."

"Are you looking to get married soon, then?" I breezily ask as we follow Lucien's strides into a small copse of ash trees, his hand lit with witchfire.

Malachite rolls his eyes. "To my work."

"Or a nice beneather lady."

"Or man," he counters.

"Or man," I agree. "Anyone particular you have in mind?"

"Someone who doesn't ask annoying questions all the time."

"Ah." I nod knowingly, ducking around a tree branch. "The strong silent type. I understand."

He leaps over a root nimbly. "You wouldn't know silence if it dueled you in the streets."

I look at him with mock offense. "Who gave you permission to be so right and so rude at the same time?"

"Who do you think?" He jerks his white-haired head at Lucien's back, and I snicker. It's short-lived, though. Malachite pulls ahead and astride with the prince, and Fione and I shore up the rear. She's bundled in so many furs I can barely see her little pink nose sticking out, her blue eyes darting this way and that for threats.

What she said before we left still haunts me. The realization that the seven High Witches are being *eaten* by the Glass Tree haunts me worse, mostly because of what Crav said. Lucien's hand, and eye—it's similar to the High Witches. What really happens when a witch uses magic beyond their physical stamina? Does the magic truly overwhelm their body, rendering parts of it inert? Or does...does the Glass Tree *eat* them?

I shake my head—the High Witches' bodies were gone. Fully and truly gone. If Lucien were being eaten in the same way, surely his affected parts would disappear entirely, too. But they haven't. If he keeps using magic recklessly…if he doesn't get enough rest…

"Zera."

Lucien's voice shakes me out of it. We've stopped walking, pausing on the edge of the copse and just beneath the boughs of a massive ash tree. His midnight eyes glimmer out at me, catching the light of the witchflames licking his hand harmlessly. It's his left hand, hard to see in the black fire. Too hard. It's a moment—just a moment, between the dancing flames, I swear his hand disappears entirely and reappears again. I rub my eyes—I must be projecting. Insinuating things that aren't there. Worried—far too much—about him disappearing, bit by bit.

I make a smile and bounce up to him. "Yes, Your Highness?"

He's in no mood to play, or kiss, or playfully kiss. Brows drawn tight, he motions to the tree above us. "Can you move this?"

My eyes widen, and I consider it. "This whole tree?"

"The whole tree," he agrees. "We need to uproot it."

"Why not just use magic?" Malachite frowns. "It'd be easier."

"He can't, obviously," Fione sighs. "Or it'd be detected."

"Pretty certain I can't lift it all by myself," I finally say. "Mal?"

The beneather shrugs his sword off his back, rolling his sleeves up. "Worth a shot."

He moves to the trunk, digging his heels in and finding a good grip.

I look up at Lucien. "It's really heavy. And all those roots…I might need the hunger."

"If you want to Weep—" Fione steps up, fingering the white mercury dagger on her hip, the bejeweled hilt sparkling.

"Can I?"

"It's not as if it'd be detected," Fione says. "It isn't magic—it defies magic. Right?"

She looks to Lucien, but he shakes his head. "I'm not sure. But if that's what will get this tree moved, then we must do it."

He pauses and looks at me. "It's…it's not painful, is it?"

I smirk. "I mean, traditionally being stabbed isn't a *pleasant* experience."

He flinches. "Yes. Of course."

"Hey," I reach my hand out, cupping his strong cheekbone. "I'll be fine."

"Someone told me once that sacrifice shouldn't be celebrated," he says quietly, leaning in to my hand and closing his eyes.

"Look at you"—I laugh softly—"using my words against me. It's almost like we're a real couple now."

His eyes go tender on the edges, black water instead of black stone. "Zera—"

"Weeping is mine, Lucien. I made it real. It's my weapon against the world, and no one else's. I choose."

The black water in his eyes swirls, thinking, worrying, struggling with being my witch, with orders and well-being and control and then…becoming my lover. Becoming proud.

"Yes. You choose."

I turn to Fione and hold out my arm. "If you love me, you'll make it quick."

"Good thing I don't, then," Fione drawls, unsheathing the dagger on her hip. She holds it to my skin, her fingers trembling around the hilt. Over the pearls of her and Varia's love.

"When did she give it to you?" I ask softly. Fione stares woodenly down at the veins in my wrist. Our embrace in Breych's tower seems so distant now. This isn't our first time in this position, her readying to stab me as she did on the mountaintop. To free me.

"Before she left," Fione answers, lost in a time I can't see. "Five years ago. *'To cut through the horseshit of the world.'*"

"Sounds like something she'd say." I laugh a little. Fione's apple-cheeked face doesn't move, frozen. We both know Varia in different ways. Me as a witch and her as a lover. Lucien knows her, too, but not like we do. He knows only a sister, but we know her secrets. Her heart.

I put my hand over the hilt with her and press harder, blood pooling and acid fire rippling through my nerves.

"We're going to get her back, Fione. Together."

This makes her come round to the present, to Windonhigh again, and she looks at me. *Really* looks. The sort of look that feels like a tattoo. And then she cuts. She cuts with memories, and pain, and hope for the future—hope for the *right* future—and I can feel it. I can feel it twisting like the white mercury twisting through my veins, beneath my skin, writhing invisibly with wildfire, with the poisonous curl of burning, consuming, *destroying*.

I hold on.

This time, I hold on.

It's not a whole sword of white mercury. It's a dagger. It's enough to weaken the magical tie between Lucien and me so that I can Weep, but it's not powerful enough to knock me out. Not like the duel. Or maybe I'm stronger.

I'm stronger this time.

Maybe, despite everything, it's possible for a Heartless to change after all.

I stagger, Fione gripping my elbow for support. Touching me again, trusting me again, and my unheart in my empty chest and my real heart in Lucien's bag shudder as one, in pain and in joy.

they hate you.

They're relying on me.

they're waiting for you to let your guard down.

They trust me.

how could they forgive you for what you've done?

I forgive myself.

The hunger disappears, clear and cold, and the world splits six times.

Between Malachite and me, we manage to uproot the tree with much swearing and straining and blood tears on my part. My claws dig deep into bark, the roots peeling up and away with angry groans and cracks, until the whole thing finally gives, and Malachite and I shove the trunk aside before it can keel over on the humans.

"Not bad, Six-Eyes." The beneather pants, wiping mud and bark off his sweaty face. "You practice?"

I catch my breath, the Weeping peaceful and silent and easy, like slipping into an old glove now. "No. You?"

"Always." He smirks, and then puts his hand over his nose, his eyes flashing with a red glow. "*Spirits.* You really smell like one of 'em."

"One of who?" Fione asks as she walks over.

"Valkerax. She stinks like 'em."

I sniff my armpits warily—bracing for the rotting meat stench I know so well from training Evlorasin. But even with my heightened Weeping senses, all I get is sweat and me.

"I can't smell anything," Lucien says, eyeing the hole in the ground where the tree used to be.

"Right, well." Malachite straps his sword on his back again. "Who's the one whose ancestors have been hunting them for a thousand years, huh? Not you, that's for spiritsdamn sure. If I say she stinks, she stinks." He looks over at me with a crooked smirk. "You stink."

"Thank you." I smile back at him with all my teeth.

Fione looks me up and down. "Curious indeed. I have no clue how valkerax blood promises work, but it seems this one has lasting effects."

"For the rest of my life, Yorl said," I agree.

"So you're basically one of 'em," Malachite groans. "Great."

"It's not like Varia can control her with the Bone Tree," Fione snipes back.

"You don't know that, Big-Brain," the beneather scoffs.

"Neither do you," she argues.

"If I get any compelling inklings to run off and start breathing fire, I'll be sure to let you all know." I cut the tension and look over at Lucien, who's still riveted to the ground. "What now, Your Highness?"

"It's beneath." He points down at the soft earth collapsing in on itself. The last bit finally sloughs away with encouragement from his boot and reveals a perfect set of stairs.

"Whaddya know." Malachite frowns. "A nice staircase leading down into the earth. Well, uh, not-earth. Sky-island earth." He pauses. "Hey, what happens if we fall through and die?"

"We fall through and die," Fione deadpans.

"At least it's an interesting way to go," I encourage him with a thump on the back.

Lucien's the first to walk in, and Fione and I move in after him, Malachite on uneasy rear point.

Just past the mouth of the stairs, the dirt quickly becomes curved stone, perfectly round, as if a tower's been pressed down into the earth and excavated on the inside. No doubt made by magic, though Malachite comments it's very good stonework. And coming from his Dark-Below-dwelling arse, that means something.

"Old Vetrisian," Fione murmurs, running a hand along the granite. "All of it."

The Weeping leaves me in increments—the blood tears of resistance growing cold and then stopping all at once. The clear, perfect clarity in my head grows the fuzz of emotion and thought again. The world comes back to being just two—left eye and right eye—and I wipe my red-streaked face on my sleeve.

Torches dot the walls down here every so often—black fire with no color to it at all. Which I find odd, considering every variation of witchfire I've seen so far has had a different hue to it, based on the witch. Or so I think. Lucien's is faintly purple. His black-purple flames engulfed South Gate weeks ago. It battled Varia and the Bone Tree's white light on the mountain peak. Varia's witchfire was faintly green. Nightsinger's was gray on the edges. The only time I've seen pure black fire was when Gavik made that fake witchfire to scare the populace of Vetris. But this fire is no fake—it sputters and gouts, eating no fuel at all considering the torch heads are completely bare and made of metal.

Actually, now that I think about it, it's the same pure black witchfire that lit up Y'shennria's apartments, and I begin to feel uneasy. What witch is powerful enough to keep so many torches burning, over such a distance? The High Witches, maybe?

Can they keep an eye on us through their fire?

"Where are we going, Lucien?" Fione asks suddenly. "This place—it hasn't been touched in a long time."

She's right. There's no dust, but the feel of the air is stale and heavy. The prince suddenly freezes on the steps, his head darting up, up to the stone steps above us and the surface beyond that.

"Something knows we're here," he says.

"Well, we *did* destroy their possibly magic door-tree," I hum.

"Some*thing*?" Malachite asks. "Or some*one*?"

Lucien doesn't answer. He grabs my hand instead, pulling me farther down the dark depths of the stairs.

"Come. Quickly. Ready your weapons. Malachite, watch the walls."

"The *walls*?" Fione frowns, the mechanical cacophony of her cane transforming into a crossbow echoing precisely. "Lucien, what's going on?"

"I don't know," he admits, squeezing my hand as if for support.

"We have to hurry."

The stairs blur, the walls blurring faster, and we finally level out to the floor. Except…there is no floor. It's glass, all of it, clear and fine and yawning into the sky. Clouds shuffle below the glass floor, slow and lazy and heavy with gray rain, night birds cutting double V's before disappearing into the water mist of the clouds and dipping back out again. Faintly, I can see green fields below, marked pale for wheat and roads.

Cavanos. Cavanos directly and miles below us. It's a terrifying and decadent floor of a room, but the only other things in the space itself are stone walls and torches. I blink into the nighttime gloom; there's something like rows in the very back walls, carved deep and lined with an unmistakable upright pattern in fading colors. Books. Just a handful. A whole room, and just these books.

"Those look important," I lilt.

"Yeah, but that's—that's a long fall!" Malachite gulps.

"It might be a trap," Fione says. "Can you teleport us across, Lucien?"

"Not without alerting the High Witches to exactly where we are," he says.

"Don't they already know?" I press, but the prince says nothing. "Could you fly across it as a crow?"

"A solid plan," he agrees shortly. "Until I needed to bring a book back with me."

"Let me check the perimeter for trap switches—"

"There's no time," Lucien interrupts Fione. "We have to move, now."

Lucien tries the glass floor with one boot, and when it stays, he instantly darts across, pulling me along. I can hear Fione's boots following us, but Malachite hedges.

"Luc, seriously—"

"If it makes you feel better, Sir Bodyguard," I call out over my shoulder, "you pass out before you ever hit the ground."

"It doesn't, actually," I hear him mumble and draw his sword, but the unsteady clip of his shoes joins us across the glass. Fione is the first to reach the books, skimming the spines with her fingers.

"Written in Old Vetrisian," she marvels. "These—all of these are at *least* a thousand years old."

"Can you translate what's inside?" I ask.

"With Lucien's help." She nods. "Some words and structures are passed down only through the royal family." Her little fingers reach for a book, pulling it out gingerly and opening the cover. "Remarkably well-preserved, too."

"Magic," Lucien asserts, head tilted as he reads other spines, "tends to do all kinds of remarkable things."

While they peruse, I watch the glass beneath our feet warily and the clouds writhing below that. It feels like the clear panes should drop away at any moment, but they stay strong. Maybe it *is* just a floor—just an Old Vetrisian marvel made for show. Maybe I'm being paranoid. But the way Lucien keeps looking over his shoulder, to the *walls*, of all things, makes me uneasy.

I put a hand on his arm and lean in. "What's wrong?"

His throat bobs. "It's in the walls."

"What is?" He doesn't say anything. "Lucien—"

"Something hungry," he finishes, fingertips dawning midnight. "Valkerax?"

"No." He goes still, voice lowering to a bare whisper. "Something older."

us, the hunger cackles. But that's impossible. The hunger is for Heartless only. Why would it be outside, made flesh, made *real*, where others can hear it? Unless...

On the opposite side of the glass floor, deep in a wall, something moves.

The granite *swells*.

"We have to go," I chirp to Fione, trying not to betray my nerves. *"Posthaste."*

"I still don't know which one to take." She frowns. "I can barely translate the titles."

"Then take them all."

"Not advisable." Fione frowns and points up to the bookshelf, where runes are carved into the stone. "That means 'large warning,' and that means 'one item,' and I don't have to know the rest to understand the gist."

"This one." Malachite points with his free hand to a green-bound book with faded silver inking. "Take this one."

Fione raises a brow. "How would you—"

"I know that symbol. It's the same in beneather runes. 'Tree.' And 'destroy.'"

"'Destroy,' or 'create'?" Her rosebud lips frown deeper. "You have to be precise—they have nearly the same shape order, but different occulants over the verb—"

I look at Lucien, but he hasn't moved—his whole body still as a deer, his onyx eyes wide and searching the walls frantically, as if seeing something I can't. And then he looks up.

And so do I.

Above us, the granite wall swells, cracking with hairline fractures.

"We don't have time," I blurt. "Just take the gamble and the godsdamn book."

Fione breathes in and darts her hand out, pulling the green book from the shelf. Like snapping out of a trance, Lucien grabs my hand and darts for the staircase, strides so long and fast I can barely keep up.

The sound comes first—screeching. Not valkerax screeching, not anything alive or organic. Not anything with a tongue, or teeth, or a voice box. It's a sound made without flesh, the screech of something dragging slowly, achingly across *glass*. The walls all around us swell, dozens of bulging rounds of stone pushing at the seams, straining.

The explosions come second.

Glass.

Raw glass bursting from the walls, cloudy and thick and moving like fast river water. Like vines alive.

Like *roots*.

The tips are ground down instantly as the roots burst through, the shattering sound of a dozen glass vases being dropped and infinitesimal shards sparkling out in clouds, raining down on the glass floor and our hair, our skin, our clothes. Blood.

"Spirits!" Malachite snarls, trying to brush the glass off, but it digs deep, the shards embedding in his face and nose and long ears. Fione's barely better, having just covered her eyes in time—her mouth bleeding and hanging open, her scalp oozing red. Shit—did she inhale? After all the pain I've endured, the faint burning and scraping as the glass shards work their way all over my body is almost nothing, but it's enough to make me wince. Once.

"Lucien!" I turn to him. The glass caught his neck, blood oozing down his throat, his collarbone, his covering halfway soaked with it. But his eyes are clear, hot, and focused on the enormous glass roots now writhing readily all around us. His fingers blossom with midnight up to the knuckles, and he throws his hand out, a massive fireball exploding from the tips and sucking in all the air as it flies, smashing into a glass root. The thing recoils like it's *alive*, melting rapidly into nothing more than a flailing stub half peeking out of the wall. The pool of red-hot glass pours down on the glass floor, eating a hole into it. The night rushes in, wet with rain and cloud and the thin smell of high air.

A beat. Glass undulating around us like a nest of vipers. And then the roots strike all at once.

12

AS THE WYRM FLIES

Malachite snarls and flings the broad of his blade with power, a brutal arc, and the shriek of glass on metal resounds as two of the roots deflect off it. Lucien thrusts his palms up, completely dark now, and a wall of animate witchfire springs to life in front of him, blazing hot and giving the roots pause. They writhe slowly just in front, looking for an opening, angling for weakness.

Fione makes a gasping noise beside me, and I lunge to her.

"Did you inhale it?" I ask. Her blue eyes dart up, withering with pain. It's all the confirmation I could want. She needs healing, and fast.

"We have to get to the door!" Malachite bellows. "You three move, I'll watch the flank!"

"You're coming with!" I snap.

"Obviously!" He deflects another root with a powerful swing, the brutal impact skidding his low stance backward. Our escape route is the way we came in this morning: the little island west of Windonhigh, connected by the cloudbridge. Lucien assured us it was a magically charged space; it would be a simple matter for him to teleport all of us down to the ground from there without exhausting himself. But how are we going to make it? These roots—they're *vicious*. Attacking viciously, as if in ironic retaliation for the tree we uprooted.

you invaded, the hunger insists. ***invaded where no one should,***

with your human pride and your human blood...

And then it hits me. Varia is the Bone Tree. If Varia can control the Bone Tree's power while being eaten by it, then the High Witches being eaten by the Glass Tree...can they control *their* tree? Are they the Glass Tree? Is that why Lucien was afraid of being overheard? The raw glass all over Windonhigh...can they *listen* through it? All that raw glass...is that *them*?

Is this seven High Witches, combining their power to stop us all at once?

Cold fear hardens my face. I pull Fione to the left just in time as one of them pierces in from the side, around Lucien's witchfire wall, and he snarls, the fire extending around us even farther in a deep semicircle. The black-purple flames reflect frosty in the glass, like candied violets with a particularly furious bloodlust.

Next to me, Fione makes an awful gurgling noise, sticky trails of blood sloughing out of her mouth and down her clothes. If the fine shards lodged in her mouth or her throat, she'll live longer. But if they got in her lungs, we're running on extremely borrowed time.

"The stairs," I urge her. "C'mon. We can make it."

She staggers, her grip on her crossbow cane white-knuckled and smeared red, her other hand clutching the book close like it's the last thing left in the world. Lucien rotates with us, defending us from the front with his witchfire wall. It doesn't stop the glass roots or destroy them, but it does make them hesitate, and that's all we need to inch across the clear floor, step-by-bleeding-step. Bloody footprints across the glass, drag marks, dripped pools. We can make it. Every step, every ring as Malachite lets out a roar and deflects, the blazing crackle of the witchfire as it eats nothing—*we can make it.*

The stairs are so close when it happens.

And that's what makes the fall so terrible.

The roots stop all of a sudden. Malachite pants; Lucien keeps the wall in place, watching and waiting. The glass roots all pull back at once, quivering, and then pierce down.

Into the floor.

Glass melding with glass. Glass roots squirming inside thinner glass, below it, peeling it apart like a pliable skin over milk.

We don't even have time to blink.

The floor opens up, wind screaming, us screaming, my insides pressing up against my outsides, and all I can think about is him.

Lucien.

My eyes are watering too badly, the speed too much to keep focused on his outline for long. But I see his arms going dark, black eating gold up to the elbows, up to his bleeding neck, black below the red, and I know he's going to lose himself. The part that deadens this time will be all of him.

fear.

Being immortal means you only have fear. But you forget what real, yawning, *mortal* fear feels like.

Until now.

It's not fair. It's not fair I can't even shout at him to stop, the wind and pressure stealing all the words from my lungs. I can't even reach him, the air battering my body around like a hated doll. He's going to die. My immortality, useless. I can only watch. I can only feel my brain slipping into unconsciousness, into nothing, into death once and for all.

Black on gold on red.

And then—*rainbow.*

Soft fur tickling my face. Smooth scales beneath my hands. The smell of rot, faintly, quickly dispersed by the relentless whipping wind. Warmth, making its way into my body from something much larger than me, all over and under.

"Starving Wolf." A voice rumbles in every one of my bones. *"Here you are, and here I am."*

I catch my breath, my ribs aching. Fione's hand in mine, still, her body unmoving and her other hand clutching the book. Lucien, passed out not far from her, and Malachite, struggling to sit up. All of us, on the finned white back of a valkerax.

And not any valkerax.

"Evlorasin!" I put my hand to its scales, feeling it to make sure it's real. "H-How—"

"I told you. I will always be with you. This was not a lie."

It's so *long*, stretching out like a banner behind us in the sky, its back so wide that all of us can fit comfortably. Evlorasin's mane flares out, all its feathers standing on end like a halo, and from that halo radiates a gentle circle of rainbow light. No wings—no wings like a flying thing should have, but lengthy whiskers beating air hard, and its lionlike paws paddling the clouds as if the stormy sky is calm water.

Words hurt, but I force them out steadily. "Thank you. Thank you so much."

"Are you talking to *it*?" Malachite rasps, clutching on his ribs with one hand and a huge pearlescent scale with the other. "Is this—is this the one that scared everybody in Vetris? The one we retrieved?"

"There is little time for idleness," Evlorasin interrupts. *"If you would look up, you would see a problem."*

It's hard with the wind, but I squint up—Windonhigh far above us. Not far enough I can't see the green, or the bottom of it—a mass of dirt and hanging roots, and most terrifyingly of all, from the tiny glass-bottomed section that's been peeled open, dozens of glass roots stretching out for us like tentacles. And moving fast.

Malachite looks with me. "Tenacious little bastards, aren't they?"

"You have angered the Tree of Glass," Evlorasin says. *"Secure yourself and your comrades to my scales, with blood if you must. Quickly."*

I look at Malachite. "Stick your sword in it."

"What?"

"The valkerax. Hold Lucien, and stick your sword in it!"

"Thought you'd never ask!" he shouts back, driving his broadsword into the scales. Evlorasin twitches but doesn't recoil, and I bring my claws out—the smaller holes I make between its scales much less painful. Malachite wraps one arm around Lucien's chest, dragging him close, and I do the same for Fione, making sure her book is sandwiched tightly between us.

Evlorasin starts to rumble-growl deep in its chest, the vibration shaking us as easily as marbles in a bag.

"We fly."

The rainbow halo around its mane bursts to life, from pastel to vivid color, blazing like seven-colored fire and expanding to thrice its size. The flash sears my eyes, and I blink it away as fast as I can only to see glass roots whizzing past my ears, past Evlorasin's tail and legs and whiskers, barely missing each time they thrust through the sky. Evlorasin twists and turns, lurching as my stomach lurches, coiling and uncoiling in split seconds, the glass roots nicking its sides, its feet. Even above the screaming wind, I can hear its excited voice like it's right in my ear.

"Hold on!"

We dive.

The world falls away, nothing but white feathers and rainbow light and the instinct to clench, to hold, to brace for something I can't stop. I hug Fione to me even harder, her bones pressing against my palms, and I know if I hold any tighter I'll hurt her, but I'm terrified. Terrified she'll fall off, human as she is. Broken bones are better than a dead friend, and I clutch, and *clutch*. A glass root shrieks over my head, and I press us as low and tight to Evlorasin's body as I can.

Another one pierces the air just to my left, so forceful I can feel the vacuum in its wake. Something warm hits my face—

blood. Not Fione's throat wound. Fresh. Against the throbbing momentum, I raise my head and see Malachite's biceps clenched around Lucien cleaved and bleeding in rhythmic spurts.

"Mal!"

"I'm fine!" he shouts. "Shut up before you bite your tongue off!"

The momentum of our fall starts to near critical, all the flesh on our bodies pulled back, away from the earth. I feel like a horse, teeth exposed, terror exposed, but no blinders. Nothing to dull the cut of reality. Just over Fione's shoulders, I can see the trees of the ground loom up, and the sharper the details the more of a warning it is. Soon. Soon, we hit the ground.

The fall, and then the rise.

Evlorasin pulls out of the death dive, shearing off not five miles above a forest. Without the force of the fall, I can look up now and see that the glass roots are trembling in the air, hesitant again.

"We've reached the threshold," the valkerax says. *"They can go no farther."*

With aching necks, Malachite and I look at each other, pure relief coursing from him to me and then to the nobles held fast in our arms. We're safe. For now.

Evlorasin flies an easy distance before descending to the earth, weaving between the trees big enough to accommodate it. It lets us off, bowed shoulders making the perfect stepping ramp down. I carry Fione to a dry patch of forest and rest her on my covering. Malachite manages to prop Lucien up against a tree trunk even with his split arm, and I feel a flash of anxiety run through me at all the tangled, still roots so close to him. So close to hurting him. Malachite seems to be thinking the same.

"Spiritsdamned trees," he says through gritted teeth, tearing a bit of cloth and wrapping his arm.

I turn and look at Evlorasin, its mane-halo radiating fainter again, illuminating the dim forest in a gentle pearlescent circle. Its whiskers undulate as I approach, and its five milk white, bleeding eyes stacked on one another watch me as I slide a tentative hand over its velvet nose.

"You really saved us back there," I mutter.

"*I saved you,*" Evlorasin corrects softly. "*The others are not blood kin.*"

"Sure," I laugh shakily. "Right."

There's a silence, the forest birds and forest animals too silent—as anything would go silent upon sensing something as large as Evlorasin. I don't know what to say to the valkerax. "Your kind are ravaging Cavanos?" "Have you seen the destruction?"

"*The Bone Tree has its chime at last,*" Evlorasin speaks first, tail tip lifting like a roused snake and down again.

"Yeah." I frown. "And we're trying to stop it."

Evlorasin cocks its head in an almost humanly confused gesture. "*The chime? Or the Tree?*"

"The Tree."

"*The Tree has many roots, buried deep and long. T'would be easier to stop the trill of the chime.*"

It means killing Varia. I feel the old guilt settle in, the old rankling. "I know."

Evlorasin thinks, puffing out rancid clouds into the crisp salt air. It starts scratching at the dirt suddenly, and Malachite, staring at it warily this whole time and very probably fighting his instincts to kill the valkerax, likes none of it.

"What exactly is it doing, Six-Eyes?"

"Ev," I start, running my hand over one of its talons. "What's wrong?"

"*One cannot destroy a Tree. It will only grow back from the other. I worry your fight will become the dust of nothing.*"

I think back to all that time I spent with it in the arena. The story-speech of the valkerax is a lot more coherent now that

Evlorasin can resist the call of the Bone Tree with the Weeping I taught it. But it still smacks of chaos and nonsense. Trees growing back from one another?

"Do you mean..." I trail off, thinking desperately. "If we wanted to destroy the Bone Tree, we'd have to destroy the Glass Tree, too?"

I can see myself reflected in Evlorasin's milky, pupilless eyes, the sixth one on the bottom a vast mess of browned scar tissue. It watches me for a long moment, and then thrashes its tail around.

"Destruction and creation are blood kin held fast in one body—they can never be separated. As the Trees were never meant to be."

I feel my whole face wrinkling with confusion. I know asking it to clarify is pointless—it's not what Evlorasin's saying that's the problem. What it's saying is true, and real. It's the fact I can't understand it. The concepts, the words. I can't understand them like it does. Another language. No—another perspective entirely, one that's been around for far longer than I have. One that knows so much more about how Arathess works at its very bones.

My eyes roam over the valkerax's pale stretch and catch on something far down its body, by its back leg. An injury. Unlike the shallow scratches of the glass roots nicking its scales, this injury is deep, dark red, and still healing. The scales are all peeled away, rotting, scabbing replacing them. I slide down and touch the edges of the wound tenderly.

"Ev, where did you get this?"

"Blood kin," Evlorasin grunts, its flank trembling with even the slightest touch I give on its exposed flesh. *"My own blood kin turned against me."*

"They bit you?"

"Teeth on flesh. I fled. They followed. They have my blood, now."

My mind screams soundlessly—something sitting unright in

its words, off-center. But whatever it is, it hangs just out of my grasp.

"What'll you do after this?" I ask. "You could come with us. Always handy to have someone who can fly."

"Your cause is noble," Evlorasin agrees. *"But I am changed. I listen to the sky. It is what I will live for, and what I will die for."*

"Well." My smirk goes crooked. "Great. Just try not to get all morbid about it too quickly, okay?"

The humor is lost on the valkerax, like most of the meanings of its words are lost on me. An even trade.

Evlorasin moves its paw, pulling me back to its face with the curve of its massive talon, like a shepherd's hook pulling back a sheep. I know what that means, what it wants—body language, even with a valkerax, is far easier to understand—and I throw my arms into its mane and hug it close.

"Be safe," I mutter into feathers and fur. The valkerax snorts, a cloud of dirt displacing around my feet.

"As blood flows between you and I, we will exist together."

"Thank you, again."

"What is gratitude," the valkerax says softly, *"but a promise made whole?"*

And with that, it pivots and winds its serpentine body through the trees, slithering loud, cracking young trees and old branches, and disappears as quickly as it appeared.

"Good riddance." Malachite waves it off.

"It saved you, you know," I blurt.

"And it'd sooner turn around and kill me, too," he drawls. "Daft thing."

I watch the last of Evlorasin go with a sadness welling up in the cracks of me—a sadness I know isn't my own. Or, it is. But it's more than that. The sadness is both of ours, Evlorasin's and mine. Connected to each other through the blood promise it gave me.

A sudden thought flashes through my brain, in Yorl's voice of all voices. Yorl, the celeon polymath genius Varia put in charge of finding the Bone Tree. He knows the most about valkerax of anyone in the world, thanks to his grandfather's research. He was there with me every step of the way, and he's here with me now, in cold, clear logic. He could help us.

"It's called a blood promise, Zera, not a blood moment."

He's right. Mine and Evlorasin's connection has endured.

"You know where the Bone Tree is. You will always know. Now and forever. Until the very moment your human body dies for the last time."

The dreams.

"Mal." I pivot, only to see Lucien staggering to his feet and toward Fione.

"Is she breathing?" he demands.

Malachite puts his fingers to her bloody throat and shakes his head. "Nothing."

My unheart squeezes painfully. So wrapped up in Ev's mystic Tree shit, I forgot who needed help. "Is she—"

Malachite looks up to Lucien. "You could...you have another glass shard, right?"

"No!" I blurt. "Mal—*no*. She has to choose it. We can't force her into it."

"Nightsinger forced you," he points out. "It's to save her life, Six-Eyes."

"No. Zera's right," Lucien manages, limping over to Fione. "It has to be chosen. We try to heal her."

"There's no pulse to heal, Luc—"

I race over and drop to my knees. "What do we need?"

"Water," Lucien croaks, rolling up his sleeves. His own neck is bloodied so badly, it looks like a butcher shop, but he ignores it. "So I can heat it. And a rabbit, if you can find it. She's lost a lot of blood."

"Uh, why a rabbit?" Malachite asks.

"Less talking." Lucien pulls off his covering and drapes it over Fione's blue-lipped body. "More doing."

Malachite and I share a look.

"Dibs on the rabbit," I say.

"Always giving me the boring jobs." He sighs, both of us splitting off in a blink. It doesn't take long for me to find a burrow, and it takes even less time to dig into the earth with all my claws.

"Sorry," I murmur.

When I get back, Malachite's already there with the water, his drinking skin bulging as he offers it to Lucien. The prince's fingers turn dark as he holds it, and a small trail of steam suddenly wafts from the skin's spout. He tears his shirt and offers me the cloth.

"Wet it with the water and clean her wounds, if you would. Gingerly."

I nod. My fingers work as fast as "gingerly" will let me, and my eyes roam over Fione's face. Her skin is sallow, her breathing so thin, I barely hear it. She's not awake, thank the gods, because Lucien cuts her wrist with his blade out of nowhere.

"Shit!" Malachite snarls. "She's already lost enough blood! What are you—"

"Rabbit," Lucien demands from me, and I hand it over. He slits the thing's broken neck, his fingers deep midnight up to the knuckles as he holds the wounds together—rabbit to girl, skin to skin.

It happens slowly at first and then quickly, like all magic. The blood from the rabbit oozes out like a hedging worm, like a thing burrowing out of winter to peek at spring. A pure liquid-red worm, thick and long, moving without spilling a drop. It almost *seeks* Fione's wound—drawn by the blood—and when it finds it, it burrows. With a sickening squelch and a slow pump, the rabbit's blood empties into Fione's cut, but not without cost. Lucien makes a snarling noise, his brow dripping sweat onto the ground.

"Can't—can't you just heal her?" Malachite asks.

"Sh-She needs blood first," Lucien says. "Or her body will reject the spell."

"Use a human's, maybe?" I offer. "I have plenty—"

"Do you see any humans around here?" he snaps.

"You—"

"I'm not human anymore. I'm witch. You're a Heartless, Mal is a beneather. All incompatible."

"Are you—" I gulp, watching the rabbit blood move into her arm, writhing like a live thing just below her skin. "Are you turning the rabbit's blood...into *human blood*?"

He doesn't confirm, but he doesn't need to. Malachite and I go silent after that, our eyes meeting wide and watching in awe as Lucien's entire hand goes void, as the sweat carves down his proud nose and over his lips. He gives a shuddering snarl again, pushing on something invisibly, and the last of the rabbit's blood ekes out, and Fione's wrist wound closes like a seam being zipped shut. Like Nightsinger used to zip shut my wounds. And then, Lucien puts his midnight hand on her throat, lightly, holding. The woods seem to go even quieter, the salt wind in the boughs dying away.

I pray like Ania Tarroux taught me. I pray like humans do. For Fione to be all right. For Lucien to be all right.

A shuddering gasp suddenly shatters the forest's silence, and Fione sits bolt upright, throat pulling in air greedily and blue eyes wide. She scrabbles for something, and I thrust my hand at her. She clutches it, hard.

"The book." Her voice is nigh tortured. "Where..."

"Fione! It's okay. I'm here—you're safe."

"The book!" Her eyes scan frantically over everything, and it's then I realize. She's not worried about herself or if she's safe. She's worried about the book. About stopping Varia, above all. Even on death's door.

I hold her close and whisper, "We have the book. It's okay."

Finally, her rigid body goes limp against mine. Next to me, Lucien wobbles, but Mal is behind him in a blink, supporting him. And the wound on Mal's arm—it's gone. Smooth skin where injury should be. Did he just heal *everyone*? The overexertion, the magic required to do that—

"*Vachiayis,* Luc," his bodyguard swears. "If I knew we were showing off, I would've gotten that water with a little more aplomb."

"Shut...up..." Lucien manages, lying bonelessly back in his arms, and Malachite smirks down at him, and then at me.

"Never ever."

13

DESTRUCTION

From my personal experience, there's nothing like a hot meal to lift the spirits. And a spirit. But alas. We're stuck in the middle of the woods (just east of the Feralstorm coast, Malachite surmises after a jaunty scout), in which the only thing resembling alcohol at all is the single half-muddied puddle of deer piss not ten paces from our fire.

The rabbit's blood is gone, but its meat isn't, and I rotate the shoddily made spit on which it sits browning in its own juices. A stew would be better, to spread the nutrition around the three mortals, but we don't have many options in terms of cookware, let alone a decent pot. Perhaps magic could conjure one up, but I dare not propose it what with Lucien looking half dead already. After he healed Fione, he rolled over and almost immediately went to sleep under a tree. The rest of us gathered around the fire are quiet, Fione most of all.

"Talking hurts," she rasps.

"Then don't," Malachite asserts, wiping his broadsword down. "Just stare into the flames and think about deep shit. That's what fires're for, anyway."

"How many nicks?" I jerk my chin at his sword.

The beneather frowns. "Way too many, considering those things were just made of glass."

"Magic glass," Fione croaks, and I hold up a finger to shush her.

"Don't make me gag you, archduchess. T'would be a *vastly* unbecoming accessory with this season's color palette."

Fione huffs, a glimmer of that impertinent, impatient huff she used to make in the before-times, in the "innocent" days of Vetris court life, and grumpily goes back to staring into the fire. I look at the green-bound book sitting at her side—she hasn't touched it, but neither has she let it out of her sight since she came back from the dead. Near-dead.

Malachite's thinking it, too.

"We were gonna Heartless you," he says without looking at her. Fione's gaze darts to a sleeping Lucien, then back to the flames.

"That would've been the logical choice," she agrees.

"But it wouldn't have been what you wanted," I say, then stop myself when she slashes a look over at me. "Not like I can know what you want, obviously. I was more worried you wouldn't get to choose it for yourself."

"Then…" Her lips curl in a tiny smile. "I'm grateful to you."

"If," Malachite starts. "If you did get turned Heartless, would your leg thing go away?"

"Mal." I sigh. "You can't just—"

"No, I'm serious. It's like, a logistics question. The magic heals everything on a Heartless when they die, right? Would it heal that? Or does it stay? Did *you* have anything that went away when you got turned, Six-Eyes?"

"Not that I remember," I say. "But that's not really the point, is it?"

"Then what is?" he fires.

"*Gods.* You always get so testy when Lucien's injured," I quip.

"Look who's talkin'."

We glower at each other through the firelight for a while, and then Fione's voice interrupts quietly.

"Whether or not my leg would heal or remain the same, I would still be me."

"Would you want it to go away?" Mal presses.

"No," she says. "And yes. It's not a simple answer. But it's mine to give—and mine alone."

Malachite studies her face for a long moment and then makes that lopsided smile, the triple claw-scars I gave him crinkling. He hefts off the root he was sitting on and goes to check on Lucien's sleeping form.

"You haven't read the book yet." I nod at the green-backed thing. She makes a small frown.

"Of course I haven't."

"I thought you could read Old Vetrisian. Or, not without Luc's help?"

"I need more than Luc's help," she says. "I can't translate an entire thousand-year-old manuscript in a void. No one speaks Old Vetrisian anymore. It's a dead language. I need reference materials, codices, Vetrisian-beneather generalized ciphers to scrape the barest sliver of information from it."

"Then we get you those."

"How? The only place that has such things is the Black Archive, and they would never—" She sees the glint in my eye. "No. Zera, *no*."

"What? It's just a little sneaking in and stealing."

"Do you think you're the first thief to think of breaking in?"

"No." I laugh.

"Have you *ever* heard of a thief stealing from the Black Archives?"

I pause. "No."

"And why do you think that is?"

"Because they're not me. Because they're bad."

"Because they're *dead*, Zera," she says, hard. "They get killed."

"I can't *be* killed." I scoff again. "And anyway, killed by what, dust inhalation? It's just a library."

"It isn't *just* a library," the archduchess insists. "Not like you're thinking. The polymaths in the Black Archives guard the information there with their lives. They're highly skilled warriors, every last one of them, equipped with the best polymath machines and strongest knowledge in the world. They can stop a body cold with the tiniest of poison threads—and their mastery of white mercury is on par with Cavanos. They can fight with all the combined knowledge of three thousand years of honed techniques from all around Arathess. You can forget about stealing. The only way we're getting any information from the Archive is if we have a kingsmedal. And those aren't given out to just anyone—"

"We're a prince!" I motion to Lucien. "And an archduchess!"

"Nobles." Her voice softens. "Of a kingdom that may no longer exist."

"I know somebody who works there!" I protest. "Yorl. He'll definitely help us."

"If he's been accepted at the Black Archive, he's theirs now. His loyalty is theirs. Besides, from what you've told me of him, I doubt he'd risk everything he worked for just to help us." She looks up from the fire, blue eyes sparking. "There's only one way to get a kingsmedal into the Black Archive."

"And?" I press. "What's that?"

Her fingers wander to the book and tighten. "The polymaths of the Black Archive deal in one currency: knowledge. You have to offer knowledge they don't already have."

It makes sense, in retrospect. That's why Yorl did all that he did: trap Evlorasin beneath Vetris, torture it, send me in to die repeatedly and talk to it, teach it to Weep. He knew the valkerax research of his grandfather was special, unique—and if he could prove it with results, with a real and true controlled experiment, it was a golden ticket—er—*kingsmedal*—into the Black Archives. He did everything Varia said, every last sordid thing, all for a single kingsmedal.

Fione's right. Even if Yorl and I did grow close, I can't ask him to give up all he's worked for—all of his grandfather's lifework—just for me.

The way Fione falls asleep on the pine needles with the book wrapped tight in her arms makes me think she wants to keep it. It's our only clue in the world to stopping the Bone Tree and saving Varia. And she's afraid. Afraid she'll have to give it over to the Black Archive in order to translate it. She could do that, but something tells me it's not just about the information inside. She's smart. She'd remember everything she'd translate, including how to destroy the Bone Tree. But to her, it's the physical book that's important, too. A symbol. A tangible object of hope in what feels like a hopeless situation.

I snake my hand up to my heart-shaped locket, to the one that lets me go a greater distance from my witch than just a mile and a half. For a while, in Vetris, the locket was that symbol for me. Something to hold on to—a taste of hope. A taste is all you need to keep moving forward sometimes. To do what needs to be done, no matter how afraid or exhausted you are.

Malachite gives a guttural snore and rolls over, flinging his uninjured arm around a root, and for the millionth time my anticipation for the moment when my guard shift ends and I can kick his arse awake builds even higher. Not that I need to sleep. But Malachite wouldn't hear of it—we were going to do shifts like normal people do. Like mortals do.

I grip the locket tighter against the warmth in my chest. Being treated like a mortal…is nice. Being given consideration, my condition and life treated as something important. Worth preserving, instead of throwing away. It's all very nice. Too nice, maybe. Maybe I'm getting spoiled. Soft.

Or maybe I'm growing. Growing up. Growing older, like I never thought I could.

The Blue Giant reaches zenith, and I gleefully lodge my booted toe in Malachite's spine. He jolts awake, muttering obscenities, and blearily staggers to take over the log I was sitting on. He stokes the half-dead coals, sparks eating air, and I make my way to Lucien's side. Still sleeping. I watch his chest rise and fall, his hair smeared with blood on the ends but his skin clean after I took the liberty of using the leftover hot water on him. He healed his own wounds—and Malachite's—all in the same moment he healed Fione. That's why he was sweating, exerting so much. And his magic healed my wounds, too, funneling into me like pure energy. I'm fine. Everyone is absolutely *fine*, thanks to him.

I watch his working hand twitch in his sleep as I lie beside him.

"But at what cost?" I breathe, my words brushing at his bangs. He's not a High Witch. The Glass Tree hasn't encased him, suspending him. What body part of his won't work tomorrow? His other eye? His nose, or his lips? Or maybe something more internal—his voice, his lungs, his stomach? How many parts can he risk, until he hits something critical and dies?

Until the both of us die, together; me as his Heartless, him as my witch?

to kill him now would be an easy thing. to end both your suffering, all your suffering. you could kill them all and spare them this impossible fight.

The hunger can't touch me. Not in Lucien's arms. I carefully brush his hair aside, fingers glancing on his cheek. I press a kiss to his forehead and snuggle beneath his chin. The night sky twinkles down on us, and I know somewhere up there is Windonhigh—Y'shennria, Nightsinger, Crav and Peligli. I can't see it. Hidden by magic, probably. All I can see are stars, and the blueness of the Giant, and my fear of falling asleep again...of dreaming. Of being connected forever to Varia—to the Bone Tree.

Malachite had a point. If I have the blood promise, the six eyes, if his eyes light up when I Weep and he smells me...am I a valkerax? Am I one of them?

Am I one of Varia's tools?

No matter how afraid I am, life still comes. Lucien is still here, with me, warm and real and handsome as ever. That feeling of safety comes, like nothing can touch me, and I drift into the darkness of oblivion.

This time, in this dream, I can feel Varia's excitement.

It's not just hers—it's her hunger's, too. That twin hunger of mine, not-same and not-different. We—*she*—is so proud. I can feel her pride blossoming in her chest like the world's biggest flower. She's done well.

Because through her eyes, I see Windonhigh.

In flames.

She's so happy—the voice is *quiet* for once. That terrible, aching hunger to destroy, to ruin—it hasn't spoken to her once since she set the last witch city on fire. She's done it. She's obeyed, and more than that, she's found out how to silence it. Zera—*I*— had Weeping. But she—*we*—have this.

Destruction.

As long as she destroys, it stops swallowing her mind whole. That's when the tides of the Bone Tree's power even out and she can surface above the waves of chaos. She can see the mousy-haired girl's face now and remember her name—Fione. Flashes of memory—of stolen kisses beneath cherry trees, of slow, never-silent touches beneath silk sheets. The smell of her is the lightest of perfumes, clover and lemongrass, and she tastes of beeswax and copper, especially when she comes in from her uncle's workshop.

Lovely Fione. Loyal Fione.

Loyal no longer.

Varia's heart pangs, but we keep our chin high. We will carve the world—a better world, a safer world—for her.

We must.

And so, we listen happily to the flames and the screams of the witches as our white wyrms circle the floating city.

Circling, in rainbow halos.

Flying.

My unheart—just mine—shudders. *Flying?!* How are they flying? Only Evlorasin knows how—how to Weep, how to fly. Peligli, Crav, Y'shennria—no, I just found them. I just left them, safe in their beds...

I'm thrown out of her body. Her eyes aren't mine anymore. I'm behind her, floating somewhere above her, and I watch in slow, dripping horror as she turns around and looks right at me. Up, and at *me*, with a smile.

"Blood, Zera," she says with a little laugh, motioning to the flying valkerax like I'm a dense child. "Remember? Blood is a conversation for them."

She can see me. Talk to me. A conversation. Evlorasin gave me its blood, and I know where the Bone Tree is at all times. Forever. I know where she is, *forever.* Evlorasin's wound on its hind leg, telling me other valkerax bit, that they followed. That's how they followed Evlorasin, that's why it struck me as strange that they could follow Ev at all—they learned. Through Ev's blood, they *learned* to fly.

And they've attacked Windonhigh. My friends. My *family.*

Varia's eyes search me, her gaze resting around me, and she breaks out in the most piercingly beautiful of smiles.

"Shall we find where you are?"

She reaches out to me, her fingers rich with animate midnight, and I panic. I step back without stepping back, trapped in the motionless torpor of the dream. My body won't respond—I don't even think I *have* a body. She's going to touch me, and it's going to end. Everything. If she touches me, *I know* she'll come to us, to Lucien and Malachite and Fione in the camp, and hurt them.

Capture them. Using my body. Using her magic. And I can't even move to stop it.

Just as the shrill panic in my head crescendos, she freezes, fingers inches from my unface. Something slithers on the floating grass island where she's standing, between her boots, and her own horror is clear as she looks down slowly. Something clear on the edges, cloudy in the middle, glinting like porcelain.

Glass.

Raw glass grows inch by inch around her boots, up, consuming it like a living thing, like a glass plant in fast motion. A thick wedge of it, boxy and smooth, encasing her leg up to the ankle. Trapping her, as I'm trapped in the dream. She tries to yank free, tries to point her blackened fingers at it to free herself with magic, but the glass stays, still and gleaming in the fire bursts from the distant battle in Windonhigh.

"What—" Her onyx eyes narrow. *"What is this?"*

I can't say a thing. My mouth won't move, or I would've told her. I would've told her the Bone Tree choker made of valkerax fangs—pressed around and into her throat like organic jewelry—is moving. *Growing.*

The fangs elongate, fanning down and outward like a birdcage around her. Bone, like vines. Living and bending and moving past her shoulders, and as the bone tendrils reach the bottom of her legs, the thick glass wedge around her foot starts to branch off. Little glass nubs like sprouts grow up to the bones, reaching for them. Both of them, like plants reaching for the sun.

Yearning for each other.

Varia's eyes suddenly widen, and her hands grow midnight up to her elbows in a split second. I don't see the magic, but I see the aftermath—a cut hanging in the air between the glass and bone tendrils, separating them, shattering them. Bone splinters and glass splinters rain down. The bone choker shrinks rapidly, back to its normal size, and the glass wedge melts away into the grass like water, freeing her.

The princess looks up at me, haggard, her hair in sweat-soaked spates on her face, the dark circles around her serious eyes magnified as she tries so hard to hide her fear with a sudden gleam of deadly determination, the dark pressure of all her incredible magic pointed at me like claws.

"You. You did this. You're trying to undo all of this, aren't you?"

14

THE CHOICE

I bolt awake, covered in cold sweat and rapidly trembling against someone's chest. That smell of honey that's now imprinted permanently on my brain. Lucien.

His dark eyes look down at me in his arms. "Are you all right?"

The dream-haze still lingers, and the black of his irises, the shape of his eyes, the thick lashes—the same as Varia. *Varia.*

I scrabble backward, panting hard. "You—"

His expression goes from soft to brittle in a second, but he keeps it from crumbling as he sits up, making his voice gentler.

"Zera, it's me."

I look him over—black hair, short. Proud nose. Broader shoulders than her. It's him. It's *him*, not her. The sharp fear scraping my throat recedes, and Lucien's frown is slight.

"Do you want to talk about it?"

I shake my head, sweat flying. "N-Not right now."

"Can I do anything for you?" he asks. "Right now?"

what can you do that I can't, little prince?

The instinct to deal with myself on my own rears up.

we know ourselves better than you.

I want him to do something. I don't know what, or for how long, but it hangs there on the tip of my tongue.

we do better alone.

I don't even have time to shake off the hunger before Lucien moves in a blur of sleeves and then I'm pressed against him, wrapped in his arms, his mouth near my ear.

"It's going to be all right."

The hardness in my body unwinds, in increments instead of abruptly, days instead of years. Feeling the heat of him against me, real and alive and human, pulls me back from the brink. He's just here.

He's just here, and that's all I need.

I don't know how much time passes. The sky is still dark outside the sanctuary of Lucien's arms. At some point, Malachite crunches over and makes some joke at me to switch shifts, but I hear Lucien's voice rumble in his chest—asking Mal to extend his watch a little longer. The beneather agrees, and I hear him shuffle off.

I can't cry.

I wish I could. This feeling is like the emotional equivalent of nausea—if I could just cry, just throw up, it would go away. I'd feel so much better. But nothing comes. No relief, just the endless purgatory of my own thoughts, my own feelings. I want to stop it, but I can't. It just keeps stretching on and on. I should be stronger than this. I used to be stronger, didn't I? But now I'm here, leaning on someone else. On Lucien. On the one person I don't want to see me weak.

I straighten, too embarrassed to look at him. "I'm sorry. For this."

"Nothing to be sorry for." The prince smiles down at me.

"No, I should—I shouldn't be putting this on you."

He pulls my hand up with his own, putting it to his heart. "You had to be strong for a long time on your own, didn't you?"

I can feel two heartbeats under my palm—mine and his. His, in his chest, and mine kept in the bag near his chest.

"You have me now," he presses. "And Malachite and Fione. But I like to think you have me most of all. Your problems are my problems. Your feelings are my feelings. We deal with them together—that's what it means. Or what I think it means, anyway. To be in love."

His face flushes red on the edges, and the sight bubbles up a laugh in me.

He cocks his head, still smiling. "What?"

"You," I say. "Just you."

He leans in, bit by bit, until he's almost touching my lips with his as he echoes me.

"Just *you*."

I don't know how long we stay up or when we fall asleep, but when I next wake, the sun's slatting through the branches from above, a particularly intense light lancing right into my face. I eke out of Lucien's arms, blinking away sun dust, and look up.

"Thank you, gods. Needed that one right in the eye."

"Oh, relax," Malachite drawls from a stump, whittling a piece of wood with his boot dagger. "You have five more of them."

I stand up and stretch, turning it into a formal bow. "Good morning to you too, grumpy."

"Interestin' approach to thanking the guy who just covered your last three shifts."

I meander to him and peer over his shoulder at the carving—a little dog. Lucien was right. I do have him. Him, and Fione, and Malachite. They're still here, after everything. Gratitude.

What is gratitude, but a promise made whole?

I sneak in a quick kiss to the side of the beneather's pale face. "Thank you dearly, dear."

He wipes his cheek with the back of his knife hand and grimaces. But when I turn away, I swear I see a flash of a contented smirk.

When Lucien and Fione wake up, I tell them. Gathered around the remains of last night's fire and a breakfast of freshly picked summer blackberries, I tell them everything I saw in my dream last night—the valkerax attacking Windonhigh, the valkerax *flying*, Varia's boot, and the glass and bone trying so desperately to meet.

"She knows where you are? All the time?" Fione presses.

"Maybe? I got the feeling she'd know if she touched me in the dream."

"Either way, we should think about leaving shortly," Lucien dryly muses. I catch him mid-eating, and he flashes one of his golden smiles at me, flooding warmth into my whole body. My return smile feels goofy almost. Blissful.

what have you done, to earn this?

Pity rabbit organs are so small, I retort back to the hunger. *Otherwise you'd be much quieter.*

"Why would the Glass Tree and the Bone Tree react to each other like that?" Malachite frowns. "They're two different things, right? Two different Old Vetrisian inventions."

"Not entirely," Fione corrects him, daintily consuming a berry with crimson-stained lips. "The Bone Tree is certainly an Old Vetrisian invention. But the Glass Tree is a witch thing. Barely any polymath contributions in it at all. Which means it's essentially pure magic."

"And that means?"

"It's more unpredictable than the Bone Tree, certainly," she says. "It has fewer rules. Or rather, the rules are not defined by any polymath terms, so I can't begin to guess at what they are."

"What about the Hymn of the Forest?" I ask. "*The tree of bone and the tree of glass—*"

"*—will sit together as family at last*," Lucien finishes for me.

I nod. "They were trying to come together—the glass and the bone. Does it have anything to do with the Hymn?"

"But they're two different things," Malachite insists.

"The Glass Tree was made from a shard of the Bone Tree, right?" Lucien muses. "So they're not entirely different."

"Perhaps," Fione muses. "It's possible they... No—"

"We have the High Witch's secret book. We head to the Black Archives and get you the reference material to translate it," Lucien interrupts her. "And with the valkerax able to fly now, we should move as quickly as possible."

"*Spirits,*" Malachite exhales. "Big teeth, big claws, big fire, and now big airborne. Perfect. Exactly what I wished for last Snowsum's Eve."

"Are you—" I look Lucien up and down. "Are you all right? From yesterday?"

His smile is small. "Of course."

"Everything's working?" Malachite looks him over suspiciously.

"Would you like to test me out?" Lucien makes a vague motion at the sword on his hip, and Malachite just rolls his eyes.

Packing up is easy when you don't have much—no utensils, no rain guards. All we have to do is bury the coals of the fire and the bones of the rabbit, and we're gone.

I've never seen the west coast of Cavanos, or if I have, I don't remember it. My parents—traveling merchants as they were— probably brought me here once or twice. The biggest maritime trade route into Cavanos runs west-east, after all. But the roads are near empty. We pass the occasional trading caravan, dusty mules and creaking wheels and terse smiles from under wide-brimmed hats, but they're few and far between. If the promise of war profit attracted them, the valkerax attacks surely scared them off.

Not to mention the ash raining down from the smoking island in the sky, visible today as it wasn't yesterday.

We start to see it when the trees clear up and as the road widens—Windonhigh. Windonhigh looming far, far above us and behind us, not much more than a speck tinted faintly green and brown and—horrifyingly—gray. Ash blown by the fires flits down, filling the potholes of the road with feathery gray softness, smearing on our skin. Lucien grips my hand tighter, and I can practically feel his unsurety of what to say. But there's nothing that *can* be said. All I can do, all I want, is to hold his hand.

Nightsinger has to be safe. Y'shennria has to be safe. Crav, Peligli. *Safe.* They have to be. That's the only thought that lets me move forward.

"No corpses fell down," Malachite offers during our water break. "That's a good sign, yeah?"

Fione jabs at his ribs with the handle of her cane, and he lets out a disgruntled yelp.

My laugh is small. "It's okay, Fione. I'm okay."

Her face softens. "The fact the island is still in the air is a good sign. They must've fought off the attack with those measures the High Witches spoke of."

"Glass Tree roots, I'm willing to bet," Malachite mumbles.

"And the hundreds of Heartless eclipseguard might've helped, too," Lucien adds.

The comfort of their words only lasts so long. We pass a trading caravan, and my unheart skips a beat when I realize it's completely *covered* in blood. The wagon leather, the wheels, the seat—all of it stained bright red. Fresh red.

"*Gods,*" Lucien swears under his breath. The caravaner tries to go past us without saying anything, but Lucien speaks up. "You there. What business have you looking thus?"

The caravaner glances at the prince the barest hint from under his hat. He sizes him up, and then whips his mule faster.

Malachite scoffs. "Should I get after him, Luc?"

Lucien's dark eyes are focused on the horizon, far down the road, like he can see something I can't. "No. Let him go."

Malachite doesn't question the decision, but I do.

"Why—"

"You'll see," Lucien asserts. "Soon."

It's a few minutes of twisting confusion until the grim reality comes into sight. *White.* White and red, long and broken open. Feathers, fur. A valkerax.

The corpse of one.

I dash toward it—Evlorasin? It can't be. It's splayed not far from the road, obliterated in the places where its body meets the ground. I hear Fione faintly say "it fell," but I'm too riveted by the sheer lake of blood surrounding it. The cacophony of a murder rings down, a cloud of black crows circling, picking at the edges of the body. *They* can eat the blood, maybe. But sentient mortals are another story, according to Yorl.

"Careful," I hear myself saying woodenly. "Don't ingest the blood. It'll kill you."

"Good to know." Malachite kicks a piece of unmentionable viscera down the road like a rock. "Except I already knew."

"Indeed," Lucien agrees. "You're the resident valkerax expert, Mal. What's the diagnosis?"

Malachite's ruby eyes flash over to Fione and offers her his hand elegantly. "Shall we, milady?"

"Don't try to do polite etiquette," the archduchess requests. "It's unsightly."

The two of them circle the corpse, mirroring the crows as they look for signs, openings. I do my own investigation at the front—inspecting its wolflike maw, its six glassy eyes. No empty scar on the sixth socket. I knew it wasn't Evlorasin in my gut, but the possibility was still there. But not-Evlorasin means one of Varia's.

"Its mane is almost completely singed off," Fione muses.

"They use those to fly," Malachite asserts. "I saw Six-Eyes's friend doing it like that."

"It has a name, you know," I press. "*Evlorasin.*"

"The day I use a valkerax's true name in casual conversation is the day I cut my own ears off," he grunts. "But thanks."

"So the mane was burned off?" Fione frowns.

"That's not fatal, though," Malachite interjects. "Looks like the fall killed it, not the witches. But what do I know? Magic can get inside where you can't see."

"There's no magic inside it," Lucien confirms. "Only the outside. Fione's right—on the mane. Witchfire, I think."

"So the witches burned this one's mane, and it fell," Malachite muses.

"That's the soundest hypothesis." Fione nods.

"That caravaner must've poached some of the parts," Lucien says.

"They sell pretty well," Malachite agrees. "But that shit's highly regulated by the ancestor council. Anything that doesn't come from beneather kills is tagged as a 'monetary threat' to Pala Amna. He'll be lucky if he can sell half of 'em before getting arrested."

"Do we just…leave it here?" I ask. I can't look away from the six glassy eyes staring into my soul.

Malachite looks around. "Didn't die belowground, where it belongs. So all the old traditions go out the window. No rune carvings needed."

"It feels wrong, though, to leave it without doing anything."

The barest of Malachite's glares flashes over at me. "It's a valkerax. Don't tell me you're on their side now?"

"There are no sides," I blurt. "It was a living thing, and now it's dead. I'm just trying to be respectful."

"Why?" He snorts. "S'not like *you* die."

"Mal," Lucien says, a sting to it. "Drop it."

"I can't, Luc." He throws his pale hand out at me. "I trust her as much as you do. But she sees Varia in her dreams, right? She's got valkerax blood in her now, *right*? What if Varia can—what if she can control Zera? Just like she controls the other valkerax?"

Lucien's laugh is chilly enough to shatter the air. "Don't be ridiculous."

Malachite doesn't budge from his stance, and all my organs settle in the bottom of me like iron ingots. Lucien gives up on him and looks over at Fione, her frown grim.

"Fione?" the prince asks, as if begging her to contradict his bodyguard.

She lets out a sigh. "I can't lie to you, Lucien. It's a possibility."

Lucien's dark eyes snap to me, and I try a smile. The memory of the dream, that ominous fear I had of Varia's touch—

"They're right, Lucien. It's...it *might* be a thing. And if it is, then I'm a threat to you—"

"You're not," he argues instantly. "You never will be."

"I've always been," I say softly.

"I know—" He clenches his working fist, reflection warbling in the valkerax blood puddle he stands in. "I know you'd never hurt me. Magic or not, you're strong. Stronger than anything or anyone I know. You'd never succumb to something like that. Gods—you made Weeping real. You did it all on your own. If that isn't—if that isn't proof..."

I walk hesitantly up to his side, taking his limp hand in mine. His whole body's shaking enough to vibrate his inactive fingers, to make the bones and tendons move when they clearly can't anymore. The old pain comes welling up like ink, like mud. I'm a threat.

we are his death in the night.

The possibility is there, even if my mind is unwilling to consider it. Even if my mind isn't willing to turn on my friends, the hunger is. I've felt firsthand how strong the Bone Tree is. I've seen it—dug deep in the marrow of Evlorasin's very being. I won't have a choice.

I'm not a valkerax. But I have six eyes when I Weep. I can see

Varia in my dreams. I can see through her eyes, like we're one. Because she has the Bone Tree in her. And the only creatures in Arathess tied to that tree are the valkerax. I don't know what I am, anymore. But I know—sadly—that it's not human. It's maybe not even pure Heartless. Fione's words at the fire the other night ring in my empty chest.

Whatever I am, however I'm shaped, whatever parts of me are here or not here, I'm still me.

"Whatever I am, Lucien," I start softly. "Whatever strength I have, I'm going to use it to stop Varia."

His onyx eyes flash—not quite betrayed, but something deeper than that. His hand darts to his breast pocket, pulling out the sack stitched with the word Heart. My real heart.

"Hold still," he says, terse. "I'm going to put it back."

"Luc—" Malachite starts.

"Lucien, *no*." I stagger back. "That's not how—that's not what I want."

"I'm not going to let my sister use you anymore," the prince barks. "I won't let anyone use you. Not her, not the Bone Tree. You're not a tool, you don't have to live like one—"

"Stop."

My voice goes hard, and Lucien's fades. The quiet is overwhelming, my words spilling out in neat, too-perfect rows. Rows that have had time to organize themselves. Nothing but time.

"These things you're saying." I look him dead in the eyes. "I know them now. All of them. But it wasn't easy. I had to meet you to really get it. And you—" I look to Fione, Malachite. "And you. The road I had to walk to get here, to who I am now—it was long. But it's not over. Not in the godsdamn slightest."

Lucien straightens, his gaze sparking. I reach out and rest my palm against the bag, against his hand, against my heart, feeling the organ contract softly. All my memories of my human life. All my burning desires to be whole again.

I push the bag away.

"No matter what, from now on, every choice I make is mine. I choose to fight Varia. I choose to continue. I choose whether or not I'm Heartless."

I put my hand on my unheart and look up at him. At all of them.

"I *choose*."

15
THE OCEAN

My words make Fione smile and Malachite shake his head and exhale wearily. They make Lucien watch me intently until, finally, he nods.

"I understand."

Just those two words. Simple, but far from easy, and said with steel pride. In me, in my convictions. He believes in me, and I hear it in every inch of his voice.

Malachite's the first to start walking, and we trail behind him. We leave the valkerax corpse behind and come across more. Dozens of them. I glance up every so often, the floating landmass waning away behind and above our heads, and then one more glance, and it's gone. No sign of the smoke, or the blackened edges, or the roots hanging from the bottom. All of it. Gone. I close my eyes and mutter one last prayer to Y'shennria.

"They've reinstated the cloaking magic," Lucien says, glancing behind him.

"So fast," Fione marvels.

"It's impressive," he agrees. "Considering how big the island is. But having met them, I know it's more or less child's play to the High Witches. All seven of them, incredibly strong and working together. There isn't much they *can't* do."

"Except get out of those glass prisons, apparently," Malachite grumbles.

The road opens up over the course of the day, gradually melting from grassland to coastline. The smell of salt wafts stronger, the grasses fading yellower and rooted in much drier, sandier soil. The birds turn from crows and sunbirds to gulls and seafalcons nesting in the rocky cliffs that've started to poke through the horizon. Fione consults a map briefly at a crossroads, pointing us to the southwest, to where the port town Dolyer—and hopefully our passage to the island of the Black Archives—awaits.

"Do we even *have* money?" Malachite asks during a water break.

"We can pawn something if we must," Fione insists, then looks to Lucien. "I could've sworn the Breych sage gave you a pouch of coin."

"Graciously," the prince agrees. "The majority of it went to the villagers we rescued, but we have enough for a charitable boat."

"A shitter, you mean," Malachite sighs.

"A local charmer," Lucien corrects.

Camp that night is quiet, all of us exhausted after three days walking on the road. It's a bone-deep exhaustion, plagued with cold and wet all because Malachite saw a few very large and very fresh valkerax tracks in the silty mud and deemed a fire unsafe. Lucien offers to warm us with magic internally, but Fione and I won't have it, insisting he keep up his energy.

"'*Warming internally?*'" Malachite scoffs. "Please, heart-breaker. Save the innuendo for your girl."

Lucien and I go rigid in our seats, neither of us looking at each other.

"Malachite-whatever-your-family-name-is!" I half shriek, half hiss. "Shut. Up!"

"Save it for the giant squids, rather," Fione chimes in and saves the day. "It's spawning season, and they oft mistake the underside of boats for other squid."

And that settles that, raunchy rib forgotten as we all chew our jerky in disgusted-expression tandem and imagine a squid trying to mate with the underside of a boat.

Thanks and no thanks to Malachite's comment, Lucien's and my shared covering-slash-bedroll tonight is more awkward than usual. Every part of him burns like a brand, too close, too radiating. At some point in the night he sits up, both of us still wide awake.

"I can sleep somewhere else."

"Don't—" I reach for his shirt and tug him back down. "Don't be silly."

"I can't help it around you." I can't see his smirk in the dark, but I hear it. It's strange. Neither of us smells very good—mud and acidic valkerax blood and the layered sweat of travel—but my body doesn't care about any of that. It wants to touch him, forever, always, no matter what. Now most of all.

"You know now," I say.

"Know what?" he murmurs against the shell of my ear.

"My choice. What I'll choose, always."

"To help me?" he asks.

"To be with you," I say. "In death or undeath."

His arms finally dare to snake around my waist, pulling me close to his chest.

"So dramatic. What do you think about talking less about death, hmm? How about you be with me in *life*?"

My laugh is small, but the bloom in my chest is sweet. "I can give it a shot."

It isn't easy to peel myself out of Lucien's arms in the morning. And, looking back at his peacefully sleeping face that cracks one eye open to find me and smile, I hope it never is.

Dolyer comes into view around lunchtime, and all four of us couldn't be happier to see smokestacks, buildings, wells full with water, and an inn bustling with an open hearth. The idea of a bath might be the most distracting, but the docks are what's most impressive about the town—sprawling and webbed over the water in pale gray salt-soaked and barnacle-encrusted wood. Everything in the village is made with gray—gray skies meeting furious gray sea, gray sands meeting gray grasses, gray buildings, and grayer horses.

But the gray only makes the splashes of color stand out more—the red of the fish gutting, the blue of the westbound ship sails and the maroon of the southbound sails, the jade green of Cavanos lawguard uniforms dotting the browns and golds of the sailors and merchants and stray dogs. The town moves and breathes in boxes—boxes being made by old men with chisels, boxes being loaded by women with arms as big as my thighs, boxes being moved by even bigger men, boxes clogging the docks of nearby ships only to vanish inside with much sweat and labor.

It's a bit of relieving normality after lurking in so much destruction—that village on fire, Vetris turned to rubble, Windonhigh attacked.

"We don't have time for the inn." Lucien sees Fione's longing look at the inn's sign.

"Where else are we going to secure a boat?" Fione argues. "In the time it takes you to find a captain willing to take us for that paltry sum, I could take three baths."

"If we don't dry our shoes, the fungus is gonna start soon," Malachite helpfully adds. Lucien looks to me to be the last bastion of reason, but I bat my lashes playfully at him.

"Just a half? *Please?*"

"Do you know where she is now?" he asks. She. Varia.

"No. But I could know. If, say, I lie down for a nap."

The prince heaves a sigh. "Fine. The inn it is. But the moment we find a captain, we're out the door."

Malachite gives a little fist pump, and Fione and I make

instantly through the gray grass to the swinging salt-spray sign of the inn. We're greeted by the stench of old beer and fried bread—a perfectly familiar smell. As we're wiping off our boots on the mat, it comes to me.

"I thought you of all people wouldn't want to slow down," I say to her. "Rescuing Varia is, theoretically, more important than a bath."

Fione's blue eyes catch on her glove as she takes it off finger by finger. Her other hand clutches the waterproof sack where she keeps the book we stole from Windonhigh.

"Your little speech made it clear to me," she says over the inn's din.

"Uh...it did?"

"My choice," Fione murmurs. "Everything I've done until now, and everything I do going forward, is my choice. But from what you've told me, and what the High Witches added, Varia doesn't have much of a choice anymore. The Bone Tree infects her. Consumes her."

With a dim sadness, I follow her to the only free table. A gaggle of sailors starts a sea shanty, and Fione leans in so I can hear her better.

"We're her only hope. And if there's any scrap of the Varia I love left in her, she knows that, too. We'll be together, always. She promised me that. And I choose to believe her."

There's a flash of iron behind her eyes—that determined iron that laced her every breath in Breych right after it all happened. But it doesn't stay this time. This time, it lightens, evaporates, as she smiles small.

"Besides. Thinking strategically becomes rather difficult when one has to stop every ten minutes to sample their own reek."

"Oh so true," I agree sagely, motioning to the tavernkeep for service.

Fione takes her bath first, upstairs in a small room, and I

decide to guard the door, what with all the drunken sailors about. I sit against it, the smell of steam and wild lavender eking out from the crack under the door, and I watch the sun spin silver in the sea clouds through the window.

Varia doesn't have a choice.

She's like me now. She's maybe experiencing firsthand what she did to me as her Heartless. But I can't be happy about any of it. There are witches all over Arathess, and plenty of them use Heartless. Plenty of them treat their Heartless well, but plenty others treat them badly. I know that now. I know, deep in the flesh of me, that it's wrong. The hunger's made that so crystal clear.

Something is wrong, this world with its Heartless in it. The wrong I feel now, and the wrong I felt in my dream of the two trees, the two pendants, the Glass Tree lonely, that feeling like if I didn't bring them together something horrible would happen... it's the same. The same wrongness.

Maybe all I'm feeling is nebulous instinct. Maybe it's remnants of the Bone Tree. Maybe it's the hunger, or maybe it's magic. All I know is it's real, this feeling.

I want to destroy the Glass Tree, too.

I can see only upsides to destroying the Glass Tree. It would release the Heartless, for one. Maybe there'll be some ripple, a tornado or tidal wave of magic like the Wave that gave the celeon sentience all those years ago. But that's a small price to pay to ensure no Heartless is ever created again. I'm sure of it.

But the Bone Tree is another matter.

Fione taps me on the shoulder, fresh and dewy, and motions to the steaming bathwater. "Your turn."

I shake my head. "I told Luc I'd take a nap."

"You can!" She pushes the small of my back into the room. "In the tub."

The room's tiny, all wood, and I sink into the tub built into the floor. No porcelain or gold like the tubs in the palace, but I've never been more grateful for one. The water's soap-murky but more than usable, and I peel off my sweat-soaked leathers and slide into the water and my own thoughts.

If we have to destroy the Bone Tree, that would mean the valkerax go free. And in my unheart I know that's the right thing to do. I've seen Evlorasin's suffering too closeup to think anything different. The valkerax, like the Heartless, have suffered for long enough as magical thralls. We live and breathe the same. Magic shouldn't be used to make thralls, no matter how much safety it gives the witches. No matter how much safety it gives a country. And that sounds mad even as I think it. I'm talking about destroying the one thing that keeps the valkerax from rampaging across Cavanos—maybe across the whole world. But Evlorasin showed me that we can talk to them; because Heartless are unique in their deathlessness, Ev and I can talk. And that's never been done before. Heartless and valkerax have never overlapped before Ev and me. Maybe we're the first of our kind. And maybe we can change the world. Talk to each other. Ambassadors, both ways.

All I know is things need to change. No more fear. Well, always fear. It's naive to say fear will never be there. But moving ahead, and in new directions, despite the fear. That's what I want. That's what I've tried to do, every single day since I left Nightsinger's woods in Y'shennria's carriage.

Alyserat, indeed.

Fione's words come softly through the door. "I'm scared, Zera."

For all her bravado, for all her determination—she's still scared. We all are.

"I know," I say. "Me too."

It's a moment, and then two. The sunshine warms the wood, my face, the water, and I embrace the light. Whatever light I can find.

Footsteps suddenly pound on the floor outside, and I hear

Fione stand up quickly on her cane. Someone slaps their hand on the side of the room's little wall.

"Get out of the puddle," Mal's voice rings. "We've found a boat for the bigger one."

The *Lady Terrible* is a far cry from the airship we took from Breych—the most obvious being that in the sky, there are no barnacles. The underside of the ship is completely encrusted with the things, the rhythmic gaping of their beaked mouths as the seawater waves lap up on them nigh nauseating.

"I knew the ocean was big," I say. "But I had no clue it was also godsdamn *weird*."

"Extremely weird," Fione agrees next to me. "The greatest variety of wildlife live in the sea, and by all polymath estimates, we've catalogued only thirty percent of them."

"My favorite are the blood-sucking eelworms," Malachite offers as he pulls astride us on the gangplank.

Fione nods wisely. "Their jaws are so strong, they can bite down to your bone and suck out your marrow."

"Okay, *please*!" I throw my hands up. "Is an entire valkerax horde after us not enough for you people?"

"There are jellyfish," Lucien says in my ear as he joins us on the ship's railing, "with tendrils so poisonous, they rot your skin off wherever they touch."

"Hello to you, too, my piquant ray of sunshine," I drawl. Lucien's laugh feels *good* to hear, soothing some worried ache I've had in me since seeing the valkerax corpse. He pulls away from me, and I instantly miss the heat over my shoulder.

"I'll tell the captain we're onboard," he says. "Try not to cause trouble."

Malachite looks to me immediately. "Duel to the death?"

"Absolutely."

Lucien's snort as he walks away is barely audible over the chanting of the sailors as they raise the anchor and adjust the sail. Unlike Helkyrisian airships, which float via aergasel balloons and propel with precise jets, Cavanos ships are very much just ships—blown by the wind, rowed when necessary. They haven't strayed from their original form in a long time. The invention of white mercury lamps is the only modern touch, and objectively much safer than open oil lamps on a fully wooden boat. The sailors we pass are curt to us, and not much more—they have work to do.

"Cargo ship, by the looks of it." Malachite jerks his head toward the barrels crowded belowdeck. "Bringing supplies up to the Feralstorm."

"The Black Archives are on the way." Fione nods. "And the sea gets more treacherous the farther northwest we go."

"Giant squids not included," I add. We put our things by the hammocks we'll be using to sleep, but Malachite keeps his broadsword and Fione keeps her waterproof book pouch. I keep Father's unassembled sword in its hemp bag, tracing it lightly.

"If we have to fight, it'll either be pirates or valkerax," I say.

"Ugh," Malachite groans. "I'd take a hundred valkerax over a ship of pirates."

"They smell equally bad," Fione agrees.

"How would you know?" Malachite raises one white brow. "You've never been out of Vetris in your life."

"That doesn't mean I haven't met *pirates*," Fione argues. "I paid scores of them for information on Varia when she went missing. I've sampled all their revolting scents."

We meander back up deck to find Lucien waiting for us at the railing.

"How long will the voyage be?" I look at the prince. "Malachite and I want to know exactly how many death-duels we can squeeze in between then and now."

"Four days, allowing for fair weather," Lucien says, and then judiciously pauses. "Please don't break anything."

"Nothing but each other's hearts." Malachite makes a swear-on-his-heart motion, then points to me. "Or lack thereof."

"What do we do if there's an emergency situation?" Fione asks. "You can't teleport us far again, like on the airship."

"Unless we need to take a bath," I chime.

"Or brine ourselves to make us tastier for the valkerax," Lucien agrees with a smirk, then fixes Fione with a serious gaze. "We stay on the ship. Defend it with everything we have."

"No magically desperate teleporting," I warn. "Promise?"

He sighs and rolls his eyes. "I promise."

The anchor finally begins lifting, Malachite jumping in on the ring of men to help winch it up. The ship backs out of the harbor, the gentle bobbing of the water becoming harsh lashing the farther out we go. Soon, the town of Dolyer fades behind us, nothing more than a gray collection of shapes on a foggy horizon.

The Western Sea is brutal.

Maybe I knew that, once upon a time. But it's new information to me now. And to my stomach.

"I wasn't aware Heartless *could* get seasick." Fione rubs circles on my back comfortingly as I heave nothing into the water.

"New God's toe skin—" I stop, lurch, and try to breathe deep. "Why am I—I didn't get airsick!"

"Air and water are two different fluids with entirely different currents," Fione assures me. Unlike her stint on the airship, she looks completely composed and non-nauseated. "No wonder witches don't live near the sea. Cavanos witches, anyway."

"What's the difference?" I choke, desperate to think about anything other than the roiling in my guts.

"You know." She shrugs lightly. "Cavanos witches rely more on Heartless than others."

"Do you think—do you think there are Heartless outside the Mist Continent?"

"Perhaps." She nods, gathering my hair gently back as I retch again. "I know in Qessen a witch having a Heartless is seen as crude and barbaric. Or so Varia told me. In Helkyris, Heartless are almost exclusively used for all kinds of polymath experimentation. Paid of course, though that hardly makes it better. Cavanos is the only place where Heartlessness is prized as a tool of war." She thinks, and then says, "Out of necessity."

I steel my throat. "I'm starting to think none of it is a necessity."

There's a long unsilence as the sea rasps and I rasp, and in a quiet lull Fione finally says, "You mean the trees. Destroying them."

I only manage to nod, but it's enough for her. She lets out a sigh.

"I've thought of that, too. But the consequences—they're too wildly unpredictable. Presumably the valkerax would be free—"

"I could talk to them," I blurt. "Through Evlorasin."

"True," she agrees. "But coming to peaceful diplomacy with them could take years. And in that time, they'd run free. With the added ability to *fly*, now—which means to more than just the Mist Continent. That's why the High Witches were so upset with you. Not because you gave the Bone Tree to Varia but because you taught one to fly. And one valkerax means more very quickly, apparently."

We shudder collectively as the sea wind blows, slicing over our grim faces. The idea of these skies being cut across by valkerax, forging new paths into unknown territories—all the stories of Old Vetris, all the myths and legends. Would it start all over? Would it be war, *forever*? The exact opposite of what any of us wants—the exact opposite of what *Varia* wants, too. Wanted, at least, before the Bone Tree overwhelmed her. I straighten, the bout of sickness passing at last.

"Destroying the Glass Tree won't make the New God's religion go away," Fione insists. "It will just take away the Heartless. And without Heartless, the witches of Cavanos would be exposed to Kavar's believers."

"I know that."

"You're willing to put them at risk? And to put the whole world at risk of the valkerax? All at the same time?"

"I—" I clench my fist. "I dunno. All I know, in my deepest heart in that bag, is that something has to change. It can't keep going on like this—magic can't be used to keep living things hostage anymore."

Fione's silent, and Malachite take that as his cue to butt in, long ear tips bobbing.

"You two look minister-serious. What's the occasion?"

"The fate of the world," I chirp.

"Ah." He nods. "Real important stuff. Well, whatever it is, you either do it or you don't, right? Right. Now come fight me."

Next to me, Fione bristles. "It's not that simple—"

Malachite instantly lopes away, drawing his sword off his back. I wipe my mouth on the hem of my tunic and straighten with a smile at Fione.

"He's right, though," I say. "We can talk about it all we want. We can debate it. We can weigh the tentative pros and unknown cons. But at the end of all things, we either do it or we don't."

Her fingers find the waterproof pouch at her hip, her nails gripping a corner of the hard book cover within. The book that holds an answer. Or at least I hope it does. For all our sakes.

"If destroying the Trees will save Varia, then I'm with you," she finally says.

"And if it doesn't?"

Her periwinkle eyes search mine. "Then I'm against you."

It's a serious moment. I shouldn't laugh. But I do. I do,

because I know if the roles were reversed, if it were Lucien and me, I'd say the same thing. Over and over again. Always. Because I know now, like she does. I know what love means.

I know what loss means.

I know what a heart means.

She and I have to follow our hearts, no matter where that takes us. So many untranslatable concepts. So many important things that would take years—whole libraries of books—to say. To even explain. That's why, when I stand up and grab a sailor's sword lying on the deck and walk toward a waiting Malachite, all I say back to her is:

"Good."

16

THE BENE'THAR AND THE STARVING WOLF

The clamor of swords echoes on the empty ocean. Empty of everything but the horizon, our ship, our breathing, our crowd of sailors who've suddenly gathered to watch the friendly duel. I blink sweat out of my eyes, the hazy cloud covering the sun doing nothing to mitigate the summer heat. It swelters all around us. The pleasant sea wind died somewhere between our first blade-swing and now. There are no shadows on the ocean to hide under, no shade, no trees. And frankly, I'm thanking the gods. Sick of the things.

Malachite has me backed into a corner, the low roar of the sailors watching a welcome sound, considering Mal's not once said anything to me. He just launched into all-out fighting the second we bowed to each other. His ruby eyes flicker dark lashes, surreptitiously watching my feet for hints on my next move.

"I know they're pretty, but you don't have to stare that hard," I tease. "They aren't going anywhere. Except perhaps up your arse."

"You talk too much," he finally says, hand tightening on his hilt.

"Aw, baby's first words," I coo, and lunge in. He isn't expecting a roundabout, but they never do. He catches it on the back of his blade, miraculously, and we hover there, straining against each other. *Kavar's tit*, he's strong. His biceps aren't particularly big—rather willowy, actually—but he pushes back with the force of a celeon.

"Alas." I grit out a smile. "It seems you're made of diamond."

"And you're made of bad jokes."

"True, and fair," I agree. He ducks, the shift in his weight throwing me off, his blade edge screeching on mine as it goes *somewhere*, so I frantically push away, make space. We established no duel rules before this—we just bowed. No Avellish rules, no Cavanosian rules, no rules at all. He's not avoiding cutting me, either, throwing his whole force into his every swing. The victory conditions are unclear. And that's the way he wants it, really. He doesn't want a duel. A duel is just a game, a diversion, a way to pass time. Despite all the jokes he made around us dueling, he isn't treating this as a game in the slightest. He's trying to show me something. But what?

A flash of his paper-white arm, and then the brown tentacles of a net. He grabbed one from the boat and threw it at me! In a duel! It's so close I can't dodge it. I swipe, praying the sword I borrowed from a sailor is sharp enough. And it is, barely. The net splits apart, ripped fibers catching on my shoulder.

The crowd shows their appreciation by wolf whistling, blasting my eardrums with excited shouts and bellows. Malachite just waits casually for my next move, flipping his broadsword with one hand and a practiced ease. That's more like the Malachite I know—a little fun. I brush bits of net off my shoulder, a laugh bubbling up.

"You'll have to excuse me—my dueling partners are usually princes, you see, and they're *very* formal. No prop throwing or anything of the like."

Malachite rolls his neck, cracking it. "Shut up, Six-Eyes, and just fuck me up. Best you can, anyway."

"*Ohhh*," I sigh, thrusting square at his face. "You know I don't do well with taunts."

He dodges, eyes wider than the heavy-lidded usual—a head shot is very risky. And very illegal. But this duel has no rules. That move was me telling him I get it—no rules. All effort. I agree to that, to it, to whatever this duel might do to either of us. So he sets his face into a lazy smile, ready.

He lunges in this time. The salt spray of a cold wave over the ship's edge drenches us, and I can barely see the flash of metal as he disguises his thrust in the water. It's hard to follow, harder to dodge, but I drop my center and pray. Something nicks on my shoulder, a split-second feeling of fabric getting caught and then freed, and my arm gapes, exposed to the air, my tunic severed on that side.

I back up on my heels as far as I can, almost slipping. The sailor crowd undulates around me, and then pushes me back into the circle. I look down—no blood. It's a miracle the stitching on my tunic stayed intact enough to cover my chest. I look up again at the beneather, his elegant face serious. He meant to nick me.

Ah—that's what he wants.

Blood.

I get it now. That's why he's going all in, every time—because the first one to draw blood is the winner. The opposite of Cavanos rules. The antithesis of Avel, and even the Endless Bog. These are his rules. The bodyguard of the prince of Cavanos's rules. No. *Malachite's* rules.

Just Malachite.

"Fine," I mutter, tearing the flapping, useless sleeve off. "I'll play."

The sailors try to grab the cloth, hooting as I flip my sword and walk in. In to Malachite. Up to him. If he wants to face me head-on, then that's what I'll give him. No Weeping. No tricks. Just me. Just Zera.

He doesn't know what to do. I see it in his eyes—no one walks right at their opponent. Lunging, stabbing, angling. All those things. But not walking. I want to show him, though. What it means to ask for me. What it means to face who I am.

I grab for him, his shoulder, his wrist, whatever I can get, but he flicks his blade at me, trying to make space between us. It's a light effort from him. But a light effort from him still hits hard. I know that, but I won't block it with my sword. That's not what he wants.

That's not what I am.

I put my palm up at the last second, the blade tip catching in the meat of my hand. Bones crunching easily, the fragile ones, and a searing pain cutting canyons up my spine. But there's still enough flesh there to stop the momentum. Malachite's eyes widen, the widest I've ever seen them, and he quickly pulls the blade out. The cheering of the sailors dulls, and I let it carry my feet forward, into the beneather. Into Lucien's bodyguard, his friend. My friend.

My hand hangs, half split, the salt wind stinging at it, the blood drawing a splattered line on the deck as I near. The closer I get, the harder Malachite's face sets, and the lower his eyelids get again. He crystallizes, ruby irises glittering in the sun. Maybe he understands. *He has to.* That's why, I think, when I near him and reach out to take his broadsword forcefully from his hand, he lets me with a gentle ease.

I hold both swords and look up at him. Just at him, and he stares back. He's so tall, so different from anyone I've ever met. And to him, so am I. I can see that, see the difference reflected in his dark pupils—see *me* reflected there. His strength is being strong. Stronger than a human, faster than a human. He can hear better, smell better. Fireproof. Those are his strengths. And mine?

Well, he says mine for me.

"You're real good"—he croaks, finally, a smile on his lips—"at getting hurt, aren't you?"

I smile back up at him. "Kind of."

This is who I am.

This is how *I'm* strong.

"Oy!" The captain's shout echoes, fracturing the ring of sailors around us. They scatter, and she marches up to the two of us, finger in my face and a cigar in her mouth. "What did I say? No fightin'!" She glances down—looking past my cleaved hand uncaringly. "And you bled all over my deck!"

"I'll swab it right away, Cap'n!" I blurt, making my posture straight and respectful, my half-healing hand already saluting at my forehead.

"We'll swab it, Cap'n!" Malachite echoes me, saluting too. "Together!"

Her dark eyes cut over to me, to him, and then she scoffs around her cigar.

"Damn right you will. And when you're done, you'll be showing me that little backhand move of yours again."

Swabbing the entire deck as punishment leaves me sweatier than I'd like—which is any. I stayed in Nightsinger's forest because I had no physical choice, yes, but also because it was cold and wonderfully dry in terms of body moisture. Sweat is the enemy. But sweets? Sweets are the ally. Gods, I hope a polymath quotes me on that one day.

When the last bucket of mop water is exhausted and the last inch of ancient wood scrubbed clean, we collapse on a pile of salt-stained ropes, panting. Malachite offers me his waterskin, and I pour a bit on my face and rub it around.

"Think she noticed you healed up right away?" he asks, jerking his head to the captain at the helm. It's a pointless question. Of course she did. The whole crew did.

"Impossible," I drawl. "Otherwise I'd be getting burned alive right now."

"Bet she's used to seeing all types, Heartless notwithstanding."

"Well, that. And the rumors of a horde of valkerax coming

back are probably far scarier than a lone Heartless and her witch."

He nods, taking a swig as I pass him his waterskin back. There's a long quiet, the lapping ocean and the screeching gulls conversing with one another.

"So," he says finally. "You gonna shake some horseshit up, huh? In the world."

I shrug. "Depends."

"Depends nothing. From the moment I heard you talk at the Spring Welcoming, I knew you were gonna do that. So. Go and do it already."

"What about you?" I ask. "Are you gonna be okay with it?"

"Yeah. So long as you don't hurt Luc, I'll be fine."

The prince is nowhere to be seen—he and Fione long gone belowdeck to try to parse the book. They didn't even come up curiously at the racket the duel made, which means they're direly serious. But I look at the shadows of the stairwell anyway.

"You like him a lot, huh?" I ask.

It's Malachite's turn to shrug. "Like, dislike, doesn't matter. He's home. My home. And you won't hurt him. Or I'll get you."

It's not a threat. Not anymore. There's an unspoken understanding—I could be valkerax. I could be susceptible to the Bone Tree. But even if I am, and I'm controlled by Varia to do something, Malachite will be here to stop me, like he stopped me on the peak of the Tollmount-Kilstead mountains that awful day. Him saying he'll stop me isn't a threat anymore; it's an assurance. A promise between friends. A promise to carry my burdens equally. And I breathe easier because of it.

No matter what, no matter what I am, Malachite has my back.

The ideas are too heavy to say, too heavy for the sun-soaked sky, wet with amber and lavender dusk. Malachite's profile against it is like marble-washed peach, delicate and refined. And then, suddenly, "If you have kids, I get to name the first one," he says.

"Shut up," I drone.

He tries to look deep and thoughtful. "I'm thinking... *Vachiayis*."

"Shut *up!*"

"Big Stinky Vachiayis the Third."

"Hold on." I stand up. "Let me go get permission to kill you."

His laughter follows me as I walk down the stairwell, my smirk affixed as I peer into rooms, storage nooks, behind pillars and boxes looking for Fione and Lucien. I find them bent over a rough-hewn table in the mess, both of them intently absorbed in the green-backed book. So intently that they completely ignore me as I bounce up.

"Lucien, quick question: Can I kill Mal? He's being annoying."

No response. Fione stutters her eyes up from the book's pages, to me, and back down to a stock-still Lucien. A Lucien whose proud hawk profile is frozen, not a blink or twitch in sight. All stone.

I slide into the table beside him. "What's wrong?" When he doesn't answer, I glance down at the page he's looking at. All Old Vetrisian symbols I can't read, clumped close and dizzying. I look up at Fione. "What's going on?"

She opens her mouth, closes it. Thinks. The unease in the pit of my stomach yawns bigger. And bigger. Until—

"We've translated some of it," she says, slowly. One important word at a time.

"And?" I lean in. "What did you find?"

The swallow of her pale throat is her only movement. "The Bone Tree...and the Glass Tree."

"What about them?" I press frantically. "Fione, c'mon—"

"They're the same thing."

Beside me, Lucien's eyelashes twitch in a half blink, like a deer frozen in the woods—watching, fearful, and yet still plagued by flies. I suck in a breath made of daggers, razors, cut obsidian.

"What are you talking about?" I nervously laugh. "The Old

Vetrisians made the Bone Tree, and the witches made the Glass Tree—"

"It used to be one tree," Fione interrupts me smoothly. Too smoothly. "They didn't make it, Zera. They *split* it. They split it and used the halves to create their new Trees."

My unheart falls into my stomach. "But—how—"

"The source of all magic," Lucien's hoarse voice finally breaks, his eyes locked ahead on a steady white mercury light on the wall, white reflecting in his black. "The tree I saw in my dream. The one that gave me magic. The one that gives every witch on Arathess their magic."

He looks up at me—calm above, and terrified below.

"They split the Tree of Souls."

17

THE TREE
OF SOULS

At this point, I'm willing to believe anything. Even things I've never heard of before.

I've seen the Bone Tree's power firsthand. I've seen how it melded with Varia, embedded itself into her very skin. I've seen myself heal from dire things—beheadings, fires, guttings. I've seen Windonhigh, like an impossible myth sprung from an old bard legend—a literal island in the sky. I've seen massive, heavy valkerax fly—I've seen them overcome the Bone Tree's brute power by Weeping.

I've Wept. I've done what I thought three years ago would never be possible.

All that to say at this point, I'd be a fool to dismiss even the wildest idea.

At the sick look on Lucien's face, I called Malachite belowdeck and gathered four mugs of cold barley ale from the tap room, spreading them among our somber table. The ship creaks in our silence.

Malachite's the first to admit confusion. "So what if they were the same tree? What does that even mean?"

Fione traces the book's page thoughtfully. "I'll need more time to truly turn it over. And the Black Archives' resources will help clarify things. But for now, the best I can do is guess. I've heard of the term 'Tree of Souls' from only one place." She looks up at me, mousy curls bobbing. "The Old God's supporters, their rosaries—they call that the Tree of Souls."

My mind flashes back to Y'shennria, to her wood-carved, naked tree rosary she kept with her at all times, stroking it in times of distress or difficulty. She's an Old God worshipper—that's why she's been admitted into the relative safety of Windonhigh at all. She adored that rosary—leaned on it like a true friend and confidant.

"What does it actually *mean*, though?" Mal presses.

"It means," Lucien says, "if we were to interfere with the Bone Tree, we could be interfering with the flow of all magic. Forever."

I go still. "Do—did the High Witches know about this?"

"Presumably," he says. "Which is no doubt the major reason they decided not to help us interfere with the Bone Tree. If we did, we'd be interfering with half of the Tree of Souls."

"And if we were to destroy both trees," Fione says, looking over at me pointedly, "theoretically, we would be wiping all magic from Arathess. Forever."

"Wait," I start. "So Gavik was wrong? The Glass Tree wasn't made from a piece of the Bone Tree?"

"Correct." Fione nods. "He was so scared by the Bone Tree, by Varia getting it, that he had his polymaths investigate as much as they could. And they came up with that hypothesis—that the Glass Tree was made from a splinter of the Bone Tree."

"But it's not." I frown.

I see Fione's hand shake, before she hides it quickly in her sleeve. "If this older text is to be believed, no."

"So this Tree of Souls is important. And the Old Vetrisians split it? So how does it still give witches their magic?"

"It's been *physically* split." Lucien stares into his mug with glassy eyes. "But its magical imprint is still intact. The Tree of Souls still exists, but not on a physical level. That's why it only ever comes to witches in dreams. Dreams are how it moves—how it communicates, and how it gives witches their magic." He sucks in a sharp breath. "But the wound of being split like that—it must be hurting. Terribly, and for so long. For a thousand years now."

pain like eternity, the hunger sneers at him.

"So, wait." Malachite holds up one long-fingered hand. "You're saying a thousand years ago, Old Vetris decided the only way to stop the valkerax was to split this super-important magic witch tree? And the witches just let them?"

"Let?" Lucien scoffs. "The Mist Continent was on the verge of ruin. They did what they thought was the right thing—they used the most powerful tool at their disposal."

"And the most mysterious," Fione agrees. "I didn't...I didn't even know it was real. All these trees, lost to time, to the crumbling of Old Vetris, and then consumed in the fires of war." She inhales deeply. "No doubt the Old Vetrisians had little clue as to what would concretely happen if the Tree of Souls was split. But they decided the short-term benefit was worth the unknown consequences far down the road. And that 'far down the road' is our reality, right here and right now."

Her periwinkle eyes dart over to me, and we share a silent moment. We talked earlier of consequences, too. About what would happen if we destroyed the trees. Both of them. That's what I want above all. I want the valkerax and the Heartless to be free. But if it means I destroy all magic, too, I—

I don't know if it's worth that.

All magic. All magic, ever. *Forever.*

It would change the world. There wouldn't be any more witches. The valkerax—who knows how they actually fly? Maybe that's magic, too. Maybe the Wave that gave the celeon sentience... Would that go away? Would the celeon revert? Would Windonhigh come crashing to the ground? What would happen on the other three continents I can't see? They have magic there, too. Everywhere. Different magic, *everywhere*. All gone.

Because of me. My decision.

There's a stretched-thin silence, like old worn skin over an older drum. One too-hard beat, and it will break—gape open into darkness.

"We need more information," Fione says first. "We could be jumping to illogical conclusions without all the facts. Or even the majority of facts. Once we're at the Black Archives I can translate more—we should wait to decide until then."

"Sure, whatever." Malachite puts his hands behind his head. "I'm leaving the thinking to the rest of you, honestly. Just keep in mind I'm team 'don't-let-the-valkerax-out.'"

I look over at Lucien, his face drawn tight. I can see the wheels of his brain working, quietly, swiftly. What would it mean to get rid of magic? What would it mean for Cavanos, for his kingdom?

What's *left* of his kingdom?

Thankfully, the tedium of dinner and cleaning dishes and waxing the seals in the hull takes over. But it's still not enough exertion to exhaust my brain—not in the slightest. When curfew falls I stay awake, staring up at the ceiling-floor of the ship, all our hammocks swayed gently by the ocean's lull. Most of the sailors snore, a few of them draped over their hammocks in impossible positions. I jolt out of my skin when one of them sits bolt upright and starts punching the air, except the air happens to be the sagging weight of the sailor's arse above him. The above neighbor is too drunk to wake. I suppress a laugh at the ridiculousness of it all, grateful for the reprieve.

Lucien's hammock is next to mine, Fione's above me, and Malachite's above his. I can see his dark silhouette breathing gently into the stale, sweaty air. I know he's not asleep. How can he be? This changes everything. Even if Fione warned us not to jump to conclusions, the questions still ring clear as bells in our heads.

If stopping Varia means destroying all magic, is that a worthy cost?

She'll be consumed by the Bone Tree in a few months. She acknowledged that herself. She'll die. We could let her rampage until she perished, but she wouldn't be the only one. People would die by her hand, her power. Untold numbers of people.

But how many people would die without magic?

The witches of Cavanos would be defenseless, truly and totally. Witches all over the world would have to learn how to piece reality together again after a total destruction of their way of life. And that's not even taking into consideration "far down the road." Anything could happen down the road. Future generations would have to grapple with the decisions we made here and now. And their battles might be far worse than ours. A chain never-ending.

It's too big to dwell on. It feels like if I give it more thought than the bare minimum, it'll bend my mind into itself until there's nothing left but fear.

great fear, and great hate, the hunger whispers.

I'm scared of falling asleep. Of seeing Varia in my dream again, connecting to her. I'm scared of the dream I had in Vetris—those two naked tree rosaries I felt I had to bring together. I know now what the thing that felt lonely is called. That feeling of wrongness that's plagued me ever since then. The Tree of Souls.

Is that what the hunger is? That "wound" from the splitting? The Glass Tree's hunger is in my head, and the Bone Tree's hunger is in Varia. Is the hunger punishment for bisecting the Tree of Souls? I know it's what's been calling to me this whole time. Not the Glass Tree. Not the Bone Tree. But both of them. The thing they both are—the thing they both used to be. It's been dreaming, reaching out to me through my dreams.

The tree of bone and the tree of glass will sit together as family at last.

I roll over again, chasing the Hymn of the Forest out of my head only to see Lucien's sleeping outline is gone. His hammock is empty. Did he go abovedeck for some air? It's not a bad idea, and I swing my legs over and stick my feet in my boots to follow him. He might need me. And even if he doesn't, I need him.

We need each other, if we're going to make it through this.

The salt air is crisper at night, gilded sharp by the full light of the Blue Giant, its cool incandescence completely unfettered by any mountains or hills or forests. There's only the sea to soak it up, and the wood of our comparatively little ship. Lucien's at the bow, watching the ship's prow carve the water white. The helmsman nods to me, and I to him, the deck guard walking lazy circles and smoking a pipe, the smell of vanilla tobacco lingering on me as I lean on the rail beside the prince.

"It's hard not to feel small," I say. "In the middle of all this. Especially with a moon that big."

The Blue Giant wordlessly looms on the horizon, dwarfing the ship, our sails, and casting a long shadow of us on the choppy water—a ship, and two people at its jutting prow.

"I wanted to be a good king," Lucien's voice comes out hoarse. "I wanted to—I saw what my father was doing to the country, and I didn't want to be anything like him. I promised myself I wouldn't close my ears to my people. I promised I'd use my power and wealth for good, not for fear."

I want to reach for his hand on the railing, but this seems important. I don't want to distract him. And, deep down, I don't want to feel his unmoving hand. Not right now. Not when I'm afraid more than ever of losing him.

He clenches his working hand. "And then I realized, somewhere along the way. Somewhere between stealing my hundredth gold bracelet from some noble's wrist to give to the urchins to pawn for food, I realized *it*. A kingdom is only as good as its king. Which means the cornerstone of the people's well-being relies on what kind of person the king is. And left in a vacuum of power and pleasure, the majority of people become selfish. Princes raised to be kings most of all."

"A king's worth is one potato," I say softly.

He looks over at me and smiles, his broad lips sad.

"Yes. It's a system doomed to untold cruelty at worst, and negligence at best."

"So...what will you do?"

His hawk-eyes pierce back out at the ocean. "Change. I don't know how, precisely, or when. But if I'm to do what's best for the people, for my people, then I must change things. Even if it means upheaval. Even if it means temporary strife. The fact that I must change it alone is a burden. But it's my burden to bear. And, hopefully, the last."

"You could just be king," I insist. "You would be a good one."

"That..." He chuckles, the sound bitter. "That's the conceit, Zera. Don't you see? Thinking that one person alone could decide justly and without bias the correct thing for millions of people...that is what being king means. It's an impossibility. But it's a convenient one, isn't it? If the king is bad, if the people are suffering, it's the king's fault, not his ministers'. Not the systems in place that make the nobles richer and the people poorer. The *king's*. An arbiter of impossible decisions and a scapegoat to place blame on all in one."

I'm speechless. His words strike deep, and are terrifying.

"To think I could rule a country alone, decide what's best for a whole country's people completely alone... I'd be no better than Varia. I'd be holding on to power fearfully, instead of hopefully, and using it as a weapon as she uses the Bone Tree and the valkerax."

"Lucien—"

"You made your decision." He turns to me, our chests close now. "You said you would choose, no matter what. That to choose was your right. And you're correct. To choose *is* your right. But to choose is everyone's right, not just yours. Not just mine. Not just the king's, and not just Varia's. It's all of ours. That's why I have to stop her. That's why, even if she's my sister, even if I love her—"

His voice splinters, throat bobbing, and he reaches out for me. I take his hands in mine, holding them close to my face so he knows I'm here. So he can feel my heat, my realness.

"This." I laugh a watery laugh. "This is why I fell in love with you."

"Self-aggrandizing speeches?" His smirk is reluctant.

"No. Your sense of justice. The way you stay true to what you believe is right. I don't think anyone can be right all the time, but you." I tilt my face and kiss his palm. "You come the closest to anyone I've ever met. You think about other people before yourself. Always. You've always put others first, me first, and I—"

I glance up at him.

"If this is what you want for yourself, then you should have it. I don't know what a Cavanos without a king looks like, but...I'll help you. I'll help you figure it out. Until the very end."

His kiss is slow, hot and lingering against the cold sea air. There's an edge to it, like a razor buried deep and begging to press into skin, and the soft sound that escapes my lips doesn't sound like me. It sounds like someone sweeter. His hands find my waist, pulling me flush into him, and that's when I know—all of him. I want all of him, no matter what that means, no matter the trembling in my body, no matter how or when or why. I want to touch him, every inch of him, and my fingers snake in his belt, under his shirt, feeling all the hard contours I've only seen up until now, only been tempted with—

"Well would you lookit that."

The voice is a bucket of close, freezing water, and Lucien and I practically leap away from each other. The watchman stands at the railing beside us, puffing on his pipe and pointing beyond our shoulders, down. He flashes a toothless grin up at us with a single word.

"Moon jellies."

Both our faces on fire, we peer over the railing. But all my fiery embarrassment sheds the moment I see the ocean—or rather, the sight *beneath* the ocean. Lights. Thousands upon thousands of flickering lights, flashing between red-blue to pink-green to yellow-orange and back again like perfectly circular rainbows. Some of them float closer to the surface, bobbing with gelatinous ease along the gentle waves, their tentacles drifting behind them like banners of the finest Avellish lace. The whole sea a dark emerald, but aglow with rainbow light.

"I've—I've read about them," I whisper, grinning over at Lucien. "But I've never seen them!"

His laugh rings as he snakes his hand into mine. "Me neither."

"Huh." The watchman puffs his pipe. "It's good luck, you know. 'Specially for lovers."

"Oh?" Lucien's eyebrow quirks.

"Ach, the usual. Together forever in bliss, etcetera etcetera."

"Look at that one!" I gasp, pointing at the water. A light a hundred times the size of the others rises up from the depths, its massive circular head an awe-inspiring umbrella of vivid color and soft light. It's nearly the size of the dinghy attached to the ship, and Lucien makes a choked noise when it floats closer and the massive tentacles prod at the ship's hull, the gelatinous lace reaching curiously up toward us. I squeeze Lucien's hand, wide-eyed and grinning huge at him.

"Oy!" The watchman barks down at it. "Leave 'em alone! They're havin' a romantic moment up here, you know!" Blithely unaware of the irony of his words, he picks up a nearby broom and bats at the tentacles with it. "Back! Back, you!"

Lucien and I glance at each other and devolve into laughter. Despite its titanic size, the moon jelly is so slow, it's all comedy and no threat, and at some point the broom gets stuck to the jelly's tentacle and the watchman fumbles it and the cleaning tool goes crashing into the water.

"Ach, fine! Keep it, then, you scoundrel!" He shakes his fist at the giant moon jelly as it floats away, dragging the broom behind it in its nest of lace. He turns to look at us. "Back to bed with you two, afore the gods send another one for ya."

I make a facetious little salute before bouncing off, pulling Lucien along with me. The lingering heat in my veins from his kiss radiates, burning my cheeks even as we settle in our respective hammocks again. Hammocks are impossible for two people. I know that. *Still*. Still, I want him now more than ever. And I know he feels the same, because he decides to sleep facing me, a knowing smirk on his face.

"They'll have real beds in the Black Archives," he murmurs. A promise.

"Maybe." I feign impartiality. "Or maybe there will only be beach."

"Then"—his smirk grows—"there will only be beach."

"You—!" My face blisters red as I roll over and hiss. "Go to sleep."

His laugh is so gentle and deep, it sends a prickle up and down my spine.

"Reluctantly, I assure you."

18

A REST

Considering the emotionally exhausting mess we've been through since the Bone Tree on the mountain, the four days on the *Lady Terrible* feel like unreal bliss. Like a break of grass between the hard, thorny thicket that's been our lives of late. Nowhere to go, nothing to do but sit and wait and work and eat. And while my mind certainly still churns around itself like a farm child's first attempt at making butter, there are distractions. In the form of a handsome prince, mostly. And his friend-slash-bodyguard who won't leave us alone.

"I know how this works," Malachite insists, trailing behind Lucien and me as we walk the halls hand in hand. "I've seen way too many hormonal nobles' kids sneak off for a quick one and come back pregnant." His ruby eyes glower at my navel. "Does that thing work?"

I shrug. "Not entirely sure. I haven't had my cycle since I was turned, so…"

"Good," the beneather breathes out. "Because two Zeras running around is a nightmare I've had before, and I'd rather eat horseshit than have it again. Or in real life."

"What about two of me?" Lucien offers mildly. "That wouldn't be so bad."

"Are you *kidding*?" Malachite throws his hands out. "Do I look like I can babysit two deluded princes at once? I have four stomachs, not ten arms!"

"Mal, please." I sigh. "If we reproduce, I promise you will be the first to know. Okay?"

"Please don't," he groans.

"We weren't planning to," Lucien drawls. "But now that you seem so invested, we might have to. Just to spite you."

"Good." The beneather throws his hands up. "Great. I'll be updeck whittling a crib if you need me." He whirls on the stairs and points menacingly. "*Don't* need me."

He storms up, his boots practically shaking the hull with every angry step.

"Bye!" I wave sweetly. "Have a nice time!" When he's gone, I turn to Lucien. "He's cheery."

"Undoubtedly," the prince agrees lightly. "He's never been good at sharing. Or letting go."

"Or manners," I add.

"Or emotional subtlety. Remind me to send him home to Pala Amna for a vacation after all this."

"And by 'vacation' you mean 'a quick roll in the hay.'" I translate.

"Perhaps. Or perhaps he finds his own romantic interest and leaves ours alone for a while."

"I'd miss him, though," I pout. "Who would we hire to spy on us while we kiss, then? It's just not the same thrill without a constant onlooker."

His eyes glimmer as he looks over at me. "Your sarcasm is sometimes unsettlingly genuine."

"Thank you." I beam.

We pass the mess hall, and among the few sailors finishing up their shift meal at the long tables sits Fione, cane resting on the bench and her head bent over the green-backed book. She reads fiercely, flipping pages back and forth with a knot between her brows.

"Don't you think she's working too hard?" I whisper to Lucien, and he sighs.

"As if she knows the meaning of the word. Especially when it comes to Varia."

"She put on such a sweet front when we first met," I reminisce. "But she was looking for Varia the entire time. Plotting. Full of surprises, that one."

"Look who's talking." Lucien curls a smirk in my direction.

I fake-huff. "My surprises were calculated. Self-serving."

A swift shadow, and I feel his lips on my forehead. "And they brought you to me."

Giddiness wells up in me, the hunger trying to claw it back down, to drag it to the afterlife instead of embrace it. It's still hard, to accept his love at the drop of a hat, without doublethinking or flinching away. Maybe it'll always be hard. But at the very least, I'm trying. I'm trying to make it work, this time, instead of running away.

This time, I lean up and kiss him back.

The whistles that go around the mess reverberate, cheers and leering, and the prince and I part at the same time, sheepishly smiling at each other. This is the only thing to get Fione's cute little snub nose out of her book, and she shuts it and walks over. Lucien puts on a modicum of a business face for her.

"Anything to report?" he asks.

"No," she admits wearily. "I still need the codices. But it doesn't hurt to memorize the letters in the meantime."

The dark circles under her eyes are faint but there. I know she hasn't been getting much sleep.

"She's—" I pause, tabulating the weight of my words. "She's thinking about you, you know. I've seen it."

Fione's face falls, and then sets grim. She can't even manage to smile. How would she? Saving Varia might mean destroying all magic on Arathess. She knows, like I know, that Varia wouldn't want that. No one wants that, except maybe Archduke Gavik and Vetris. But Vetris is effectively gone. Gavik is dead. New God, Old God—it doesn't matter anymore. All that's left are the valkerax, and Varia, and stopping both of them.

I promised Fione. My promise shines back at me in her hopeful blue eyes, hopeful despite everything—I promised I'd find a way to get Varia back alive, no matter what. But what if it's a promise I can't keep? What if all promises are things people can't truly keep? We make promises to make people feel better, to give them hope, and when the time comes to fulfill, it's often impossible. Promises themselves are just empty words.

What is gratitude—Evlorasin's voice rings in my head—*but a promise made whole?*

"I promised, Fione," I try into the stiff air. "And I don't intend to break it."

She shutters the light behind her eyes, the hope there dimming to shadow.

Lucien steps in then. "The Black Archives will have answers, Fi."

The archduchess nods. "Yes. But I'm not sure they'll be the answers we want."

We watch her go up the stairs to abovedeck, the book clutched under her arm.

Lucien inches his fingers into mine slowly. "Do you think we make her sad?" he asks. "Being together like this?"

"Yeah," I agree. "Probably."

"Then that just means we'll have to get Varia back." He smiles wanly. "As fast as we can."

The last two days on the ship feel like they go by in a pleasant, perfect blur. Perfect blue sky, perfect sea, perfect moments soaking up the sun in Lucien's arms. Malachite braiding my hair, grumbling the whole while. Fione, smiling small when I finally, *finally* make the right joke.

Only when the crow's nest calls "land ho" does cold reality start to seep in again.

The entire ship crowds abovedeck, straining at the railing to see the island. The scuttlebutt among the crew is that the *Lady Terrible* doesn't make frequent stops to the Black Archives—or at all—but the Cavanosian war and the subsequent valkerax attacks changed that. The usual ship routes were overturned as captains scattered to calculate profit versus risk. So this is a rarity for them. To see the fabled island of the scholar-monks now is their first.

As it's mine.

The island itself is a little green jewel tucked far and away in the pocket of the ocean. The greenery is so tall and fresh as it cascades down the mountainside, because that's all the island really is—a mountain. A considerable peak rises up from the beaches, jungle between, and while it's nowhere near the height of the Tollmont-Kilstead mountains, it's more vertical height than we've seen in days on the flat ocean.

But the peak isn't the most impressive part. That title belongs to the thousands of steps carved into the peak, all of them leading toward the black tower embedded firmly at the very top. As the ship bobs closer, I suck in a sharp breath—the tower isn't built on top of the peak at all. The tower *is* the peak. From between the gentle roll of the earth as it ascends come windows, balconies, long terraces growing crops, and waterfalling streams, all of it made of shimmering black rock. Beside me, Fione's voice takes pride in its knowledge.

"They hollowed the mountain and used the volcanic rock to create the Archives inside it."

Malachite whistles, muscling in next to me. "Not bad earthwork, for a bunch of bookworm humans. Almost reminds me of Pala Amna."

Fione turns to face him. "Where do you think the beneathers learned earthwork?"

Malachite's white brow skyrockets. "Here? Yeah, right. We're way older than some library—"

"It's not 'some' library," Fione corrects. "It's *the* library. The library before Old Vetris. Before the beneathers took on the burden of living underground and guarding the valkerax. Your people *learned* earthwork from this library."

Malachite's face sets hard, and he stares at the mountain-library with a well-disguised smidgen of newfound awe.

"Raise sails!" The captain trounces around the deck, flinging orders. "You there, Heartless! Get on the winches. Beneather, help the men ready the anchor. Archduchess, what can you do?"

Fione pauses thoughtfully. "Calculate the angle of approach? If you haven't already."

"Do that, then. The port's on the west side. But it'll be dark."

Malachite and I look at each other, and I mouth *dark*? Fione seems to understand, though, pulling out her brass seeing tube and peering at the island as she says, "Aye aye, captain."

Between hauling stiff, salt-stained rope over and over, I see the captain walk up to Lucien. She says something, he nods. The raucous excitement of the crew is infectious—whispers and murmurs between grunting about what the Archives look like.

"I've heard they make you strip down and get sprayed before you step foot on land," a sailor says.

"Oh yeah? I heard they're blind as bats from all the reading. Every. Single. One."

"Ach, well, if they cannae see, that means more fancy books for me!"

The laughter shatters the quiet of the ocean, bouncing off the black-stone cliffs as we approach. I look up at Fione, at the helm with the captain. Where are they leading us? A port's supposed to be in calm water, but the ship is bobbing worse than ever. We could just anchor out by the beach and ride the dinghy in—that would be far easier than navigating such rough water so close to land. After all, who knows what kind of rocks are just under the surface? The sailors seem equally confused, glancing around nervously at one another and the looming cliffs above as the cool shade envelops us.

And then we see it.

The island is far bigger up close, and the cliffs far taller than I originally thought. But beneath one cliff, there's a gap. A gap between the ocean and the land, the cliff sticking out and hanging over, leaving a perfect height for the *Lady Terrible* to slide under. The sailors and I watch in awe as the helmsman takes us into the gap, the masts almost skimming the rock, flirting with the danger of snapping in two. Every heave of the ocean below us feels twice as dire now, and some of the sailors clasp their hands and start praying to the New God. Others watch overboard as the water turns from choppy blue to an incredibly clear turquoise color, milky hordes of shrimp and kelp-babies floating on the surface. Essentially, it's a cave with a sea for a floor. And we sail along it, carefully and quietly, every single one of us is on edge that something will scrape against something and capsize us for good.

But the reef formations under the water are surprisingly scarce, and the deeper we go, the darker it gets, until there's nothing but black. The only light comes from the water, refracted turquoise and up to us by the sun. I look over to Lucien, his proud face illuminated from beneath by the eerie light as he stares silently into the nothingness.

"What's wrong?" I approach him, touching his elbow. He starts and shakes his head.

"A lot of magic here. None of it friendly."

"Like, poised against us?" I ask.

"No." He frowns. "Not yet."

"Well." I try a smile in the darkness. "That's not ominous at all."

I trot back over to the ropes as the sailors call for help, the hunger straining against my muscles and my common sense in tandem as Lucien lets the reins go, and I rein it back in. The combined strength of the hunger and the nervous sailors is just barely enough. I suddenly feel a warmth behind me, another body, and turn my head to see Lucien pitching in to haul the very end of the rope. I smile, and on the captain's signal, we heave and twist until the winches clatter in place, and the sails come down entirely. Belowdeck the sailors start to row, wood cutting turquoise water rhythmically.

Finally, through the gloom and the chanting of the rowers, lights start to appear. At first I think it's the other side of the cliff shelf, but then I realize it's *too* white. Too bright to be sunlight diffused all over. A torch? But it's not a dot of light at all—it's a line, long and arcing like a rainbow with none of the color. When we get closer I realize it's built into the rock wall, above an entryway. And below that entryway is a port made of volcanic black rock waiting for us, polished smooth and jutting strong into the lapping ocean water.

The ship pulls gently into one of the many black-rock docks, though it doesn't seem like rock at all with how sleekly it's been sanded down. It smacks of glass, and specifically of the raw dark glass in the High Witches' tower, and I suppress a shudder. *These aren't the witches*, I remind myself. *These are polymaths.* Correction: warrior-polymaths.

The best in the *world*.

And they're waiting for us.

A row of figures in silver robes, just...*waiting*. Hoods up. It's more than a little intimidating. The captain orders the anchor dropped, and half the sailors are busy lashing rope between the dock and the ship when the first figure steps forward and lowers their hood. It's a woman, her face thin and lean and yet heavy with two large, gray eyes, like sacks of translucent fog.

The captain looks between her and us, then jerks her head.

"Go on. We've got no business with them, just their cargo." She turns to the sailors. "All right, start unloading, boys! The faster we get these damn barrels off the ship, the faster we can go home!"

The sailors scrabble, and the four of us straighten and ready ourselves, Malachite letting the gangplank clap down on the glassy dock. Fione hefts her waterproof book pouch higher, her fingers on the laces gripping white.

"Nervous?" I ask her as we walk down.

She murmurs through gritted teeth, "Let Lucien do the talking."

"No fun," I pout.

"Please."

"All right," I sigh, putting my hands behind my head leisurely.

Malachite elbows me as he passes. "Hands down. Try to look interested in what they're saying."

I feign innocence and outrage. "Why is it *me* you're all harping on? I'm capable of not ruining things, too!"

"In theory," Malachite groans. Fione's too nervous to say anything more, and we all follow Lucien as he draws even with the line of silver robes. I see him square his shoulders minutely, head high. The prince has arrived.

"I am Prince Lucien Drevenis d'Malvane of Cavanos."

"You are greeted." The woman with the limpid eyes looks him up and down. "What do you seek from the Black Archives, Prince Lucien?"

Lucien's dark gaze slices over to Fione for a split second, and she steps up and says, "We wish to find a way to interfere with the Bone Tree."

The line of silver hoods look to one another ever so slightly. Most of them stare straight forward, and I can't help but wonder where Yorl is in all this. The woman herself doesn't so much as blink.

"And what knowledge have you brought to replace the

knowledge you will take?"

I see Fione take a deep breath, steadying herself. She unlaces the strings of her pouch with deliberate slowness and pulls out the green-backed book. She opens it to a page, holding it out so the woman can see.

"An Old Vetrisian book. It speaks of the Trees."

The woman steps closer, pulling a monocle out and peering at the writing, and then at the writing on the spine. She straightens quickly, eyes hardening on Fione and her monocle dropping on its chain.

"We have this book already. The rough draft, to be more precise. What we will gather from your book will be too slight a repayment for what you seek."

The line of silver robes suddenly speaks all at once, scaring me out of my skin: "So it has been deemed."

And just like that, the line turns. The woman makes a soft bow, the goodbye sort—utterly dripping with finality—and Lucien looks at me and I look at Malachite and he looks at Fione but she's frozen, hands trembling on the book cover.

"Magic?" Malachite snaps at Lucien. "You could tell 'em about that skinreading shit. It's rare, right?"

"Not rare enough." He shakes his head. "Surely you know a few tricks about hunting valkerax, Mal. *You* could tell them—"

"No way. Every kid in Pala Amna knows—"

With each step the silver robes take, Fione's face falls further, deeper into a pit of despair. I can see it happening right in front of me. In her mind, in our reality, Varia is slipping further and further away.

"Wait!"

I shout before I think. The silver robes pause, the woman looking over her shoulder with a decidedly anticipatory aloofness. Waiting. I settle mentally, deep in the sand, sinking to the bottom of the ocean of stillness inside myself. The hunger falls away, down into darkness. When I open my eyes again, it's six worlds. Six views of the world, of the woman's gray gaze going wide. Hot blood tears sluice down my cheeks, one from each eye.

"Weeping," I say. "I can tell you about that."

Next to me, I see Lucien watching me. Nervous, and yet proud. There's a beat before the woman walks up to me, pressing the monocle into her eye and looking me over. I feel like a piece of meat hanging on a butcher's hook as she circles me slowly.

"We already know of Weeping," she says tersely. "We know of the valkerax who Weeps, we know of the Heartless who Weeps, and we know of its mechanisms. This was our newest initiate's kingsmedal project."

Yorl. She *must* mean Yorl. He detailed it all, it's true—my every interaction with Evlorasin, my every thought about Weeping and how to do it. The whole time he was scribbling in that dungeon arena beneath Vetris, he was signing the death warrant for this moment. Even through the perfect emotional peace and stillness, my chest deflates. My one advantage, gone. Just like that.

Fione darts forward. "Please, whatever I can do, the book, my uncle's white mercury research—"

The begging sounds wrong in her voice. Unnatural. Fione is sweet, she's smart, she's determined. But she's always had her pride. Until now. Until her hope and her love for Varia were cut away all at once with this woman's words. The woman doesn't look at her, doesn't so much as acknowledge what she's said. She turns, and it's a decision. A rejection. The sound Fione makes at my side tears me in half—like a lone wolf dying on a winter's night. She sinks to her knees, her tears splattering on the volcanic glass. Lucien's posture sags, the hope draining from him, too. Malachite's face twists and his mouth opens but he never gets the chance because the woman speaks again, clear.

"However, our newest initiate failed to mention a Heartless with six eyes like a valkerax."

Fione's head snaps up, gaze glimmering fiercely through her tears. Lucien helps her to her staggering feet, and she juts forward instantly, voice breaking. "Does that mean—"

The woman turns to face us, extending her hand to me. In her palm is a black-glass medallion, etched with a dizzying gold and silver symbol of some sort, like a flower opening or a star exploding.

"You may enter," she says coolly to me. "And you may learn from our books. As we may from your body. Is this trade acceptable?"

I glance at Lucien, and the worry is clear on his face. What are they planning to do to me? I can see it flash across his mind. He tries to speak first.

"We—"

"Yes." I cut him off. The woman nods, and the silver robes suddenly speak, so loud this time it thunders around the sea-lit dock.

"So it has been deemed."

19
THE BLACK ARCHIVES

"Can I be the first to say these guys are freakin' weird?" Malachite offers under his breath as the silver robes lead us under the white-mercury-lit arch and into a long black glass hall.

"Like a cult," Lucien agrees softly next to me.

"And the New God churches aren't?" I posit lightly. "Let's just get what we came for, and go."

Fione's totally quiet, marching on the heels of the woman with a single-minded determination. I try to keep up with her, no matter how much the fear is pulling me apart at the seams as the Weeping fades. Lucien offers me his handkerchief, and it's a wordless moment of comfort as I wipe the blood tears from my face.

"I've ruined so many of these," I laugh as I hand it back to him. "Sorry."

"Hopefully you won't have to ruin any soon," he says, dark eyes roaming over my face. He thumbs away a speck of blood, smiling as bravely as he can. But he's just as scared as I am. Maybe more. Whatever these librarians want to do to me, I can endure. I'll survive, no matter what. That's what being a Heartless means. And enduring the pain is the choice I've made. I can do it, if it's for him. For the good of everyone. But he needs to hear that.

"If it'll get Varia back, I can do it," I reassure him.

He stares, then lets out a breath. "I know. But I don't want you to get hurt."

"Hey, c'mon. It's the only thing I'm good at. Let me have it." I wink, and then go somber when he doesn't smile at all. "Let me do this."

"I already know there's no 'letting' you do anything. You're going to do what you're going to do, because you're Zera Y'shennria, and you never listen to anyone who isn't your own unheart."

My smile mirrors his—wry and knowing. The white light flashes over his face as we ascend a wide staircase, and I've never been more grateful to have him. To have someone who knows me, what I'm like at my very core. I used to be afraid of it. And maybe I still am. But right now, I'm just thankful.

The silver robes lead us deeper and up into the Archives, past what look like blocks of countless dizzying dungeon cells and up, up into a winding staircase lined with white mercury stripes. They've figured out how to make the lights into glass bars, instead of the glass lamps I'm used to from Vetris, and they wind around the walls in efficient, stark, otherworldly patterns, almost like blocky, precise veins in a body. This place feels...*ancient*. Deep and old, like the valkerax. But the technology screams of bleeding-edge newness—newer than even Breych with its airships and ultra-efficient white mercury lights—and the contrast makes me uneasy more than anything.

"It's like a fortress," Lucien marvels.

The leader speaks again, voice echoing. "We are about to enter the central library ward. Please keep your voices down to a minimum, and refrain from touching anything—"

"The usual," Malachite grumbles.

"And, if you would, do not look directly at the machinery. It makes them rather uncomfortable."

Malachite and Lucien and I all share a wary look. Uncomfortable? Since when do machines feel *comfort*?

Fione is still unmoved, her gaze straight ahead and fixed on the woman she follows stalwartly up the stairs. Not knowing what to expect, I lace my hand into Lucien's, relieved when he laces his fingers in mine. Together. Together, at the very least.

The stairs finally flatten out, the view widening into a cavernous room of black glass. "Cavernous" doesn't really cut it—this place is *massive*. The ceiling is so tall it utterly melts into forever-darkness. You could fit a hundred of the arenas where I trained Evlorasin into this one space. But the polymaths of the Black Archives have decided to fill every available inch of this seemingly infinite space with books. Not in the usual bookshelves, though—rather, the entire shell of the cavern is carved with hollows in which books are perfectly slotted. Thousands—no, *millions*. There are scrolls, too, stored in the traditional Avellish style—which is to say strung from copper rods by flax strands bookended with wooden slats. Dozens of scrolls hang from just one strand, looking like a string of butterfly cocoons swaying gently in an airless breeze.

And then there are the things that don't even *look* like books— rotating copper orbs with specifically patterned indents, crosscuts of gelatin the size of walls with ink spirals of all colors frozen within them. What I presume to be polymaths in silver robes gather around these contraptions, peering into them and turning them with handles this way and that, as if…reading them? But that's not possible—those things don't even look like language. Language is with ink and words. Stranger still, no matter how high the bookshelves extend up, no matter the daunting distance the scrolls hang from, there are no ladders. But that—that doesn't make any sense.

Malachite echoes my sentiments.

"How do they get up to those books when they need 'em?" He glowers. The line of silver robes accompanying us start to peel off in all directions, some toward the books, others to shadowed nooks.

"We approach the machines," the woman says suddenly. "Walk with care."

We feel them before we see them. The rumbling of the black stone floor is gentle at first, and then crescendos to a quaking, undeniable presence. Something is coming—something reminiscent of a valkerax with the way every gargantuan step shudders the bone. But it's the sharp, acrid smell that makes me cover my nose, that makes Malachite hiss a soft swear under his breath.

"White mercury," Lucien murmurs beside me.

"Highly refined," Fione corrects him, but her next words are cut off as the source of the heavy steps rounds the corner. Slowly, a brass giant comes into view, shaped like a human and yet impossibly heavier, bulkier. Its face is smooth of all features, save for a small slot on the bottom where a mouth would be. The sheer clumsy bulkiness of it seems out of place among so much careful order and arrangement. With every movement of its pendulous arms and creaking knees, curls of white mercury steam exhale from its joints, spiraling up into the archive air.

"Don't stare." Mal elbows me.

"And how do you propose that?" I breathe. "When it's a man made entirely of metal?"

"Is there a man inside?" The beneather squints.

"Obviously not," Lucien says.

"It's moving on its own." Fione's determined facade slips for a moment, her marvel sparking her eyes with pale blue fire. "Incredible! It's...*automating*!"

"We call them self-motivators." The woman looks over her shoulder at us. "Though I suppose it's been agreed to call them 'matronics' in the common vernacular."

"Automatic motion, fueled by highly refined white mercury." Fione leans in to look at the woman. "What type do you use? Qessen-red? Or perhaps starscreed? Is starscreed even strong enough to power something like this? What method of expulsion do you use to generate the energy?"

"Such questions are not of the sort you have traded information for," the woman insists. "We move on."

The gleam in Fione's eyes doesn't fade, her face riveted to the heavy steps of the matronic. It moves like a person, its gait wide with metallic hip flexors, but I'm more than a little put off by the fact it's moving without seeing—no eyes on its face or anywhere else I can see. I can't tell which sense it's using to navigate, if any sense at all. A senseless creature made of metal, moving simply because it's been made to. I can't help but feel kinship with it.

"They aren't...*alive*, right?" I ask the woman.

"They do not possess sentience," she affirms, turning a corner and leaving the matronic behind even as all of us are surreptitiously glancing back at it. "Manmade sentience has only ever been accomplished by the Wave."

"Then why do they not like being looked at?" Lucien asks. "Surely things without sentience cannot have preferences."

"Does a bird not have a preference for gentle wind and sunny days?" the woman asks. "We have created life in the matronics, and so they prefer it a certain way."

Malachite and I share a thoroughly worried look. Fione, meanwhile, appears lost in her imagination, thrilled at the polymathematics of it all, and Lucien looks likewise intrigued. But the beneather and I know better—if the Black Archives are making these matronics, then that means they're the only ones who know how to control them. It's worrisome. What are they making them *for*? I doubt they'll ever tell us that. I glance back now and then, and it appears the matronics are here to lift the polymaths up to the higher shelves. There's an indent in their backs well-suited for stepping on, and mortal-sized metal handles on their shoulders. The carved shelves turn into perfectly spaced footholds for the matronics to clamber effortlessly up, the polymaths pointing towards the book they require. That's why the polymaths don't need ladders. They've invented *walking* ladders. Walking ladders that have no eyes, but can still see. Walking ladders that aren't flesh, but still have preferences.

And Fione just won't stop *staring*.

"Fione," I murmur to her. "Maybe don't."

The archduchess barely spares a glance at me, but I reach for her elbow carefully, trying to gently remind her of what we're here to do. Thankfully, we don't have much more time to dwell on the disturbing matronics, as the woman leads us away from the main library ward and into a thin-cut hall cleaving into the volcanic rock with many doors on either side. Once we're out of sight of the matronics and their bulk, Fione seems to regain herself, the sparkle in her eyes hardening to determination once more as she walks.

After what feels like an unending trek down a repeating infinity, the woman finally stops in front of a specific door and motions for us to go inside. We squeeze in tentatively, the room barely big enough to accommodate a small polished table with four chairs.

"Please wait here." The woman makes a bow. "I will return with the polymath of relevancy in a moment."

"The polymath?" Lucien's brow wrinkles. "We came here for books, for matrices. We need a codex to translate—"

Fione's hand on his arm stops him cold. He looks down at her, but her gaze never wavers, and he finally gets the message and sits back down. The woman bows slightly and leaves, the heavy door clunking behind her. When she's gone, Malachite props his muddy boots up on the table.

"So, good parts," he starts. "They haven't killed us thus far."

"Bad parts," I counter. "They're making metal Heartless, essentially."

"Not Heartless," Fione argues. "Not really. It's not as if they're controlling something that was already alive. They made those matronics, from ore to metal to the legs and every other part of it. They've *created* it."

"Like gods," Lucien murmurs, and those two words ring powerful enough to make us all go silent.

The little room has a slot for a window, the bright sunlight squaring through no bigger than a peg. I stand on my tiptoes to see out of it, and feel a support underneath me as Lucien picks me up by the waist with his broad hands and lifts.

He smirks up at me. "Is that any better?"

"A little." I feign disinterest, peering through the window. Outside is a lush expanse of vivid green, the sweltering humidity of the outside air so different from the coldness of the Archives—they must keep it cool to preserve the books. We're closer to the meridian here, and so while the ocean is still relatively cool, the land is a different story. Palms and tallferns reach for the sun, piercing blue and purple and gold blossoms bursting from every crook of every shadowed canopy. Vines slick with viscous pink sap creep over bark, over the forest floor, over any rock they can find. It's a different forest than I'm used to compared to the chilly pines and old moss of Cavanos—more alive, more active.

And I too am more active, considering my beloved's arms are securely around my waist and his face perhaps the closest to my body it's ever been. I motion for him to put me down and turn to him with a pout.

"Who taught you to approach ladies in such a brazen manner?" I look over at Malachite. "Was it you?"

"Oh, c'mon." The beneather rolls his eyes. "Like Luc ever takes my advice."

"I take it sometimes," the prince argues lightly. "When it's relevant. Which is, well…never."

Malachite throws his hand up. "My point exactly."

Something about the moment sobers us. Maybe it's the black

rock fortress of our tiny room, or maybe it's the height of the view outside the minuscule window. Whatever it is, it makes Lucien's dark gaze wilt on the edges as he looks at me.

"I'll be there with you. Sending magic. So. If they try to hurt you—"

"I'm sure some of it will hurt," I cut him off. "About as badly as a scraped knee. They're dusty old librarians, for Old God's sake."

"If anything, it will be a thorough cataloguing," Fione adds, leafing through the precious green-backed book idly.

Lucien ignores her and pulls me flush to him, my waist against his, my forehead against his. Malachite makes a discontented noise and struggles to face his chair away in the small room, and Fione's smile is the smallest saddened hint, but Lucien doesn't seem to care. His eyes are on me, his gaze never wavering as he speaks, low, like I'm the only person in the room. In the world.

"If you need me, I'll come for you."

"You don't—" My breath catches as he kisses a soft pond-skip from my cheek to the corners of my lips. "I'll be fine."

"I know," he asserts, kissing the fullness of my lips. "But I want you to be fine with me."

"You'll—" His kiss this time feels like a slice, where the others were paper cuts. "You'll have to let me go *sometime*."

"Yeah, Luc," Malachite grumbles self-righteously. "Who's the one who's 'bad at sharing' now?"

"Heard that, did you?" Lucien lilts.

Over the prince's shoulders, I see Malachite tap his ears.

"I hear *everything*, dolt. And if I have to hear you two smacking over there for one more second—"

The door opens, framing three people in silver robes. Malachite kicks his shoes off the table and exhales.

"Oh thank spirits." He jerks his head at us. "Do something about them."

The silver robes enter wordlessly, and Fione closes the book and stands. I try to make what little space I can between us, but Lucien won't let me go, his grip around my waist tight and high-strung. He's worried. Worried like I've never seen him worried before. About me.

My unheart tries not to melt at the idea—worry is a natural part of caring about someone. He's worried for me many times before this. But, still. *Still*, this feels different, deliberate, painted in absolutes and with two high-contrasting colors. He cares. About *me*. It's a foolish thought, after everything, but he cares for me out of everyone in this world. He's chosen *me*, out of all the Spring Brides, out of all the eligible, witty beauties of the world, and that makes my chest glow with buttery gold joy. As the silver robes take their places standing against the walls of the room, I lean up and whisper in his ear.

"You have strange tastes."

He gives me a look, lips crinkling with a smile. "As do you."

"The six-eyed Heartless will come with us to undergo preliminary examination," one of the polymaths suddenly says. "The duration of our study will be approximately two halves. If the results of the preliminary examination prove the presence of further information, you will be allowed access to our materials."

Malachite snorts. Fione stands, hands folded over the book, and the book to her chest.

"You won't harm her?" she asks. The polymath's silver-robed head tilts to her and pauses, as if it's a question they've already answered, or maybe one so obvious it doesn't *deserve* an answer. Fione, worried about me, and Malachite in his own way. All of them, caring for me.

I ease Lucien's hand off my waist, slow and reassuring, and give him my best smile. "I'll be back."

"You have to be," he insists, the black of his eyes near-matching the volcanic rock. "We have a beach date."

My laugh goes nowhere in the cramped room, and as I pass

Malachite, he pulls on my ear softly. "Don't put up with it if it stinks."

"Yes, sir," I agree, patting him on the head. The silver-robed polymaths follow me out the door, and I can hear Malachite's grumbling all the way down the hall as he fixes his hair, the sound a comforting accompaniment into the unknown.

The polymath who spoke leads me down the hall, but not to the central library ward. This time we hang a far left, arcing down and around a ramp built on the edge of a massive chasm, in which a huge pendulum made entirely of what looks like clear quartz crystal rocks gently side to side. It's a miracle the thing doesn't just ram through the walls of the room, but I suppose that's all due to the polymaths' careful calculations.

The rocking of the pendulum soon fades, our steps the only things daring to break the black silence. The hallway narrows down to a single ominous door, and the silver robes open it for me with a ring of keys from their belts. This room is far more spacious than the reception cell they put us in, but also sparser. The only things in the room are a large chair seemingly carved straight out of the volcanic rock, and what looks like gutters carved into the ground, centering around the chair. A single shaft of white sunlight pierces in from a hole in the ceiling, illuminating only the chair.

"Please." One of the silver robes motions. "Sit. This will not take long."

"Two halves, right?" I say, tempering the nerves in my voice as I sit on the cold, ominous throne.

"That was a generous estimate, to allay the fears of your companions." The polymath who speaks is a new one, seemingly stepping out of the shadows. But when they step, the sound isn't clipped, as boots or armor might be. It's soft, silent. I look down—ochre paws, a vermillion furred tail tip thrashing excitedly between them. My eyes travel up to their hood, but before they lower it I know who it is already. I try to say his name, but my voice cracks down the middle, and it comes out true.

"Ironspeaker."

There's a pause, the darkness falling away from his feline face as the light spills over it and his own voice fills the gaps.

"Starving Wolf." Yorl smiles, returning his true name with mine, all his fangs showing and his whiskers crinkling. "Missed me that much, did you?"

20

THE IRONSPEAKER
AND THE
STARVING WOLF

I t's been only a week and a half, bordering two, but I've never been more relieved to see the smartest being in the world.

And Yorl Farspear-Ashwalker is, objectively, the smartest being in the world. Or at least, the smartest I know. He and Fione tied, maybe. There might be others, too, but his dedication to helping Varia solve the mysteries of Heartless-valkerax communication made it possible for her to get the Bone Tree in the first place, and for me to get to know Evlorasin. We'd conspired together in the hopes I'd get my heart back, and his end of the deal was being able to conduct one-of-a-kind research—specifically, to finish his grandfather's life's work—in order to gain entry and ratify his grandfather's findings in the Black Archives forever.

All of this is to say Yorl was there for me during the hardest parts of Evlorasin's training, and, when I'd shoved Fione and Lucien and even Malachite away, he was there for me. When I was in the depths of loneliness, Yorl was my only source of levity, of positive interaction. He's relatively new in my unlife, but after what we've been through, our friendship feels so old.

He bends the knee at the base of the throne.

"Finally," I drawl. "The respect I deserve."

Yorl's laugh is deep, ragged in that celeon way, as he claps metal restraints onto my wrists and ankles.

"Strange way to show respect, isn't it?" He plays along.

"Very." I act puzzled as I look down at the metal, then slide a glance at the silver-robed polymaths bustling around the room. "Your new friends don't trust me much, I take it?"

"My new friends don't trust one *another*," he murmurs. "Let alone total strangers. Interdepartmental feuds are the air we breathe."

"So sad." I try to draw a tear down my face, but the wrist restraints clang. The polymaths all look at me at once, alarmed, and I smile. "Sorry, sorry! No more sudden movements, I promise."

Yorl smooths my hair away from my eyes because I can't—a kind gesture, in his own way.

"If this was my project, I could ask them to forego the restraints," he sighs. "But the high-running valkerax fears have been one of the only things from the mainland to take root here. The bastion won't hear of it."

"The bastion being your boss, I imagine," I say.

"Something like that." He nods, his vermillion-shot mane bobbing on the ends. It looks silkier than when I saw it last.

"You look better, at least," I press. "It's almost as if you don't have anything to desperately prove anymore and can focus on the little things like eating and sleeping and keeping your body functioning."

"It hasn't even been a quarter-half," Yorl grumbles. "And you're already patronizing me."

"Lovingly," I assure him. "So what are you going to *actually* do to me? Flay me alive? A bit out of style, but I'm game. Hmm... draw and quarter me? That's always fun."

"Nothing that extreme." He shakes his mane. "They're going to take the ten biological samples required for a full analysis. Blood, bile, liver, saliva, brain—"

"Brain?" I hiss. "How exactly do you plan to—"

A polymath walks up to Yorl bearing a full leather canvas

packed to the brim with wicked hooked needles, and all the blood in my body curdles away from it.

"Yes, well," Yorl sighs. "Because you're technically a 'dead' specimen, they voted against the far kinder live-gathering methods."

"But you voted *for* them, right?" My voice goes high as the polymath pulls out a hooked needle and wipes it clean with alcohol. Yorl snatches it from the human's hand almost too quickly, and they look utterly shocked. Yorl's green feline eyes widen, too, like he's alarmed at what he just did, but his voice remains smooth.

"Please, scholar. This is technically messy, menial corpse work. Let an adjutant like myself ensure your hands remain clean."

He's good at covering, but the scholar doesn't buy it, snorting as his thick eyebrows wrinkle under his hood.

"'Menial corpse work'? You must be joking. If our suspicions are accurate, she's the first nonhuman Heartless specimen in Arathess history. Surely even an adjutant like yourself can see how important she truly is."

"Not important enough to spare her pain, though," I mutter, perhaps a bit too loudly. The scholar's dark eyes snap to me, a flicker of familiar Fione-like curiosity in them.

"Can you hear the song, Heartless?" he demands suddenly.

"I'm from the Vetrisian court, where a quartet accompanies every breath," I chime. "I've heard a lot of songs—none of them particularly noteworthy."

"No," he presses, leaning in. "*The* song. The one all valkerax hear."

he means us.

I pause, the hunger echoing. "You mean the Bone Tree's hunger?" He nods, and I tilt my head. "I'd love to tell you. But on the condition I get a painkiller or three."

"There are no conditions," the scholar snaps. "We will take

your information, and your friends will receive theirs. So it has been deemed."

I glance at Yorl, but from the way his green eyes slide around, I get the feeling he can't interfere or assert himself. Not without risking his own position. Organizations are fickle like that. But thankfully, I'm a free agent.

I make a sweet smile. "Oh, sure. You can take all my information. Slice me up, take bits of me all you want, look at me under a lens. But my parts won't tell you what my mouth can."

"We don't need your words," the scholar insists, "to know you."

"Yes, I'm certain you're very good at sussing things out," I agree placidly. "I saw your matronics, all your little machines. But that must be so much *work*. So much effort, so many long nights in your laboratories. So much brainwork, trying to analyze *my* brainwork. All my experiences, all my perceptions. I could just tell you and save you the bother."

I've got him, and I know I've got him because he pauses on the brink of leaning in farther, like he's pulling himself back from temptation.

The old me would have let them hurt me. The old me would have gladly thrown herself into the fire to achieve a means to an end.

But the new me has different ideas. The new me has people who care about her.

Twist the knife, Zera, salt the wound, make him want to wash it out. Save yourself.

being kind to yourself? The hunger laughs. **a pathetic escape attempt.**

"The first nonhuman Heartless in the world," I murmur, looking down at myself. "Wow. That's so amazing. Who knew?"

I look over to Yorl innocently, wide-eyed with my faux wondering. He can't assert himself, but he *can* play along. He nods solemnly, an emotion he's incredibly good at showing. Perfect, really. And it tips the scholar over the edge, the hooked needle in his hand retreating into his sleeve.

"Fine," he assents calmly. "We administer pain relievers, then."

"Will that work on her Heartless body?" Yorl asks, and I'm simultaneously flashing eyes at him to shut up and curious about it myself.

"We'll use the formula intended for large game." The scholar motions to the other silver robes on the wall, and they scatter out and back in, wheeling a tray with multicolored bottles on it. "It's not as if overdosing will kill her."

"Good point." I flash a wink at Yorl as the scholar tips a bottle into my mouth. The taste is scathing tar and ferment, but it works almost instantly—all the muscles in my body unwind like coiled snakes, and I sink into the black rock throne far more relaxed. Yorl is an ochre blur above me, the muscles in my eyes drooping.

"I've gotta say, Ironspeaker, this stuff is way better than what you used to give me."

"Shut up," Yorl says, not an ounce of anger in it, only gentleness.

"Not quite yet." The scholar steps in, holding either side of my face in his hands. "You have your painless time, Heartless. Now tell me; do you hear the song?"

I have no filter anymore, my thoughts spilling out faster than I can make them.

"I hear both songs. Glass and bone. But the bone song only ever in my dreams."

He blinks. "The Heartless hunger is not the song."

"It is," I argue, my head lolling uselessly back as he lets go of me. "I've heard them both. They're the same thing. Different notes, but the same music, deep down. I can feel it."

"That's—that's utter nonsense."

I laugh, rolling my head to look at him. "I sound a bit like a valkerax, don't I? But don't *you* know? The Old Vetrisians split the Tree of Souls."

"Of course." He pulls a shining scalpel out of his pocket, testing my skin. "But it's been more than a thousand years. By all deductions, the Trees' connection to each other should've completely eroded at this point."

I go quiet, watching the silver blade split my skin and hot blood ooze out. Yorl holds my wrist softly between his paws, steadying the work. I want him to push the hair off my face again, but he's Yorl. He has a job to do, and polymathematics to aid. It's enough for me that he cares enough to be here, that he came to this at all. I'm starting to slip in and out of consciousness, the world blurring on the edges. Better to pass out, I suppose, because I'm not particularly fond of the idea of being here when they take my slice of brain.

to be together, the hunger slithers. *to undo what you did, weak things afraid of death*.

"They want to be together again," I mumble. "More than anything. So they sing. They sing to punish us...to—to *guilt* us. To make it unbearable. To make us undo what we did."

The darkness claws around me, but softly, folding interlocking talons one by one over the light until there's only shadow and the hunger left—two hungers, same but different and both ringing clear as winter rain in my head.

together.

TOGETHER.

The feeling of someone's leathery pads pushing my hair off my sweating face gingerly, and then nothing.

As with most people I've met, once they have what they want, the scholars of the Black Archives are far nicer to me. In that they leave me the afterlife alone.

"Humans really are *humans*, no matter where they are or how smart they think they are," I groan, massaging my head as Yorl undoes my restraints. When I wake up again he's the only one left in the room, the instruments and blood all cleared out and cleaned up. It's like nothing ever happened—like I just sat down here and fell asleep. With leather wristbands on, but still.

"The entry hole closed almost instantly." Yorl jerks his hairy chin to where I'm massaging my skull. "In a way that suggests your new witch is either very powerful, or very attentive to you."

"I want it to be the latter," I admit. "But I think it's more likely the former."

"Or a combination of both," Yorl suggests.

"I forgot I can always rely on you to be the stark realist," I tease, poking his wet nose lightly with one finger when my hand works free. "Yes, it's true. I'm in love with my witch."

Yorl mechanically undoes my other restraint, not a single twitch on his face.

"No applause, please," I add.

"Wasn't planning on it," he deadpans, offering a spare shift. "Do you want new clothes, or what?"

"Here I am talking about direly important things like *love*," I huff. "And all you want to talk about is which burlap sack would look best on me!"

"I doubt your love's going to appreciate it if you come back looking like that." He motions to my blood-smeared everything, and I sigh, grabbing the shift.

"You're right."

"I usually am."

Ignoring his infuriating confidence, I slip behind the throne to change.

"So," I start, pulling blood-soaked cotton over my head carefully. "How've you been? What've you eaten? How many other girls have you experimented on while I was gone?"

"You'd think a recent death experience would make you *less* chatty, not more." He sighs. "Come. We need to vacate the surgery."

I walk around the throne, now far drier and cleaner-looking. "Personally I'd call it a dungeon, but all right. You're the boss. Although apparently not enough of a boss. Do you always let the other polymaths in here push you around?"

"I'd like you to realize earning a kingsmedal whilst also bypassing initiate and going straight to adjutant is a feat no one has accomplished in the history of the Black Archives ever."

"Goodness! Both firsts in history, the two of us." I walk out with him, his silver robe swishing along the floor. "When will I get my results back?"

"They aren't yours to get back," Yorl says evenly.

"But you're going to tell me what they think about them."

"Obviously," he agrees. "Depending, of course, on how long you plan on staying here."

"As long as it takes to translate a book we stole from the High Witches," I say. "We think it'll tell us how to stop Varia and the Bone Tree."

Yorl's quiet, the white mercury lights of the hallway glittering in his large green eyes. "I hope you don't expect me to feel guilty."

My laugh bounces off the walls. "Nah. I'm done with guilt, too. We did what we had to. But say that enough times and it starts to sound like a terrible excuse, so I've started to tell myself 'what's done is done' instead. Convenient *and* catchy."

The comfortable quiet that fell between us all those times walking down to Evlorasin's arena falls now. He's not the type to talk unless excited about something, so when he starts, I know it's important.

"When I was helping Varia get the Bone Tree, I didn't anticipate I'd make Arathess's first nonhuman Heartless."

"I mean, I'm still human."

"Yes," he starts slowly. "But not entirely. You're also technically valkerax."

"Because of the blood promise, right?" I ask. He gives me a dull *obviously* stare, and I laugh. "Fine, sorry. Continue, master polymath."

And so he does, between sighs.

"I told you before—blood promises are like conversations for valkerax. They communicate thoughts, concepts, entire memories through ingesting one another's blood, given willingly."

"Right. But if a mortal ingests their blood, they die."

He nods. "But if you survive... We don't know what happens if a mortal survives. We didn't know. Until you."

"Six eyes, it turns out. And a weird connection to the Bone Tree." I smirk.

"A connection?" Yorl frowns.

"I can..." I pause. "*See* Varia. Well, *through* her. In my dreams. And she can see me. Any ideas what that might be?"

"Your guess is as good as mine in that regard. It may very well be the Bone Tree sensing the valkerax blood promise in you and tying you to itself." Yorl's sigh is practically thunderous. "I underestimated the power of the blood promise. I thought—because you were a Heartless—that your witch's magic would overturn the promise. Valkerax blood promises work because they remain in the blood—but a Heartless's body is constantly regenerated by magic. And by that, I mean you're not like a human."

"You don't say," I drawl.

"Mortal blood is very efficient." He ignores me. "And their bodies only replace it with fresh blood when blood loss occurs. Their heart pumps the new blood around. But as a Heartless, your blood is replenished by magic. That's how you survive—not through circulation, but through constant magic replenishment."

"So you thought the valkerax blood promise would be cycled

out of my veins eventually," I finish, and Yorl's sigh this time is pleased.

"You've gotten mildly smarter."

"And you've gotten slightly longer with your explanations," I tease.

He snorts, but I know him enough by now to know that's his version of laughter. The hall becomes familiar eventually, going thin and entirely lined with dozens of doors.

Yorl pauses before our door, looking over at me. "I'm…I have to confess. I'm nervous."

I cock my head. "What? Why?"

"Your friends are in here, aren't they?"

I pat his broad shoulder. "One of them's out here in the hall, too."

The flicker of his lashes against the gloom of the hall tells me everything I need to know—surprise. He's not one to be easily surprised, Yorl. He's like me. He knows things, and accounts for things, and predicts things ahead of time. To keep safe, to accomplish goals. We're both planners, schemers, and that's what I like best about him. Us. As I push the door open and Lucien bolts up from his chair and Malachite hefts off the wall and Fione grips her cane and stands, all their eyes fall on me, not him.

Lucien's over in two strides, taking my hands, glancing his way down my body as if studying me, his gaze heavy with onyx concern.

"Did they—"

"I managed to wheedle some painkillers out of them," I lilt. "So ease up on the worried look, okay? It doesn't suit Your Highness."

His laugh is small, but the kiss he leans into and gives me is anything but.

"I warned you about that title," he murmurs when we part.

"And I warned you about kissing girls," I whisper

conspiratorially back. "Who knows what's going to happen after this. I might even fall in *love* with you."

"Here we go again." Malachite rolls his eyes to the ceiling. On their way down they catch on Yorl. "Who's this?"

"Yorl," I pull myself out of the intimate spell of Lucien and motion to the celeon. "He's my friend. And, by some stroke of luck, he works here."

"Luck had nothing to do with it," Yorl snorts, then realizes everyone's looking at him. He makes a quick, polite bow. "Yorl Farspear-Ashwalker, Adjutant of the Black Archives. I was—" He shakes his mane. "I *am* the one who aided Varia in getting the Bone Tree."

"Ah!" Malachite muses. "I knew you looked familiar. You're the guy I helped catch the valkerax for."

"One and the same," Yorl agrees. "Thank you again for your aid."

"Psh." The beneather waves his hand. "That was nothing. I could capture valkerax in my sleep. With eleven other beneathers also sleeping," he adds.

Yorl goes stiff upon seeing Lucien, and I remember their flash of a confrontation, back before the Bone Tree was found. But this time, Lucien nods at him, and Yorl eases into a nod back.

"You're all right then, Zera?" Fione's frown crumples her heart-shaped face.

"Right as rain, Your Grace." I tap my cheek. "You can kiss me too, if you want."

Her expression lightens minutely. "No, thank you. I'm saving them for someone."

It goes unsaid, but it makes both of us smile. Varia. The Varia we'll get back when we translate the book. The Varia who's this much closer now that I've returned and given the Black Archives what they want.

Fione turns to Yorl, then, and puts on her best Vetrisian smile.

"It's a pleasure to meet you at last. I've heard much of you from Varia, and more from Zera. Both of them seemed to insist we'd get along."

"I have likewise heard of you." Yorl nods at her.

"Show 'im the white mercury dagger, Fi," I urge.

Yorl's eyebrows instantly shoot up. "A white mercury weapon—it can't be."

Fione, shier than I've seen her in months, pulls the dagger out and unsheathes it before Yorl. He leans in eagerly, whiskers twitching.

"It took a little reconfiguring of the mathematics," she admits sheepishly. "My uncle thought it was the metal's ratio to the mercury from which the common base had to be built, but in actuality, it was the gradual introduction of the ore compound through acid—"

"Through acidic methods," Yorl finishes for her, and as he looks up at her from the dagger, his eyes widen. "How did you realize that?"

"I had help," she assures him, a blush on her cheeks from all the attention.

"From whom? Who else would know? The smithing methods have never been recorded. Which means...you discovered it on your own. You're—" He pauses. "You're *incredible*."

"Oh." Fione makes a high, wavering laugh. "Well, I wouldn't go that far—"

I lean in and elbow her with a wicked grin. "I've never once heard him use the word 'incredible.' I didn't even think compliments were in his dictionary. Live it up."

Fione pauses, Yorl's eyes shining at her, and when she looks up this time, all the sheepish modesty is gone. Her face is set, ready.

"Will you help me, Sir Farspear-Ashwalker?"

"Just Yorl is fine," he hurriedly insists. "Help you with what,

Your Grace?"

She holds up the green-bound book in one hand, and our kingsmedal in the other. "This. Seven hundred pages of Old Vetrisian, some of it mixed with Qessen, and half of it near-illegible."

"We'll have to wait for the results of Zera's testing, but...yes. Gladly. It sounds a true challenge." Yorl laughs. Really *laughs*, a soft growl-purr under his breath. Fione looks equally pleased, eagerness beneath all her iron willpower. The celeon looks back at me, at Mal and Lucien and me, and nods.

"This may take a while. Let me show you to the beach."

21

THE LITTLE ROOM BY THE SEA

The island of the Black Archives—Rel'donas, Yorl calls it—is the most beautiful place I've ever seen. But I said that about Vetris once upon a time, didn't I? Maybe I'm just the sort of person to be easily impressed by shiny new places. Even taking that into consideration, Rel'donas does nothing *but* impress; Yorl leads us out through a door of the Archives that guards a staircase cut straight into the side of the black volcanic-rock mountain, zigzagging and switchbacking until it reaches a black sand beach at the very bottom, the emerald waves lapping at mollusk-eating birds with mind-bendingly long beaks and hordes of minuscule horseshoe crabs the color and texture of glossy pink confectionaries in a box. Thickets of mangroves guard the litmus between sea and sand, their roots like bark soldiers standing alert and waist-deep in gemlike water.

But it's the sound I like most.

No one tells you the ocean sings. They say it's there, and that it's big and dangerous and deep, but never that it has its own orchestra, constantly playing a soothing symphony as the waves scrape across the shallows and back again. It's almost like breathing, like the *world* of Arathess itself is breathing.

"It's—" I pucker my lips, my hands wet with cupped seawater. "It's salty!"

"Of course it's spiritsdamn salty!" Malachite shouts from his place stalwartly far away from the water's edge. "It's the ocean!

You were on a ship for like, three days! How'd ya miss that?"

"No one threw me overboard to taste it!" I shout. "That was *your* job!"

"Come in, Mal!" Lucien calls, his pants rolled up as he wades the shallows with me.

"So the two of you can pull me under and drown me?"

"With love!" I insist. "Drown you with *love*!"

"Ugh." He wrinkles his nose. "Pass."

Lucien shoots a sly look to me, and I to him.

"On the count of three?" the prince proposes.

"Absolutely," I agree.

"One, two, three—"

We dash out of the water and make a beeline for Malachite, and he tries to run to the safety of the tidepool rocks, but with Lucien holding his arms and me grabbing his weak spot ever so slightly (ears), we manage to drag him down the beach.

"You little—" He quickly pulls his sword off and throws it in the sand as the water approaches, desperately trying to do the same to his chainmail. "The salt's gonna ruin my armor—"

"And we've had quite enough of you ruining our fun!" I chide, helping him unhook his chainmail and tossing it in the sand. With his massive strength, he could fight us off anytime he wanted, ear-captured or not, and that's how I know he's all right with it. Secretly. Deep down. Where no one else can see.

With Mal shed of his metal, Lucien smirks at me in an unspoken plot as he cries, "Heave, ho!"

We crash into the water face-first, dragging Malachite down with us. Salt floods my ears, my nose, the ocean so much warmer with the sun on it. It's not bathwater, but it's close, and the sensation of the tide pulling and pushing is perhaps the closest my unremembering Heartless arse can come to recalling what being a child in a crib was like. Malachite squirms, and I let his ear go, Lucien releasing his arms, and we surface, the waves tossing us as playfully as we splash the beneather's face relentlessly the second he comes up.

"Stop!" Malachite snarls, eyes blinking rapidly with the assault. "Stop, stop it! I'll duel the both of you!"

"Revenge is sweet!" I tackle him from behind and smack my mouth. "And a little salty!"

Lucien stops splashing, and there's a moment where Malachite glares daggers into him, me hanging like a monkey on his back and grinning around his shoulder. Lucien's smirk lights up his handsome face as he dares to flick one last tiny bit of water onto Malachite with two fingers, and Malachite explodes, scrabbling for the nimble prince as he swims away. I'm too heavy to swim with, and Malachite claws for me.

"You flirty little shit! Get off me!"

My shrieking laughter echoes up the beach, Lucien's light taunts sending Malachite into a hilariously frothing rage as he tries to swim after the prince with my added weight. At some point I decide to let go and allow the boys to kill each other, Lucien's taunts turning to pleas and Malachite gloating as he gives the prince a terrible underwater noogie.

And I just…float. The sun beams in the blue sky, blue-green sea rising up to kiss it. The water in my ears mutes the world, covers it in a muffled, gentle blanket so that all I can hear is the sand swishing and the sound of the air in my body moving in and out. I feel so small, in such a big ocean. In such a big world. Vetris had been my everything for so long, and the forest before that. Always confined to cramped spaces, wasn't I? But I've seen more of Cavanos now than ever. More of the world than ever.

I remember on the ship Fione said something idly about saltwater being easier to float in, and she's right. Floating in the warmth of the ocean is nothing like trying to float in the bone-chillingly cold rivers of a Cavanos forest. The spring Lucien and I bathed in was beautiful, certainly, but the ocean has its own charm. I start to think, as my conniving brain is wont to do. If I could live anywhere, if at the end of all this death and destruction I could start over like I'd always wanted to, in a shack somewhere no one knows me, it would be on the ocean. Somewhere close to the ocean. I'd adore this view every day. To fall asleep to the sound of the waves, and wake up to the sound of the waves, to bathe in sun and sand and a sound that drowns out every worry—that's my new idea of perfection.

The blue sky—Evlorasin's up there somewhere.

Varia's out there somewhere. Killing people. Causing suffering. Suffering herself.

The tide brings a soft something against the top of my floating head, and I look up. Dark, wet hair, a proud chin.

"Lucien," I say, staying still. His smile is soft as he puts his hands beneath my back, holding me as I float and he stands, acting as a rock, a dock, an anchor to the world. *My* anchor. I don't know where Malachite's gone—probably to the beach to dry off like a disgruntled puppy. But really, I don't need to know. All that exists now is Lucien's comforting presence, the sweet warmth of the water's embrace and his hands on my back. I can feel my hair floating all around my head like a halo, flickers of gold catching in the sun and in his dark hawk eyes.

My own voice sounds muffled through my submerged ears as I ask quietly, "What will we do? When it's over?"

"A question for the ages." There's a beat, and then Lucien smiles down at me. "Eat? What's the human food you like most?"

"Cinnamon sweetrounds," I answer immediately.

"Then the lady will have a plate of them," he asserts, then pauses. "We could always get married."

"After all that fuss I went through being a Spring Bride?" I huff. "Absolutely not. We can do a few hundred years of trial runs, first."

"I might not be around for all of it." He laughs. My smile pulls at my lips, my eyes.

"And with any luck, neither will I," I say.

It's more than just a dry joke. It means, after it's over, I'll be human. No matter what, once Varia and the valkerax are stopped, I'll become human. My life with Lucien after this, all human. All mortal. All pain and slow healing and wrinkles and old age and sagging. And I'm dying for every bit of it. Repeatedly. Until our goal can be achieved.

Lucien seems to always know when I'm getting too lost in my own unheart. I don't know who taught him, or if he just knows me by now—my tells, my expressions. The price of showing him my best and worst moments, I suppose. He scoops me out of the water easily, arms straining but strong, and smiles down at me.

"Busy thinking, are you?" he asks lightly. My face heats, unbearably hot despite the water.

"Trying to," I sniff. "But a certain someone with his hands on my thighs is making it very difficult."

He leans in, dark hair dripping into his eyes, dropping cool water on my burning face as his lips skim mine.

"Shall I make it more so?" he murmurs.

"And why would you want to do that?" I ask innocently.

"Because you're gorgeous, you silly thing."

His fingers tighten into my legs, pressing the lush skin there like feather pillows under strain and all I can think about is a bed, with him in it, with me in it, and I give in first, for once. He tastes like salt, like honey and bread, and a flick of my tongue on his and the moment changes. His eyes search mine, and I search his face, looking for permission.

We give it to each other with wordless smirks.

And then I'm squirming out of his arms and both of us are racing for the sand, for our shoes, for the steps, Malachite calling after us but both of us ignoring it, ignoring everything but peering into each volcanic rock room of the Archives' long hall looking for somewhere safe, somewhere just for us. A perfect room is the one with a bed— a cot, really—and a window overlooking the sea. When Lucien shuts the door, all our frantic energy suddenly closes in, solidifies, and in the quiet, the prince just stares at me, and me at him.

New God's eye—he's beautiful. He's grown, somehow, from the boy I first met at the Spring Welcoming. It hasn't been long, but experience has changed him. Magic has changed him. Or maybe it's just my unheart beating for him that makes him look so devastatingly perfect. The edges of his sharp jaw, the curve of his proud nose, the deep dips of his thick brows as he looks back at me curiously, questioningly. The bright sunlight catches every raven part of him—his hair, his eyes somehow both darker and brighter than the volcanic rock of the room. The outline of him calls out to me from beneath his clothes. A tense knot vibrates in my chest, in the hollows of it, every hair standing on end as I reach up and, shaking but determined, pull my collar open.

It's just a little skin. Barely anything, really. It's a pallid move considering all the seduction techniques in the world. But I can smell myself—salt and cotton coming off my throat—and maybe he smells it too, or maybe it's the sight of me doing it, because he's stock-still one moment and then striding across the room in the next, pulling me in to him and kissing every exposed bit of flesh. Hard. Hard in a way I know will leave marks, and at the thought, the vibrating knot inside me suddenly feels like it unfurls, reaching its buzzing tendrils into my bloodstream at the idea of me welcoming his bruises on me.

A slow smile overtakes me. He's been like this since he met me, hasn't he? Wanting me.

wanting your body and nothing more.

I waver. Like he can hear it, feel it moving inside me, Lucien makes a snarl and a flood of magic pulses into me, so torrential and huge I can feel it *move*, spread rapidly, and it dulls the hunger to an insignificant buzz like a hand over a mouth.

"No more," the prince pants. "No more hunger. You are not the hunger's. You are yours. And you are *mine*."

Of all the ways I've died, I've never been struck by lightning. But this is how it must feel—this hot, sweet relief lancing through my spine down to my softness, to the place between my thighs. We've kissed before, certainly, but the hunger I kiss him with now is all mine, all blazing, all promises and gratitude and love.

"Zera." He pulls away suddenly, panting and putting his forehead to mine. "You— Please—"

He can't even speak anymore. I want him. I *can* want him now, and the feeling is like flying. Like throwing off something incredibly heavy. I can take what I want, for myself. For my own happiness. And so it's my turn to kiss his neck, beneath his ear, gently moving up to the shell of it and whispering, "All you had to do was ask nicely."

The soft noise he makes at my words, the sudden breath he sucks in—it's like music. The best music I've ever heard, all the finest quartets in Vetris paling to nothing in comparison. I've plucked a string in him and he sings and I do it again with a whisper, the better to hear him with.

"I'm yours."

It's a blur. It's a blur of very pointed moments, sensations—his mouth on me everywhere, so furiously hot and eager; his hardness against my hand; our mouths in and out of each other's, dipping and scraping like two valkerax in death dives. The smell of his skin, no, *our* skin. This belongs to us. To me and no one else. Not the hunger. Not Cavanos. Not the war waiting outside, not the world. There's that moment, *that moment*, and we're connected, and I understand what it truly means to have a heart, *finally,* when we're moving together as one, the sea breeze and the silly little cot and the two of us making it happen, together, making this moment in time all our own.

Forever.

22
BLOOD AND PROMISES

There's always this strange unspoken opinion that floats around Cavanosian society, and it's that one's first time changes a girl. That lying with a loved one in the carnal sense is transformative, somehow. I wish I could report that this was accurate, but alas—it barely changed me at all. It really just made me more, well, *me*.

"Is it *hard* to eat?" Malachite drawls at dinner, a fish-and-rice affair of the Black Archives' mess hall. "With a permanent shit-eating grin on your face?"

I grin even wider and bat my eyelashes at him across the table. "I wouldn't know."

Malachite rolls his eyes and looks at Lucien. "You've created a monster."

"I can hardly claim to take credit." Lucien smiles contentedly into his water glass. "When she's worked so hard on it herself."

His black-glass eyes catch mine over the candlelight, knowing and full of himself and I can't stand it one second more and neither can he, apparently, because we both stand and dump our trays with some muttered excuse to Malachite. The halls that were buzzing an hour ago are now empty, everyone at dinner, but an unfortunate (or should I say fortunate?) silver-robed polymath rounds the corner and catches Lucien pressing me against the wall. Nothing lewd, of course. Just simple kisses. All over my body.

I watch the polymath round the hall corner, then murmur

breathlessly down at Lucien, who's currently thoroughly engaged with my collarbone.

"We could—we could find a room, you know. A broom closet, even."

He rumbles his assent against my skin. "Forgive me my impatience."

"Forgiven," I tease, pulling him by the hand. "But not forgotten."

There's a giddy urgency to it all this time. And the next. And the next after that. The novels in Nightsinger's library never spoke of the intricacies of it—the way you learn someone's body, freckle by freckle and line by line and scent by scent. They never spoke of how different and yet the same people are in their love, in their wants and needs and lusts. The novels never warned me of the sheer glow, the incredible feeling of an empty mind and a full heart.

We've been forbidden to each other for so long that being together feels like a dream. We relish in each and every moment, and a day passes like this, wrapped in kissing and holding and just lying, just being with each other. Someone will find us if they need us, but we try so hard to pretend the world doesn't exist for just this short time. And it works. He knows exactly how to touch me, and where, and when, and part of me faintly realizes that's probably his handy little skinreading ability. Used for good this time. Oh so good.

But reality always finds a way in. It needles at first, piercing tiny holes in our joy through our conversations afterward—me tracing the gorgeous planes of his stomach and listening to him worry. About Vetris, about Varia, about the war, about everything.

And then, it punctures with an arrow.

I'm brushing the dark hair off his neck, kissing a line down his spine when I reach for his hand. The unmoving one. I miss, but my eyes are on his back, so it's understandable. I flounder around for his hand again, feeling for it everywhere, but it's not there. My fingers follow the line of his arm, his elbow, knowing it will lead me to his hand. Because it has to.

Except it *doesn't*.

I feel down to his wrist, but that's it. There's nothing after that. Just air. I recoil at the smooth stub, the lack of fingers and palm and—and *anything*. I thought he—I thought it was there! It was, wasn't it? It didn't work, but it *was* there...

"Y-You—" I stammer. Lucien straightens instantly on the cot, his expression taut as he looks up at me. With one dark eye. The other socket is empty, perfectly smooth just like the stub where his hand should be. Not wound-smooth, not scar-tissue smooth. Just...*smooth*. Like the skin's been unnaturally sanded down to an inhumanly perfect flatness.

"Godsdamnit," Lucien breathes softly. He tilts his head to shade his missing eye with his bangs, cradling his missing hand with his other. "I didn't want you to see this."

"I thought they—they just stopped working." My voice cracks. "But have you been hiding this? The whole time?" I swallow nails. "Were they *always* gone?"

The prince won't look at me, his one eye thin and entirely focused on the far wall.

"Lucien, please," I beg, reaching for his other hand and bringing it to my unheart. "Please talk to me."

He swallows too, our throats mirror images, mirror-bruised with the ghosts of lingering kisses, of our love, and he nods slowly.

"Yes. I did the magic. Overdid it. And they just...disappeared. But I knew if you saw that, you'd never tolerate me using magic again."

"You hid it," I finish for him. He nods again, a flinch to it this time.

"Illusion spells are difficult. But they're much easier if you're filling in the natural gaps of appearance, rather than altering it to something completely different." He pauses. "It doesn't take much magical effort, is what I'm saying. So don't worry."

"I'm not," I blurt, and his wounded look turns into a sardonic one for a moment. "Okay. So maybe I am worrying. But gracefully, and with a shit ton of poise."

"Varia did the same thing," he continues. "Before she went missing all those years ago, she used a spell to kill her guards and make it look like a Heartless attack. But it was beyond her skill at the time. We found only a few parts: her leg, two index fingers. But when I met her again, she was missing far more fingers. No doubt they'd been—"

"*Eaten*," I repeat, pressing down the rising panic. Lucien nods, the sunrise coming through the little window painting his profile in rainbow translucence.

"I felt it. When I met the High Witches. They willingly offer their bodies to be consumed by the Glass Tree. To power it. But if any witch attempts to use a spell beyond their control at the time, the Tree will consume them, too."

"As punishment?" I ask.

"No." He shakes his head. "The feeling I got when I used the spells was more like…*repayment*. Like I owed the Glass Tree something for reaching too far. Like my reaching hurt it, and so it took from me to stem the wound. It felt as if it was making some kind of exact equilibrium."

"But the Tree of Souls gives you your magic, right?" I say. "Not the Glass Tree. The Glass Tree is only for Heartless. So why would the Glass Tree consume you?"

He shrugs. "Perhaps when the Tree of Souls was split, the Glass Tree became the arbiter of the magic flow on Arathess. Or maybe it's simply how magic works; I don't know. I'm not the one translating the book with all the potential answers right now."

There's a soft quiet. And then I reach my breaking point.

"You won't do this again," I say. "You won't use magic you

get consumed for."

Lucien doesn't say anything, and that sets my unheart on fire even more.

"Right?" I press. *"Right?"*

"I don't know what you want me to say, Zera." He sighs. "You chose to use your Heartlessness to fight her. I choose to use my magic. All of my magic, if it comes to that."

Every inch of my skin feels as if it shrivels at once. "No. No, not all of it. You can't. I'm not going to lose you."

His dark eye seems so distant as he moves to stare out the window. He suddenly feels a million miles away, like a mirage through a heavy fog I can't navigate.

"I've realized, lately, that you may have to."

"But—" I leap up. "All our plans! You're going to change Vetris, right? Cavanos? We're going to rebuild together what it means to lead your country. I said I'd help you. I *want* to help you." I scrabble for his other hand, but it feels cold as I press it to my cheek. "I can't help you with it if you...if you aren't here anymore."

He finally looks down at me, his smile wan. "I know. I want to be here, after it's over. You know I do. I want to be here with you. But she's my sister, Zera. Family. Perhaps the only family I have left. I can't let her destroy herself like this, not for one second more. If it comes to it, I'll use all of myself to save her."

"It won't come to that." I stick my chin out.

His laugh is gentle, sad in the sunrise. "You're so stubborn."

I crawl onto the cot again, shivering. There's a moment where I'm afraid to approach him. Afraid to get closer, only to lose him.

he will leave you, like everyone else.

I squeeze my eyes shut and force my body to move, to curl up on his lap and hold him down, hold him here with my weight, with my everything. My murmur is small, unsure, fractured. "So are you, Your Highness."

I say it because I want him to kiss me. And he knows. I feel a gentle hand lifting my chin, and the short, salt-scented curtain of his hair envelops my face, his lips on mine like a goodbye and the sunrise bathing both of us in its weak, fragile pearl light and I make a decision like a hammer stroke, then and there.

It won't come to that.

That night isn't an easy one. Even with Lucien at my side, I can't sleep at all. I slip out of bed, careful not to wake him. He needs all the rest he can get for the...*everything*. Everything ahead of us. The fight. The fall. And the rise, after.

The halls of the Black Archives are patrolled by the matronics at night, but the smaller halls where they can't fit have night watch polymaths, their silver robes softly illuminated by the handheld white mercury lamps they carry. Word of newcomers carries fast in an enclave dedicated to knowledge, and they all nod at me as I pass—well aware of who I am, of what I am. It's almost strange, to be treated like nothing special. Like a non-threat, when Vetris treated me as everything but. Breych, this place. Only recently have I learned Arathess is much bigger than its hate for Heartless.

The cool stone floor feels good on my bare feet, and the windows display the midnight ocean like a proudly sparkling black jewel. Bit by bit, I can feel my body settling even as my mind buzzes—Varia's out there still. The stars in the sky look less beautiful and more like spears pointed dead at all the world.

Dead.

All of them.

All of them, if we don't do something.

Windonhigh, Helkyris. Other continents. Everyone else is too busy protecting their own. But our own is us—one another. Fione, Malachite, Lucien, and me. Yorl. Varia, too. She's one of us, no matter what she's done. She's in over her head. She needs us.

All of us, protecting one another in our own ways.

If the world won't fight, we will.

Out of the corner of my eye, I catch a flash of ochre tail rounding a corridor. But...the only celeon I've seen here is Yorl. And that color, it's definitely his. But why is he up? Shouldn't he be where we left him—studying the book with Fione? Is he resting, maybe?

"Yorl!" I call out, trotting after him. "Wait up!"

I round the corner he disappeared behind, but there's nothing. No one, as far as I can see down it. I do a pivot, catching another flash of ochre to the right.

"Hey, Yorl!" I shout. "Seriously, slow down!"

My words echo hollowly about the stone, but I lunge around the corner this time, determined to catch up with him. My burst of speed is cut short as the right hall widens into a massive, polished balcony of volcanic glass. It overlooks the ocean, the long stretch of it disappearing at the moonless horizon: pitch-black on pitch-black, streaked with silver starlight.

Except in the very center is a tall streak of yellow fur with vermillion patches. Yorl. No—not him. Too tall to be him. Too bent-backed. Whiskers too droopy with age, tail silvered on the very end like an old man going white. Dewclaws too long and hard to be young.

The celeon turns and smiles at me, voice a rumbling purr.

"Ah. Zera. We meet at last."

Green eyes, a broad muzzle, the same coloring. It has to be Yorl. But it's not. It's more like an elderly version of him. It might just be the starlight, or the reflection of the white mercury lamps off the black-glass balcony, but I swear the celeon's outline shivers like water. Like hot gas. Like he's not all...*real.* He seems to follow my thoughts and looks down at his own body, then back up at me with a wry, white-whisker smile.

"I see you've noticed my curious state. You're the first one—the first mortal to notice me at all. And that's a comfort, in its own way."

"Who—" I stop myself. "There's no way! Are you Yorl's—"

"Where are my manners?" He cuts in smoothly. "I am Muro Farspear-Ashwalker." He motions with his paw to the balcony railing. "Please. Join me."

"You're supposed to be—"

"Dead?" He laughs with all his yellowed fangs. "Yes. But then again, so are you, are you not?"

Muro—or the ghost of him, I can't decide—turns to face me head on, the shimmering near obscuring him. But it can't obscure his face, every clear whisker and bristle and old scar between the fur. It can't obscure the way his emerald green eyes replicate twice down his face, and then twice again, three eyes on either side of his long, proud, lionlike nose.

Six eyes.

My brain spins, but he just laughs softly. "We seem to have the same ailment."

He looks like me when I turn into the monster. When I Weep to control it. Six eyes. But that's like...a *valkerax*. Did he...

"You..." I gulp, stepping closer to see him better. "Wait, how did you get a—" I stop, mulling over the strangeness. "Blood promise?"

Muro's smile is more approving than Yorl's. "A blood promise. Correct."

"*How?*"

"The same way you did: I befriended a valkerax. Not as effectively as you did, I'll admit. You, it seems, were much more skilled at it. You could simply talk! I, on the other hand, had to spend years in the Dark Below watching, baiting, cajoling, getting bitten."

"Hey!" I protest. "I got bit, too."

Muro's laugh is louder this time, so loud it scares a frog

from a nearby tree.

"That you did. Many times. And terribly."

My mind churns. How does he know that?

"I've been watching," he admits. "Not you, though you are very interesting. Yorl. I've been watching over him. I saw it all—his journey to replicate my research, the way he helped Varia and worked with you and that valkerax."

"Wait, you were watching us that whole time?" I swallow. "Are you...*dead*? Yorl said you were. And if you've drank a blood promise, then—"

"Yes," he agrees, but his expression never changes from its mildly pleased state. "I died an old man, when Yorl was young. My age finally caught me in some sickness. But I'd held on to the blood promise my valkerax friend gave me all those years ago, during my research. And in the name of polymathematics, and with little life left, I took it."

Muro motions down to his finely silvered fur. "It wasn't a blood promise given under sanity, so it wasn't as effective as yours. But it was effective enough."

I frown. "You're worse than Yorl! Haven't either of you ever heard of the expression *curiosity killed the cat*?"

At this, Muro's laughter echoed. "That it does. Quite literally. He takes after me so fiercely, the silly thing."

Muro. This is *Muro Farspear-Ashwalker*, the brightest celeon polymath to ever live. Or die. Lucien's parents called on him years ago to try to heal Varia's habitual nightmares of the Bone Tree. His research helped make the white mercury blades during the Sunless War. He was the one who brought the Hymn of the Forest to Gavik's attention, an act that kickstarted Gavik's vendetta against Varia, trying so hard to kill her before she could get the Bone Tree and destroy the kingdom.

With a cold chill in my spine, I realize she succeeded in that one.

And Muro knew. He knew she was chosen by the Bone Tree. He knew about valkerax, more about them than anyone. I walk up to the balcony tentatively, my frame dwarfed by Muro's sheer height. Even old, he's tall as sin. Was. I still can't decide if this is some sleepwalking dream of mine or not, but the way Muro's outline shivers each time he blinks makes me think it has to be.

"Is this…a dream?" I ask.

The celeon thinks hard on this, and then holds his paw up lightly. "I'm not sure. Perhaps, and perhaps not. I know very little and can explain even less. Time is a fickle thing, in my state."

"How can I see you, if you're dead?" I blurt.

"Because of our blood promise—we are connected. A blood promise is a conversation, forever. Surely Yorl told you that. The Tree of Souls connects us all, and the valkerax understand this best."

I wrinkle my nose. "I can see who Yorl got the 'talk frustratingly cryptically' trait from."

"Indeed." Muro chuckles, tail thrashing. "He's a good boy, and a strong one. Even stronger now, in no small part because of meeting you. I thank you for that."

"I didn't—"

"Please," he interrupts kindly. "Spare me the modesty. I've seen enough of it from you for a lifetime. Or a deathtime."

I knit my lips, and it twists into a smile. "Okay. You got me."

"For a while, yes," he agrees mysteriously. We watch the sea together for a second, and then, "Do you know what a soul is, Zera?"

"Uh." I glance at him. "You? Shimmery, kind of here, kind of not?"

"Possibly. I'm not sure what a soul is, myself. Here in Arathess, we talk of the 'afterlife,' but rarely do we speak of what part of us goes there. Is it our bodies? Our minds? Or something else? Our feelings, our essence, our memories, a great mishmash of our lived experiences—it could be any of these, or all of them."

The ocean laps below us, the sound soothing against his cryptic words.

"I may not know what a soul *is,* Zera, but I may be able to tell you *where* they are. In humans, their soul resides in their heart. In valkerax, it is in the blood—the marrow that makes blood."

"Their...bones," I say slowly. "The marrow in the bones?"

He nods. "It's why the Bone Tree is made of their bones, and why the Glass Tree must have a sliver of itself touching a human heart for it to create Heartless. They are Trees made to control two different creatures, and the only way that is done is by the soul."

I blink, reeling. "How do you know all that?"

"When you look past all the labyrinthine twists and turns here"—Muro smiles—"there's really much to be learned on the other side."

I don't get it. I don't get it, but he smells like Yorl—copper and sun-warmed fur—and that's the only clue this might not actually be a dream.

"The Tree of Souls," Muro starts patiently, "is a special creature. It is alive, as you or I. Well, you." He smirks. "Regardless, it is a creature. It, too, has a soul. And it gave that to us, at the very beginning of Arathess. It gives that to us every day—but only some of us are able to grasp it, hold on to that great gift."

He tilts his maned face over to me, six eyes gleaming. "I'm speaking, of course, of witches. Of magic."

"Magic," I breathe. "Are you saying—magic is the Tree of Souls'...*soul?*"

He chuckles. "Perhaps I went too quickly in too short a time. You'll understand for yourself, someday, when you join me here. But you've already taken the first steps to understanding, haven't you?"

I knit my brows at him, confused.

"The dreams," he clarifies. "Of the Tree."

"I mean, sure. I've had a dream about the Trees. The two tree rosaries," I say slowly. "But I haven't had any grand, spontaneous moment of understanding, nothing like you're talking about—"

"Truly? No feeling of sureness in you? No strange feeling that seems like it comes from outside of you, but one that is so sure of itself regardless?"

I freeze, then mutter, "That feeling of wrongness, like if I didn't put the trees together—"

"—something terrible would happen," he finishes for me, leaving a beat for digestion. "The Trees communicate through dreams. The Glass Tree speaks to witches. The Bone Tree spoke to Varia in her dreams. But when you arrived in Vetris, it was neither the Bone Tree nor the Glass Tree that spoke to you. It was their mother, and their true self. The origin. The Tree of Souls spoke to you."

I remember every dream-moment painfully—the tree covered in stained glass crying out in pain, in loneliness, turning the glass on me when I got too close. *That* was the Tree of Souls? The origin of all magic on Arathess? The tree Fione and Lucien looked so wary talking about on the ship?

"Why me?" I instantly demand. Muro's chuckle is despairing this time.

"I cannot do much more than guess—it may have known. The Tree of Souls is connected to us all, and perhaps it knew what you would become."

"Beautiful?" I try. "Smart? Stylish?"

"It knew you would be touched by both the Glass Tree and the Bone Tree."

"So is Varia," I argue. He nods.

"True. But she is only witch. You are Heartless and valkerax, all at once. She has felt the Bone Tree's pain but not the Glass Tree's. She has not felt the pain of both the Trees as you have. You have felt the Tree of Souls' pain as no one else in the world has."

I watch him tilt his muzzle up to look at the stars, and he shimmers so violently, the ochre of his body almost entirely melts into the black.

"Ah. Time is so fickle." He pivots to me, that eternal smile in place. "I will see you again, Zera, someday."

"Wait—" I reach out for him, but my hand passes through him like air, my fingers making the shimmer worse. "There are a million things I want to—"

"Tell Yorl I am proud of him, would you?" he interrupts, soft and yet determined.

I catch his emerald eyes, all six of them gentle, and I nod. "I will."

And then I blink, and he's gone. No increments, no fragments. Just there and then gone. But somehow, as I trace my steps back to the cool bed and Lucien's arms, I know he's not really gone at all. It's the blood in me, the promise in me. It's a feeling. A knowing.

I know I'll see him again.

I'm tempted to write off Muro's appearance as a dream. Wipe it away clean as a passing fancy, as my mind trying to explain everything to me neatly, wrapped up in a bow. As a convenient dream. I want to forget, and snuggle deeper into Lucien's embrace in the morning. But Muro's words linger, insisting realness into my blood, staring back at me as my dusty feet from walking the halls late at night.

It's a feeling, deep in my unheart. My soul.

I just...*understand* it was real.

Lucien tries to ask me about it, but I have no words for it, offering him my wrist limply. He holds it, and the air thickens with the hum of magic as he skinreads me. He can see what I've seen easily—it's only thought-reading that's truly difficult, or so he's said. And I trust him. I trust him enough to let him see, now, and he frowns.

"Who was that? It looked like—"

"Yorl?" I offer. "Yeah. I think it was Muro, his grandfather. Like, his ghost or something. Or his...soul. Is that even possible? With magic?"

Lucien looks as lost as I feel. "Perhaps. I know so little, compared to any other witchblood my age. But why would he appear to you now?"

"I don't think he chose to." I frown. "It just...happened. He said I could see him because of our blood promise."

"Well then." The prince nods. "That's Yorl's territory, isn't it?"

My murky thoughts carry over into the morning meal in the mess hall. The polymaths are poring over some shoddy pieces of paper, all of them strangely identical in their black ink letters. A "printing," I hear one of them call it, though I have no idea what that means. As far as I can gather, it carries news, because the polymaths won't stop whispering among themselves.

"Helkyris has fallen—"

"Naturally. If their western armada falls, Helkyris falls. That's a given—"

"If the armada succumbed to the flying valkerax, then Avel's spear-runners have no chance."

"The Mist Continent is done for. The valkerax will move on to the Star Continent next, no doubt—it's the closest."

"Where are the beneathers at a time like this? Surely they're not sitting on their thumbs in the Dark Below letting all this happen—"

"With the political anarchy they have no one to rendezvous with above—not Cavanos, not Helkyris. It takes more time than you'd think to deploy their forces up from the Dark Below, and their ancestral bureaucracy ensures a mired response to say the least—"

At our table, Malachite throws a very effective glare at the polymaths. They shut their mouths near instantly at his dangerous eyes, going back to their porridge and hushed discussions of whatever experiments they're working on.

"I hate it here," the beneather scoffs. "All this sun, and nasty sand. This whole place is basically one big barn for people who wanna act like they know everything." He looks at me and shoves a scabbard across the table. "Here. I got a polymath to put it together."

I quirk a brow up at him, the hilt so familiar, the grooves of it—

"You didn't," I breathe, pulling the blade out. Father's blade, or the replica of it, the handle still the original but the blade remade by Lucien. Mal got the pieces I'd been carrying around for so long put back together. My heart swells at the feeling of it in my palm.

"I did." Malachite grunts. "No mushy thanks needed."

I immediately jump up from the table and pull him into a hug across it. "Thank you! Malachite, thank you so much."

"What did I just say?" the beneather squawks awkwardly, freeing himself from my grip and sitting back down with the biggest flush on his cheeks. "No fuckin' thanks. Just use it to defend Luc. That's all I ask."

I throw a smile at Lucien, and then back at Mal. "Understood."

"When is Fione gonna be done, anyway?" The beneather tries to quickly change the subject. "I keep checking on 'em, but they just tell me to stop bothering them."

"We should check on them together, then," Lucien agrees. "Knowing Fione, she's probably conveniently forgotten to eat or sleep this entire time."

"Yorl's the exact same," I sigh. I slip one last liver in my mouth and stand, picking up the clay jar of honey tea on the table. "Right. Operation Rescue the Bookworms, begins!"

Malachite makes a facetious salute and heads the charge,

Lucien walking beside me. His hand is back, and his eye, and while I'm numbed by the illusion of normalcy, knowing he's using magic to make them seem there churns my guts. He doesn't want Malachite to know, for anyone to know but me. And I can keep a secret—I'm just not sure I *want* to.

I watch the beneather's broad chainmail back walking ahead of me. Malachite's devoted his whole life to protecting Lucien. He's tortured people, killed people for him. He deserves to know about Lucien's state more than anyone. Malachite, of all people, would unite with me if I told him Lucien's self-sacrificing strategy. I'd feel better having someone on my side, someone other than me guard-dogging Lucien's willingness to throw himself away for his sister.

If Lucien dies, what will Malachite do?

What will *any* of us do?

I don't want to think about it. I can't. It yawns like an open valkerax mouth, thousands of teeth and all of them promising mind-bending pain. Not right now. I raise my head and grip the warm clay jar for any shred of comfort as I walk.

Thankfully, Malachite is much better at navigating tight, dark corridors than we are. He leads us to the same door we left Yorl and Fione in yesterday, and knocks his pale knuckles against the wood. The sounds echoes, and we wait anxiously for one beat, two, before the door creaks open. One periwinkle-blue eye peers out from the dimness inside, the skin around it ashen. Fione.

"Oh," she croaks, voice hoarse. "It's you."

"Pardon the insult, Your Grace," I push into the room before she can shut us out. "But you look like shit. How about some warm tea?"

I take one step forward, my shoes crinkling paper. It's so dim, but I squint to see the floor entirely covered in parchment—some crumpled, some flat, layered on top of each other like thousands of nonsense-scribbled cream leaves. They've closed the shutters, blocking out the daytime light so that a single white mercury lamp on the table is the only thing struggling to illuminate the room. And the table—Yorl's bent over it, yellow mane peeking out from behind towering piles of books and scrolls, the sunny color the one bright thing in the pale-washed room.

His ears are drooping, tail not so much as twitching—a clear sign he's tired. I bite my tongue to stop from bombarding him with the fact I saw his beloved grandfather roaming around last night. Not now. Not when he looks so haggard.

"Gods," Lucien breathes into his sleeve. "It smells terrible in here."

"Acid-wash," Fione blinks, gratefully gulping the bowl of tea I pour her. "To remove the lacquer decomp on the book's untreated pages. We couldn't see the letters through the stains." She looks at Lucien. "The phrases you gave me on the ship helped immensely, by the way. Thank you."

"Anytime." The prince tries a smile. "Zera's right, though. You look exhausted."

"Almost done," she insists with as few words as possible and shoves the bowl back at me before walking to the table and sitting down again. She looks over at Yorl. "The four-point remedy?"

"Close," he says back, voice even rougher than usual. "Need a second adjudicator on the sentence structure." I pour another bowl of tea and offer it over his shoulder, but he waves it off. "No. Can't risk the papers getting wet."

"Oh, c'mon. One little drop won't hurt 'em," I insist. "But one drop could do wonders for you, Sir Large Brain."

He glares up at me with emerald slits, then down at my boots. Those are Muro's eyes, through and through. No wonder everyone can tell he's Farspear-Ashwalker by just looking at him.

"Move. You're standing on Willem dal-Braal's verb-transfer theorem."

"Well, Willem dal-Braal will have to wait for a bit, then, won't he?" I shove the tea bowl under his broad nose. "Go on. The price for me moving is three sips."

Yorl's glower is far worse than any valkerax's. His ears lay flat as he snatches the bowl with his claws and barely puts his muzzle to it.

"Big sips, mind you," I singsong.

He makes a snarl and chugs, shoving the empty bowl back at me. "Begone, you irritating mother hen."

"He's proud of you, you know."

His eyes snap up to mine, confusion there for just a moment before he realizes who I must mean. His grandfather. *Message sent, Muro.*

I smile cheerily and hop off the parchment. Yorl unfreezes and shakes his head, deciding I'm talking nonsense again. He leans over in his seat to scoop the paper up, comparing it to the book page under his paw and muttering quietly to himself. I shoot an exasperated eye roll at Lucien, and he smiles with the bare corner of his lips back at me.

"So what's our time estimate for some answers? Because I'm pretty done with this place." Malachite sits at the only other open chair at the study table, managing to prop his boots on the paper-strewn surface for just a half second before Fione instantly raps her cane against his shoes and he lowers his feet back down.

"You can't rush this process," the archduchess says wearily, and it's then I notice both her and Yorl's voices are more even than I'd like. Even in a way that shows no enthusiasm. At first I chalked it up to them being exhausted, but the lack of a single inflection in their tone starts to worry me. Yorl looks like he's far along in the book, almost done with it. The fact they got so far in such a huge book in only two days is mind-blowing. Then again, they *are* the two smartest mortals I know.

But that means it's almost over.

The ultimatum is almost here.

The hairs on my arm stand up straight, hot with nerves. Whatever they've found thus far probably hasn't been good news—or they'd be way more chipper. Fione especially. I send her a meaningful asking glance, but she won't meet my eyes. Another bad sign.

"You're in here, you know." Yorl looks at me and waves his paw at the green-bound book.

"Little old me?" I blink.

"*At the end of the world, there will be empty-stomached wolves,*" he recites. "Didn't Evlorasin say your name was Starving Wolf?"

"The High Witches said something like that, too," Malachite grunts. "When they questioned her."

"'Questioned.'" I make air quotes. "It was more like one of your torture interrogations."

"You don't even know what those are like," Malachite drawls, and then adds, "yet. There's still time."

"This all certainly feels like the end of the world," Lucien murmurs. "Helkyris has fallen. Cavanos is..." His voice catches, but he straightens. "Avel will be next. And then the rest of the world after that."

"Someone will stop it," Malachite assures him.

"And that someone is us," Fione asserts, exhausted voice unfurling a little stronger.

"Surely the beneathers are mobilizing." Yorl looks at Malachite, and he nods, long white ears bobbing.

"Definitely."

"But they're mobilizing to kill the valkerax," I interrupt. "Not the source. Not the Bone Tree. They're gonna throw themselves at everything but the root of the problem."

"Literally." Lucien makes a pallid grin.

"Literally," Fione brushes past the joke and agrees. "Because as far as we've found from the book, our best bet is something called the First Root."

"What is it?" I ask.

She motions to Yorl. "He's finding out, right now."

"Then we wait." Lucien moves to me, taking my hand in his and stroking his thumb over mine. There are moments when two people share a look, and then there are the times when everyone in the room shares a look, and it ripples through us now. Red eyes, periwinkle eyes, green eyes, black eyes, and my pale gray-blue ones. An unspoken hope, passing among all of us.

Malachite settles against a far wall, chin down in his armored collar, the same pose I always saw him with in Vetris: his intimidating waiting pose. Fione sits across from Yorl sipping more tea, her bowl ever so slightly shaking as her fingers do. Nervous. How could she not be? The fate of her beloved depends on this last bit. The fate of the world, maybe, depends on it.

Lucien and I sink against the wall, sitting with each other and against each other, our hands intertwined tightly. It's so quiet, so dim, a moment suspended in time. I wonder if the history books will talk about this someday. If we succeed, if we destroy the Bone Tree or the Glass Tree or both and change the world, will the books talk about this still, gray moment—the moment before everything changed? No. They'll talk about everything else—the battles, the struggles, the deaths, the rise and fall of kingdoms. But not this. This will be lost to history.

This belongs only to the five of us.

Somewhere along the way as we wait and worry and wait, my head falls on Lucien's broad shoulder, and, exhausted by thought, the embrace of sleep pulls me under.

23
BETRAYAL
LIKE DEATH

I know what this cold, salted darkness is now. The ocean.

In my dream it's all around me, pressing down hard on every inch of my skin. In dreams I don't breathe, but even so, I know it'll be fine if I try. The water breathes for me, passing through slits in my neck I've made with magic.

Magic.

I look down, down into the murky darkness all around me, to see white beneath me. White fur, white scales, glowing softly against the depths of the ocean. I'm riding a valkerax. No—not me. A girl with wooden fingers is riding a valkerax.

Varia.

I'm in her mind again, the two of us connected by the blood promise and the Bone Tree and my dream.

Far and away in the water other spots of white scales glow, a rainbow tint valiantly radiating out from their manes against the crushing black. *Hundreds* of them. Hundreds of glowing white spots in the water, all churning in one direction. The current is strong, and sometimes the valkerax have to change course against its furor, but the goal remains the same. All of them, swimming toward something at once.

I—we—look over into the abyssal darkness, the flicker of rainbow light catching the visage of a massive fanged fish half as large as the valkerax. It scatters quickly, knowing danger when it sees it. Or perhaps it doesn't see at all—the other lifeforms at the bottom of the ocean seem to have milky white eyes, much the same as the valkerax. Darkness doesn't beget vision, but that doesn't mean the ocean creatures don't sense the incoming valkerax horde. A sawshark flees too late, caught up in the carelessly violent jaws of a passing valkerax. Black blood clouds in the black water. The skeleton ruins of old ships flicker past— wood and metal and a pearly material Varia recognizes as Old Vetrisian but I don't. Massive crabs as big as bears sit on the ships, picking off fish and swinging claws menacingly to no avail—the valkerax slither past and swallow them whole as easily as blinking.

Varia and I both know the valkerax are comfortable, down here. Darkness is their home, depth is their home. The bottom of the ocean is perhaps the only place on Arathess anywhere close in scope and feel to the Dark Below. The water rushes past our face, past our ears, but our hearing is drowned out at all times by the Bone Tree's hunger.

<u>DESTROY</u>. <u>DESTROY</u>. <u>*DESTROY*</u>.

anything, my hunger joins in. *everything.*

Ruination. That's all it wants, and it screams that into Varia's mind without ceasing, without a single second of rest. Her own thoughts and feelings are submerged in unrelenting pain and anger and lust for carnage, the same as mine. Louder, maybe, and more insistent. But the same intent.

Except I have the Weeping. I have a witch and organs to temper my hunger.

She has *nothing*.

She's alone.

She bears the brunt of everything, alone.

But that was her plan all along. She thinks that, she knows that. To bear the worst of it, so others wouldn't have to. So the girl she loves wouldn't have to. So she can change the world for that girl, to make it safe for her.

The girl—what's her name? Ruin? Destruction? No, she has a *real* name, and I can feel Varia's mind start to claw out frantically for it, combing through the Bone Tree's bloodlust, struggling to hold on to even a scrap of reality, of memory, of self. *Her name. Her name, her—*

Fione, I think, loud and intentionally and clear.

And just like that, we split. The dream-me peels out of Varia, and I can see myself floating beside her in the dark water, floating along with her speed as if I'm invisibly tethered to her, as if I'm one of the valkerax surging toward destruction, too. I can see the princess properly now that I'm outside of her—her long black hair streaming behind her in the water, the slits on her throat like gills on a fish. Her eyes are bloodshot, her gold skin bruised, and not just by the umber of the dark water. Great green-gray bruises have started to bloom on every inch of her body, as if she's rotting from the inside. Is that the Bone Tree eating her magic? I think my voice—or Fione's name—gives her a moment of clarity, because she looks up and right at me. Lucidly.

"You," she speaks, her mouth moving but only bubbles coming out. Her black eyes go wild, furious, and I hear her voice more in my head. "You made the Trees touch in Windonhigh. They touched because they felt you."

I'm quiet. She's not.

"You're trying to stop me." Her voice is far deader than deadpan. Lifeless, even as her eyes burn. "If you make them touch, it will go away."

She keeps one hand knit in the valkerax's mane, but the other hand rises to her throat, to the bone choker strangling her. The Bone Tree, wrapped tight around her neck.

She traces it lightly, as if making sure it's still there. "You're trying to take it from me. So I'm coming for you."

"All right," I say patiently. Patience is what she needs, now most of all. She's not herself. She doesn't even remember what herself was like before the Bone Tree. But I'll wait, patiently, and remember for her.

For Fione.

For Lucien.

For the girl who knows what it's like to make a mistake you can't take back.

"I've...I've killed them all." Varia glances down at her hand. She means Helkyris. Cavanos. Everyone the valkerax meet. "I'm going to kill them all."

"I know," I say. She clenches her fist inward, nails biting. Blood in the water.

"They have to die," Varia snarls. "All of them."

"Is that you talking?" I ask softly. "Or the Bone Tree around your neck?"

Her wooden fingers move up again to the choker of valkerax fangs ringing her neck. Wringing. Her weapon. Her advantage. Her leash.

"The Varia I know had a plan," I say. "And it wasn't wanton carnage like this. She was going to carve the wood of the world, not throw it all in the fire."

Her black eyes go wide, deep pools in the deep ocean, and she recovers, bristling.

"You are under my command—you will not speak! You will *kill*! You will kill them like I want you to!"

Something in me buckles, my unheart spasming. My blood thrums hot in my ears, every sensation suddenly very real and not dreamy in the slightest. She's *making* me feel. I suffer everything intensely, no longer dream-detached, my body growing heavy and my mind becoming aware of my eyes, six of them opening on my cheeks—

"Varia, stop," I plead. *"Stop!"*

Her fingers twist out at me, a cruel, delighted smile on her face. But it's not her smile. It's older than her, somehow. It's lined with so much more pain than a mortal could experience—hundreds of aching years, not two decades. I watch in horror as the bruises on her body start to throb, expanding in their discoloration even farther up her neck, her chest, her wrists and arms, as if they're...*consuming* her. A bruise on her scalp moves to her eye, shriveling the white of it instantly, her socket bleeding bright and the shriveled eye hanging loose and useless, a mirror of her brother's.

"You will destroy," she rumbles. "For us. You will hurt them, as they have hurt us."

This isn't her. It's the Bone Tree. I can hear it in her voice, her words. That's not a witch, or a d'Malvane, or even a person. It's a hunger. It's something beyond life and death, beyond magic and machine and mortals. Something bigger and older and wounded. Lonely.

I just know.

I just...*understand*. Like Muro said, it's that feeling. That feeling of wrongness I sensed first in my dreams. A feeling that isn't mine, but is so sure of itself anyway. It's that feeling I felt in my dreams sent to me by the Tree of Souls, according to Muro. It wells up now, aching.

"Are you...lonely?" I manage through my squeezing throat, through the hunger's sudden urge to rip and tear and consume.

Varia's eyes go wide again—her withered one bleeding profusely with each inch the lid moves up. A trail of red blood banners behind her, curling around her stream of black hair. I swallow hard and fight to hold on to my thoughts—with how strong the urge to destroy is, I don't think I can Weep, but the principal of sinking into myself helps keep my mind above water. Or below it, in this case.

"You sound lonely," I press. "I'm sorry. I'm sorry you're alone."

Two rosaries, two trees, and the feeling that if I didn't put them together again, something terrible would happen. That wrongness. The Tree covered in stained glass, and the aching feeling of loneliness it exuded just before all the shards stood on end to stab me. It's the same. Varia's face now—*no, the Bone Tree's face*—it's the same loneliness.

And the same stabbing.

I'm sure of it.

I understand now.

"One of them!" Varia snarls in her unvoice. "You're one of them. You want to hurt us again! Split us again!"

"No," I try. "No, I promise, I don't—"

"EMPTY!" the Bone Tree screams, bubbles streaming out of her mouth and her working black eye darting madly around in its socket, wildly, like a berserk animal in a panic, as if it's trying to escape its lid, driven to the final edge by fear. "EMPTY! PROMISES!"

The force of her scream feels like it's tearing me apart, tearing my skin off my body as the valkerax ascend rapidly, hurtling up through the water, the pressure becoming less but the burning becoming more, and the explosion of water as they surface, and right before us is an island.

An island of volcanic black rock.

I jolt awake so hard, my brain feels like it ricochets in my skull, my gasp so loud it sounds more like tearing cloth than breathing.

"Zera!" Lucien's voice faintly rings through my panic, close. "What's wrong?"

I blink, forcing my eyes to focus on him. Six eyes. I freeze. Varia made me *transform*. Not just in the dream. But in reality, too.

I'm not in control.

And she's here.

"We have to go!" I shriek. "Now!"

"Whoa, whoa," Malachite hefts off the wall. "Go where? What's going on?"

Fione moves like a cat, collapsing at my side with a hurried hiss. "Did you dream with her again?"

I nod, hair sticking to my cold-sweat forehead. "She's here. Hundreds of them. We have to *go*. You have to—you have to tie me up. Knock me out. Something. Hurry!"

Yorl stands, hurrying over to me. "Is it Varia?"

I nod. "I can see her in my dreams. Through the Bone Tree. Look at my eyes—she did this. Not me. *Her*. She can...I can feel her. Inside me."

"Shit," Malachite hisses, lightly punching the wall next to him. "Shit, shit, *shit*! I told you!"

"Now's not the time, Mal," Lucien says, voice eerily calm.

"He's right." Fione looks at Yorl. "We need a sedative for her."

"It's not gonna be strong...enough," I manage. "She's... Together she and the Tree are so strong." My eyes flicker to Lucien. "You have to command me."

His onyx gaze hardens in an instant. "No. Absolutely not."

"Luc." I wince as a deep pain clenches around my unheart. "She's trying to. You have to combat it, or—"

"I promised you." His face burns golden, every determined ridge hot as the sun. "I made a promise. I may have your heart, but I'll never have your free will, Zera. That's yours, and yours alone."

"Well, she'll kill us, then!" Malachite snarls. But Lucien doesn't budge an inch. He means it, down to the last syllable. Even if it means I hurt him, he won't command me. And in some sick, twisted way, I feel tears of happiness prick at my eyes.

He won't strip me of my freedom like the others.

He's not like them.

you're not one of us, the hunger sneers at me. *you never were. a traitor to the very end.*

Fione is a clear voice of reason through the haze. "Either way, we need to tell the polymaths the valkerax are—"

From outside the shuttered window, the cold call of a bell

starts to reverberate. Just one, and then two, and then ten, and then the island erupts with frantic warning rings and frenzied shouts. Malachite throws the window open, peering out and then back in, his face even more paper-white and grim.

"Too late."

My throat feels like it's in my mouth, Lucien's hand squeezing mine barely legible through my mounting panic. I thought I had it under control. I thought I was free of her, of everyone, free to make my own choices, but now she's reaching me—

"Zera, look at me," Lucien says, gently capturing my face with his palms. "It'll be all right. I can put you under."

"But—" I look out the window. "You need me. You need me to fight. You need me to help you escape—*ah!*"

A lance of white-hot agony rips through my chest, up to my teeth. All my Heartless teeth sprout in an instant, longer than I've ever felt them, and far sharper. So deadly sharp, my lips bleeding as I clench them shut, refusing to bite, refusing to give myself the slightest opportunity. It's not just human teeth—I can feel rows of teeth behind those teeth, spiraling all the way down and into my throat.

Like *valkerax*.

She's changing me. Calling out to the blood promise in me. She's forcing me to obey, like every other valkerax must obey her, obey the Bone Tree.

you betrayed them, and now you betray us.

"A sedative it is, then," Yorl says after a single glance at my mouth. He whirls to a bag on the wall, rummaging in it before coming up with a vial of blue liquid. "This is enough to keep you under for a quarter-half. He doesn't have to command you, but if he can slide a magic suggestion that you sleep—" The celeon looks up at Lucien, and they nod at each other. "There's a good chance not even the Bone Tree would be able to wake you."

I let out a strangled cry-laugh through my gritted teeth. It's a sweet attempt at putting my fears to rest, and I want to trust it. I want to trust him, and Lucien, but I've felt the Bone Tree. It's doing unimaginable things to me—things it's not supposed to be able to.

"Sleep? It's feeding off Varia," I pant. "Getting stronger. Don't—don't put me to sleep. She'll see me again, control me. The dreams...dreams are how they talk—"

"How *who* talks?" Malachite frowns.

"If we put you under strongly enough, you won't dream," Fione assures me.

"But—"

"Hush," Lucien murmurs into my hair, lips pressed to my head in a kiss. "You've done your part. Rest now."

Yorl holds the vial to my chapped lips, and I can't think. My teeth arc so many, my claws growing strange and white and long. I have to down it. It's this or rampage as a valkerax, with the valkerax. It's this or hurt the people in this room, maybe.

And I promised I'd never do that again.

I promised I'd never lose control and hurt someone again.

you were meant to hurt, the hunger laughs gleefully. *you were born to hurt others.*

The fourteen graves, bells and ribbon swaying in the mountaintop breeze—

I gulp greedily and a wave of magic slides through me, the warmth of the sedative harmonizing with it to weave a deep, dark, utterly inescapable slumber. The panic still buzzes to the last—they need me. They *need* me to fight with them. They're mortal. I'm not. I'm going to be nothing but dead weight, unable to help like I want to, like I have to. I'm the only one who can survive if I die. I'm the only one who can protect them, protect him, Lucien—

"Lucien," I whisper. His blurry smile beams down at me, golden and soft, his murmur slowed and drawn-out by the looming sleep.

"Let us protect you, this time."

The sedative is strong—of course it's strong. It's Yorl's. The magic, too, is strong.

Of course it is; it's Lucien's.

Their attempts to put me under are so *strong*. But the Bone Tree is strong, too. Varia is weaker, but the Tree has only grown. It flutters my eyes open in momentary bursts, sound and light and sensation coming through. Someone carrying me in their arms—the smell of honey. Lucien. The *swhick* sounds of Fione's crossbow cane firing heavy bolts, Malachite's ferocious battle cries, and the air-shredding bellows of valkerax in return. The sound of stone crumbling, the feel of wet droplets on my face, half of them salted sweat and the other half metallic blood.

There's a terrifying moment when my six eyes open fully and I see a copper giant—a matronic—swinging massive fists into the scaled serpent body of a valkerax. A silver robe is perched inside each matronic, a polymath sitting inside it and maneuvering it like a suit of armor a dozen times their size. *That's why*, my human brain chimes. *That's why the Black Archives made them—not to bring them up to bookshelves, but to fight.*

The valkerax try to bite down on the copper titans, to rip and tear like they would flesh, but the matronic is metal, harder, and my own new teeth chatter with the urge to bite, to help, to *destroy.*

<u>DESTROY.</u>

<u>DESTROY IT ALL.</u>

Above me, I hear Lucien shout something, but my mind's battle between sleep and wakefulness is too chaotic. I can't understand. I can't understand any of it—why me? Why me, of all people? Why am I the valkerax-Heartless?

Why, Trees? Why give your lonely dream to *me*?

Why am I the wolf at the end of the world, and not someone else?

someone braver, someone better, the hunger slithers. Lucien, Fione, Malachite—any of them would've been better.

why are they friends with you?

Why are they friends with me?

Why am I still asking this when I know the answer?

I have to trust them. They're friends with me because I'm worth it. Because, despite all the flaming horseshit I've put them through, I'm worth it to them. I'm worth it, period.

My friends chose me because they believe in me.

The Trees, maybe, chose me because they believe in me.

I can't give in. Even as the Bone Tree beckons me to battle, keens for me to pick up my claws and tear the one holding me apart, to tear this whole world apart, I fight it.

DESTROY. DESTROY. DESTROY.

Fight it. Fight with everything in you. Fight by the light of the moon, of the sun, whatever faint light you can find.

I battle the urge to destroy with every memory I've gathered—Fione's apple-cheeked smile, her gentle hands. Malachite's smirk, ruffling my hair. Lucien kissing me, the hollow of my throat, the way he breathes when he holds me—all the memories stand like soldiers, like the soldiers once gathered outside Vetris's walls, like the eclipseguard gathered in Windonhigh, like the valkerax gathered in the Dark Below obeying eternally the Bone Tree, like Crav and Peligli and I in Nightsinger's forest, waiting to fight for her. To die for her. Over and over again.

Love. Not-Love.

TOGETHER, the Bone Tree's demands go soft, for just one moment. **together.**

It wants to be together. Of course it does. Everybody wants to be together with the one they love. Fione wants to be with Varia.

I want to be with Lucien, with all my friends. Malachite wants to be with us. Crav and Peligli want to be with me.

The Bone Tree wants to be with the Glass Tree, again.

Because it's lonely out there, isn't it? It's a lonely world if you aren't together. And the Trees have been lonely for a thousand years.

I'm sorry, I think. *I'm so sorry you're alone.*

And then it lets me go.

For just one second, the magic and the sedative come roaring back against the Bone Tree's suddenly weaker grip, and the darkness of sleep consumes me in one fell swallow.

I see it all.

In that one moment of the Bone Tree's vulnerability, I see it all, like looking into a deep, clear, still pond. I see the Bone Tree, its roots tangling back into the roots of a bigger tree, so much bigger and standing alone. I see the Glass Tree in the distance, roots tangling into the same tree, the same massive tree, and the roots of that tree spiral outward, like millions of hairs connected to each and every one of us on Arathess—every human, every witch, every celeon, every beneather, every frog, every bird, every leaf, every berry. Everything. Everyone.

Not alone.

Muro stands under the great tree, smiling.

The great tree, connecting us all. Pulling us back in when it's our time, and growing us back out, over and over again.

The Tree of Souls.

No one is ever really gone.

Muro reaches his paw out, six eyes smiling brighter. And above him, the Tree of Souls with two gaping wounds in its trunk, bleeding black. And like a conversation, like an embrace, I know it's the source of everything. The destruction. The anger. The hunger. Yearning, wounded, alone. He was right. Muro was *right.* He's there, waiting for me, and he's right. I've felt both Trees' pain.

They're alone. All alone, and hurting.

I know what I have to do. Because I know what it's like to be alone.

I *understand* now.

I have to put the Trees back together.

24
WATER RUNNING RED

Without me awake to perceive it, time moves rambunctiously. The sound of the waves reaches me first, grinding my worries smooth with that great gentle symphony. When my eyes flutter open again, I'm on a beach, the golden glow of a bonfire lighting the velvet-blue sands. And around me sit three figures, their backs to me as they look out at the sea moonlit by the half-full Red Twins.

I take a moment before I say anything to let them know I'm here. To just admire them, admire the fact they're here for me when I wake up. That they're still here at all, alive and well enough to sit on a beach even after a valkerax attack.

Brave Malachite, armor stained slightly red—bloodied and then tried to wash it off. He'll be fine, won't he? He'll protect Lucien, no matter what. No matter how old they get or how much they argue—he'll always be there for the prince. And I'll never be able to thank him enough for it.

Sweet Fione—wrapped in a woven blanket and trembling, her mousy curls still frazzled with the chaos of battle. She's stronger than even Lucien, than anyone I know. She'll understand better than anyone that I did what I had to. She understands love. And she, too, understands what it's like to be alone. She'll do great things for Cavanos—whatever grand, fair Cavanos Lucien decides to build.

Serious Lucien. Lucien, in all his midnight glory, black hair and black eyes piercing out into the night. It hurts to think about him alone. But he won't be. He'll have Malachite and Fione, and someday, a girl who reminds him of me. A girl who can pierce that dour, sad look on his face, who sweetens the bitterness of his life. He'll never be alone. He'll have me, no matter where I am or what happens to me. I'll be with him, always. I know that now. The Tree of Souls—that strange thing that's kept calling to me, giving me dreams—it connects us all. And even if it didn't, by magic or by my own sheer will—I'll be with him until the very end.

Because I love him.

With a great wrench, I pull myself together. When Lucien touches me, he'll read my thoughts. I can't think about anything. And certainly not about what I have to do, what I saw in that locus of perfect understanding. He'll try to stop me if he knows. They all will. This is my choice.

So how do I keep it mine?

A wolf to eat the world, Evlorasin's words drip in.

That's it. If I think about it like a poem, like Evlorasin and all valkerax do—it will sound like nonsense, and not a plan going against his concern for me. It's *not* to put the Trees back together. It's to eat the world. *I am the wolf, and I eat the world.* There. Nonsensical. Perfect. A perfect mantra.

Armed with it, I clear my throat. "Ahem. Why so pensive, children?"

All three black silhouettes on the sand round instantly, the bonfire melting gold across their tense, worried faces.

"You're back!" Fione chimes, smile blooming in relief.

"And just two eyes," Malachite adds with a smirk.

"Thank the gods," I exhale. "Do I look like the sort of girl who has the time to put makeup on all six of them every morning?"

"Absolutely not," Lucien agrees, swooping in to help me sit up with one arm around my shoulders. He anticipates the question in my half-open mouth. "We lost a dozen polymaths."

I quirk a brow. "A dozen? I was expecting far more."

"The matronics are machines capable of terrifying power," Fione says, looking me over for wounds with a polymath's sharp eye. "But even they were being overwhelmed by the sheer number of valkerax. We would've lost the entire Archive if they hadn't stopped."

"'*Stopped*'?" I blink. "What do you mean 'stopped?'"

Malachite shrugs one shoulder. "Halfway through the battle, all the spiritsdamn valkerax just froze. Jaws open, tails thrashing, but no hostile movements. Varia was sitting pretty on a flying valkerax, circling the whole place, but Fione saw her freeze up, too."

I glance at Fione, whose hand nervously moves to the brass seeing tube hanging from the chain around her neck.

"She was just...*staring*," the archduchess murmurs. "Just staring at nothing, her jaw slack, like she was—"

"Seeing something. Hearing something we couldn't," Lucien finishes for her. "They all were. We seized the advantage, and by the time they came to again, we'd killed more than my sister could stand. She turned tail and left when she realized how depleted her forces were."

If they froze...was it because of what I saw, too? What I felt? That moment of the Bone Tree's softness...did that freeze them? For one second, did the bloodlust fade? But *why*? All I did was say sorry. All I did was apologize. Maybe the Trees have never heard a mortal apologize to them. For what we did. For the horrible way we split them a thousand years ago.

Maybe that was the first time the hunger—the song—has ever heard an apology.

I lean against Lucien's strong arms, grateful for the support. My blurry eyes catch on the ocean water—red. Not deep blue. The waves lap pink foam on the shore. I follow the red water with my eyes far down the beach, to another stretch of sand where hundreds of polymaths in silver robes are gathered around a hulking mass of white serpent flesh. The mountain of carnage bleeds rivers down the beach, the sand and sea stained red in a ring around what seems to be the entire island. The mangrove trees rejoice, their long roots in the shallow water soaking up the blood. So many valkerax, dead. My stomach churns.

"What a waste. They were too easy," Malachite scoffs. "Not even a challenge. Almost made me sick, killing 'em when they couldn't fight back like that."

"I thought you lived to kill them," Fione says.

"Yeah." He frowns. "But in a legitimate fight. Beneathers train to be warriors, not butchers. We're not meant to kill 'em brainlessly like that."

"The polymaths didn't seem to mind how they died," Lucien mutters. "As long as the books were kept safe."

"They want the parts," Fione agrees, smoothing down a strand of my stray hair.

"Your Yorl friend wouldn't shut up about all the parts," Malachite insists. "Kept blathering on about how they'd be great for 'making a cure' for you, or some crap like that."

I watch the polymaths, picking out a single one in the crowd with ochre ears and a swishing tail. Yorl's so kind. Kind in that thorny way of his, but kind nonetheless. He wants to make a cure for my valkerax blood promise. A cure that will come too late, when I do what I have to. He'll be fine, too, won't he? The Archives are smoldering, the fortress of black volcanic rock crumbling and smoking in some places, but still mostly intact. He'll have his books, and he knows my friends, now.

All my friends, united. They'll be able to help one another when I'm gone.

"Fantastic." I flash a winning smile at Lucien. "At this point, I'll take anything that'll make me more human and less warbeast."

Everyone falls silent, the sound of the waves filling in. Fione's periwinkle gaze is somber, lit by the moons and sadness as she looks at the valkerax body parts strewn and bleeding.

"I wish it didn't have to be this way," she whispers.

"Wishing and doing are two different things." Malachite's words are hard, but the way he puts his pale hand on her shoulder is gentle.

"What do we do, then?" Lucien asks. "You haven't told us what the book's translation said."

Fione looks to me. "I wanted to wait until you were awake. It's important."

"I am now." I smile at her, but it feels strained. She stands, her skirts skimming the sand and her shadow thrown long by the bonfire. She folds her hands, working her fingers in and out of one another nervously, and then all at once she drops them, going still.

"We can't destroy the Trees," she says.

"Can't. Like...definitely can't?" Malachite repeats.

"It's impossible to destroy the Trees," she insists. "There's nothing that can destroy them. No fire, no weapon, no magic."

"Then how do we stop Varia?" Lucien asks.

Fione inhales and steadies herself. "The Tree of Souls is the origin of all magic on Arathess. And the First Root is one of its roots—the only one that we've ever seen. It may have other roots; research suggests it *must* have other roots. But even the Old Vetrisians couldn't find them."

"So there's only the First Root," Lucien murmurs.

Fione nods. "There is only the First Root. To make another Tree, one must split the First Root. That creates a divide in the magic, and from that divide grows a new Tree."

I frown. "Like pruning a rosebush. Cut back one stem, and it makes two new ones."

"Exactly," she says. "Using the First Root, the Old Vetrisians split the Tree of Souls once to make their Bone Tree, and the witches used the other side of the split to make their Glass Tree.

The split weakened the Tree of Souls considerably and changed the workings of magic as we know it." She looks over at Lucien. "It's why witches inherit their magic in pubescence and not from birth. And it's why the Old Vetrisians were able to do so much more than modern witches can now. They were simply more powerful."

"I see," Lucien starts. "So we find the Tree of Souls and the First Root. Then what?"

"We split the root again. That will weaken the Tree of Souls again—and by proxy the Bone and Glass Tree—and theoretically release Varia."

"You mean…" I trail off. "Split them into a new tree?"

She won't meet my eyes. "Into *two* new trees. We must split the Bone Tree's offshoot and the Glass Tree's offshoot to weaken the Tree of Souls as a whole. This process will create two additional trees."

"So…so that *what*?" I can feel my hackles rising. "So that mortals can use them to magically control *more* creatures?"

"Zera—" Lucien starts.

My fists are shaking, and I clench them hard. "Two new voices. Two new types of Heartless. Two new ways for people to inflict magical suffering on others. Is that what you're saying we have to make?"

Fione doesn't flinch, meeting my gaze now with a steadiness. "It's the only way to free her, Zera."

"The valkerax won't be freed though, right?" Malachite asks.

I simmer quietly as Fione nods.

"Most of them will still be tied to the Bone Tree, obeying its primary command to remain in the Dark Below," she clarifies. "A few might escape its hold—hopefully not enough to be a threat to the upworld. The same goes for the Heartless." She looks pointedly at me. "A few will be freed from their witches."

A few. Not all.

"We save Varia and stop the valkerax from being controlled by her," Lucien murmurs. "It sounds like the best option."

"The best—" I whirl around to look at him but go quiet at the expression on his face. He's smiling down at me, at every part of me, with a faint look of hope in his dark hawk eyes, and all my anger drains instantly. I love him. I love all of them. They want so badly to save the people they love, to save the world they love. They know, now, what they have to do.

But so do I.

The Bone Tree helped me see. That moment under the water, feeling so sorry for it—I know what I have to do now. A gentle burn—a peaceful flame of surety. Maybe I've always known.

Maybe this is what I was born to do. The witches made old sayings about it. Evlorasin knows about it, like it knows so many other inexplicable things—my true name least of all. Muro said maybe the Tree of Souls knew what I'd become.

At the end of the world, there will be wolves.

A wolf to eat the world.

I can't let it happen again.

we won't be hurt again, the hunger whispers.

I flash a glance up at Lucien. Nothing. His smile fades, and he looks at me curiously. I don't know when he does skinreading, but I know it's not often. We agreed to that much during our walks in snowy Breych. But he will read me *sometime*, and I have to be prepared for it. I will be, so long as it's all just a wolf eating the world in my head, mouth dripping with blood, eyes and fur luminous. If I make my intentions a valkerax story, a poem, a madness, he won't understand. I breathe deep and turn to Fione.

"How do we split the Trees, exactly? I imagine we don't use an ax."

"No." Her return smile is wry. "No axes. There are a few requirements. Firstly, we need to find the Tree of Souls. The book said the Tree itself disappeared after it was split from the Bone

Tree, but the First Root remained. There are old stories as to its location: a city filled with flowers."

"Pala Orias," Malachite mutters. Fione looks over at him with surprise.

"You know it?"

"How could I not?" He snorts. "My grandma never shut up about it. I just thought it was a fire-brained story of hers: 'a city of flowers?' Sounded freakin' ridiculous. There are no flowers in the Dark Below."

"There used to be," Fione asserts. "Before your grandmother's time. Before *her* grandmother's. A thousand years ago, it was called Pala Orias—the birth city. And it's where your people came from. They lived in the Tree of Souls' trunk for millennia."

"*Spirits*," Malachite breathes. "Your dinky book said all that?"

She nods. "It might be one of the last surviving records of your ancestors' beginnings. The rest were destroyed by the War of White, weren't they?"

He nods, scratching his pale hair absently. I look to Lucien for translation, what with his brain full of princely tutoring lessons.

"War of White—when the valkerax first rampaged and destroyed all the beneather cities," he clarifies. "The beneathers lost most of their history."

"There's another requirement," Fione speaks up again. "We need Varia to be close by the First Root to have any hope of splitting it again."

"Why?" Malachite asks.

"At least one of the Trees must be physically present for a splitting to work. The Tree of Souls would work, but it's physically disappeared. And considering the Glass Tree is being hoarded in Windonhigh by the witches, the Bone Tree is our only hope." She looks to Lucien. "The book said it would act as a large-depth anchor for the splitting spell."

Lucien muses this over, chin in his hand. "Right—because otherwise the cast radius would be impossible."

we will not be split again, the hunger snarls soundlessly at them.

"If I'm understanding this right, we're bound for the Dark Below," I say. "And we have to lure Varia there."

"Not without me." Yorl's voice. We turn to see him drying his paws on the bonfire. "I have my grandfather's guidebook from his ventures there. I know the safest ways in and out."

"I doubt that," Malachite sneers.

"And you *do*, Mal?" Lucien looks at him with one brow quirked. "You haven't been back for a decade."

"A beneather never forgets the Dark, Your Highness." Malachite drawls his title. "I can guide you better than the furball can."

Yorl's teeth start to show, and I pipe up cheerily.

"Or both of you can work together to guide us doubly safely down there!"

Yorl and Malachite glare at each other, but Yorl relents first with a twitch of his whiskers.

"Fine. We could use your sense of hearing, regardless."

Malachite's almost taken aback, and his shoulders relax as he snorts. "Your sense of smell's better than mine, anyway. Useful for the bloodbats."

"Ah, true love." I wink at Fione. She giggles behind her hand, and for a blissful moment on the beach, me in Lucien's arms, a plan on the horizon, Varia beaten back, this feels like peace. An echo of it, a tantalizing promise of things to come. For them.

For all of them.

They have a plan.

And so do I.

I look up at the prince, cupping his cheek. "You protected me. All of you."

Lucien's eyes crinkle, and he leans down, planting a soft kiss on my forehead. "And you trusted us to. Thank you."

I don't tell Lucien on that night-lit beach, but I tell it to myself in the days afterward: it's not about trust.

What comes next for me isn't about trust. And not telling Lucien, or any of them, isn't at all like what I did in Vetris after I was discovered as a Heartless. This is different. This isn't us forced apart, forcing one another apart—it's my road leading one way and theirs the other. It feels more peaceful than pushing them away for their own good ever did. This isn't me pushing them away at all. It's us walking the same path together, for as long as we can.

And I plan to enjoy every second of it—of them—until our paths part.

In the bustle of the mist the next morning, the silver robed polymaths gather on the docks of the Black Archive, their ship for us bobbing gently in the blood-tinted waves. Several polymaths in matronics load supplies onto the ship, carrying far heavier loads than any mortal could, their copper armor dented by the valkerax attack but still gleaming in the sun. The polymath leader who greeted us first says farewell first, too, her face much less severe now but her robes more bloodstained.

"You have given us learning, and we have given you learning in return. Until we know you again."

"Until we know you again," the polymaths behind her all say at once and bow their heads, and at my side, Yorl does the same. The polymaths begin to walk up the steps of the Archive and back to their books and machines and no doubt even mustier intellectual pursuits. The woman remains, though, and she steps forward very suddenly and takes my hand. Her gray eyes pierce mine with a fearsome determination that reminds me intensely of Fione.

"You will bring Yorl back to us in one piece."

"Sage," Yorl scoffs quietly, more like a purr than anything derisive. "Please."

"I will," I assure her, trying to match her fierce eyes. "I'm not going to lose anyone anymore. None of us is."

"Thank you." Her expression softens minutely, and then her eyes dart to Yorl. "Make sure you parse the runes in the Dark Below correctly, and you can finish reading Tolwin's *Theocratics* on the ship. I had the kitchens pack dried ginger to chew in case of seasickness—"

"Sage," Yorl repeats, his muzzle pulling into a rare smile. "I'll be fine."

She steps back. "Yes. Well. Off with you, then."

As we walk up the gangplank, I look over at Yorl. "You didn't tell me your mother's human."

He rolls his eyes. "She's not my mother."

I chuckle, and then, "Is it really okay? You worked so hard to get here, and now you're leaving."

His tail thrashes. "Grandfather would've wanted it. He spent his whole life trying to unravel the mysteries of the valkerax. If I go with you, I can see his life's work through to the end."

I open my mouth to tell him about his grandfather, that I saw him. But I *did* tell him, didn't I? I relayed the message that Muro is proud of him. That's all he asked of me.

If I tell Yorl about seeing Muro, he'll ask what Muro said. He'd press and press me, and I wouldn't be able to resist him. I trust him. I would tell him; I know I would. I'd tell Yorl every last thing about the Tree of Souls, and how Muro implied it might've chosen me to put it back together.

But I can't let him know that, can I?

It must be a poem, a story. His path, one way. My path, the other.

I pat him on the shoulder, and we watch the island float away from us. Even as we raise anchor and lower the sails and start to drift away, his green eyes hungrily take in every inch of Rel'donas, every grain of sand of the black volcanic island devoured by his gaze.

"You'll be back," I say, certain.

"You don't know that," he scoffs. "No one knows that."

I look out past Rel'donas, at the gray horizon peeking through the mist, and laugh a little, shaking my head.

"I do, Ironspeaker. I *do*."

25

THE WOLF
WHO WILL
EAT THE WORLD

It doesn't take long for a handful of bored half-children, half-adults to find the very cool giant metal man in the cargo bay.

"They packed you a present!" Fione chimes to Yorl, stepping delicately around the matronic laid out on the wood, as if sleeping. It takes up nearly the entire floor of the bay, arms and legs as thick as tree trunks splayed out and gleaming in the white mercury light.

"Do you even know how to control this thing?" Malachite grunts, dubious. Yorl jumps with catlike alacrity onto the matronic's inert body, kneeling down on its chest to look at the copper metal gears there.

"In theory," the celeon agrees. "I'm still a season away from my piloting test, but I've logged a month of practice. Enough to know how to make it stand and lift a box."

"That's all we'll need from it," Lucien says, dark eyes roving over the matronic with curious awe. "I gather that—at the *very* least—it's going to be an extremely large, extremely shiny distraction for the valkerax to gnaw on."

"And you know how much we love gnawing," I agree cheerily.

Yorl jumps nimbly down from the matronic. "That reminds me. I should set another batch of sedatives to simmer for you."

"We can't be drugging me every time Varia shows up," I say.

"So you *want* to rampage around?" Malachite shoots.

"So you *want* to fight the final battle all by yourself?" I fire back.

He ignores me and looks to Yorl. "Maybe brew something to keep her awake. If she falls asleep, Varia will find us again like she did on the island."

"Mal," I whine. "You're being mean."

"Yeah, well." He folds his pale arms over his chest. "You're being too laid-back about all this."

"I'm not!" I argue. "I'm just trying to lighten—"

"If Varia dream-tracks you again, or whatever, it's my people who'll get the worst of it," he snarls. "She'll see into your brain and head for the Dark Below and start destroying Pala Amna."

"Mal," Lucien says. "That won't happen. We'll get there first and warn them."

The beneather snorts. "We better."

"Surely Pala Amna is best prepared for a valkerax attack out of every city on Arathess," Fione says.

"Yeah." Malachite shrugs. "But not all the valkerax. And sure as shit not all at once."

"Why does she want you so badly anyway?" Lucien muses at me.

"A very good question," Yorl agrees, then looks to me. "Zera?"

"I—" I falter. Just for a second. "I don't know. I know she attacked Windonhigh right after we were there and then the Black Archives while we were there."

"Seemingly tracking you," Lucien says. "Is it because—you don't think it's because she still hates you, right?"

no, foolish prince. it's because she's afraid of us. of losing her power because of us.

"I don't think she remembers her own name most of the time, let alone what it's like to hate someone," I insist. "If there's any hate fueling her, it's the Bone Tree's. And if there's any reason that thing hates me, it's because I'm part valkerax and not obeying it."

I meet Fione's periwinkle eyes, the sole gaze that cuts right through me. She's the only one who knows both Varia and me intimately. She knows something doesn't sit right in my words.

"Anyway, I don't need sleep," I quickly blurt. "But what if— she's destroyed Vetris. Helkyris's capital. Maybe she's destroying Avel's right now. After that, all that's left on the Mist Continent is the beneathers."

"Pala Amna," Lucien agrees.

"She could go to the Feralstorm," Malachite argues.

"No," Yorl says. "There are more beasts than people there. Disregarding her going out of her way to stalk your group of late, there's been a pattern to her attacks. The cities Zera just listed are of the greatest population densities. Varia seems to be going by descending order. And the fourth largest is Pala Amna. She's headed there eventually, regardless if we are or not."

Malachite's face goes even whiter, the cargo bay's shadows clawing at his cheekbones. The silence between us is filled by the creaks and groans of the ship, the pressure of the ocean bearing down like iron. Lucien looks somberly at the matronic. Yorl studies his claws with a frown, and Fione gazes at a far crate with hard eyes. Malachite looks sick at his own thoughts. I clench my fist.

"What if we lure her?" I ask. Fione's the first to snap her gaze to me.

"With your dream?"

"She's been following your *dreams*," Lucien murmurs.

"Yeah." I nod. "If we get to Pala Orias first, and then I dream, she'll track it, and skip over Pala Amna to come right for us."

"She might. Or she might raze Pala Amna on the way down," Yorl murmurs behind his paw.

"She'd want to keep the bulk of her forces for us, though, right?" Malachite asks, hope creeping back into his voice.

"She could split the horde," Lucien offers. "Most of it for Pala Amna, the rest for us. We're just five people. Logically, a handful of valkerax would be enough."

"But she's not operating by logic anymore," I blurt. "She's being consumed by the Tree." I see Fione flinch, but I barrel forward. "The Tree's dominating more and more of her thoughts as time goes on. And all it wants to do is destroy. Except, that moment at the Black Archives where all the valkerax went still—I think I might've done that."

Everyone's eyes go wide, Malachite's just narrowing.

"You?" Yorl blinks. "How?"

"I was—" I swallow. "I told it I was sorry. Sorry it had been alone for so long. And it seemed so...*shocked*. Shocked someone like me would apologize. That *anyone* would apologize. I think that's what made it—and all the valkerax—freeze up. It was confused. Or sad. I dunno. But it worked, right?"

"You think you can do it again?" Lucien squeezes my hand.

"Maybe." I grin grimly at him. "If I can make it sad, I think I can make it mad. And if I make it mad enough, Varia will ignore everyone else and come right for us."

"If we can go to the ancestor council and get their help, we can mount a defense before Varia gets there," Malachite says. "Lay a trap for her in Pala Orias."

"Lure her, and trap her there so that we split the First Root," Fione says and looks to Lucien. "Can you do that?"

Lucien shrugs. "I won't know until I'm there, feeling its magic. There's a good chance the Old Vetrisian witches split it with a combine weave."

"Translation?" Malachite drawls.

"More than one witch," Yorl clarifies, "pouring magic into the same spell."

"It's what you're supposed to do for teleports, too." I look pointedly at Lucien, and he flushes and scowls.

"Regardless." He assumes a princely tone. "I'll do what needs to be done."

"You're not going to kill yourself doing it," I snap.

His chuckle is gentle. "Not planning to, heart."

The nickname melts me like hot honey over cream, but I won't let it distract me. I hold his gaze stubbornly.

"We can send for help," Fione says, looking to me. "Nightsinger would help, wouldn't she?"

"We can't trust any of the Windonhigh witches," Lucien says. "You saw them—they don't want things to change. They want their Glass Tree and their Heartless to defend against outsiders. If they find out we're going to weaken the Glass Tree, they won't be keen on helping us."

I feel a sting in my unheart. "But Nightsinger might. She'd want to help me—"

"We can't take the risk." Lucien looks to me. "You understand, right?"

I breathe in shakily and nod. Lucien strokes his thumb over mine, as if trying to comfort me. He's right. We have to do it before any interested party can find out and try to stop us. Nightsinger's and Lucien's combined magic would have better odds at splitting the First Root, and Lucien wouldn't have to lose himself over it, or worse—die. But he won't die. He won't need to split the First Root on his own. They think that's how it will go, how it must go. But it won't.

They have to live. All of them. They have to live, and the world has to change.

The Tree has to be put back together.

the wolf will eat the world, the hunger hisses.

Yorl's stomach gurgles just at that moment, a welcome reprieve of levity as Malachite snickers and Yorl's ochre face tints darker with his blush.

"All right, enough serious talk." I grin. "Can't plan strategy without something to eat, now, can we?"

I usher everyone up the stairs and set about delivering the

dried meat and fruit the Black Archives gave us to the few polymaths working the ship. I come back to the captain's quarters with rations and a bottle of wine to lift everyone's spirits, and as soon as I open the door, the sound of arguing filters out.

"What do we tell the beneathers, then?" Yorl demands. "How do we get them to carve a way into Pala Orias for us? Any actual ideas, or is it just empty battle-lust in that head of yours?"

"Battle's not the point, arse-licker!" Malachite bellows. "We won't have to carve anything anywhere if we use Six-Eyes' dream thing right! We tell Varia where we are at just the right time, and we won't have to lose so many spiritsdamn beneathers to the valkerax!"

Fione's buried herself in the green-covered book again, trying desperately to do something useful instead of adding fuel to the argument. Lucien looks up when I come in, flashing me a tired grin and motioning for me to sit by him. I flop into the chair next to him and clunk the wine bottle down on the table.

"Do I need to put you two down for nappy time?" I chime. "Or can we talk about this like civilized folk?"

Yorl and Mal both open their mouths, but Lucien smoothly interjects with all the effortless authority of a prince.

"Zera will stay awake for as long as it take us to get to Pala Amna. I'll make sure of it. When we arrive, we inform the ancestor council of our plan first. We travel with their reinforcements to Pala Orias, allowing us to lay down traps and ambushes for the valkerax. Only when that's done will Zera sleep, informing Varia of our plan."

Yorl's huge green eyes narrow at me. "Can you truly stay awake that long? It's an instinct for Heartless to sleep when they become emotionally drained—"

"She can do it," Malachite interrupts him, his voiced laced with a thread of pride. "I'm sure of it."

"But that means we can't risk sedatives," Fione offers without looking up from her book. "If Varia calls her again—"

"She won't," I say. "I think—I think after the last battle, she might be afraid. Of me." I scramble to cover. "Of what I did on the island. Stopped her valkerax, you know?"

"It's not just her in her body, though," Lucien argues. "It's also the Bone Tree."

"I don't think the Bone Tree is as keen on trying to kill us at the moment, either." I smile, but it feels paper-thin. "I felt it recoil when I said I was sorry. It's confused. It might get unconfused shortly, but I think we have a little leeway."

"And if we don't?" Malachite grunts.

"Well," I breathe in. "Then chain me to the rudder and throw me in the sea and let me drag along out there. Much less likely to kill someone if my excessively toothy mouth is full of seawater and fish."

"You're not—" Lucien's handsome face hardens with a frown. "No. You're here, with us. And that's final."

"She got through my Weeping, Lucien," I say gently. "Your magic won't be enough."

His onyx eyes meet mine, studded with steel. "I will make it enough."

"Not at the cost of your body—"

"At any cost."

His last words ring in the captain's room, ricocheting off the glass wine bottle, off the windows and bedframe and my cold hands. Fione looks up from the book. Malachite looks pained, and Yorl just looks at me. It won't come to that. I won't let him consume himself for me.

He stares at me, unblinking, sure of himself, his sacrifice. But that's not how this story in the history textbooks goes. Lucien lives to rebuild Cavanos greater than ever before. I know it.

"What do we do now?" Fione whispers the question.

I tear my gaze from Lucien's fiercely burning one, moving

to the iron Eye of Kavar nailed to the wall above the captain's bed, and nod at it.

"We do what the rest of the world is doing."

"Dying?" Malachite offers cynically.

"Praying," I correct softly.

"Do you believe in the gods now, all of a sudden?" Fione scoffs, the uncertainty getting to her, too. I feel for Lucien's hand under the table, and he holds me.

"I believe in what people do and what people don't do. I believe in our power to come together and to come apart. And that's all. That's all I know for sure."

The words hang, nervous and young and small. They sound ridiculous in the face of so much importance. We're talking about the final battle, the last stand, and all I can do is give platitudes. All I can do is stay awake, stay strong, stay ready. I have to be ready for the moment, because it will come in all the chaos, and I have to snatch it from between the fingers of my well-meaning friends.

because you did this, the hunger whispers. *you freed the valkerax. all those cities, all those people—dead because of you, wolf.*

That beach running red. All those valkerax dead because of me. Lucien's grip tightens. He's skinreading me, I know it. The horrible guilt is a more effective armor for my intentions than even the songpoem of the wolf who eats the world.

Not me. I didn't do this. This horrible web was spun long before I was even born. The Old Vetrisians, the witches. Decisions were made by scared people, by power-hungry people, by *people*. I didn't do this; we all did. All of us fed into it and out of it, like a constant polymath machine. A cycle. A cycle that feels too big and too ingrained to ever break. Breaking it would mean breaking the world apart, throwing every previous rule into chaos. The end of the world.

No—the end of *this* world.

And the beginning of a new one.

A new one for Lucien, for Fione and Mal and Yorl. For Varia. Varia was wrong. We can't just carve the world into a shape we want. That's not how things change. One person can't hold the chisel. There's no point in holding the chisel at all if what you're trying to carve is the bare tip of the iceberg.

The whole iceberg has to break for the river to flow again.

I am not a chisel. I won't use a chisel. Not like everyone else. Maybe it's the valkerax blood promise in me, but even my littlest thoughts are clear and certain and like poetry, like songs—my mind moves like a song and I finally understand Muro. His words. Evlorasin, too. Everything the valkerax ever said that sounded like nonsense becomes so *clear*.

Two hungers are in me, and they drive me forward. I was born to starve. I lost my parents to starve. I was brought to Vetris to starve, I fell in love with Lucien to starve, I killed those fourteen men to starve, and my hungers drove me to my friends, and my choices, and they drive me now to the river, and the iceberg, and the end of all things.

True names are true.

I *am* the Starving Wolf.

And I will eat the world.

26
THE WOUNDED

It's the nights that are the hardest.

But I always knew that.

In Nightsinger's woods, the deep cold and the deep darkness ate away at you. They gnawed like the valkerax gnaw, like the Bone Tree gnaws at Varia even now. I'd stay awake, listening to Crav and Peligli breathing in their unneeded Heartless slumbers, their cheeks and eyes puffy with childhood. A childhood suspended in midair, like a dewdrop off a tree branch.

Remembering how I used to watch them sleep, I understand. I understand the witches of Old Vetris and their desire to freeze their beloveds in time. To never have them age or grow sick. To have them by their sides, always. But isn't that cruel? The witch would die eventually, taking all the Heartless with them. Wouldn't it be so cruel, to ask people to tie their fate to yours like that?

Looking around the ship at night, at Yorl serenely in the crow's nest with his tail hanging and Lucien and Malachite at the prow talking, I realize it's not unusual. Isn't that what friendship is? When you become friends, you ask one another to stay. To tie their fate to yours, until that same fate rips you apart.

So when, I wonder, did Heartlessness become a tool for war and not love? Was it *ever* love? Did inflicting the hunger on a loved one make them love you more? No. Less, surely. Living with the hunger is not a fair exchange, ever. Not even for immortality. And those who became Heartless in the more peaceful days of Old Vetris still would've lost their memories of being human. They would've forgotten the very people who made them immortal, their family and friends. They would've had to start over.

Love doesn't take things away. It gives. I know that now.

I'm glad I got to know that in my lifetime.

I watch Lucien's broad back, he and Malachite laughing together about something. I watch him transform into a crow, black hair growing long and swirling around him and turning white, his clothes bleaching white and his body shrinking small and feathery. He does a quick circle around Malachite's head before turning back to human, boots thumping on the wood of the deck. Malachite looks pissed, but Lucien just laughs, smile bright under the brighter moons.

Trying so hard to steal moments of laughter, even though we all know the end is coming.

I watch his hand, the one I know isn't really there. He'll have to tell, eventually. And Malachite won't be pleased, to put it far too lightly. Neither will Varia, when they get her back.

I laugh under my breath. *Varia.* Oh, the princess is gonna be piping-hot fish-pie mad when she comes back and finds out it was *me* who did the whole world-changing thing, not her. She'll hate me more than she does now, if that's even possible. I can just imagine her walking through New Vetris and constantly spitting on whatever silly statues of me Lucien decides to erect.

"He better make me look good," I mutter to no one and pat my chest. "But then again, with this figure, how could he not?"

"How lucky it is you developed a habit of talking to yourself *outside* your time at the Vetrisian court," Fione's voice comes from behind me. I whirl to smile at her.

"Indeed, Your Grace. Can you imagine the scandal I would've started if someone caught me muttering about eating cow's brains for lunch?"

"Utter mayhem," she agrees, the stars twinkling in her blue eyes.

"I would've died," I say. "Again."

"For good, maybe."

"Oh, no one dies for good." I wave her off. "Haven't you read any books? Characters live on forever."

"You're not a character, Zera." Her voice goes flat. Does she suspect? No. She couldn't have. I haven't let anything show.

"*Obviously.*" I motion at my everything. "I'm larger than life. And, occasionally, my own corsets."

Her face doesn't move, and that's how I know she's thinking about it. Of course she is. Out of all my friends (what a luxury, that sentence), she's always been the whip-smart one. Yorl is just as intelligent, certainly, but Fione *knows*. She has uncanny intuitions and she follows them, because she's a creature of heart. Some part of me still connected to Varia knows that's what the princess loves best about her.

"You can't leave," Fione says finally. I lean on the railing of the ship, watching the sea churn black, embroidered white by our froth.

I grin at her, small and faint. "Why would I?"

"I meant what I said, Zera. I don't want to lose anyone anymore."

"Neither do I," I agree.

She leans beside me, staring into the water with me. "You can't keep doing things on your own."

"Oh, I'm not—not this time. I have all of you."

My smile doesn't reach her, her gaze searching the ocean desperately. "I promised, you know. I made Varia promise we'd name our first child after you."

I laugh, watery. "Bet she fucking hated that."

"More than a little," Fione agrees. "But when this is all over she'll probably come around, considering you're going to save her."

There's a pause in her voice, like she's waiting for me to correct her, to let her down, to shatter the little bead of hope I gave her with my promises to save Varia no matter what. But I'm done doing that. So I just chuckle instead.

"I am, aren't I?"

I watch her compose herself, noble training ramrodding her back straight like I've seen Y'shennria do so many times. To recover. To look strong.

"There will be a celebration when it's over, of course," she says in her best archduchess voice. "And you will be there."

I stare out at the moonlit horizon and imagine it. A half-rebuilt Vetris, full of sawdust and rubble and almost-finished buildings. The brown-patched lawn of the palace, unkempt but spread with a blanket of delicious snacks and cakes and drinks. Fione making flower crowns with Varia, giggling and laughing. Yorl and Malachite bickering about something with a wine-flush on their cheeks. And Lucien, offering me his hand to dance a slow dance in the new buds.

It's a beautiful idea, and I hold on to it like a dream. I hold on to it as Fione leaves and Lucien joins me at the railing, his kiss like honeyed fire. I hold on to it as he pulls me into the captain's quarters, the feather bed consuming us and him consuming me. I hold on to it even as—with every incremental sink of the moons and rise of the sun outside the little window—it slips like seawater through my fingers.

A wolf kisses a rose.

"What are you thinking about?" Lucien murmurs, his dark hair mussed and his eyes heavy. Just looking at him, every worry melts away from me. I smile at him.

"Nothing, anymore."

He strokes my hair from my face, his return smile more glorious than moonlight. "Good."

I don't like to think of them as the last days. I can't think of them as the last days, or Lucien will catch on.

So I think of them as the first days.

The first days of the rest of my life with my friends and with my love. The first days of my life in the new world we're going to make.

Together.

together.

Sometimes, when I'm staring at the ocean depths, at the dolphins cutting paths beside the boat joyfully, I get sad. Not terribly sad. But a little sad that I won't see the new world, that I won't get to see what happens to it, how it moves, what it looks like in the years to come. And when I get too sad, I go to Lucien and he holds me, and I hold him, until both of us feel better. He asks if it's about Varia, the Trees, and I nod. Because it is. That's not a lie at all. I was done lying to him a long time ago.

Sometimes, Lucien's presence doesn't work. Going to him bandages the wound but doesn't heal it. I think that's the nature of love, really—no one can heal you but yourself. Your love for yourself is what is most important, above all others.

"I've gotten so wise in my old age," I drawl to myself, bent over a parchment with a quill in my hand. Sequestered behind a crate spate in the cargo bay with only the brass-gleaming matronic as company, I write. Drafts and drafts of a letter, just one, for all of them. The words don't come out right, or at all sometimes. But I try. I pull blood up from my veins, tears up from my eyes, and I write. It takes days, and many close calls of being discovered by Lucien and his thief-instincts and me-instincts, but I manage to finish alone. I rip up each draft when I'm done for the day, opening the waste shaft to drop them into the sea and be rid of them for good.

It's not an easy thing, to keep a secret from a worrier like Lucien. But I try—he tries to stay up with me, but he's still a mortal. Sleep claims him as it always does. He touches me, trying to skinread out of sheer concern, but all he hears are the faint whispers of the hunger, the wolf who will end the world, a poem orbiting my thoughts like a shield.

In the end, the hunger shields me.

we will protect ourselves and no one else.

The empty wine bottle makes a good hiding place for the letter, and a word to the helmsman polymath to deliver the wine bottle to Lucien when it's over is all it takes.

It's easier for me than most people not to sleep, but that doesn't mean I have to like it. And on the sixth day of travel, I like it even less.

"Hi," I announce as I walk into the mess hall and toward the table where my friends eat hot oats and syrup. "I'm grumpy."

"What'd he do this time?" Malachite drawls, shooting a look at Lucien.

Lucien smugly takes a sip of his tea. "Nothing wrong, I can assure you."

"*Land ho!*"

The cry is exactly the one we've all been waiting for. Our eyes flash up at one another in a suspended second of disbelief, and then everyone bursts from the table and we make one mad dash together up the stairs, crowding the railing for a better look.

"Ow! Stop stepping on my tail!" Yorl yelps.

"Quit putting your tail under my boot, then!" Malachite snaps.

Fione stamps her foot. "Both of you, behave, or I'll put my heel in the two of you!"

"*Heel time, heel time, heel time!*" I chant. Lucien's the only one not taking part in the cabin-fevered fight, his onyx eyes focused on the strip of green in the distance, his whole face washed by relief.

"Cavanos," he breathes.

I watch it grow closer with him, my hand intertwining his on the railing as if to silently say, *I know how much you missed it, how every day away from it has been eating you up.* Because it has. How could it not? He's its prince, and he's always longed to protect it. To protect everyone. Varia destroyed Vetris, but his people are still in Cavanos, and his heart belongs with them.

And to me, too, I think with a wry smile. *We can share it.*

"The Sea Gate is the main entrance to Pala Amna—" Malachite clears his throat and points. There, not far from the beach is a dirt road utterly packed with people, so many they overflow onto the beach, into the thin gray forest bordering it.

"New God's throat," I mutter. "Look at them all."

"Refugees from Cavanos," Lucien says, black iron in his voice. "Perhaps even Helkyris. They think the beneathers can save them from the valkerax."

"And we can," Malachite insists. "Just slowly. With periods to repopulate."

"We don't have that time," the prince insists.

Mal sighs. "I know, Luc. It's called a joke."

"How will we get through that crowd?" Fione frowns. "They must be backing up the entire road into Pala Amna!"

"The Fog Road is the ancestral council's special entrance and a more direct line to them," Yorl offers. "It's highly guarded, but when we announce who we are, I'm sure we'll have no trouble."

"*No trouble*?" Malachite's white brows knit hard. "Yeah, no trouble getting past the guards at the entrance. But there are no guards inside. There's *nobody* inside but the bones of thieves and assassins, because it's booby-trapped to the afterlife and back!"

"Why?" I wrinkle my nose.

"Well, I'm glad you asked, and the answer is because it's less of a gate and more of a *maze designed to destroy anyone who doesn't know the specific route.*"

"Even without the crowd, it saves us hours of travel time in the Dark Below." Yorl ignores him and insists to the prince, "Speed is of the essence."

"Is *death* of the fuckin' essence?" Malachite asks him lightly.

"We'll be fine! We have me." I jerk my thumb to my empty chest and wink. "I can die a few times."

"You upworlders don't seem to spiritsdamn understand," Mal says faux patiently. "The Fog Gate is where we send our defectors and criminals to *die*."

"So then we take the safe route," Fione says softly. "And risk Varia attacking in that time."

"No!" Malachite blurts and then heaves a sigh so massive, it squeaks his chainmail. "Fine. Fine! This is total death-wish garbage, but I'll go along with it because *why not*?!"

"I have my grandfather's map." Yorl taps his head.

"What map?" Malachite growls.

"He bought a rudimentary map of the Fog Road from a beneather on his travels in Pala Amna."

"You know who else bought a rudimentary map?" Malachite motions to the land. "All the dead skeletons in there who were naive enough to give up a gold piece for some hungry kid's attempt at gouging tourists! *There is no map!* The ancestral council are the only ones who know the way, and they make sure of that!"

Yorl looks thoroughly shocked, his ears pulling back. "Are you saying my grandfather—the smartest mortal in all of Arathess—was duped?"

"I'm saying I was seven when Muro Farspear-Ashwalker came to Vetris," Malachite fires back. "And he was a laugh-happy old croak of a man who tripped over his own robe a lot!"

Yorl goes a shade darker under his whiskers. "How dare you—"

"He's not all wrong, Yorl," Lucien murmurs from the railing.

"Your grandfather *did* laugh a lot."

I think back on Muro's night visit. He certainly did laugh a lot, the jolly old cat. As in life, so in afterlife.

"A real hoot. Complete opposite of you, frankly," Malachite bites at Yorl.

"All right, break it up." I step between them. Malachite throws his hands up just as the polymaths bring the sails down, and Yorl's huge green eyes quietly watch the sea below us. The ship slowly glides into a rickety wood dock covered in moss that looks as if it hasn't seen traffic since the Sunless War.

"You okay?" I touch Yorl's paw as we walk down the gangplank.

The celeon looks over at me, heavy-lidded. "Yes. It's just strange. To hear of someone you hold in such high regard as being..."

"Not like you envisioned?" I ask.

He nods. "Not anything like I envisioned."

"He tried to help Vetris, and Varia. I didn't know him, but I'd say he was a good guy."

"He helped design white mercury swords to kill witches."

"We all have our faults," I chirp. "Your grandpa's was laughing."

Yorl breathes out and then turns to say something to the helmsman polymath—about moving the matronic down to Pala Amna via one of the larger surface-to-city air ducts.

"They'll make camp here and wait for me to return," the celeon says when he rejoins us. "So let's ensure we all make it back."

"Affirmative." I salute facetiously even as I feel Fione's eyes dragging on my back the whole way up the beach. She hasn't told anyone, Lucien least of all. She wouldn't. She wants Varia back no matter what, and I know she's struggling with the idea of losing one of us. Me, or the princess. A hard choice to make, certainly.

But Fione won't really lose me. None of them will. I'll be here, always. The valkerax know it, the Tree of Souls knows it, and I know it too, now. Nobody's ever really gone.

Evlorasin said it best.

This is never-goodbye.

Life is a garden that must flourish, and we will water its soil. The valkerax bodies, cut apart and piled on the beach of Rel'donas. The blood watering the sea, the sand, the mangrove trees growing greener as their roots soaked up crimson.

Evlorasin said it best, and most truly.

Something pretty on the not-red sand catches my eye. I bend down and scoop it, skipping up the beach to draw even with Lucien. I hold the tiny, brightly blue iridescent shell up to his face.

"Isn't it pretty?" I ask. He doesn't spare a glance my way, eyes determined and forward, but one corner of his lips perks up.

"This is the part where I'm supposed to say 'not as pretty as you,' right?"

"If you want to sound like a rehearsed theater performance," I sniff. "Then yes. By all means, follow the script."

"Can I deviate?" he ribs playfully.

"Are you capable of deviating? Or is it all just princely business in that head of yours right now?"

There's a popping sound, and the shell disappears from my hand and reappears in his.

"Hey!" I pout. "No fair!"

His smirk grows, and the fingers of his working hand grow midnight void up to the first knuckle.

"I'll give it back later," he assures me.

I point accusatorially at him. "You're a thief!"

"You're a worse one," he lilts. "Considering you stole my heart."

"Ugh!" I tamp down the pleased rush in my chest. "You really *are* sticking to a theater script!"

His laugh fades as we walk over the sandy roots of the forest and toward the crowd. People with bandages over their eyes, their hands, some of them missing legs. Burned skin peeking out, children huddled together without family. The crowd is brimming with the injured, the old, the sick, and the hungry. A little boy tugs at Lucien's overcoat, and the prince puts a hand on the boy's head and offers a bit of jerky from his pouch. He takes it eagerly, chomping, and Lucien looks back to me. His smile is sadder this time.

"Right now, it's princely business time."

My unheart steels and I nod, carefully maneuvering through the crowd with him. People cry out when they see our swords, our clothes that aren't rags. Some cling and beg for food, for shelter, thinking we're with some authority, and I watch Lucien's heart break one shard at a time. He reaches out to all of them with his food and coin pouch, but the crowd starts to frenzy around him, and I know instantly he's in danger. Like a synchronized performance, I feel Malachite at my side as we step in between the prince and the crowd, making a ring with our backs and arms.

"Keep distance," Malachite bellows. "And maintain patience! There's room enough for all in Pala Amna!"

"Is there?" Fione whispers at my side. "It seems half of Cavanos is here."

"Pala Amna is a fortress city," Yorl assures her. "There are wings built into the Dark Below for just such an occasion."

"And the food?" Fione presses.

"The beneathers are expert preservers and fermenters. They can stretch their stores to last for several weeks, even with this amount of mouths."

"Enough time, then," Lucien says, fists gripped tight at his side as he strides through the crowd and we follow. I can tell he's trying desperately not to look at the people, lest he break again. "For us to do what must be done."

"Won't be able to endure a siege, though," Malachite muses.

"If we do things right, there won't be a siege," Fione says. I clear my throat.

"Varia doesn't want a siege anyway. That's slow death. She wants immediate and total destruction."

"Comforting." Malachite throws a smirk at me, and I throw one back.

"I try."

"Advocate," he suddenly barks at a passing guard beneather. "Where's your adjudicator?"

The beneather narrows his ruby eyes through his helmet. "Who's asking?"

A dimness creeps into Malachite's gaze, stifling the usual bite and wit in them. "The Malachite of House Olt'reya."

The change is instant. The guard goes from suspicious and low-stanced to tall, clutching his spear rigidly and his visor almost too comically falling with his shock.

"Mala—" The guard chokes. "Second Son Olt'reya! *Faldinis arn!*"

"*Tor-arn faldinis cet,*" Malachite sighs back. "Now, pretty please tell your adjudicator to get these people processed and inside the road as soon as you can. And if he asks who's being bossy, it was me."

The guard nods and whirls on his heel, ushering the people of the crowd forward and into the massive mouth of a distant cavern with more fervor. I've never seen beneather armor before—I thought it was all chainmail like Mal—but their native design seems a lot more organic. Ivory, but of what? Every piece of their armor is made of smoothed bone, ribbed at the joints with a rubbery substance for what must be great mobility.

"Valkerax, in case you were wondering," Malachite answers my lingering gaze. "That Bone Tree's a pain in the arse, but it's got the right idea—nothing stronger than valkerax bone. And it pulls double duty in disguising our scent from them."

"It isn't easy to shape," Yorl chimes in beside me. "It requires years of precise acid-soaking to make it bend even the slightest bit. And to remove the glow it incurs in the dark."

"So it's sturdy, but hard to replace or repair," I muse.

"Exactly." Yorl's green shining eyes look almost...proud of me?

"Are we going to ignore the part where you hold considerable sway around here, Malachite?" Fione asks innocently. "Did he forget to mention something, Lucien?"

Lucien looks over at his bodyguard. "Should I tell them?"

"What does 'second son' mean, anyway?" I frown.

Yorl is practically vibrating, gaze a little less hostile toward Mal all of a sudden. "Each house has a hereditary hierarchy. Tourmalines are the first sons of a house. Malachites are the second sons of a house. You're...Malachite Olt'reya. I thought the name was ironic—no second son would leave Pala Amna."

"Kept it out of sentimentality, I guess." Malachite massages between his feathery white eyebrows. "It's not even a big deal. I'm technically disowned in all the chronicles."

"Thankfully, beneather politics are quite petty, and branches hoard information from other branches for years hoping to gain political edge in the ancestral council," Yorl murmurs.

Malachite's ruby gaze softens at the celeon for once. "Yeah. Can't get past the bloodpriests or the orators, but the advocates and adjudicators apparently still don't know shit."

I nod like it all makes sense when it absolutely doesn't. "We move quick like bunnies, then, before anybody catches on."

Malachite steers us through the sickly gray forest, great boulders becoming more and more frequent, small rocks making it difficult to walk without pain. An ancient riverbed, maybe. Lucien maneuvers with ease, but Fione and I lag behind, helping each other pick out sturdy surfaces. Up an incline and around a dusty corner of the forest, the dried riverbed carves a path straight to the mouth of a cave, the stone overhang worn blade-sharp smooth by old water. The darkness inside looms as deep and indecipherable as a throat.

And Yorl was right. It's *slightly* well-defended. Sixteen beneather guards in their bone armor stand at the ready, spears and swords aloft, and five more pace atop the cavern with intimidating longbows at the ready.

"Is it always like this?" Fione marvels.

"No," Yorl asserts before Malachite can. "This is very unusual."

"High alert." Malachite makes a *tsk* noise. "Probably because of the refugees."

"Not like they'd shoot them, right?" I ask nervously.

"Nah. But the Fog Gate is ceremonial—which is as close to 'sacred' as beneathers get."

"And it'll kill anyone who goes in unwittingly," Lucien reminds us. I smile.

"Including us!"

"*Especially* us," Malachite corrects. An extravagantly robed figure walks through the guards and he ducks farther behind the boulder. "*Vachiayis.* Bloodpriest."

"What are they doing upworld?" Yorl's whiskers droop with his frown.

"No clue," the beneather spits. "Sorry—can't wave the bloodline around here. They know."

"How bad would it be if you walked up and tried it?" I ask.

"I mean, my aunt had my father's side of the Olt'reya house branded an eternal traitor to the spiral—"

"Sooo..." I trail off. "You're a criminal, then?"

I practically hear the cogs line up in Fione's mousy-haired head next to me. "Perfect, Zera."

"What's—" Yorl stops, mouth twitching. "Oh."

Lucien laughs a little, shoving Malachite out from behind the boulder. "Go on. We're right behind you."

It takes Malachite a bewildered few steps to get it, all of us trailing behind, but when he does he rolls his eyes and grumbles, "Shut it. This brain shit isn't my strong suit."

"We love you all the same," I tease. Fione's giggle resounds, and even Yorl's muzzle pulls into a faint smirk. Lucien pats Mal on the back reassuringly. But the hard-won moment of laughter fades the closer we draw to the Fog Gate, every pair of beneather eyes on us. We fall silent—a cool arrow stepping over the dry riverbed, drawn tight with sheer determination, Malachite spearheading us with his best fiery glare.

27
HUNGER LIKE FIRE

I skid on my elbows onto the vicious stone floor of the Fog Gate. "Ow!" I shout at the beneather guards retreating into the white light of the cavern's mouth. "You didn't have to arrest us so *exuberantly*!"

"As if a scraped knee matters to you," Malachite scoffs, wiping blood from the corner of his mouth. He took several fists to the face in the scuffle to make it all look convincing.

"I happen to like that knee, thank you," I sniff. "It's the sexy one."

"I'm surprised they didn't question why you'd returned so specifically now, and with so many friends." Lucien dusts himself as he gets up, offering his hand to me. I wave him off and he gives it to Fione, instead. She takes it, frowning at some invisible scratch on her cane.

"Mindlessly following orders makes people feel as if they're accomplishing something with their lives," she says. "Ask any of the polymaths who worked with Gavik."

Another thought rests unspoken on my tongue: Varia's killed far more than Gavik. She destroyed Vetris, razed it to the ground. She destroyed Helkyris. Yes, she's under the influence of the Bone Tree. Yes, she had no idea just how strong it would be, how much it would consume her mind. But she still made the choice. The princess still reached out and touched the Tree, hoping to change the world.

Just like I made that choice to kill all those men, when I was first turned.

When she gets back, there will be much to atone for. And, just for a moment, I wish I could be there to show her how.

We brush ourselves off, the Dark Below yawning huge and cold in the descent of the Fog Gate's throat, the gray light from outside fading into pure velvet darkness. Lucien passes around his waterskin to each of us, a thoughtful gesture that gently says "prepare yourselves."

"The guards didn't even hesitate to throw us down here." I marvel.

"The Fog Gate kills all who do not know," Yorl recites. I puff my chest out and draw Father's sword, striding down the slope.

"Right, then," I say. "Ladies and undead thralls first. Lady undead thralls first of all."

"Be careful, Zera, *please*," Lucien calls, boots scrabbling on the stone to catch up. Not being able to sleep on the ship wasn't a problem for the Heartless part of me—my body's primed and ready to go. But it's a moderate difficulty for the Weeping part of me—my brain is buzzing with disorderly thoughts, with fuzzy worries and tangled strings of plans. The background chatter of the hunger isn't loud because I've been eating organs, but trying to ignore it or push it down feels like lifting an iron carriage with only my pinkies.

I grasp for silence, for any shred of the quiet peace of Weeping, but my own mind fights against me, a tight, close, me-shaped chamber lined with dagger-teeth, every prick worth a scream that echoes eternally.

The farther down we go, the sharper the Dark Below sinks its fangs into us and the more the blackness becomes impenetrable, until Lucien finally has to witch-light his hand, his purple-black fire lighting a faint sphere around us. The cavern walls aren't smooth anymore—faint carvings like runes peek out from between the moss and unfathomable age of the place.

"Sound-activated traps," I hear Malachite murmur. "I don't make noise when I walk, but the rest of you sound like horses."

"I object," Yorl hisses. "I'm far quieter than you."

Malachite pauses, listens, then nods. "Okay, not bad. But unless the rest of you grow hairy feet like Bookworm over here, we're going to trigger one of the sound traps sooner or later."

"I can muffle us," Lucien offers.

"Isn't that difficult?" Fione asks. "Three people, for who knows how long?"

"Not as difficult as you'd think. The stone down here is hungry for anything—sound most of all."

"Whatever that means." Malachite shakes his head. "Just go easy on yourself, Luc."

The witchfire suddenly illuminates a split in the path—one tunnel going left, the other going right. Malachite stops us, he and Yorl listening carefully with their long ears.

Yorl looks at him first. "Nothing."

"The other way, then," Malachite asserts.

"But—" Yorl stops, listening to the other side. "There's nothing there, either."

"There is," Mal insists. "Faint clicking. You just can't hear it."

"Clicking?" Fione's voice cracks nervous. "Doesn't that mean there's a trap down that way?"

"The ancestral council is made up of beneathers," Yorl says. "Beneathers have the best hearing in the world. They can hear the clicking as no other mortal can—not even celeon."

"It's how I used to spy on you two." Mal grins at me and Luc. "Didn't even have to be close. Could be blocks away and I'd still hear every word of your vapid flirting. There's a trap both ways," he clarifies. "Probably. It's just one of them beneathers can hear, and the other is silent. So we go the beneather-way."

"If it was that easy, every beneather not on the council would've navigated the Fog Gate by now," Lucien points out.

"S'not gonna be easy to disarm the trap," Mal agrees. "But it's better than nothing."

"If we get lost down here—" Fione starts.

"We won't," I assure her. I try to summon the Weeping again as we walk down the imperceptibly clicking left path. If things go wrong, I can always dig into the stone with my claws, create them a shelter or a new tunnel. Nothing of this place looks valkerax proof, and certainly not Heartless-valkerax proof—

"What was that?" Yorl stops. I freeze at the front, peering uselessly into the dark ahead of us.

"The clicking," Malachite says.

"It's getting louder," Yorl agrees. "But it's…that's not mechanical—"

I take a single step forward, Father's blade at the ready. Behind me I hear Malachite unsheathe his, too, and the metallic ring of Fione's crossbow unfurling echoes.

Lucien's eyes widen at my side, and he sucks in a breath as he stares down the tunnel. "It's alive."

"What is? Is it a valkerax?" Fione whispers, loading a bolt.

"No." Malachite narrows his eyes, and I see his pale hand shaking around the hilt. "Something worse."

Worse? I grit my teeth and step forward, the clicking finally loud enough to reach my ears. It's getting closer. And *faster*. Not a valkerax—not in the slightest. Something far quicker, and with far more legs.

"The stone down here might be hungry, but the darkness is well-fed," Lucien mutters, sweat beading on his temple. He strains, fingers turning dark as his witchfire struggles to spread its sphere of light outward. I step forward without thinking, my boot crunching something—bone. A skeleton hand; human or beneather or celeon, I can't tell. Gnaw marks deep in the bone.

Bones as far as the witchfire can illuminate—*thousands*. Ribs, feet, legs, half-mangled skulls.

The whole of the tunnel floor is made of mortal bones.

Fione suddenly releases a shot, the bolt whistling past my ear, and I expect it to clatter down into the empty darkness, the bones, but there's a wet *crunch* and fear eats me alive. Close. So *close*. No cry of pain, no sound other than the clicking getting faster, angrier. Somewhere in my brain, just before the chaos, a clear and rather helpful thought rings out.

How is it moving through the bones without making them clatter?

Two impossibly long spears jut at me out of the darkness, and I move to intercept them with my immortal body, but they don't pierce. They give softly around me, slithering past me like tentacles, or whiskers. No—*antennae*. Fione cries out, recoiling, and I hear Malachite swallow the most uncharacteristic whimper as one curls up his face. He's stared down full-grown valkerax effortlessly, but this thing has him frozen in fear.

"It comes!" Lucien bellows.

The rest of it bursts into the light, smooth and long and brown and glinting like polished armor, every part of it, every part of it segmented, millions of legs clicking against the stone of the ceiling and clinging to it effortlessly. Its head, nearly as big as the tunnel, glints with a set of massive serrated mandibles the width of two of me. The head waves madly back and forth, a bolt stuck in its plate-size eye bleeding blue.

It's not a valkerax at all.

"A migtratus!" Yorl snarls. "The mandibles are deadly venomous!"

It's charging for us with a single-minded fury—right for the mortals. This tunnel is even smaller—even worse than when Evlorasin escaped and Malachite and I stopped it. There's no space to fight *at all*, the tunnel essentially a feeding tube funneling right to the giant insect. Definitely a trap.

We can't back up. It's so fast—so much faster than I'd be able to dig a hole through the stone. I have to stop it here. Right *here*, where it meets my blade, because the mortals are lined up behind me like a row of perfect sweetrounds. I don't know how thick the armor on its head is, but I don't have a choice—

I feel Lucien's hand on my shoulder just then, a liquid warmth running down it and through my body, curling up my arm and lighting the darkness brighter—witchfire. Purple-black witchfire slithers up my arm, unburning, and moves to my hand, wrapping around the hilt of Father's sword and up to the blade.

"Run," Lucien whispers.

And I trust him.

I trust him, to the end of the world and back again.

Cloaked in black fire, I hold the sword high through the fear, running full tilt at the insect. The fire banners out like a flag, the tip of the sword grinding sparks against the stone ceiling, and I can see every hair on the thing's body now, every drip of poisonous saliva glinting on the mandibles, every hexagon of its unwounded eyeball, its blood the smell of tar and vinegar, and with all my Heartless strength I brace and let out a roar, my hands death-gripping the sword's handle for all they're worth. I feel it hit, blade meeting between the mandibles, the fire burning into what the blade can't reach.

we are hungrier than you.

A second of resistance, a hitch. It writhes against me, the force of its long body condensed into this one point. I strain with all the words and muscles and teeth the song gives me.

"I am...*hungrier than you!*"

And then the give.

Freed, the sword carves through the insect and I sprint, cold black blood raining down on me but unable to extinguish the witchfire, to extinguish my momentum as I slice through all of it, the whole length of it until the spiked tail.

For a moment, the insect still clings to the ceiling.

And then the split; the long, twitching corpse falling to the ground.

Panting, I look behind me, the witchfire lighting up Lucien's face—the gentle curve of his beaming smile, the rise and fall of his likewise panting chest, the way his eyes glint out like black diamond from the other end of the tunnel. We've done it. Together.

I can taste the kiss he's giving me without ever touching him. His expression in this second is clearer than any signpost, any flag.

He loves me. *Me.* The hungry me, the fighting me, the blood-stained me. I cup it like a desert-dying man cups water—preciously. I'll always be here, with him. I know that.

But I will miss this look.

Malachite has to sprint through the bones and between the bisected body of the giant insect to get to the other side.

"Massive wyrms with six eyes and an ancient bloodthirst, no problem," I say, catching up with his hurried steps down the tunnel. "But give you something with more than six legs and you suddenly take issue."

"Don't even start," he snarls, face even more bloodless than usual. "I'm not proud of it."

"Who would be?" Fione asks as she, too, catches up. "I gather no one on Arathess is partial to giant insects."

"They aren't insects," Yorl corrects. "A common mistake—they're more akin to crustaceans. It's a clever trap of the ancestor council's—they're highly repelled by the scent of juniper. You could walk through a tunnel full of them with a single bough and they'd all scatter."

"Remind me to pack an array of very specific tree branches next time," I chime.

"Whatever they are, whatever they hate, they're horseshit," Malachite mutters.

Lucien draws even with him. "You did well, Mal."

"Ugh. Don't patronize me, Luc."

"I think it's kind of cute, actually," I tease, wiping the black blood off my mouth with Lucien's offered handkerchief. "The most badass of badasses in all Vetris is weak to creepy-crawlies!"

"What did I *just* say about the patronizing?" the beneather snaps.

"Everyone has a weakness," Fione agrees. "Yours is understandable, at the very least. I've known him since nursery, but I *still* don't understand Lucien's obsession with fictitious novels."

"Or yours with the color pink," Lucien drawls.

"Or mine, with cake!" I add. "Actually, I understand that one intimately."

"A pink room filled with cake and novels," Yorl murmurs. "Why not arrange it when this is over?"

Lucien beams at the celeon. "A fine idea. Maybe a rousing duel for Mal, and what will it be for you?"

Yorl waves his paw. "I require little. But I do indulge in a peppermint cordial from time to time."

The pleasant idea floats around us all, sanding down the grumpy look on Malachite's face and warding off the growing chill of the Dark Below as we press on. They don't know if they'll die here, or later, or at all. They think none of them might survive. It's a brave thing, to think about a nice future in the terrifying present.

I smile to myself and lead on, first in line for the deadly traps; my friends are so brave. Brave and silly.

Of course they'll live.

Because I'll make sure of it.

28

THE DURANCE
OF THE
ANCESTORS

The other traps of the Fog Road are no less gut-wrenching—and occasionally, actually gut-wrenching. I look down at my flayed-open stomach and at the bit of hanging intestine there with faint amusement through the ripping pain.

"H-Hello again. I'd n-nearly forgotten what you looked like."

The heavy, rhythmic *thwump* of the blades swinging in and out of slots in the wall drowns out Lucien's shouts to me. We've tripped something accidentally, and the blades don't seem to be stopping. I dodge out of the way of another swinging for my head, blood squelching down my legs. Five, six—seven of them, all of them longer than my entire body and sharper than my most deadly incisors. How do I stop them? The mortals will never make it through here, and Lucien can't teleport us—his witchfire has been flickering wildly the farther down we go. Magic is hard to do in the Dark Below; Varia had the same problem when she was trying to capture a valkerax to find the Bone Tree. Malachite swings his broadsword with a weighty overhead strike, meeting the first swinging blade head-on, and for a second he makes it pause, the veins in his biceps and forehead straining.

"Go!" he bellows. Fione and Yorl and Lucien all duck beneath it, to the space between it and the next blade. I claw into my mind, trying to pull up the Weeping, but it's even harder than it was near the surface—like someone's been moving it away from me bit by bit this whole time I've been walking. Malachite whirls, letting the swinging blade go and joining the others in the in-between space.

"*Body!*" the beneather mouths at me. "*We trade off!*"

His ruby eyes flick to the next swinging blade, and I get it. I don't *like* it, but I get it. Lucien hates it, but his shouts for me to stop are drowned by the grinding of metal and stone.

"Gods bless this absolute mess," I mutter, waiting for the next blade to swing down, and I jump between it and the wall slot. The impact knocks the wind out of my lungs, and the sharp edge of the blade knocks my lungs out of my body quite literally, honeycomb-gray peeking through my ribs and the wall behind me splattering red with my blood. But still the blade doesn't lose momentum, grinding me against the wall with vicious fervor. It's worse than being speared by any human, but not nearly as bad as being ripped apart by Evlorasin's thousands of serrated teeth. I can manage—or at the very least, I can hold the blade back for a few seconds.

Faintly and through the pain, I see Malachite and the other mortals blur by, Lucien's dark eyes razors of worry as he reaches out for me. The beneather shuffles him along, and I hear the screech of metal on metal again as he stops the next blade and lets them through. He's close enough now to hear his yell.

"Your turn, Six-Eyes!"

This is the worse part—ripping free. I let my weight down, fall to my knees, the blade yanking up through my shoulder and cold air slicing through warm, screaming flesh. I duck along the wall, Lucien's magic healing me only in slow trickles down here. Flesh knits in small increments, bones cracking back into place in slow motion. The slow healing hurts far worse than the blade's impact. But eventually, there's enough meat of me again to stop the next blade. My body's ready, but my mind isn't as prepared as I'd like—the next hit gets my spine through my stomach, bile and blood in my throat, and I black out.

But the magic won't let me rest.

The Trees won't let any of us rest.

I wake up again to Malachite's shout, Lucien's hand in my blood-drenched one. I can feel all of them helping me—Yorl's paw on my back, Fione's hand on my arm, pulling me out of the blade and into place for the next as Malachite stops the second-to-last one, his face pouring sweat and his veins glistening under paper skin.

"Last one!" Fione encourages, blood-flecked face determined. Her tender touch is so different from her fearful hyperventilating just a month ago. It gives me something to hold on to as I fling myself into the path of the last blade, marking the wall with my blood one last time.

We make it through, and they pull me out yet again. A handful of hands, helping me. I collapse on the ground, laughing blood. Lucien kneels at my side, cradling me, and I can feel him pouring all his concentration into the magic flooding into me and stitching closed my injuries.

"What's so godsdamn funny?" he whispers down at me, the words hot but his tone cool.

"Thank you." I smile up at him, touching his face and regretting the blood-finger marks it leaves on his golden cheekbones. "For letting me get hurt. For letting me do what I can to help."

"Implying anyone could ever *let* you do anything, you stubborn wildcat." He holds me close, my chest wounds closing against his own chest.

The pain was worth it this time, and it's nice because that's never a guarantee; pain isn't often wrapped up in a neat bow of purpose. But the benefit of immortality is a second chance at everything. Now that we've sprung one trap, Fione and Yorl know what to look for—the mechanical triggers hidden in the stone and littering the tunnel moving forward. They steer us around every horsehair tripwire, every deadly gas vent, and soon the tunnel changes, morphs and widens and opens into a yawning chasm—darkness as far down and far as we can see. The tunnel continues as a thin stone pathway from one side of the gap to the other, barely room enough for two people to walk side by side.

"I'm no expert, but this room sort of screams 'trap.'" The buzzing in my head chooses the exact moment I step into the cavern to intensify, crushing me with a flood of random thoughts and pressures. It's like someone's crashed cymbals in my head and turned it to mush: strings of jokes I can barely hold on to, one argument replaced with the next, one thought laced with another, and the hunger beneath it all, conducting it like the head of a dark, chaotic choir.

"Definitely a trap. Not for us, though." Malachite points at the distant, faintly lit walls on either side of the chasm. They slope up to the infinite ceiling and down to the infinite drop, but Lucien's flickering witchfire illuminates them enough to see the very deliberate carvings in the stone.

"Beneather runes." Yorl squints, his catlike pupils dilated so large his eye color is just a faint ring of green around black. "This room is a *hevstrata*."

"Hev-what now?" Fione frowns.

"Beneather runes are the only things that can affect valkerax— hold them in place or keep them out of a place—"

"I know that," Fione interrupts, but Yorl presses on.

"They become unreliable against large masses of valkerax. Which is why these *hevstrata* were made in the early days of the War of White: choke points full of beneather runes meant to disorient groups of them."

"It messes with their brains," Malachite clarifies. "If a hunting party's being chased by a bunch, they come here to throw 'em off. It works. Most of the time."

"Well, good news—it's working right now." I wince, holding my scalp. "Bad news—it's *working* right now."

"Are you all right?" Lucien asks.

"Oh, I'm fine. I just can't—" I pause, gulping air and trying to remember what I was going to say next. The noise is like a cloth over wood, sweeping away the crumbs of the sentence cake I was trying to build. "I—I can't think straight."

"Then think crooked," Malachite snipes. "We just need to get across the gap, and it'll get better."

"Maybe," Yorl adds.

Malachite sends a withering look at him. "*Maybe* move your arse."

"I'm just being factual," the celeon hisses back, beginning to mince down the thin pathway with an effortless ease. His tail swishes, no doubt giving him a balance advantage. Fione stares warily at the thin pathway and then her cane.

Malachite sees it and offers his pale hand to her. "C'mon, Your Grace. I'll carry you on my back."

"I can walk just fine," she sniffs.

"I know you can," the beneather sighs. "It's just to be safe. C'mon."

She studies the impossibly long drop for a second more and then slings her cane beneath her pack, climbing on Malachite's kneeling back. He straightens, holding her like it's nothing, and looks back at Lucien and me.

"I'll leave you two slobbering lovebirds to figure out who goes first."

"Eternally thankful," Lucien drawls and tips an imaginary hat. He turns back to me with a smirk. "Jealous, you think?"

"Irascibly so," I agree and motion for him to go first.

"Don't fall," he advises.

"If I do, I'll shout up and let you know how deep it is." I smile. I'm making jokes, but the second I take two steps onto the precarious line of stone, I feel my stomach drop out. A cold wind whispers up from the abyss on either side of my feet, and I finally get it. It wasn't the traps or the suffocating darkness and closeness of the tunnel. It's this yawning nothingness that crystallizes my understanding of the Dark Below—it goes on *forever.*

It's not a place but a feeling, the deep and unsettling feeling of eternity. I've felt it before in my darkest moments of hunger—the hopelessness of my situation. The hopelessness of immortality. No change. No end. Only pain like dark, without rest.

I look up from the fall and to Lucien's back. Because of him, I found rest. Because of them all, I found change. But other Heartless aren't so lucky. And the valkerax aren't lucky at all—dying in scores for a Tree they can't disobey.

We make it to the other side of the fall, the cavern narrowing again, and I look back once at the runes all over the walls. Runes that tell me to forget, to think, to run chaos in my own mind. Runes that presume I'm like the other valkerax, like every other Heartless, like everyone else who can't disobey.

Like everyone else who wants to continue the cycle.

A single blood tear falls off my cheek, and my soft laugh is swallowed up by the abyss.

Finally, through the bones and the traps and the shadow, we come to a door.

The complete lack of sound in the Dark Below started to break apart long ago, interrupted by faint hissing, bangs echoing, the sounds of footsteps. Civilization. Even the smell changes—moss and sterile stone replaced by cooking oil and metal and tobacco smoke. The door is made of stone like the tunnel is, like everything in the Dark Below is.

Malachite turns to us, knitting his fingers in his broadsword handle. "If they ask you questions, don't say shit. Let me handle it."

"I thought you've been disowned?" Fione lilts.

"I can speak to them," Yorl asserts. "My grandfather was a prominent figure here—"

"If I hear you say 'my grandfather' one more time, I'm gonna make you meet him," Malachite snaps.

I slide in and put a hand over Malachite's mouth, smiling at Yorl. "I'll go first. I'm a great talker."

"A greab horbseshitter," Malachite grumbles through my fingers. But when I release him he plays mild and leans on the stone door to crack it open for us. I blink away the light, everything so bright and sudden, and walk over the threshold.

The feeling of a blade at my throat is almost immediate, but I can't see them through the eye-searing light. Sound works a little better.

"Who are you? Identify yourself immediately or face death!"

The voice means business, so ragged and furious, the joke in my throat dies. The clink of bone armor and the feel of cold steel against my neck. I adjust slowly to the sight of a beneather holding a fanged dagger to me, the same dagger design I've seen on Malachite's hip. The room is well-lit by clusters of brightmoss in clay jars, the kind I grew used to in the underground arena where Yorl and I trained Evlorasin. But this moss is much brighter and all in the same golden-orange color, nearly simulating the hue of fire torches. Incredibly intricate and rich tapestries line the walls in the hundreds, made of what looks like white valkerax hair stained in differing shades of green and rust. Remarkably, they've gotten the persistent valkerax-y smell of blood out of it; the whole room thick with the saccharine smell of incense and oiled metal.

"My name is Zera Y'shennria," I say slowly. "And I have some information for the ancestral council about the valkerax horde."

The eyes of the guard holding the dagger to me widen, the

ruby a darker wine-red than Malachite's but their skin the same paper-bloodless-white, if a little grayer. Their eyes dart to the door behind me, and the guard barks, "The rest of you come out. Now."

Lucien, Fione, and Yorl ooze around the door, but when Malachite comes out, the guard's eyes narrow.

"Olt'reya," they say with a full snake's worth of venom.

Malachite's eyes widen, his grin lopsided and more nervous than I've ever seen. "Lysulli," he murmurs. "You... Look at you. Full ancestral regalia. Since when did you get good?"

"Shut your mouth!" Lysulli demands. "What are you doing here? How did you get through the Fog Gate?"

Malachite looks over at me and grins. "I had a little help."

Lysulli makes a furious exhaling noise, grumbling. "What are those idiots thinking? Has the crowd made them lose their mind? Sending a group down into the Fog Gate. *P'eqeq*."

"Madness," Malachite translates under his breath, then speaks up. "Listen, this'll sound *p'eqeq*, too, but you gotta let us talk to the council."

"And why in the afterlife would I do that?" Lysulli snarls. "You're a disgraced Malachite who didn't even stick around to make an appeal. You just left. You abandoned us."

"Abandoned *you*, you mean," Malachite says softly. Lucien and I look at each other, and Fione's brow furrows. Malachite being genuine? The world's ending. Lysulli and Mal clearly know each other, but Lysulli plays the tough card.

"The council has no interest in unloyalists like you." They sniff.

"You should let the council decide that," Lucien says. "Considering you're a guard, and not one of them."

"Who is this human?" Lysulli's fury rivets to the prince. "And why does he talk like he's above it all?"

"Oh, that's just Luc. You'll get used to it." Mal laughs.

"No, I won't," they snarl. "Because I'm throwing all of you in the cells." Their hand moves for a whistle around their neck, but Malachite's hand suddenly shoots out and encompasses Lysulli's on the whistle gently.

"Lys, please," he murmurs. "You gotta trust me."

Lysulli's wine-colored glare pierces up into his for a tense, drawn-out moment. And then they smack Malachite's hand away, reaching up to take off their helmet. Their long white hair waterfalls out, revealing a fine, vulpine face with a high nose and thin lips with rouge on them. A sharp face, like a honed blade.

"What do you have?"they demand, but it's less harsh this time.

"We've got a way to control the horde," I say. "And it's not the Bone Tree."

Lysulli's eyes slice over at me, suddenly rapt with interest. "Truly?"

"I don't lie to gorgeous people." I smile.

"You just flatter them thinking they'll like you for it," Lysulli scoffs. They remind me so much of Malachite when I first met him in Vetris; as thorny as a burr stuck in a tunic. Their eyes find Yorl. "You, that pelt color—Farspear-Ashwalker?"

Yorl makes a bow. "His grandson, Yorl."

I watch Lysulli put something together in their head, and they look back at me, clearly ignoring Malachite.

"Fine. I'll bring you to the council. But if they execute you, don't come for me in the afterlife."

"No promises," I chime. Lysulli scoffs again and turns on their heel, the sound of their bone boots clicking sharp against the stone floor. We all scrabble to catch up. Without even looking at him, Lysulli's sure to keep a careful distance from us, and Mal most of all.

Lucien and Fione march determinedly, but Yorl's head is on a constant swivel, taking in every tapestry and door and piece of stone-cut furniture lined with scaled cushions.

"Never been down here?" I ask.

"Not in the ancestral council building," he says, green eyes gleaming with the reflections of a gem-encrusted wall that forms a mosaic of the beneathers fighting the valkerax. "It's where they keep the majority of their historical records and artifacts. Only the ascendants of the beneathers are allowed here."

"Ascendants?" I tilt my head.

"Beneather culture is based on a merit system." Yorl touches a tapestry lightly with his paws. "If you contribute greatly to the culture by some measure, whether in trade or an invention or by battle, you're granted the title of ascendant, and given privileges not allowed to others. The Olt'reya family, for example, are a family that's had many ascendants, so they're known as an ascendant family, and kept in high regard."

"So, it's the beneather version of high society," I muse. "Like Vetris and their nobles, except based in practicality, not the luck of being born into a bloodline."

"Precisely," Yorl agrees. "Though such a system puts passive strain on the culture as a whole to contribute, and creates much negative bias against those who can't, or don't."

"Like Malachite," I say. "Who just left upworld to be a bodyguard for a human prince."

Yorl doesn't say anything to that, whiskers twitching, and that's all the confirmation I need. Lysulli leads us past a long line of guards dressed in the same armor as them, and it's then I realize that, unlike the beneather guards upworld, these guards have beneather runes carved into their armor. Something deep in my gut recoils at the sight of them, and I realize my body starts making space between me and them as I pass, an instinct, a tic I disturbingly can't control. It's like a goose following true north—I must avoid them. I have to avoid them.

"Valkerax repelling runes." Yorl watches me move as the guards do, though the guards' gazes are filled with far more suspicion. "Try not to be so obvious about it."

"Big words," I mutter, sidestepping another guard, "from the guy who made me like this."

"By accident," he insists.

"Well then. I *accidentally* forgive you," I tease, only really half listening at this point. Between the runes on the armor and the strange architecture, I can barely pay attention—the stone here is carved butter-smooth and elegantly, shaped into incredible helixes and spirals that wind down the hallways. The helix shape seems to be popular—stitched into banners and made into fountains. Occasionally, the hallways open up to underground courtyards deprived of sun, but they're no less beautiful in their vegetation; swathes of moss like rich quilts, spidery mushrooms curlicuing down from the ceilings, and pitch-black ferns gently bleeding great globules of iridescent purple liquid. There's even one of those sapphire, gemlike mushrooms growing that Fione and Malachite lost their minds over in Windonhigh, but this one is far tinier.

Lysulli leads us through one of the garden courtyards and up a staircase to a massive steel door. Out of the corner of my eye, I see Malachite looking at all the plants, and for the first time I see a drop of wistfulness in his eyes. This is home for him, isn't it? He's been gone so long.

"We're here." Lysulli stops in front of it. "I'll do the talking until one of the council acknowledges you."

"Much obliged." Lucien nods with no hint of sarcasm, but they glare at him as if he dripped with it. They turn to the guards on either side of the door.

"Adjudicator Lysulli, reporting. I've got upworlders here who claim they have a contribution to the spiral."

The guards look us up and down, and one says, "And what credentials have they?"

Malachite steps up, thumbing his nose languidly. "I'm

Olt'reya Malachite."

The guards looked shocked through their visors, hands tightening around their spears. I clench my fists, ready, Lucien's body going stock-still in that way it does before he magics. But Lysulli squeezes between us.

"At least let them in so the council can decide the defector's fate," they insist.

The guards move slowly to the door, eyes on Malachite the whole time as they winch it open. This whole "outcast" thing must be a huge deal, with the way everyone's looking at him like humans look at a Heartless. I almost feel bad we came to Pala Amna, but it's fleeting. We had to. Malachite knew that, too.

The steel screams as it parts, the embossed valkerax on the doors beckoning us into shadow with their stylized claws and teeth.

"Any advice?" I lean in and ask Malachite. He's not the type to be comforted by a held hand or a touched shoulder, but standing at his side feels right. And it helps; I can tell in the way his posture goes soft even as his whole face hardens with something like pain.

"Don't let them make you feel like shit for being you," he says. It's a sentence with the weight of years behind it, but I don't dare ask.

"Noted."

There's a pause, our shoes clipping on the polished stone floor as we walk through the entranceway heavy with precious gems.

"I like you," I start. "For being you."

"You're the only one down here who does," he says, his smirk lazy. "And the only one who matters."

It's a moment of sweetness before the bitter reality sinks in. The gems of the entranceway expand into solid emerald walls shot with gold, bands of lapis lazuli and topaz glimmering here and there in a trenchant pattern. I'm half expecting the council to be encased in glass like the High Witches, eerie and suspended. But thankfully there's a stone table in the center, and the ancestor council sits at it in old stone chairs, their robes overflowing long on the emerald floor.

"For a moment, I was worried it was glass," Fione whispers to me when she sees me staring at the floor.

I nod emphatically. "Me too."

"Mind yourselves," Lucien warns, and I look up to see the ancestor council's frozen in their talks to stare at us.

I've never seen old beneathers before—just Malachite, and he's young. The council, though, is elderly, their faces so heavily wrinkled it's hard to see the slits of their eyes; still ruby, but with massive pupils, nearly as big as Yorl's were in the Dark Below. They're much smaller than I thought they'd be, too—human-child-size, like Crav. Beneathers must shrink drastically as they age. Their ears are just as long as Malachite's, but pierced and hung with heavy garnets.

"Who approaches the durance of the ancestors?" the elderly beneather at the head of the table croaks. Despite how small he is, his voice booms like a drum in the near-empty room. Lysulli steps up instantly, making a rigid salute in their bone armor.

"Ancestor," they start, "these upworlders claim they have information for the spiral. And one of them is—"

"Olt'reya Malachite," Malachite says, stepping forward with them.

The ancestors at the table raise their wild white eyebrows, clicking their ringed fingers in their earrings as they glance at one another knowingly and unhappily.

"Outcasts return on punishment of death," the head ancestor croaks out. "They have been torn from the spiral and deemed unusable. Is that why you have come? To die?"

I flicker my eyes to Lucien. Would they really kill him?

"I'll happily put my head on whatever chopping block you've got." Mal lifts his chin. "After you hear what my friend the prince of Cavanos has to say."

He motions at Lucien, and Lucien approaches the table carefully. Lysulli's face falls, and they snaps their eyes accusatorially to us, as if asking *why didn't you tell me he was a prince in the first place?*

"He has the look of a d'Malvane," an ancestor agrees in a birdy, high-pitched wheeze as they look Lucien over.

"Do we have time to entertain him?" another ancestor asks in a guttural growl. "He offers nothing. Vetris is lost, their armies ravaged, and so shall we be if we do not finalize these battle plans."

One of them scoffs. "We are in the spiral, but not so entrenched that we are empty of common manners for foreign royalty."

"Welcome, then, Lucien of House d'Malvane," the head ancestor announces. "You bring us information?"

"What is this 'spiral' they keep talking about?" I whisper to Yorl.

He leans in, whiskers tickling my cheek. "It's what they call the eternal fight against the valkerax. Everything goes to the spiral. Everyone who dies returns to the spiral. And so on."

"That explains the decor," I whisper back, staring at the massive helix of carved emerald around the door.

Lucien looks over at Malachite, and then bows to the council. "Your Honors," he starts. "I would gladly share my knowledge, but I fear for Malachite's safety. Would you consider sparing him his punishment?"

The head ancestor shifts in his pool of a cloth robe. "Human word holds little sway in the Dark Below, Your Highness. Our laws are our laws, subject to no royal favors."

"Outcasts must be disposed of, lest they rot the spiral!" An ancestor's wrinkly fist beats the stone table.

The birdy-voiced ancestor speaks up. "Consider this, fellows; they bring a Farspear-Ashwalker with them—a great scholar who aided us many times before with the valkerax."

All eyes flicker to Yorl, his mane flaring a little in stress or pride—I can't tell. He really does look like Muro. The birdy-voiced ancestor smiles, face melting into a pool of wrinkles.

"If Farspear-Ashwalker's information justly aids the spiral, as it has before, will we not consider mercy for a defector this once?"

There's a stretched quiet, the ancestors looking to and from one another. They murmur, but not in whispers—far, far lower than a whisper. A breath. I can't hear a single thing beyond the slight hiss of air, but I'm sure with their long ears, they hear one another's words perfectly well.

Malachite shakes his head at the prince. "Don't worry about it, Luc. I'll be fine. Just tell 'em."

"I won't let them kill you, Mal," the prince insists.

"Me either," I agree.

"I came here figuring it'd happen." Malachite's voice turns to granite. "Just tell 'em. We don't have time to sit here and stop everything just for me."

Fione steps up then, cane tapping on the floor so loud, it sounds thunderous among the council's soft whispers.

"You will allow Malachite to walk free, or we will never tell you how to stop the valkerax coming for your last city."

The ancestor council's huge black pupils focus on her perfect posture and gleaming brown curls, studying her as she defies them, defies Malachite's insistence and the world's insistence that we sacrifice people to make things better.

I've never been prouder of her than in this moment. My memory flashes to her timid, tiny frame at the first banquet where I met her, and now, in contrast, she stands like an apple tree grown gargantuan, like a queen, like Archduchess Himintell.

No.

She stands like *Fione.*

"We know how to stop them," she continues. "For good this time. And you will trade this information for Malachite's total exoneration from your spiral. He will never be executed by you. He will be allowed to walk free in his homeland for as long as he lives, and you will condone this."

"Insolent little—" an ancestor hisses.

"The spiral you have bled and killed and died a thousand years for," Fione interrupts them like a glass cut, deep and precise. "This information can stop it. Forever."

Yorl's brow twitches minutely, but the rest of us are stone-faced. Yorl knows she's not following the script—splitting the trees again won't stop the spiral. It'll condemn the valkerax to the Dark Below again. Not as many of them, but most. That's not stopping the spiral—it's simply continuing it. He thinks she's making promises she can't keep, Malachite and Lucien, too. They just have the court training to hide it.

But she's not lying. She knows.

Out of everyone, she knows what I'm going to do.

And when I do it, there will be no more spiral anymore. The spiral will change. The beneathers won't have to shoulder it alone—it will be everyone's burden. Everyone's fight. It may not even be a fight; maybe this time, without the Bone Tree screaming madness into their ears, the valkerax will be calm. Maybe this time, it will be different.

This time, we can try again—without using the Tree to control them. To control anyone.

"You." The head ancestor points to Fione with one gnarled, tiny finger. "You will tell us, then. Tell us how you will stop the spiral—"

Lucien steps up. "Your Honors—"

"Alone."

The shift of the beneather guards behind us is clear by the sound—bone armor boots stepping to us over the floor.

"Fione," Lucien starts. "Will you—"

"I will, Your Highness," she agrees without turning to look

at us. "Every last bit."

The plethora of guards hover, waiting without words, telling us to leave with just their towering body language.

Lucien stares at Fione for one last beat, and then turns to us. "Let's go."

Our footsteps ricochet down the entrance tunnel, bookended by the clamor of the guards, Yorl looking confused and Malachite looking uneasy and Lucien looking ahead. Just ahead. He wants answers. He'll try to skin read me if I put my hand in his. I know that—I can feel that. I know him and how he works.

But the answers are a song now.

I put my hand in his and smile. "It'll be all right. She's going to tell them what we know."

He nods and squeezes my fingers close to his palm. He's worried it won't be enough to save Malachite's life, to persuade them to help us, but it is. She'll tell them what we know. What she and I know. What she knows I'll do when we get to the First Root.

I won't split it. Not again. And she knows that.

This is Fione and me—together—wordless and word full, working as one.

In a way, it's her telling me she approves of my plan. She's telling me she's chosen to trust me, that she's done hedging between Varia and me as she did on the ship, and now she's made a choice. She's given me her trust.

I smile at the floor and hold Lucien's warm hand, hold the boy who's trying to read my skin so hard, and I *understand*. Love doesn't take. It gives.

She's given the wolf her trust.

And the wolf will give her Varia in return.

29

AMETHYST

Waiting's far easier when you're an immortal thrall with all of eternity ahead of you. The mortals, on the other hand, have it a little rougher.

"I would've been just fine." Malachite throws his hands up. "If you'd all kept your mouth shut and let them imprison me for a day. They woulda been distracted by my arse long enough for you to creep down to Pala Orias."

"And when we came back, you'd be beheaded," Lucien finishes. "Like *Vachiayis* I was going to let that happen."

"It's too bad only humans can be Heartless," I mourn, batting my eyelashes at Malachite. "We'd do well suffering together, I think."

"Well?" Malachite arches a brow.

"Stylish, at the very least," I insist. "By far the most important thing."

Yorl's claws click across the stone floor of the reception hall as he paces. What looks to be an entire valkerax skeleton encased in gold is suspended from the ceiling above us, vertebrae countless and serrated jaw dozens of feet in the air and yet *still* too close. Beneather guards walk the perimeter of the room, keeping careful ruby eyes on Malachite all the while.

Lucien puts his hand to my forehead. "You must be exhausted."

"Just a little." I smile at him.

"With any luck, you can sleep soon," he says. "And lure Varia to Pala Orias."

"If she isn't on her way here already," Yorl murmurs. "The Bone Tree having her cunning brain at its disposal is a terrifying thought."

"'Cunning' coming from someone like you truly means something," Lucien interjects. Yorl looks over at him with massive, terse green eyes.

"Don't feign innocence, Your Highness. You d'Malvanes have cunning in excess. It's how you've held on to power for all these generations."

"So we did," Lucien agrees softly. Past tense. The King and Queen are dead, for all we know. If Varia dies, that means he's the last d'Malvane. "And for what purpose?" he continues. "To lose the faith of our people? To tax them into starvation? To decide only the nobility worthy of care and respect? We were a family of a thousand years who did nothing but rot from the inside, who drove our people to kill one another in fearful wars of religious difference." His laugh is drill. "No—that won't be our lasting legacy. I'll see to it."

"Lucien—" I start. He straightens, sword clinking at his hip.

"I'll be a better king than any of them were—by being no king at all."

His words strike hard in the vaulted ceiling, in the bones of the valkerax. My unheart swells with that sweet pride, and Malachite looks at him with nothing but admiration.

"I'll help, Luc," he says.

Lucien's rigor softens, and he grins at his near-brother, all-friend. "Who else will motivate me with their constant harping?"

The stone slab doors slide open then, soundless save for the triple tapping of shoes and a cane. Fione walks to us slowly, gaze fixed to the ceiling and the valkerax there. Lucien's the first to run up to her, Yorl's tail swishing as I follow.

"So?" Yorl presses.

"Malachite's sentence? Is he free? Did they agree to help us?" Lucien asks. Fione's eyes move down to me, and then flicker away to Luc. I pray the prince didn't catch it.

"Yes," she says. "They're sending two battalions to escort us to Pala Orias."

"Just two?" Malachite grunts.

"It's all they could spare," she says.

"And Malachite's life—"

"His outcast status will be revoked," Fione cuts Lucien off. "On the condition we stop Varia."

And put the Trees back together, thus freeing the valkerax to roam upworld, and simultaneously freeing the beneathers from the spiral. She doesn't say it, but it lingers between us and only us. She promised them freedom, and it worked. She managed to convince the council. Of course she did—she's Fione. And the beneathers have been fighting in the spiral for so long—they no doubt jumped at the chance to shuffle the valkerax responsibility equally onto the rest of the world, where it belongs.

"*Revoked*?" Malachite's pale jaw goes slack. "That's never— that's never happened in the history of—of *ever*." He pauses, thinking. "What exactly did you say to them, Fi? We ain't getting rid of all the valkerax—we're just putting 'em back where they belong."

I tame my frown, unsure if it's my rational human thought or my valkerax blood making me bristle at his words.

"What does it matter?" I ask. "We have forces enough to make a stand at Pala Orias. Let's focus on preparing for the impending bloody confrontation, shall we?"

Fione doesn't sneak looks at me anymore. Probably for the best—Yorl and Lucien don't need more fodder to doubt.

"She's right," Fione backs me up. "The council gave us a stipend—we're to take it to the quartermaster in this building."

"Fine. When do we depart?" Malachite sniffs.

"By the tenth-half. They said the battalions will meet us at the River Gate."

"Spirits," the beneather swears. "We better hurry, then. River's across town."

"I'm going to need somewhere to lie down and take a quick one," I say. "Eventually. No hurry."

"No hurry indeed," Yorl agrees. "We must be absolutely sure every last one of our defenses is ready in Pala Orias before you lure her."

"And you gotta do it well," Malachite presses. "Make her real mad, so she just comes for us and not anybody else."

Not Pala Amna, not his city. I nod reassuringly. "C'mon, Mal. When have I ever let you down?"

"Constantly?" he offers.

"And *lovingly*," I tease.

Our shuffling footsteps resound as Malachite leads the way down a corridor and into a huge saferoom reinforced with bars of what look like sparkling diamond. The light's so fractured and pure, it hurts to look at it directly.

"Metal in short supply down here or something?" I ask with a wince.

"The valkerax destroy a lot of it with their fire breath," Malachite points out.

"And the digging of the valkerax routinely unearths large deposits of gemstones otherwise inaccessible to mortals," Yorl adds. "Making it the primary source of the beneather's wealth in upworld trade routes."

"It all goes to the spiral, anyway," Malachite huffs. "Every last piece of gold."

"And it seems to be the main selling point of their architecture," Fione marvels under her breath at the gems glittering in the ceiling.

"Gaudy doesn't even begin to cover it," I agree, following Malachite past the guards and farther into the barred room.

"You have no idea how long it took me to get used to the way humans 'ooh' and 'aah' over the pathetically tiny gems in their jewelry," Malachite snorts.

When we come to a solid diamond set of doors, Fione shows a guard a topaz orb dangling with red thread, and the guard nods. I watch in awe as the bioluminescent moss glitters in the diamond, in all its facets and rainbow crevices. Rainbow, like Evlorasin when it escaped from Vetris. Like the rainbow aura that clings to valkerax when they fly.

"It's the strongest gem." Malachite sees me ogling. "But beneathers consider it the unluckiest."

"Because it's rainbow," I mutter. "Like valkerax when they fly."

He blinks in surprise, and then ruffles my hair with a grin. "Smart is a real bad color on you, Six-Eyes."

"What color would you prefer, then?" I sniff, but my indignation is short-lived as the diamond doors finally yawn all the way open, revealing a perfectly square room loaded to the ceiling with weapons of all shapes and sizes—Cavanos-style swords, Avellish spears, pneumatic Helkyris harpoon guns using the same jet technology as their airships do, circular throwing blades, jade-encrusted rapiers, swords and axes and knives bent over and around one another, tied together at the ends, so old and bizarre and foreign they might as well be indecipherable puzzles of steel and leather.

"Celeon *belduri*. How do beneathers even use this?" Yorl muses, strapping on a pair of bladed foot gauntlets. "You don't have the auxiliary tendons for it—or the paw shape."

"Nobody *uses* all this shit—we just like to collect shiny upworld things." Malachite throws me a wicked toothed dagger just like his, and I strap it to my thigh. "You know, just in case the upworlders accidentally invent something real good at killing valkerax."

"Aren't you going to use the matronic, Yorl?" I chirp.

"The council said they'd bring it to the rendezvous point," Fione says.

"Generous of them," Yorl murmurs thoughtfully.

"Yeah, well. They're not the High Witches," I say. "They *want* us to succeed."

"A white mercury sword," Lucien marvels at a pale, gorgeous ruby-inlaid blade mounted on the wall.

"Not the real thing," Malachite asserts. "An old prototype."

"Still functional as a blade," the prince insists.

"You're better off with a piercing weapon with valkerax, considering you humans aren't strong enough to cleave through their scales with something heavier."

"Are you calling your prince weak?" Fione calls from across the room. She sits on a stone table, a polymath tool in one hand and her crossbow cane in the other as she tinkers with its gears and levers.

Malachite shoots a smirk at Lucien. "Yeah, real weak compared to me. He's a flexible little shit, though, I'll give him that."

"I'll give him that, too," I muse thoughtfully, looking innocently back at Malachite as he glowers my way. I make a little finger wave at him to rub salt in the wound and duck just in time to avoid his throwing knife. He wasn't even trying hard—it quivers in the wall miles away from my head. "Rude!"

Lucien's heat envelops my shoulder as he walks up behind me and plucks the dagger from the packed earth, inspecting it nonchalantly. "What are you taking, heart? Something flashy, I'd imagine."

"Nonsense." I smile up at him. "I've got Father's sword and my own teeth. Anything else would just slow me down."

"Not even this?" Fione dangles a bracelet of stunning amethysts.

"Oooh!" I coo, hurrying over and grabbing it appreciatively. "You know me so well, Your Grace!"

"Doesn't look like a weapon," Lucien muses, taking it gently from my hands and fastening it around my wrist for me.

"S'not," Malachite agrees brusquely. "It's an offering."

"For what?" I blink.

"A grave."

"Amethysts for the dead," Yorl agrees softly. "Always."

A quiet descends. Lucien starts to take it off me, but I stop his hand.

"Everyone who's died: Vetris, Helkyris. Y'shennria's family. Mine. Yours. Everyone who died because of these Trees. I'll keep it. I'll fight with it. For them."

Lucien squeezes my hand tight. Yorl nods, satisfied, and Malachite seems proud of me somehow—a thin grin on his pale lips. Fione catches my eye, and then looks somberly away. I stare down at the gleaming purple stones as we leave, Malachite directing us to the River Gate.

This bracelet will be my offering, too.

It's a pity we don't have time to sample the wonders of Pala Amna, because it is *wondrous*. Malachite leads us through only half of it, the great stone widow'swalks we march on looming high over the city of stone and gems. It's nestled on the bottom of a fearsomely huge cavern, something Yorl calls a "lava tube,'" the buildings stacked and mashed into one another like huddled stone children. Protecting it are seven stone gates, all of them accented with fierce lines of weapons similar to the one I saw in the ceiling of Evlorasin's arena—a spear mechanism wound tight inside a hole, ready to spring forth and huge enough to pierce even the largest valkerax. Smaller weapons adorn the belts of every guard, and unlike Vetris, every civilian is armed to the teeth with broadswords, axes, and curved blades—the glint of metal bright in the thronging streets below.

An entire city, devoted to the spiral and ready to fight at a moment's notice.

Like a grim reminder of a fang, a spire sits in the very center of Pala Amna—a huge stalactite of limestone jutting up out of the earth. Intensely incandescent brightmoss curls around it, creating a luminously golden spiral glowing over the city and providing what seems to be the majority of the light to the citizens.

"An artificial sun," Fione marvels. "I'd heard of it, but to see it is something else entirely."

"Yeah," Malachite agrees wistfully, ruby eyes reflecting its brilliance.

"Is that brightmoss?" I squint at it.

Yorl shakes his head. "A distant relative that grows only on limestone. Much rarer. It requires near-constant supervision—the beneather lightsmiths tend to it."

"Lots of shamed ancestor councilmen flung themselves off the peak," Malachite snorts. "Or got pushed off by an angry mob."

Lucien looks mildly impressed. "Certainly one way to do politics."

"We're almost there." Malachite points ahead to a spear-lined gate. It's nearly three times the size of Vetris's main gates, the stone so old it makes my immortal arse feel as young as spring grass.

"I'm surprised things aren't mustier down here," I say as we descend the widow's walk via a curlicue flight of stairs.

"Brightmoss creates ample fresh air," Yorl offers. "Though, yes—the air itself doesn't move. The flow has to be maintained by heavy duct usage and a few polymath machines powered by white mercury."

"Must've been awful before the invention of those," I muse.

"Not all bad," Malachite insists dryly. "As kids we used to draw stick figures in the dust."

"And come down with the occasional fatal respiratory disease." Another voice joins ours—Lysulli, their long, pale hair swinging as they walk up to us. They've changed out their heavy armor for something lighter, the bone thinner but no less protective.

Malachite practically squawks. "What are you doing here?"

"What else? I'm heading your little mission," they snort.

"Why *you* of all adjudicators?" He groans. He was so happy to see Lysulli at first, but now he's sullen, and I know him well enough to know why. He didn't want them at the final battle—not when there's such a good chance we could all die. But Lysulli ignores him and the subtext completely, pushing him out of the way a little, and I start to like them even more. They might be brushing Malachite off lightly, but the double daggers sheathed in a cross over their tailbone look deadly serious.

They study me with piercing bloodstone eyes. "The council entrusted me to watch you. You better not fuck it up, Heartless, because I've got a promotion waiting for me when I get back."

"Got it!" I salute. Lucien chuckles and follows suit.

"This isn't some little promotion game, Lys." Malachite frowns. I see Lysulli smile for the first time at him, all acid sweetness.

"If you want my battalions, then it is now." They sweep past him, bashing into his shoulder on the way.

"History?" Lucien asks, trying to sound as disinterested as possible.

"A bit," Malachite grunts. "Let's just get this over with."

"And miss all the drama and fun?" I pout. "Nonsense. Who are they? How do you two know each other? Why are they so pretty? What's their haircare routine like?"

Malachite does his godsdamndest to ignore every question I chirp as we follow Lysulli under the massive stone gate with all its embedded weaponry. Lysulli motions at the massive copper matronic waiting for Yorl a little farther in, and he strokes its armor affectionately before pressing some unseen button. A mortal-sized compartment hisses open on its back, and Yorl jumps in it, the sounds of levers being pulled echoing. Finally, he jumps back out and catches up to us. There's a split second before I ask him why he isn't taking the matronic with him when thumping footsteps resound, nearly scaring me into dropping my waterskin.

Yorl grins at me. "It'll follow."

"G-Good," I gasp. "Great."

The cavern ceiling of Pala Amna narrows down to a series of smaller caverns still lit by brightmoss and evened out on the bottoms by smooth stone roads. The matronic's hissing and thumping is the only real noise once the bustle of the city fades. Stone signs carved with beneather runes dot the landscape here and there. There isn't much wildlife to be seen, just the occasional skitter of bugs, which Malachite doesn't seem to mind nearly as much as the big one we killed. But then Lysulli dislodges a brood of ghostbats from a stalactite and I shriek. Lucien draws his sword, Fione's crossbow unfurls in a second, and Yorl hunkers down, ready to strike with his bladed foot gauntlets. Nothing. Nothing but my voice ringing around our heads. It echoes ceaselessly in the caves, folded in on itself and fading even slower than the bioluminescent trail the ghostbats leave behind in the air. The party looks at me, some more pointed than others, and most wincing as my shriek comes back around again on the stone.

"Oops." I smile sheepishly.

"Pair of lungs on that one," Lysulli admires begrudgingly.

"And here I was," Yorl murmurs, "thinking your voice couldn't get any worse."

"Wait till she sees some fool dress," Malachite scoffs. "Then you'll know real eardrum pain."

"Ahem!" I draw myself up to my full height. "I'm no master

socialite, but maybe consider shit-talking me when I'm *gone*, hmm?"

"Never." Lucien's low voice is in my ear. It's supposed to be comforting, but I turn to look at him and his gaze is heavier than comfort warrants, probably because I used the words "me" and "gone" in the same sentence. I can't help but remember the suspicious look he gave Fione and me before we left her to talk to the ancestor council.

He knows? No. He can't. I've been careful—singing the song-poem in my head every time we touch. He suspects, but he doesn't *know.*

He doesn't know I'll never really be gone.

"Luc won't shit-talk you." Malachite hefts his pack higher. "But I will. Because I have the good sense to."

"Is that what you're calling your inborn urge to make fun of people you find attractive?" Lysulli's voice resounds. "I thought ten years would mature you, not keep you exactly the same."

From what I've seen thus far, beneathers don't really blush, but that doesn't stop Malachite's pink cheeks from trying not to. The color gathers around the three scars I gave him, now almost entirely healed, the long, puckered marks starker white against the flush. And it reminds me.

"I gave him those scars." I point at them and smile at Lysulli. "So if Malachite wants to make fun of me, he can make fun of me. You know?"

Lysulli looks between the beneather and me, then turns away with a disbelieving scoff that sounds suspiciously like "upworlders."

When they've gone ahead, Malachite breathes out a single word in my direction. "Dolt."

I trot over to his side, blinking innocently. "You called?"

"I think he means to say 'thank you,'" Lucien offers.

I act shocked. "What is this 'thank you' you speak of? And why have I never heard it in beneather?"

Fione and Yorl shoot each other smirks, and Malachite huffs and starts striding so long it takes all my leg-length just to keep up with him.

The Dark Below isn't so dark near Pala Amna.

The brightmoss ensures that, but there also seems to be more natural light clustered around the city—reflections on water from little bioluminescent creatures and flora that live below, or above. Maybe that's why they built Pala Amna here. It's most certainly why, when the twists and turns around stone and abyss finally come to a stop, we see the waiting battalions clearly—a small crowd of beneathers armored to the teeth in valkerax bone, with spears and massive broadswords like Malachite's. They wait patiently, nursing strands of jerky as their commanding officers meander through them checking equipment readiness.

"The fabled valkerax-slayers, in the flesh." I whistle.

"Hurry up!" Lysulli demands from ahead, waving us over. The closer I get, the more I realize just how many of the two battalions look to be Lysulli and Malachite's age. Young.

"Much younger than I thought they'd be, but no less impressive," I murmur to Yorl, who nods.

"Beneathers don't have a very long expected lifespan. The spiral takes most of them before their time. Getting older than three decades is a rarity."

"Aha." I nod, and think to myself that's perhaps why the ancestor council was so eager to agree to Fione's offer—tired of seeing their young succumb to the valkerax, only to be replaced by the younger. And it explains why Lysulli is in a position of power and still so young. I watch them salute the two commanding officers of the battalions by placing their pale fingers together, lightly interlaced. From where I'm standing, the points of Lysulli's fingertips almost look like a spiral. Always the damn spiral.

In a way, the beneathers are imprisoned just as much as the valkerax they fight.

As much as Heartless.

The battalions are much less impressed with us than we are with them—but the matronic definitely catches their attention and awe. They shoot looks at it as they march, and we march with them. At some point, we pass a long, low, flat expanse of stone, almost like a field. Amethysts have been carved into various shapes of various sizes, embedded in the stone in a way that's all too familiar. In a way I saw that day I left Nightsinger's forest, along the Bone Road.

Graves.

Graves innumerable, stretching into the darkness.

But these graves aren't from the Sunless War. They're from a thousand years of fighting. Of dying. Of sacrificing.

The bracelet of amethysts jangles on my wrist as if calling out to its brethren, calling out to the place we all go in the end. The place we're all marching to. A place I refuse to let my friends go to. A place I've been many times. A place familiar to me and yet, at its core, still unfamiliar. Frightening. Comforting. A spiral.

Malachite's scars. Evlorasin's blood promise within me. Lucien's memories, of a cool little room overlooking a black sand beach.

No one is ever really gone.

"This is never-goodbye," I whisper.

30
TO PALA ORIAS

The trek to Pala Orias is far easier than the maze we traversed after the Fog Gate. Or so it feels. Having two beneather battalions of highly trained warriors cut down every hungry crawly that decides to slither toward us is a true blessing. As is having Lysulli. They know the way to Pala Orias with a bird's mind for navigation, steering us through tight weaves of rock tunnels and devastated canyons so huge and wide, they put infinity to shame.

The canyons are more unsettling than the tunnels, frankly— the darkness stretching on forever and holding all manner of unknown horrors spun entirely by mind. My thief-brain screams that we could be attacked from any angle, at any time, and the brightmoss torches the battalions bear would detect such an attack far too late. But I suppose that's why beneathers developed such good hearing in the first place.

And I'm not the only one worried—everyone is on edge in the canyons, Malachite walking with his sword drawn, Fione with her crossbow unfolded. Yorl holds a handkerchief up to his nose, blinking away dust and stale air as he desperately darts his low-light vision in every direction, the matronic thumping after him mindlessly. Even the battalions seem on edge this deep down—beneathers twitching in their armor at the faintest sounds I can't hear.

Lucien seems to, irritatingly and wonderfully and as always, know how I feel. He walks beside me, close, his body heat a welcome thing in the clammy cold of the Dark Below. He must be even more nervous than I am, considering magic becomes more difficult the farther down into the Dark Below a witch goes. One of his defenses, gone. And one of mine, too. If his magic is weak, he can't heal me as quickly if I get injured. But I know he'll try anyway, to his detriment. He smiles sideways at me, his working hand sputtering with witchfire—not strong, but enough to contribute light to the path.

"It's good news," he assures me when he catches me staring at the weak fire. "It means that Varia might not be as strong as I thought, either."

"But stronger than you," I say. "Because of the Bone Tree."

"I wouldn't count me out just yet." He makes that cocky smirk I love, but it pulls at deeper heartstrings. Worried ones. He'll have to struggle, to pour so much magic into just fighting her. If I'm not fast enough in my own plan, I could lose him. He could do something brave and foolish and noble and—

I suck in a breath, then let it out slowly. The must of ancient things cloys my lungs and helps none.

"Don't look so worried," Lucien assures me, a playful, Whisper-esque edge to it. It almost riles me, how hard he's trying to be casual about this, but it fades quickly when I hear a popping sound, and feel something solid appear in my fingers.

I look down to see something blue. A gorgeous blue, deep and vivid and familiar. The shell. The little shell he took from me when we landed off the coast. It's hard to see in the brightmoss, but he moves his witchfire closer to reveal ridges. It's been carved with the most delicate touch into an iridescent blue rose, now peeking off a silver band.

"A— You—" I blink at him. "Is this—"

"A ring," he says simply. "In case you couldn't tell."

My unheart clamps down on itself, making it nigh impossible to breathe. "Luc—"

"When this is over, you'll think about it, won't you?" He smiles. "We were supposed to, anyway, before all this happened."

"Supposed to what? *Marry?*" I squeak out.

His smirk widens. "What I mean is, you were a Spring Bride. And I did, technically and forever, choose you."

I gape. "You realize that—"

"I realize everything," he assures me, smirk softening. "And I realize, mostly, that I want to realize you. Every day. For as long as you'll have me. I don't intend on transferring the old Cavanosian notions of what a wife should or shouldn't do to the new realm I'll build. Not that I think you'd ever ascribe to those in the first place."

His onyx eyes glitter mischievously, terribly and beautifully, and my blood sings choruses with him in it.

"Will you marry me, Zera Y'shennria?"

I can practically feel my bagged heart in his coat pocket rear up, bucking against its seams. Together. Together for as long as we'll have each other. Never in a thousand years did I think someone would ask me this—that I would be important enough to someone, to their life and their own heart, for them to consider me their partner. Happiness like that—being important to someone I love, and crave—was never possible in Nightsinger's woods. It was a dreamy fantasy I read about in my witch's books, tucked away between the garden rhubarb and spring onions, dirt smears on my knees and on the pages, but I was so lost in the fantasy I didn't care. What would it be like, I thought, to be asked such a monumental question, and by someone I loved? What even *was* love? I didn't know.

But now, in this canyon pulled wide by time and disaster, coated with shadow and mosslight, I do. The world turned upside down, in just a few years that felt more like ages.

I'll never really be gone. Still. Still, a shred of sadness tears at me.

But I have to hold on to any light I can.

I smile for what feels like the very first time and slide it on my finger.

"I'll perhaps consider it."

"Just perhaps?" He quirks a brow above his smirk.

"Just perhaps," I assert playfully, pretending haughtiness until the very last second, when he pulls me in by my waist, quick and sharp, while his kiss is slow and velvet.

I'm still dizzy from it when we stop for a water break. Lucien's chatting with Malachite, the biggest smile plastered on his face as Malachite demands to know why he's so giddy. Lysulli chimes in that it's obvious; he's in love, and Malachite in all his stone-headedness wouldn't know what that means. It quickly becomes a sniping contest between the two of them, Lucien watching and chuckling at it all.

Fione sees me fiddling with the ring. She swallows her water, wiping her chin delicately before she speaks. "It's his way of trying to persuade you to stay."

I laugh under my breath, staring into the blue of the rose. "Am I being that obvious?"

"No. But he's always had good instincts. For terrible things most of all."

"It won't be terrible," I insist. "Just...different. New. I won't pretend it'll be easy, but. He'll learn."

Fione stares at a scarred canyon wall, at the black moss growing there. "No one wants to learn alone, Zera."

"He won't be alone." I press down the clawing in my gut. "He'll have all of you—Yorl, Malachite, you, Varia."

At the last name, Fione closes her eyes, as if it's caused her pain. Or maybe she's imagining having Varia back. Longing.

"It's not—" Her voice, trying so hard to be regal and composed, cracks. "It's not a fair trade."

Me, for Varia. My laugh comes again, softer. There's a silence filled by the shuffling battalions opening their helmets to drink, opening their armguards to wipe off sweat, adjusting the metal of their swords and spears. Lucien's laugh. Malachite's grumbling. The hiss of the matronic letting off steam, Yorl's faint busy purr as he scribbles observations about the canyon on a pad.

I brave the silence first. "I know it's hard to believe. I know you don't believe in the gods. You believe in polymathematics, in reality. But I've lived it and died it. No one's ever really gone, Fione. We're all connected. I know it. Maybe by the gods, or not by them at all. All I know is I've seen it, Muro's seen it—the Tree of Souls connects us all, through our memories, and our love, and our feelings. That's what a soul is: a root. It's memories and love and feelings. And that can't be destroyed. I promised you then and I promise you now—no one is ever really gone."

She opens her mouth to say something, closes it. Opens it again, closes it. She stares out at the darkness, finally, the deep stretching thing with no end, and I watch her luminous periwinkle eyes fill with tears. Eyes I hope she gives her children. Eyes I hope see a new, peaceful world born.

And then, silently, she nods.

Pala Orias sits at the nexus where the five great-canyons merge, or so Lysulli says. Yorl looks thoughtfully around at the canyon wall, then murmurs to Lucien and me, "It stands to reason, then, that these five great-canyons were created when the Old Vetrisians split the Tree of Souls in two."

"Probably," Lucien agrees.

"These?" My eyes bug out. "But these canyons are *huge*!"

"So is the Tree of Souls' power." Yorl nods. "Or, so *was* the Tree of Souls' power."

I make a frown. "What'll happen if we split it again, then? More canyons?"

Yorl and Lucien share a look. It's a silent answer but a thorough one. No one knows. More destruction, maybe. Maybe the whole place will collapse in on us and kill us.

All hypotheticals that'll never come to pass, if I have any say in it.

I'm so mentally exhausted that my boots start to drag on the stone. No sleep, no rest, my mind listless and everywhere and droopy. I'm not even sure what's keeping me awake at this point—Lucien, probably. He leans in and offers me his shoulder, and I take it. His working hand smooths my hair, his murmur of "soon, heart" the only thing forcing my feet one after another.

And then they catch on something.

I stumble forward, Lucien gripping my arm and pulling me back to standing at the last second. A string caught me and snapped—no. Not a string. A *vine*. A root.

A flower.

It's not a real flower—it can't be. It wobbles and wavers like a heatwave, made of what looks like golden mist so faint it could be mistaken for a mirage, a water spray suspended overlong. But its root caught my shoe, so it must be real. Real enough to trip me.

There come more of them the farther we walk—dotting the canyon floor like hesitant golden dreams, bunching together and apart. The strangest bit is that they bob in some invisible wind, and it's surely invisible because the air down here is deader than I technically am.

"Flowers," Malachite laugh-marvels, "in the Dark Below. Gran was right."

"Our grandparents knew all along," Yorl asserts, then turns to me. "They'd heard the stories. This is as far as I've been—

Grandfather's notes advised against getting any closer to the Pala."

"Yeah, the place is a ruin—it could crumble at any time. But I've never—I've never seen these flowers in my life." Lysulli frowns. "And I've patrolled here countless times. It's…it's usually just a crater."

"The Tree of Souls is the source of all magic," Lucien insists. "It disappeared physically, but its fingerprints still remain."

"You talk like it's alive." They huff.

"It could be." Lucien shrugs.

"Why would these flowers appear now, then?" I ask. "All of a sudden, when we come down here? Isn't that too coincidental?"

"Coincidental indeed," he muses, staring right at me.

I answer my own question wordlessly; it's because the Tree of Souls wants me here. It gave me that dream ages ago, of the two tree pendants, and that overwhelming feeling of wrongness. It's wanted me for at least that long—maybe even before that, Muro said. I try not to let the nerves overtake my thoughts. Lucien can't know. He *can't*. I can only be the poem-song, the mantra.

Finally the prince breaks his crushing gaze on me, and he inhales, exhales. "Gods above—I feel like I could do anything here."

"What does that mean?" Fione inquires at his side.

"The magic's unstable, but there's so *much* of it. So much more than anywhere else, than even Windonhigh." He marvels, dark eyes catching the faint golden glow of the flowers. "It's like—like I've only ever stepped in puddles, and now I'm swimming in the *sea*."

"So you've got full capability, is what you're saying," Malachite grunts.

"Which means Varia will, too," Fione murmurs.

"We're setting up the perimeter, regardless," Lysulli interrupts. "I'm splitting the battalions into fourths and stationing them in a phalanx formation surrounding the centerline of the Pala. We'll back ourselves against the north canyon wall."

"Depending on the terrain, we can hide some of the archers for an ambush farther up," Lucien says.

Lysulli looks at him, mildly approving. "Agreed. Clever move."

"We can follow the centerline to the First Root," Yorl says. "It should be there, at the axis of north and west."

We soldier onward, the flowers becoming so thick under our feet, we can't step without crushing some. They bounce back quickly though, bobbing cheerily and spraying an ethereal, half-real golden pollen of some sort. The canyon finally starts to narrow, but the flowers do the opposite, growing bigger and bigger until they're waist-tall and thick enough to hide our legs entirely. Fione struggles with her shorter height until Malachite puts her on his shoulders without a word. The light of the collective flowers grows stronger, illuminating our faces with gold from below.

The first time I see Pala Orias, it feels like home.

It's the valkerax blood promise in me, probably. A sweet, buttery feeling settles on the void in my chest the moment the golden flower-light reveals it—an old, crumbling ruin. Arches, plazas, chipping supports of houses long collapsed. The architecture is entirely different from Pala Amna—far smoother, taller, lots of domes and curves and strange pillars of coiled stone. Not spiraled but coiled tight. Malachite can't stop looking everywhere, and neither can Yorl, but I look at only one place—ahead.

here at the cradle, the hunger whispers. *here at the grave.*

At first I think it's me—my eyes going bad. But then I realize it's a warp in the air. You can see it only when the golden flower-light hits it just so—a shimmering, rainbow-esque outline of something. Something huge, something looming gargantuan over the ruins, over us, spreading far and wide with many sturdy limbs and without a single thrown shadow. It gives off a faint rainbow light in a pattern like veins, pulsing gently in time to some unseen heartbeat, to some unseen music. To an unseen song.

The song. The one in my head, the one in my heart. The one in Evlorasin's head, Evlorasin's heart.

Our song.

"The Tree," Lucien breathes.

"Spirits." Lysulli's ruby eyes bug out. "It's...it's *real*."

"Shit," Malachite manages to grit out. "It's *huge*."

"Like nothing I've ever seen," Fione agrees in awe.

"They say it began here." Yorl's green eyes shine with the Tree's light as he takes it in, tail swishing madly. "Life. They say the Tree of Souls was the first thing to ever grow on Arathess."

I look up with an awed sigh at the shimmering veins—no, they're *branches*. Branches bigger than entire rivers latticing the darkness above us. "And I godsdamn believe it."

Lysulli gets over their awe first, and immediately begins shouting orders, the clamor of the battalions splitting to their positions drowning out the ethereal peace, their bone armor thundering over the stone ruins as they take their places.

"Prince!" Lysulli shouts, standing in front of a swathe of waiting archers. "Can I trust your terrible human eyesight to oversee the ambush placement?"

They motion to the archers and Malachite bristles, but Lucien starts.

"Yes! One moment!" He throws a smile at me. "I'll be back."

"Far too soon," I tease. He gives me a last squeeze of my hand, then jogs over to the archers. I watch them clamber nimbly together over the debris of the ruins for a moment and then disappear up a cliff face.

"We should position ourselves near the First Root," Yorl advises, wading through the ruins as the matronic trudges behind him, displacing rocks and rubble with its huge bulk. "So that when Varia approaches within terminal range, we can act."

"Lucien can act, you mean," Malachite says.

"Same thing." I wave his grumpy arse off and turn to the celeon. "Lead the way, Master Polymath."

"Not a master yet," Yorl corrects. "An *adjutant*."

I laugh and step around a boulder. "You mistake me for someone who gives a shit about any titles ever, darling."

"I thought you're engaged." Fione sniffs. "Shouldn't you be calling fewer people 'darling' now?"

Dead silence. The matronic hisses a little. Malachite makes a sputtering noise behind me.

Oops.

"E-Engaged? SINCE WHEN?"

"Keep your voice down!" Yorl hisses at Mal. "Lest you start a rockslide!"

"Being buried under a rockslide would be preferable to listening to him chew me out for the next seventeen months," I lilt.

"Months?" Malachite chokes out. "Try *YEARS*! Decades! I can't believe you two are so thickheaded! Who gets married in a time like this? Who even proposes? What do you even eat at a stupid upworlder's wedding?" He pauses his rant and looks at me with the tiniest of plaintive gazes. "Why didn't you tell me first?"

"It was literally a half ago, Mal." I pat his shoulder sympathetically. "Fione just noticed because she's observant about jewelry."

Malachite glances down at the blue rose on my finger, and his eyes widen. "Oh."

"Hurry up," Yorl insists. "We're almost there."

He points one claw into the distance, to the very middle of the ruin. We follow a decorative line in the ground, glazed reddish tile long buried in dust and fragmented by time. The smell of flowers is everywhere—so faint it's more of a suggestion than a true scent. Half vanilla, half cinnamon—it's a smell I've never smelled before. It changes moment to moment, wildly swinging between sharp rosemary, to musty lavender, back to vanilla and everything in between.

"Are those the flowers, you think?" I ask Yorl. He's covering his nose.

"Hopefully not," he says, muffled by his handkerchief. "They reek."

"I don't think they're so bad," I muse, watching as the ghostly golden blooms bob like a sea lapping at our waists.

"You're a Heartless. Of course you think the smell of rotting meat isn't so bad," he grunts.

I blink once. Twice.

"They smell like rotting meat to you?" I ask.

Yorl's green eyes over his handkerchief freeze on mine. Fione catches up to us then, and chimes in, "Definitely rotting meat."

All three of us look at Malachite, who, though still wrapped in his own thorny disgruntlement, blurts words. "Yup. Bad meat."

Yorl glances at the flowers, then warily back to me. "Let us continue, regardless."

I sniff hard and wait for unpleasant, but while the scent cycles, it never changes from utterly delightful. Could it be...the Tree of Souls? It feels like this scent is welcoming me, and only me. I look up as we walk, the shimmering branches suspended high above and the not-quite-there trunk so massive it seems to hold up the entire world. It connects everyone; I saw it. I don't know how, or why, or what it really is, but it isn't just magic. And it isn't just a Tree. It's more than that.

A god.

No, not a god. Because a god can't be split, or hurt, or wounded by mortals. But it's the closest thing to one I've ever known, ever felt, ever dreamed of. It *gives* magic to the entire world, visiting each witch in their dreams when they're ready for it. It's the same one that Lucien saw in his dream before becoming a witch. Nightsinger, Varia, the High Witches—all of them. They got their magic from this wounded Tree. Such powerful magic, from a wounded thing.

Such a powerful, torn soul.

"Are you the one who sent me those dreams?" I ask the branches softly.

I don't get an answer, but the scent of lavender-vanilla tickles my nose, and I suddenly don't need one.

Yorl stops in what must be the center of the ruin, his paws hovering over the red tile line in the earth. He bends down, and we gather around him. Just in front of his clawed toes is a hole, barely the width of two humans. It slithers down into a shallow cave, the light of the Tree and the flowers illuminating the dimness inside enough to see something sticking out of the earthen wall of the cave—something that looks to be made of pearl. It snakes in and out of the soil, a single strand, the origin of it shimmery and not-quite-real like the Tree above is, but the very end...the very end is solid wood. Solid, white-ish wood like birch, with veins of what look like pearlescent sap.

It's a root.

And it's split.

At the very bottom of the hanging root is a rift, the wood curling off in two different directions. The wishbone split itself is open and raw, bleeding pearl liquid onto the thirsty ground in a steady drip.

"It's...smaller than I thought it would be," I admit.

"Something that tiny did all this?" Malachite quirks a brow at Yorl, and the celeon nods.

"The First Root, of the first thing to ever grow on Arathess. The origin of perhaps all sentient life."

"All sentient life?" Mal wrinkles his nose. "Isn't that a little much?"

"The Wave gave celeon sentience." Fione bends down to look at the root, mousy curls bobbing. "And the Wave was magic. A combine witch spell. Who's to say the Tree of Souls didn't radiate enough magic over time to turn humans sentient? Or beneathers? It's just a hypothesis, but it's not an undue one."

Muro said the Tree of Souls gave us all its own soul, at the beginning of time. The roots I saw in that vision, connecting all of us... I stare at the pearl-bleeding thing, my own bones aching. It's so close. I can't do what I need to without Varia here, though. But neither can Lucien split it again. A Tree has to be here to affect the First Root.

"So we wait for Varia," Malachite says. "And then send Lucien down there to do his thing?"

"Presumably." Yorl nods. "It's quite lucky this place is teeming with magic—enough that it won't be a struggle for the prince."

"What won't be a struggle for me?" Lucien appears on top of a rock in a whirl of white crow feathers.

"Marriage, apparently," the beneather grumbles.

Lucien looks taken aback. "Oh, c'mon, Mal. I told you it was coming."

"Yeah—the first day you saw her!" Malachite snarls. "*Months ago!* I didn't think you were serious—"

A joyous, golden laugh escapes Lucien as he jumps down and ambles to my side. "When am I not serious? Practically never."

"Are the archers in place?" I ask. He looks over at me and nods, kissing my forehead.

"Yes. The beneathers have tranquilizer arrows for the majority of the horde."

"The same tranquilizers I used," Yorl clarifies. "Darkmoss syrup and acidified talhut blood. If they shoot well, they should be able to keep some of the valkerax asleep and at bay."

"Long enough for me to do my job," Lucien agrees.

"The rest we'll have to fight," Fione says, oiling her cane ominously with a rag.

The prince rummages in his pocket and hands her a fistful of bolts. "Tranqs for you, too."

"Much obliged." She makes a facetious Vetrisian noble bow, so out of place here in the bottom of the world, and the two of them grin at each other.

"Make no mistake," Lysulli says, appearing out from behind the rubble. "We'll have to kill most of them. The tranqs just stagger their rate of death."

My chest sinks. And here I was, thinking the beneathers were being charitably kind about the whole thing. They exist to kill valkerax, not put them to sleep.

"Is there a *hevstrata* we can retreat to if shit hits the vent?" Malachite asks them.

"No." They shake their head. "Runes don't work near Pala Orias."

"Ah, I see," Yorl murmurs, chin in his hand. "The magical influence of the Tree of Souls could unravel the Old Vetrisian word-binds."

"So this is our last stand," Lucien says.

Lysulli fixes their bloodred eyes on him. "Yes."

A beat. The flowers bounce excitedly in their invisible wind, and we go still in our own dread.

"I assume everyone's in place?" Lucien asks.

Lysulli nods. "The alert's gone round—we're just waiting for them to show up now."

Yorl, Fione, Mal, and Luc all look to me. I can see their worry, their fears, their tension drawn tight like bowstrings in their eyes. Fione most of all. Lucien most *most* of all.

I make my smile as big and warm as I can. "Well, then. Time to take a nap."

We find a quiet place behind a boulder, and Lucien sits. He motions for me to put my head in his lap, and I do. Rest, at last.

I thought it would be hard, this last sleep. But it's the easiest thing I've ever done. Surrounded by friends. Cradled by love. Lulled by the Tree welcoming me. The smell of lavender, of vanilla, of Lucien's honey.

His kiss to my cheek, and then I'm gone.

31
THE WYRM, COILING

The first time I ever see the beautiful seaside country of Avel, it's in dreams. And covered in blood.

Blood drips from my fingers like slick, gleaming syrup—half of my fingers made of wood. Varia. I'm in her body again, watching through her eyes and feeling what she does. A port town in front of us on fire, the proud redwood of Avellish buildings charring quickly to black. Valkerax circle above, ten of them flying in rainbow halos—no, twenty. Thirty. *Fifty*, at least, catching high air above the port town like a lazy tornado of untold death. Their tails fly out behind them, the white banners of victory giving us only a fraction of satisfaction before the clenching pain of the maddening song returns.

DESTROY DESTROY DESTROY DESTROY DESTROY DESTROY DESTROY DESTROY DESTROY DESTROY DESTROY—

I focus on it, focus on how it's not my hunger, not my song, and pull myself out of Varia's body. Floaty, and visible to her now. She can see me and I can see her, but neither of us is happy to. Her body is drenched in blood—the rags of her dress so far gone, barely covering her at all, her skin caked in blood and dirt and rubbery, fleshy patches that I know aren't hers. Parts. Parts of *people*. Her cheeks are sallow, gaunt, her wrists thin and her collarbone stark. She looks famished—starving, her ribs showing through in her shreds of dress. But her face is the worst of all, her expression hollowed out, empty of anything resembling thought or emotion. Like a doll. No—emptier than even a doll. A glass shell, transparent and thin. It hurts just to look at.

Varia, I think to her.

She doesn't blink, her deep black eyes staring at the same space over my shoulder, the flames of the Avellish port burning gold in her irises. I try to get closer to her, even if the idea scares me more than any nightmare—if she touches me, she could turn me to her side. I felt it last time, and I can feel it now. She's more Bone Tree than mortal. I can feel it ringing in the air. *Powerful.* So powerful that as a fire-cracked beam falls from a nearby house and onto her, she barely twitches one finger before it instantly explodes into a fine cloud of ember splinters.

"Varia," I say softly. "It's me. Zera."

Her eyes move only at the last word, flickering over to look at me. All my insides turn to ice at her gaze—there's nothing. None of Varia behind those eyes. No mirth, no pride, no grace, no determination, no cruelty. Just...*nothing.*

"Th-They're worried about you," I stammer. "Everyone. Fione most of all."

Another flicker of her eyes, this time inward. She still recognizes names. That's good—she's not too far gone. I can still bring her back. But first, I have to goad the thing inside her. Draw it out like a poison.

My ghostly, half-dream gaze travels down to her neck, the Bone Tree choker made of valkerax fangs seemingly tighter in her skin, digging points into her flesh that drip blood. Her own blood, for once.

It really *is* eating her.

"I heard"—I try a smile—"you're going to name your kid after me, aren't you?"

Varia blinks slowly but betrays nothing.

"But what if it's a boy?" I hum softly. "Hmm. Zeran might work. With an *N*. Fione might hate that one, though—you'll have to confer with her."

Varia's face twitches as if something is fighting inside her, thrashing with no escape, so deep down, it can only ripple her surface. She's still in there. Her love for Fione, her hopes for the future—she still has hope. Hope that I'll save her. That this will end, and that she'll live to see another world made with her love at her side. An impossible wish, she must think.

But nothing's impossible at the end of the world.

It's time to twist the dagger in the wound.

"I've decided I'm not going to save you anymore." I inhale. "I'm not going to put you back together."

Her head tilts slowly, eerily. I try desperately to keep my dream-voice even. Honest-sounding. Luring out the Bone Tree, one root at a time.

"We're going to split you again."

"*No.*" Her voice rasps out instantly, but it's not hers. It's deeper, darker. Far older than she. Than me. Than anyone.

"Yes." I lift my shaking chin. "It's the only way to stop you. I tried to help you, but you killed too many people. You can't be allowed to keep hurting others like this. You deserve to be punish—"

"*YOU,*" the Bone Tree thunders at me, Varia's canines flashing in her rotting gums. "*YOU. DESERVE. TO BE PUNISHED.*"

The valkerax circling in the smoke above suddenly roar in tandem, an earsplitting symphony conducted on high. A valkerax lunges out from the sea, striking its long body across the beach and to Varia's feet in an instant, all its thousands of teeth bared at me and its six white eyes snarled up into one another. Looking right at me. Dream-me. But I have no doubt if it tried to eat me, it would succeed, because I'm more than just a dream. I can speak, think, feel. I'm connected to Varia. We all are.

we are her fingers. we are her swords.

I fight against my own hunger as it turns traitor for her. It belonged to her once. She was my witch at one time, and the hunger remembers that, reaching out for her furious face with my hand, my dream-body leaning toward her like a plant leans for the sun—

Black hair, black eyes, long lashes, proud nose. Even in anger, even in hunger, even in ancient thrall to a Tree, she looks so much like Lucien.

Lucien.

I wrench my body back, pinning my hand to my side with my other arm.

"I'm going to split you apart again and again!" I thunder. "I'll split you until you're nothing, insignificant, too small to even see! Until you can't hurt Varia again! Until you can't hurt *anyone* ever again, you hear me?"

She turns away, putting her half-wood hand gently on the valkerax's side. Shaking.

"YOU HURT US FIRST."

She whirls. What's left of Princess Varia d'Malvane's face contorts into a wrinkled, skull-hollow horror, her black eyes gleaming, blood pouring from beneath the tines of her collar in frenzied rhythm with her furious heartbeat.

"BUT WE WILL HURT YOU LAST."

Her hand snaps out faster than I can move my torpor dream-body, fingers digging deep and instant into my chest, as if I'm made of cotton. Fire. Fire everywhere, in my flesh, in my veins— the otherworldly fury burning out of her eyes and into me as she speaks with a triumphant rasp.

"THERE YOU ARE."

The pain is so great, it wrenches me out of the dream gasping for air. And unlike most dreams, it follows. Lingers. The motion of the jolt up from Lucien's lap sears across my chest—five small holes buried in the flesh there, and about the exact size of fingertips.

"Heart, I'm here," Lucien murmurs comfortingly, pulling me close and putting his hand over the wounds. I can feel his magic pouring into me like molten salve, numbing and easing all at once. He wasn't lying—magic here is easy and strong, like the finest well-decanted alcohol instead of the usual water.

"What happened?" Fione asks, brows knit as she hovers over me. "Did you see her?"

"She's...she's on her way," I gasp between breaths. "And she's not happy."

"Good." Malachite narrows his eyes at the darkness all around us. "They get sloppy when they aren't happy."

"You included," Lysulli cuts in. Malachite opens his mouth to retort but Lucien cuts him off with just a look, holding my hand firmly in his.

"Everyone should spread out and take positions," the prince says. "I'll head into the cave and wait for Varia to approach."

"We have to let her near the Tree," Yorl muses. "But not so many valkerax near that we're overwhelmed. A tricky thing."

"How will you know when she's close enough?" I ask Lucien, my breathing finally evening out as the pain recedes and the fingertip wounds close.

"It's a feeling." He smiles wryly at me.

"This battlefield will be unpredictable." Lysulli frowns, pale lips thin. "So stay flexible. The valkerax could do any number of strange maneuvers under a singular commander."

"The Tree of Souls might seem tame now," Yorl agrees. "But it's very likely to react to Varia's presence."

"Hopefully to our benefit." Fione perches on a boulder,

crossbow deadly at her side.

"Nothing to do, then"—Lucien looks to me—"but wait. Would you care to join me?"

He motions to the First Root in the little cave, and I nod, following him into the low hole. This dim little crevice…our last haven. The two of us, sitting aside the gently bleeding First Root, hands in each other's hair, around each other's waists. Our last moments.

Our first moments.

I make sure to think it, but Lucien's skinreading doesn't seem to notice the slip. Or if he does, he doesn't say anything, looking me over with gentle onyx eyes. Thinking. Thinking about us, him, Cavanos.

He can't know.

He'd talk to me otherwise. Because this is our last chance to.

But he's afraid like me. Nervous like me. How could we not be? His sister, the most powerful being in the world, maybe, is coming to kill us. And all we have is a hope, a prayer, and a plan made of an old book.

Time drips on, slower than the pearlescent sap collecting in the little pool to our left. It reflects us, our outlines wavy and tense, but clinging to each other to the last. Something like exhaustion pulls me under and into the darkest lake. It's a different tiredness from the mental toll of staying awake for days—this feeling is more dire. More pointed, and pointed right at my core.

you will die here, forever.

It's dug deeper than a thorn in my unheart, my empty chest stone-heavy all of a sudden. Resignation? Maybe. Or maybe this is simply what the beginning and the end of the world feels like.

monsters have no soul. you have no soul.

I've done so much. Learned so much. Been so many things to so many people. And now here I am. But who is "I?" Am I really me? Did I spring from my forgotten mother's womb as me, or have my friends and loved ones made me?

pointless.

The sum total of me is every moment I spent with Lucien. With Fione. With Crav, Nightsinger, Peligli. Every loss. Every gain. Every smile and joke and tear. Undeath tried to stop me. Tries to stop me still, whispering despair into my ears.

you are nothing, nothing, NOTHING.

I am everything.

Life has made me. The world has made me *me*.

And it's my time to return the favor.

"Our time. Together, Starving Wolf."

I start up, the familiar voice echoing in my head. I heard it for so many weeks, in that pitch-dark arena below Vetris.

Lucien blinks drowsily, gripping my hand harder. "What is it, Zera?"

The clamor outside the cave comes instantly—the clash of bone armor on bone armor, beneathers shouting in their language, the sound of bowstrings being fired. Lucien and I jump up as one just as a shadow appears at the mouth of our cave, folding itself in half to look in at us with ruby eyes.

"Valkerax," Malachite pants. "Nearby."

"Is she here?" Lucien demands.

Malachite shakes his head. "No sign. But if the valkerax are here, she isn't far behind."

"Wait." I swallow. "I don't think—"

"Ready the first round of tranqs, for the love of the spirits!" Lysulli's shout from outside dumps cold water into my veins. I dash for the cave exit, squeezing past Mal and running furiously to the front line, legs pumping over rubble.

"Wait!" I screech. "*Wait!* That valkerax is a friend!"

A beneather soldier looks up from his bow like I'm absolute batshit and scoffs. "Yeah, and it's here to politely ask us to dance."

"Prepare yourselves!" Lysulli's faint orders resound as they stride up and down the firing line, and I sprint around broken pillars and piles of traveling packs to reach them. The archers draw their bows tight, eyes focused and scanning the silently howling darkness just past the golden glow of the flowers. No shadows, no light. Just yawning nothingness out there.

I freeze when something moves.

Deep in the black, something slithers. I hear it, so they definitely hear it with their long ears.

Yorl comes skidding to my side, nose twitching madly. "It smells like valkerax. Is it Evlorasin?"

I nod. "We have to get Lysulli to stop—"

"There!" a beneather soldier suddenly cries out. "*P'ashath ora*!"

The whole firing line rises up with cries of *"p'ashath ora,"* and Yorl breathes an unthinking translation beside me, his green orbs locked in the distance.

"The wyrm cometh."

From the depths rises a white line, slow at first, slithering over and under rubble, into and out of the ground. It's massive. I still viscerally remember just how massive Evlorasin was, is, but with it surrounded on all sides by the giant canyons and headed off by the monumental, ghostly Tree of Souls, it looks no more than a toy. A string. Something quaint and small, until it darts in closer, its five white eyes catching golden-flower light and glimmering in the darkness and all of a sudden it's huge and everywhere.

"Starving Wolf," Evlorasin says in its calm, guttural voice. *"I've come to aid you."*

"Fire!" Lysulli yells.

"No!" I spin on my heel, wrenching a beneather's bow out of their hand. "No, *no*! It's friendly! Stop!"

But the line doesn't listen to me—only to Lysulli. They nock their bows, and I watch in horror as a hundred archers pull, tense, and then fly loose their arrows. Some tranq, some not, but they all soar toward Evlorasin's exact location, exactly at its five white eyes and undulating whiskers—

And then they stop.

The hail of arrows stops just before Evlorasin, who slithers fully out of the darkness, white scales and long halberd claws on display, its wolflike paws pattering down the earth in heavy thumps as it nears, leaving prints the size of horse wagons on the canyon floor.

"Didn't you hear her?"

The voice seems to boom around the stone, and Yorl and I watch in shock with the archers as a white crow flies to the front, hovering just before the wall of unmoving arrows frozen in space.

Lucien.

The crow's feathers meld to his armor, his cape, his smirk as he looks back at us.

"This one's a friend." The arrows suddenly bunch into one dense knot in the air, floating back toward the line of archers and landing softly on the ground just before them. He's so powerful. This place...it's made him a giant. That's supposed to make me feel happy. Satisfied.

But all it does is terrify me.

will he be strong enough to stop us?

Lucien just throws me a small grin. "Always wise to save ammunition in a time like this, isn't it?"

"Prince!" Lysulli booms. "What the *fuck* do you think you're doing? The thing's next to you—"

Evlorasin slithers just behind Lucien, and joy pierces me as the prince turns to pat it on the nose.

"See?" He looks at Lysulli. "Gentle as a rabbit."

"It's the one I told you about." Malachite sprints over to Lysulli far easier than I with his beneather agility. "The one Zera tamed."

Yorl hems and haws. "'Tamed' isn't really the correct phraseology—"

I push through Yorl's words and the firing line and dash toward Evlorasin and Lucien, half-real gold petals scattering as I throw my arms around the prince and then bury myself in Ev's chest mane.

"Thank you," I mutter. "I didn't think you'd come."

"I felt the yearning of you," Evlorasin rumbles. *"And so too did it become my yearning."* The great wyrm narrows its five eyes at the firing line, the beneathers clearly jumpy and still ready to attack at a moment's notice. *"Will they have me?"*

"I'll make them have you," I laugh, teary.

"Any bit of help is welcome," Lucien says, a twinge of uneasiness to it as he tries to speak directly facing the valkerax. He can't hear it speaking like I can—to him it's just hissing—but he must be guessing how the conversation is going based on my words.

Evlorasin blinks down at Lucien, slowly and scrutinizing, sniffing the air around him intently. *"This is your mated?"* Ev snorts. *"It seems rather...small."*

My laugh bubbles up, and I hug the beautiful beast closer.

It takes more than a little negotiation on all our parts to get Lysulli to stop ordering the archers to keep constant aim on Evlorasin. Especially when it breaches the firing line with me and circles my body like a lazy dog assuming its place before the hearth. But somehow, between Malachite's cajoling at Lysulli and Lucien's fearless, careful touching of the valkerax to communicate its friendliness to the battalion, we make it. None of the beneathers looks happy about letting the valkerax through and behind them, constantly checking over their shoulders as it curls up on the rubble and waits with us.

Lysulli won't even approach closely, shouting from the firing line instead. "If it kills my men, I kill you!"

"Fair enough!" I shout back, and then put my hand on Evlorasin's velvety wet nose. "You'll have to be careful when the fight breaks out, Ev. They won't be able to tell you from the rest."

"Then I will battle deep." The valkerax thrashes its tail. *"Where arrows cannot reach."*

"You have to be careful! There's a lot more of them that can fly, now. I saw them."

"Care cannot be afforded against blood kin." Ev's whiskers undulate in a deceptively calm rhythm. *"We are of the song and will only cease for it."*

"Still!" I pout, patting down its mane. "You've gotta be—"

The five white eyes slick over to me in their sockets, nictating membranes blinking. *"I will not die, Starving Wolf. Not until my kin are free."*

I know how stubborn Ev is. How stubborn I am. A small smile pulls at my lips. "It's a promise, then."

Ev drapes itself over the mouth of the cave, and I duck beneath it to join Lucien again. Our fingers intertwine just near the pearl puddle, waiting. Waiting for maybe-death. For all of us.

The amethyst bracelet on my wrist, the heart locket around my neck. Both of them glimmer.

"Will they write books about us, you think?" Lucien asks softly.

I put my head on his shoulder and laugh. "Gods, I hope not."

32
TOGETHER

In war, there is no grand moment of beginning.

The bards like to sing about it—that still second before the world turns on, the gears of mortals grinding as two armies face each other, and then the horn. Always a horn, announcing the charge, and two glorious lines of steeds and men charging at one another.

But that's song. Fantasy. Not reality. Maybe it happens in mortal war. In wars between humans, not between humans and witches. Without magic. Maybe, somewhere across the sea from the Mist Continent, war has that grand horn and that majestic charge. But what comes after is nothing poetic.

Be wary always of bards who sing about beautiful war.

Because it's nothing but pain, and death, and horrible, horrible disfigurement. Because, when the valkerax finally arrive, it's in secret, through the canyons and from crevices below, and we never see it coming.

Peace one moment, and furious chaos the next.

Varia doesn't stand on her valkerax valiantly or line them up and charge them in like a mortal might. She doesn't gloat or pose dramatic before her victory. She fights with her wyrm weapons like a beast fighting for survival, for revenge—ragingly, the bulk of the horde descending on us in what feels like an instant. Fire suddenly everywhere, licking invisible flowers and eating what wood is left in the ruins of Pala Orias, snaking up the corpses of beneathers far too young to die. Beneathers who have only ever known war.

The archers shoot frantically, the white valkerax swarming over the canyon walls and staggering at the tranqs in their scales, passing out dead cold and tripping the others rushing in behind them. Pileups of wyrms writhe around one another, snapping and scrabbling to get their bearings and charge, claws ripping one another apart as much as they rip the beneathers.

Evlorasin immediately ascends, roaring out a vicious battle cry as its mane shines rainbow. Up, and up, and then I lose sight of it.

"*Be well*," Ev says to me, but the words fade all too quickly. I watch its pure white feathers drift softly down to the earth with something like regret. Lucien stands, and I stand with him and watch as the fingers of his working hand turn black up to the wrist.

"I put a barrier around the front line," he clarifies. "A bubble. It won't stop the valkerax, but it will slow them down marginally. Make them easier targets."

"Is Varia nearby?" I ask.

"Yes." He narrows his eyes out of the cave's mouth. "But not close enough. She's staying just out of range. It's like she...*knows*."

"Shit," I hiss. "I can lure her out. Make her angrier, make her come right for us—"

"By sleeping again?" Lucien frowns. I should say yes, but I can't. If I sleep, and lure her, and Varia gets close enough, I might not wake up in time to stop Lucien from splitting the First Root again. I have to be here to interrupt him. To put it back together before he splits it apart.

I can't go to her in the dream. But the only other way I have to communicate with her, to lure her, is the hunger. My valkerax blood promise, and the Bone Tree song inside her, calling to me. The hunger here is muted by Lucien's powerful magic. Just a little more from me, and I can push it down entirely. But if I Weep, that valkerax part of me comes out, too. The six eyes. It could make me *more* vulnerable to the Bone Tree's command, not less. I could communicate with her, goad her closer, but she could also just grab my reins, force me to hurt and kill like she almost did in the Black Archives.

"Zera, no," Lucien starts. "What if—"

"I won't," I say. "Trust me. Please."

He hedges, black eyes sliced thin. "I can't lose you."

"You won't." I say it, and unsay it. "It'll be only for a second. *Please.*"

I feel the grip of his magic loosen before his expression does. "Only a second."

I suppress my smile and dive straight into the silence. Of the silence. One foot in front of the other, one step deeper at a time. Falling, like falling into a weightless ocean. I've seen the ocean now.

What a beautiful unlife it's been.

I surface into absolute stillness, into the world being split six ways, six eyes looking at six Luciens. Magma-hot blood tears streak down my face, eye-corner to eye-corner, the blood dripping to the floor and mixing with the pearl blood of the Tree of Souls. The hunger in my head is gone, gnawing at me no longer, but I understand it better now. It's not really gone. Weeping doesn't get rid of the hunger. It just lets it rest—from the pain. From the anger. From the guilt.

Weeping isn't to suppress the hunger. It's to embrace it.

To embrace all of myself, no matter how dark or terrifying.

I'm here.

I'm here, I think loudly and clearly. *Come and get me.*

I look at the First Root sticking out of the dirt, crystallize its sundered shape in my mind. The connection between Bone Tree Varia and the valkerax part of me twinges, a harp string plucked too fast and too hard. She's seen it. She knows I'm looking at the First Root. So close to splitting it again. *Too close.*

The impact is instantaneous. I hear Malachite shouting outside, Fione wailing, the hiss of steam as Yorl's matronic moves, the battle raging outside as my unheart splinters into a thousand shards. Lucien's face looks ashen and fearful—scared of losing everyone. Of losing me.

But we can't move. We can't go out and help them. We have to be here, at the First Root, to fix it all. To end—and begin—it all.

I have to trust that they're still alive. I can't let the emotion of fear submerge me. Drown me. The ocean is so big, so full of life, but I won't drown in it. I can swim. I've *learned* to swim now. Reginall taught me. Ev taught me. The fourteen men I killed taught me. Lucien taught me.

Everyone in my life taught me to swim in the ocean of myself.

I can swim now, and there's an island I have to reach—that black-rock island of Rel'donas, that small, peaceful room where I found rest at last.

Fire starts to lick at the cave's mouth, and the ground rocks us to our knees as two valkerax entwined in furious combat writhe over each other just outside, slamming into the cave and away from it, blood spattering over earth and our clothes and staining the First Root. Dirt and dust fall from the precarious ceiling, white feathers and fur flying.

Ev.

Ev, tearing into the stomach of its brethren, as its stomach is torn into, too.

And then Varia.

She appears out of nowhere—teleporting? I don't know, but she feels like she's gone, far away, and then she's in front of us, sallow and hungry and mere rags, a skeleton of the princess I knew and the sister Lucien loves. It's clear to read on his face—he doesn't move. He can't. She looks like a corpse. Dead. *Worse*—

sucked clean of all life. The bone choker around her neck is nearly decapitating her now, the red flesh of her windpipe showing, the white tendons of her throat column exposed. She looks a waif, but the power around her is harder and heavier than lead.

And her milky, shriveled eyes are on me.

In a way, Lucien's shock, that one moment of hesitation—his love for his sister sealed the world's fate. He could've gone for the First Root the moment she appeared. But his love roots him to the spot for just this one second. And I take it.

He has never starved. But he has loved.

And that's why, at the end of the world, there are wolves and not mortals.

That's why I reach the Root first. That's why Varia lunges for me, my hands gripping the slippery pearlescent blood as I try desperately to push the two halves of the First Root together again. To hold it there, to heal it there. She's only destruction. She doesn't know—she can't know of healing. Of what I'm doing.

But the bones of her choker spear out of her and into me all the same.

Four, five—I can't count how many points of pain, of entry. Maybe a thousand. It feels like a thousand, the agony ripping through muscle and organ and every undead part of me. My skin tries to curl away from itself, vomit and hot-cold blood like nausea, a tide that moves with my inhales and exhales. Each breath, pain.

Every year of the thousand this Tree has had to endure—pain.

"*NO!*" Lucien bellows, and the flash of black light dizzies me. He does something—I don't know what—but Varia staggers back woodenly, like a doll, and lunges for me again.

This time, her half-dead visage freezes. Completely unmoving, her withered eye sockets focused only on me. Her bones still spear my body, but I manage to turn my head over my shoulder to look at Lucien. His entire body is eaten by the void, up to his neck, to his jaw, creeping over his lips as he trembles, shakes, holding his sister in place with all his magic.

"Lucien!" I scream, blood spattering out of my throat. "Let go!"

He doesn't.

"It'll kill you!" My voice shatters. "LUCIEN!"

His eyes flicker from his sister to me, just that one movement so impossibly hard for him. "You...let go..."

"I have to put it together!" I shake my head. "You have to trust me!"

Varia's eyes are dead. But his are alive and burning. Burning alive with his love for me, his worry, our memories together. The two halves of the First Root start to keen in my hands, close, their wounds touching and reaching out for one another all at once. Something booms beneath us, around us, above us. It sends out shock waves, little tremor warnings, and I know.

I know like the valkerax know. Or maybe it's the fact I'm holding the First Root itself in my hands. Maybe it's talking to me with its soul, its magic. However it's doing it, I can see it like a clear dream. Like I'm dreaming lucid, awake. Images, feelings. I can see the battle unfolding below, valkerax dead, beneathers dead, blood smearing the ghostly gold flowers. I can see the now and the future. The Tree of Souls won't heal without first hurting. It'll collapse the cavern. All the canyons. The destruction will be huge.

Everyone will die.

"Lucien, take them," I beg him. "Everyone. Take them and go."

Spittle and blood foam in the corners of his mouth, the animate void crawling steadily up his throat, Varia's limbs beginning to twitch.

"I won't leave you...behind...again," he hisses.

"Take everyone," I say. "I can do the rest. You have to—you have to get away. To Pala Amna. As far as you can get."

His black eyes flicker with great effort over to Varia. I make a smile.

"I'll send her along," I say. "When the Tree lets go of her. I promise."

"You...can't—"

"I can," I assure him. "I know it's selfish. But I can—"

"You will let go of the First Root."

His command hits me like an arrow to my chest already riddled with them. But this one hurts more than any. He promised. He was different from the others—he'd never use me like this. He said that. He showed that. But now the magic rises up, curling around my arms, forcing itself through even the peace of my Weeping—his magic is so much stronger here at the Tree of Souls. Strong enough to defy my Weeping like Varia does. He doesn't have a Tree in him, but even being near one is enough to give him the magical power to brute force through my will. But it's killing him. Holding Varia *and* making me obey this command is...it's too much. It'll kill him. The hunger laces razor threads around my wrists, my fingers, pulling them apart without my will.

"You said—" I gasp. "You said you'd never—"

"I will not." He pauses, gasping for breath. "Lose you again."

I see it in his eyes, and the hurt drains from me one feather-touch at a time. Love.

He's doing this for love.

He's commanding me for love.

Not like Varia did. Not in his best interest or in mine. In ours. He wants a world with me in it, as I want that world, too. Desperately. More than anything.

We teeter on the edge of a knife, the past and the future. Our past together, our future together. The battle rages outside, Evlorasin's roar cracking the deadly tension in the cave.

A tear slips from my fifth and sixth eye, my human eyes, as my smile widens and the words tumble from my lips, tragic and hopeful all at once.

"Wait for me."

The wildfire in his gaze roars higher, eating me like kindling. The ring—*his ring*—around my finger feels so solid, so wonderful, the only unpainful thing in the world as every little muscle in my body strains to force the First Root back together. The tremblings of the ground grow wild, nearly throwing us off-balance, but Lucien refuses to let even the earthquakes tear his gaze from my face. The ceiling of the little cave starts to collapse in places, chunks of dirt and stone leaving puckered holes into darkness that reveal the glowing rainbow tree above. It seems more real, somehow—its branches now strongly shimmering.

Varia suddenly breaks free of Lucien's spell, her wooden-fingered hand darting out for my throat. She squeezes and squeezes so hard I fear my head will come off—squeezes like I'm the source of all her rage and fury. But Varia's grip is nothing compared to the iron grip of Lucien's command, the hunger peeling apart my willpower like it's nothing more than dry lace. He knew all along, maybe, what I was going to do. But he had a plan, too. He didn't want to command me, but he knew he would if he had to. He'd pour all his magic into that one command if he had to.

I can't stop him.

But I can love him.

"If I don't do this, Lucien," I gasp, "I'll be hungry forever."

It's not the *I love you* he wants. It's not the *I'll stop, and let you do this instead*. It's not the *I will consider my own safety above all others'* he wants to hear. He wants me to be with him, to be us, together at last, and in peace.

And I want that, too.

Varia's grip closes in around my windpipe. I breathe deep, for maybe my last breath, and say, "Please trust me. Wait for me."

It's a promise, and a cry, and a prayer.

It's unfair to ask him. Selfish.

But maybe I've earned a little of that, at the end of all things.

Whisper isn't the type to linger, but Lucien is. So I know it's Whisper who pulls him away from me, who breaks his eye contact, who is there one moment and then gone in shadow the next. The sound of popping, everywhere, outside the cave. Clattering as swords fall to the floor, as bowstrings unwind sharply, the clank of metal as Yorl's matronic falls, as every beneather and friend is teleported away by Lucien's sheer power, the sounds of battle emptying in a split second, and all I can think is *thank you*.

I love you.

Varia digs into my neck. I feel it happen, but she can't stop my hands. I press with all effort, all breath, into my two palms, forcing the First Root's wound flush against itself. My neck creaks, groans, resisting her force trying to decapitate me. Around her fingers buried deep in my neck, blood and life leave me, and I see her face. I see her expression—no, the Bone Tree's expression—as she realizes I'm putting her together instead of taking her apart.

I've never seen joy. Not really. Not until this moment.

It's a deep, old, eternal joy, the sort the New God priests crow about in the temples. Divine joy. Joy that makes moving mountains possible, that makes the sun rise and set and rise again by the buoy of sheer gilded ecstasy. She—no, *it*—looks at me, milky, shriveled eyes somehow filled with gratitude.

"Thank you."

The bones sticking out of Varia's choker and piercing into me suddenly retract, small and slender and like jewelry again. There's a clicking sound, and the bone choker comes loose, one fang at a time, until it falls to the ground and disintegrates into white dust.

Varia staggers as if she's been cut free from some string holding her, her knees tumbling to the ground and her body unmoving, her head on her chest. My six eyes start to blacken at the edges, but I force myself to focus on my hands, on holding. I can feel the Root's wound starting to close, inch by inch. The tremors are worse now, great clots of dirt falling on our heads, cracks and crashes beyond the little cave as boulders fall and the canyon faces start to shatter.

"V-Varia, wake up," I stammer, throat scraped raw and open. "Your Highness...wake up, *please*."

Lucien's magic can't reach me—not anymore. He's gone from the Tree of Souls, not a scrap of the power it was giving him to be found. He's far, too far, so far my heart necklace can't even help. I can feel the white rush of noise crawling up my half-broken spine, ready the moment I let my Weeping down to freeze me in place, keep me here screaming soundlessly for all eternity. He can't heal me. He can't help me. He's gone.

Fione, Mal, Yorl. They're all gone.

No—not gone. Safe.

I have to keep my promise to Fione now.

"Varia!" I gurgle. "Please! Get up!"

Nothing. The wound is closing in my hand, the First Root mending itself quickly and the pearl liquid coming to a stop. It coats my hands, makes them slippery, my own blood spurting out of my neck not helping, but I cling on, dig my claws in. If I can't get her to wake up, she's done for.

"HEY!" I scream. "ASSHOLE!"

To my utter relief, she jerks up, eyes wild and plump and black again as she looks around like she has no idea where she is or what's going on. Her skin is still sallow, but the skeletal hunger in her cheekbones is gone, and her neck wounds are dire holes that will leave scars, but nothing fatal.

"What—" The princess blinks at me. Black eyes full of suspicion, of pride. She's back. She's herself. "What are *you* doing here? Where—"

"There's no time," I blurt, blood bubbling out of my nose. "This is the Tree of Souls. You can use more magic here. Use it, teleport away. To Pala Amna."

She looks me up and down, at my mangled body "But—"

"I'll be right behind you! Hurry!"

It's just a second. Just a blink. But I know. How could I *not* know? She was my witch; we have history. She hurt me, I hurt her. But she led me here in the end, didn't she? Her sheer determination to make the world better, no matter how misguided, led me here, to the Tree of Souls. It led me to make things right, once and for all. Varia held my hand, didn't she? The whole way. She was the one who helped me stop the song.

"I know you wanted to do it alone." I wheeze a laugh. "Change the world. But Fione's waiting. So. I'll take over from here."

It's just a second, but her onyx eyes soften. "You—"

"Go."

Varia is her brother, but she's not at the same time. She doesn't linger, ever. No waiting for that one. Things to do, people to see, lives to change.

But she lingers now, face broken and soft as she says, "Don't you dare die."

All the animosity between us, all the history. It pivots on those words, and I smile. She's there, and then in a faint popping noise, she's gone.

And I'm alone.

"Never alone." I can hear Evlorasin's faint voice outside, struggling. Injured. *"Never-goodbye."*

Through the massive holes in the cave's ceiling, I see the Tree start to glow. Hundreds of feet up, and through the darkness, the Tree of Souls grows hard, full of color, real. A pure white streaked with rainbow like oil, like blood, branches regal and extending for what seems like forever. Roots below, extending forever. Connecting us all.

And it all starts to *glow*.

It's a hum. A hum that reverberates in my insides, in my unheart, replacing the hunger, blowing it out and away like a sweet wind. No more guilt. No more anger. No more pain. The golden flowers become real, whole, shining like little suns in the darkness, their faces bobbing even more happily in an even more joyous wind.

Wind I can feel now.

The glow becomes so intense that it turns to light, white light shafting through the holes in the cave's roof. One beam shines down directly on me, and it feels warm. I can see a six-eyed face in it, a celeon maw and a wise smile, a paw reaching for me. To help me.

Never alone.

The light consumes my eyes—pure white. No matter which way I glance, all white, and the heat of a thousand suns bearing down on me, full to bursting, full to burning me alive. Or burning me undead, as it were.

I laugh at my own joke, here at the end of everything, and hold the First Root together tighter. Nothing can escape the light—the sound of my laugh scorched away instantly.

together, my hunger—the Glass Tree—sobs.

TOGETHER, the Bone Tree shrieks.

I look up. "Together."

Never alone.

A wolf to end the world, Evlorasin said. And it was right. I'm here, at the end of the world.

And the beginning of a new one.

EPILOGUE

It is said that in the year 34EA, in the very middle of the summer season, a powerful earthquake rocked the Mist Continent as far as the Gold Shore in Avel and as high as the scholar-city of Breych. This cataclysmic earthquake, whilst capsizing much of the land surrounding it, heralded the rise of the King Without Crown, who went on to build the greatly peaceful and greatly influential Vetrisian Empire and who, by scheme or by purpose, has lost his name to the sands of time.

But in what scraps remain of the seminal history annals entitled *Recordings and Observations from the War of Trees* by Yorl Farspear-Ashwalker, there resides significantly more detail on the event, and it is as follows: in 34EA, on Highmoon day 17, a category three earthquake gripped the Mist Continent for exactly seven seconds, the epicenter of which was the beneather city-fortress of Pala Orias. When it subsided, there were approximately 142 aftershocks over the course of five days. Yet this ushered in a prominent era of peace for the major nations of Arathess, politically spearheaded by the newly formed Vetrisian Empire, and such a time of growth and prosperity as we now live in is referred to as "the Contentment."

—Excerpt from Archsage Tessal Miroux's dissertation, entitled *A History of the War of Trees, or, an Attempt to Trace the Five-Hundred-Year-Old Origins of Arathess's Great Change.*

...

Lucien,

Try not to get too angry at the polymath who's delivering this to you. I asked him to. He's just the messenger. Shoot me, if you must. With an arrow of love. Ha-ha!

It's strange, isn't it? Trying to write to someone you talk to all the time. I feel like I can be much more serious in letters—it's the lack of body language options. Or maybe the lack of my body, period. How can I make jokes if all I have is ink and not my wonderful bosoms? Oh, does a lady not speak of her bosoms in a letter? I'm terrible at this. Send me back to Y'shennria for five more years.

I'm writing this, mostly, because I'm nervous. And maybe that's a bad idea, because you know me—I get to blabbing when I'm anxious. Too many words, but none of them with any meaning.

So. I'll cut myself off and cut to the point.

I love you.

Did you know that? Even if you did, I wanted to say it one last time.

But no one is ever really gone.

I wish you the happiest of lives. A long life, too. But not too long. You know how I feel about eternity.

Wherever you go, I will be.

Yours,

Elizera Y'shennria

Sitting in his chair at the high table of the negotiations room of the palace, Lucien d'Malvane felt as though the Pendronic ambassador was looking at him with the eyes of a hungry hyena.

"Surely Your Highness is aware he is approaching twenty-two years of age now." The ambassador licked his lips uneasily. "The Golden Empress wishes to express her high regard of you, and of your ancient bloodline, and begs you consider her daughter—"

"And I'm very flattered, to be regarded so highly by the Golden Empress." Lucien wove his voice in the careful silks politics required. "But I'm sure I've sent out more than one notice of the dissolution of the kingdom of Cavanos and its noble hierarchy, sir. All noble families are in the process of being formally stripped of their lands and birthright, and the assets redistributed among the commonwealth. This, of course, includes the royal bloodline."

The ambassador's fine red mustache twitched as he made a small bow in his chair, ruffled collar barely containing his hidden disdain. "Of course, Your Highness."

"Then, if the royal family is dissolved," the former prince began slowly, but not too slowly as to offend, "it seems there's very little need to call me 'Your Highness,' am I not correct?"

"You are, your—" This time, the ambassador caught himself, and he coughed into his sleeve. "Your Excellency."

The tall, pale beneather sitting against the wall among the ambassador's silk-clad guards rolled his ruby eyes. Lucien prayed to whatever god was left that Malachite could hold his tongue long enough for the former prince to drill the facts of the new Vetrisian Empire into the ambassador's head.

"Ah-ah." Lucien put up one finger and waved it playfully at the ambassador. "Excellency is still a noble title."

"Th-Then—" The ambassador stuttered. "What should I call you, sir?"

"Sir will do nicely, I think." Lucien smiled at him brightly.

The man practically went beet down to his boots. "B-But—but you are the ki—"

"Head of State," Lucien interrupted him smoothly, a chuckle on his lips. "Though my people do still cling to tradition. Have you heard? They call me the 'King Without a Crown.' Silly, really. And so...*theatrical*."

Lucien could swear he heard Malachite scoff a soft "you love it," but the rest of the room was quiet, uneasy at the unheard of shift of etiquette. The constant knocking of hammers on the palace walls and the deafening hiss of white mercury machines was but a dull undercurrent of noise here in the negotiations room, the shouts of workers and the stomps of the metallic matronics doing heavy lifting ringing far louder along the half-finished marble halls.

Lucien stood and made his way to the window, his black robe sweeping out behind him. He touched one finger to the sill, the paint still fresh. He'd ordered that the palace be the last thing to be rebuilt—housing and infrastructure first. And to his joy, the city had blossomed in the three years since. Well...since the end.

He shook himself out, holding his wooden hand tightly to his side.

New Vetris had sprung up around the crater of the palace slowly, but also in a blink. Time worked strangely in that way—constant negotiations, drawing up papers and trade requests and refugee inventories, sleepless nights of city planning with Fione, with Yorl, with the People's Council. It all blurred together, melded and stretched and compressed until he was standing at the window today, in the fresh sunlight of spring, watching the city hum below. The horizon still looked different with the Red Lady gone, with the temple's spire much smaller. Sometimes he'd blink and expect it to be there, wished it to be there, if only because that meant *she* would be there, too.

Time, reversed enough to give them time.

He scoffed softly under his breath.

Of all the rebuilding and restructuring New Vetris had accomplished together, the People's Council was his proudest achievement. It was comprised of sixteen representatives from every walk of life, elected entirely by the people. The disenfranchised nobles had snuck in their man, of course, but outnumbered fifteen to one, his entrenched opinions barely held much sway. Bribery had tried to happen, naturally, but Fione had made the very prescient suggestion Lucien strip said nobles of their land rights. And so that had begun in earnest. T'was only doable because the nobles' landed armies had been wiped out in the War of Trees—otherwise, civil war would've surely descended.

Lucien smirked to himself. Fate had given him the perfect time to step in and change things.

So, too, had it taken every other happiness from him.

But she'd be proud of him, wouldn't she?

His sharp onyx eyes fell on the black rosebushes of the former Y'shennria manor, properly trimmed and maintained. It was an orphanage now, for all the children orphaned by the War of Trees, with Lady Y'shennria managing it gladly and well and as warmly strict as could be. He could hear the children faintly shrieking, scrambling about in the yard as they played.

On the difficult nights, Lucien would wander over to the orphanage and pick a single black rose to put in his room, to let the fragrance fill the empty spaces in his bed.

"My apologies, sir." He turned from the window and back to the ambassador. "I'm afraid I grow weary. Shall we continue this on the morrow? Does midmeal agree with you?"

"Verily." The ambassador stood, his guards standing to

attention with him. "I would appreciate such kindness thoroughly, your—sir."

"Then." Lucien nodded and smiled as he swept past him and out of the room. "Farewell for now."

His boots clipped on the sawdust-strewn marble, joined quickly by another pair with a far longer, lazier stride.

"The Pendrons think they're so big," Malachite scoffed at his shoulder. "Just because Varia forgot to touch them during the whole thing."

Lucien laughed. "To be fair, not even the valkerax want to cross the Redlands."

"They could've just taken the ocean," Malachite grumbled.

"The ocean is very, very big, Mal."

"So I've heard."

"So you've seen." Lucien laughed louder. The quiet descended quickly between them. The ocean. He, of course, meant Rel'donas. The Black Archives. That little island full of fond memories. A tender place now in his heart.

Together they walked through the palace, nodding at workmen carrying great loads, chopping and sanding and refitting walls. The two young men passed a particular room being rebuilt—a room that once held old portraits of an older family, and then burned portraits of a family made suddenly much smaller. Lucien had started to forget their faces halfway through year two, his father's face last, his mother's first, nothing left behind of them but their blackened skeletons in their beds. They had been terrible rulers but kind parents. Forgiveness, and longing, and gratitude that they were gone enough for him to undo the damage they had done. His family had become but a dust devil in his busy mind—a tremor of a memory.

Lucien was glad, at least, that the ashen smell had gone.

The valkerax were a distant concern in the aftermath. Many had died at the explosion that occurred at the Tree of Souls, and the earthquake afterward. Scattered to the wind after the Bone Tree's disappearance, it was hard to say what had happened to their remnants. Some people said they sunk down to the bottom of the ocean. Some romantics said they flew up to the sky, to the Blue Giant, and were living on the moon now. In the distant corners of the Star Continent, it was whispered a valkerax with five eyes could be seen flying high on particularly starry nights. But sightings had been few, few enough that it would be years or more before any real threat came of the valkerax, if at all.

Perhaps they'd learned, as Lucien had, to forgive.

"Watch it!" a workman snapped at his fellow, the beam they were attempting to set in the ceiling wavering. Lucien threw out his hand, the fingers instantly black, and the beam righted itself into place.

The workman looked down and waved. "Much obliged, Your Highness!"

"It's 'sir' now," Lucien insisted up at him, smiling.

"All due respect, *sir*." The man chuckled. "You'll always be 'Your Highness' to me."

"Plucky little shit." Malachite scoffed. "What do we even pay them for?"

"For their hard work, Mal," Lucien said patiently. "Now do me a favor and leave me alone for a bit."

"Depends on where you're going."

"The streets. For some air."

They stopped at the grand front doors of the palace, the entrance hall coated in plaster and ladders and discarded tools. She had walked through this place once, hadn't she? She must've thought the former decadence all so ridiculous.

"Are you going this year?" Malachite's question rings.

The work-flurry sounds dulled in Lucien's ears. He meant Rel'donas, again. After the end, Lucien found himself visiting the island once a year, welcomed heartily by Yorl. Lucien gave them information on how he was forming New Vetris each time in exchange for two days' allowance to roam the Black Archives, though roaming wasn't solely what he came to do.

He came to count the thirty-second door on the left, in the west hall, facing the ocean. He came to open the door, to dust off the floor and chairs and table, to leave fresh flowers on it. He came to sit on the cot, and watch the ocean, and remember.

Sometimes, in the light, he could still catch the ghost of her scent.

"Maybe," he answered Malachite. "Maybe not. Depends on how busy I am."

"You always find time for it," the beneather muttered. "Somehow."

Words failed the former prince, sadness succeeding them, and he walked down the steps and out to the lawn.

To call it a lawn still would be a disservice. Where once nobles spent leisurely time walking among the thin, artisanal waterways carved into immaculate grass, a garden had replaced it. The waterways made only to impress now provided great irrigation to a dozen acres of vegetable gardens, flowerbeds, grain fields, and fruit orchards. After he'd entered the ruins of Vetris, after he'd cried enough and shouted enough and stared long enough at the last memories of his childhood, it had been the first thing he converted—a food supply for his people. The fish of Vetris held what survivors he gathered well enough until the first sprouts of quick-growing sugarleaf began to blossom, and then followed the young beans, and the red lentils, and even the weeds between the garden gave them sustenance—bitter dandelion greens and pithy butterbur filling grateful, hungry mouths.

He could scarce believe, somedays, the bounty such a garden had become. He remembered shoveling barrels of manure, of what horses still lived, into fertilizer until his whole body ached. He remembered pulling water up from the broken irrigation channels, carting bucket after bucket under the sweltering sun, Malachite and Yorl and every refugee citizen healthy enough to work at his side. He remembered most keenly the moment they'd realized they had grown enough greenery to supplant the mulch with vegetable chaff. A luxury, truly, that had now become almost laughably commonplace.

He breathed deep the smell of ripening cherries, almond blossoms, swathes of young garlic and green onions and the honey of the beehives just beyond the vegetable garden. Potato flowers grew thick and white, covering the ground in spring snow, and rows of sweet radishes and strawberries had begun to shamelessly peek their rosy countenances out for all to see.

From the scorched soil of hopelessness, they'd together made New Vetris bloom. And so did his heart learn to heal. To move, when it wanted not. To beat, even if all it desired was to stop. What kept him moving, shoveling, eating, breathing, was the thought she'd chide him for thinking such things.

You have a heart in that handsome chest of yours, and you don't want it? So terribly ungrateful!

He smiled at a daisy, the words coming from nowhere and everywhere at once. But he didn't want them to stop. They'd be with him for the rest of his life, of that he was sure.

Of that, he hoped desperately.

His fingers wandered of their own accord to the breast pocket of his vest, in which he kept the empty bag. He pulled it out, studying the rough burlap and, most importantly, the golden threads that sloppily stitched out the word Heart on it. The mere sight of the bag and the word brought back a flood of memories, held by the tenuous dam of time and work and distraction.

But the jewelry inside, he had no dam for.

Lucien took them out now: a bracelet of amethysts in the beneather funerary style, and a golden heart locket embossed with stars and the three moons. The locket was so familiar and dear to him, like seeing an old and wonderful friend. The bracelet was a sadder friend, one spoken to in whispers and tears.

He'd found the jewelry on his return to the Tree of Souls. After the great quake subsided, after the surviving valkerax came pouring out of the earth and flew in all directions, freed at last, he'd been the first to lead a party down again. Down to the massive crater that yawned into darkness. Malachite and Fione had convinced him to rest for only an hour, but eventually caved and went with him. Yorl opted to stay with Lysulli and patch the wounds of the surviving soldiers. It was a long trek, and a furious one on his part. He didn't remember any of it, or even how he navigated, but he remembered how it felt—the searing rush of terror, the frantic praying unending that went through his mind until he stepped foot yet again on Pala Orias.

Or what was left of it.

The ground was still unstable, and Malachite had to hold him back. The bottom of the massive crater was so deep and wide that only the faintest suffusing of light managed to illuminate the destruction. Rock. Nothing but rock, and stone, and dust, for miles in a ruined radius.

But through it, in the center of it, the Tree of Souls still stood.

Tall white branches splayed out, greedily soaking in the light, the sun, as it hadn't for maybe thousands of years. Magic pulsed beneath its snow bark, rainbow flashes of light traveling up and down and back again. Only the highest golden flowers still peeked from the rubble, white manes and white bones of valkerax crushed beneath.

He'd tried to reach out, to use the Tree's great imprint of magic to teleport himself to its roots, to the First Root. But it wouldn't let him. There was a block, an iron door closed between tree and witch, now.

So he tried to walk.

He took four steps, then collapsed from the exhaustion.

Malachite hadn't taken nicely to it, and with Fione's help, they took him to Pala Amna and rest. In the following weeks of his recovery, and even after, they tried to get him to leave each day— to return to Vetris, to rebuild. After all, Fione said, there was no chance anyone survived. It was just miles of rock, miles of earth.

And besides, her heart was gone.

He'd noticed it the moment he teleported every soldier and friend back to Pala Amna, at her desperate request. The burlap bag in his breast pocket was suspiciously light. And when he opened it, it was empty. Not even the glass shard of the Glass Tree still remained. There was nothing. Not a smear of blood, not a single bit of flesh.

Her heart was gone.

And so was she.

But he wouldn't accept it. Not until he went back to the First Root and saw for himself.

It was a fevered journey. Malachite was the only one who stayed with him—Varia had come to fetch Fione. He was glad to see his sister, truly, more whole and healed and free of the bone choker, but even she couldn't pierce the steel around his mind. She was no longer witch. Her magic had gone.

The First Root was gone. Buried under rubble so far down, not even Malachite's strength could get very far. They dug until they hit a crevice, and then another, and then one incredibly deep and right on top of where she would've been. The hot glow of magma at the bottom cauterized his heart shut.

Somewhere between the days and nights that passed of his crying beneath the boughs of the white tree, Malachite found the jewels—her necklace and her bracelet. But not the ring. And that gave him the only hope he could cling to. Her ring—she still had it, maybe. She had said to wait for her.

So he would.

He would, until the end of the world again.

Her heart had disappeared, but so had every other Heartless's heart. Every single witch lost their Heartless at the same moment he lost her—every bag, every jar, every box. All of them, emptied out in an instant. Every heart magically teleported back into its body, rendering each Heartless human again, the flower-shaped scars on their chests like badges of joy.

"Luc!"

He quickly stuffed the jewels back in the burlap bag and looked up, Varia's smooth voice ringing over the garden as she caught up with him. Her cheeks were flush with spring and happiness, her black hair long and lustrous as always. It'd taken years for her to recover to this state—to have enough flesh on her bones again to walk, to talk, to laugh. And he was glad of it.

She was still thinner than she had ever been before, a gauntness to her cheeks, and she couldn't breathe as well as she used to. Her wooden fingers and leg still remained under her gauzy green dress. All traces of her own magic had been wiped away the moment the earthquake happened. She could no more spell a fireball than she could a pebble, and her wooden prosthetics had been unfeeling, drained of her magic. At first, the loss was devastating. She was happy to be with Fione again but seemed listless, and struggled to eat well or sleep well, the loss of magic deep in her.

It was harder still when she had to teach him, struggling and without the ability to demonstrate, how to forge a wooden hand of his own to replace the deadened one, and how to reanimate it with a constant low hum of magic. He figured out the latter mostly on his own, with Nightsinger's occasional help, and together, the two of them finally managed to breathe enough magic back into Varia's wooden parts that she could move them again—not nearly as well as if it was her own magic, but enough. That seemed to cheer her, if only a little.

She wasn't the same, but then again, no one was. They were

all new people, in a new world, learning. Magic still remained in Arathess, but different. It was not quite the same dark whisper, but it was there, nonetheless. It was more difficult, deeper, harder to pin down, and all witches in the world had to readjust accordingly. It would take years, perhaps decades, to return to the status quo of magic again, but he knew it'd be better this time. Truer.

He'd refused Varia's idea of making him a glass eye that moved, too—he wasn't particularly partial to glass anymore. He preferred his eyepatch, if only because it gave him an intimidating edge in negotiations with foreign lords.

"There you are!" Varia breathlessly smacked her wooden hand on his shoulder, and he staggered at the force. "How did the Pendronic meeting go?"

"Awful. They tried to marry me again."

"Bastards, the lot of them," she determined breezily. "Where are you off to?"

"More importantly, why do you need me?" he drawled.

"Because you're my beloved baby brother, baby brother." She laughed, head back, the indent marks of the Bone Tree's choker now nothing more than faded, whitish scars on the skin of her throat.

"Speaking of babies." He blinked. "How's my nephew?"

"Oh, fine." Varia sighed, flipping her hair over her shoulder. "Just fine. They tell you the twos are the worst age, but everybody says three comes around and then you know the true meaning of pain. And sleeplessness." She smiled at him in that pleading way. "Any chance we could reinstate the royal nannies before then?"

"No," he said flatly. "You made that child, and now you get to lie in his shit."

"Woe!" Varia put a hand to her forehead and feigned fainting before instantly bolting upright. "Very well. I'll tell Fione you heartlessly declined our request for a day off. She'll be disappointed, but I'm sure Zeran will be overjoyed to get the chance to vomit on us some more." She paused. "He hugs now, you know."

"Marvelous. I'll make an appointment."

She'd noticed his flinch at the word "heartless." Of course she had. But even with all her mellowing after the War of Trees, she still had that edge of pride that never allowed her to take back what she said. Though she did tend to apologize more now.

"Sorry, Luc," she started. "I didn't mean—" She stopped herself and smiled on his behalf. "Honestly, though, if you keep sneaking out to the city, I'm going to start to think you hate the palace."

"Never." He chuckled softly. "It's just…the memories."

Varia blinked her dark eyes. His same eyes. Their mother's eyes. "Right. I get it. That's why I go out to the Bone Road, you know."

"I know," he agreed.

Every month after the end of the War of Trees, Varia would trek out to the Bone Road. At first it was by foot, a hard task with one leg and a cane. But then they found the surviving horses, and it became easier. And then he learned to spell her leg, and it became even easier after that. He wasn't sure what she did out there, but she insisted she had to do it alone.

He'd asked Fione, and she'd only shaken her head, saying something about offerings. He never went out to the Bone Road when Varia did, but he did once go a week after her visit, and found the hundreds of graves spread out over the marsh—*every single one*, the new ones from the War of Trees and the old ones from the Sunless War—newly and neatly cleaned of moss with a brush and salt, and each adorned with a little bouquet of fresh wildflowers.

Penance, he supposed. Or her way of doing it. To watch over the dead—the ones she killed, and the ones who killed in the service of their family all those years ago.

The d'Malvane siblings watched the gardeners go about their business for a moment, the air laden with heavy honey scent, before Varia put a hand on his shoulder.

"You'll come for dinner tonight. Fione's making some sort of heartfelt stew abomination, and I'm terrible at suffering alone."

"She's gotten better," he argued in her defense.

"Oh, absolutely. Just not at the rate my bowels hoped," Varia agreed. "I'm leaving for Windonhigh in the morning—they've made a new monument for the fallen. So I must be there. And so you must come to dinner to see me off."

"I will," he assured her.

"Good."

She held his hand, her wooden fingers in his wooden palm for a long moment, and her smile crinkled on the edges. A smile that said more than words ever could; a smile that told him it was all right to be sad. But that they—the world—had been given a second chance, her least of all, and that to not forge forward in it was a waste.

"She'd want you happy, Luc."

It was a hard thing to say, and a harder thing to respond to, but the gift of siblings was that one knew you didn't always have to. Some words were just meant to be said and left to the wind, and as the two of them parted—him to the city and her to the palace—that knowing was most poignant of all.

He buried the loneliness frequently in the rush of the New Vetrisian crowd. The capital was still called Vetris, for convenience and something for the country to hold on to in the midst of rapid change, but it resembled little of its old self. The waterways were perhaps the one constant feature—too entrenched to be removed but not entrenched enough to resist an update. The pipes had been relaid in white mercury alloys and the pump systems completely overhauled thanks to Yorl's efforts. Fione helped where she could, but for the first year while she was heavy with pregnancy, it was

Yorl who did the majority of the work.

He went off Fione's blueprints she drew up in bed, and the two had revitalized the city—a major pipeline system allowing for indoor bathrooms not just in the palace, but in every home. Running water to cook with, to bathe with. The effects were immediate; the people became healthier and had more time to spend with their families and on rebuilding their lives. The watertells became more efficient, hissing faster and delivering messages at untold speeds. Thanks to Yorl's knowledge of beneather stonework, the buildings of Vetris were three stories taller now, allowing for more space and more shops. Connecting bridges to the buildings, such as he'd seen in Breych, allowed foot traffic to be split between the roads below and the bridges above. It was a wondrous and strange outline to see on the horizon at sunset, but Lucien felt proud of it.

The temple, of course, was remade. But Lucien's stipulations of a free worship meant that it belonged both to the New God and the Old God, to the beneather spirits and the celeon *morgus*. Lawguards patrolled nigh constantly, yet it was naive to say there were no conflicts among the people—the tensions still ran high. But Lucien stood for none of it and installed punishments severe enough that the intolerant now thought thrice.

As he walked the streets, he fended off as many roving bands of merrymakers as he could—women offering him fruit from their stalls, shopkeeps holding out legs of cured lamb to him, a girl with a flower basket floating a ring of lilies over his head with a giggle. It was harder to blend in to a crowd now, what with his eyepatch, but part of him was at peace with it. He no longer felt the need to skulk around in Whisper's gear, stealing trinkets and redistributing the wealth to the poorer. He was helping in far more overt ways, on his own accord, and that required no disguise.

But that didn't mean he didn't hear the call of the shadows anymore.

He managed to slip away down an alley, cleaner than the ones he remembered but no less cramped and surreptitious. A new city meant a new layout, one he hadn't memorized as well as he'd liked, but he'd taken to using such breaks to wander, to map in his head the streets and curbs he loved so much. His boots clicked down the cobblestones, around puddles of piss and piles of discarded junk. The smell of horse dung and old vomit was almost a welcome perfume—it'd been quite disturbing to walk the alleyways at their clean, odorless inception.

And then he heard the footsteps behind him.

He whirled around, convinced it was another overeager citizen, but the alley behind him was empty. Nothing but cobble. He shook his head and chalked it up to a stray watertell hiss and continued his way down the narrow path. It branched out into a little plaza with a snake fountain, a newer one replete with silver binding and fewer gems. With water so plentiful in homes, people rarely used the fountains anymore, but this left them to be admired, and this he did for some time before crossing the plaza into another alley.

The former prince was so busy mentally tallying the left turns of this alley that he almost missed the soft rustle of fabric behind him. He whirled again, and this time his suspicions did not fade.

"Who's there?"

Crime was crime—ever-present as long as mortals were present—but he'd done his best to catch the swindlers and conmen who tried to prey upon the rebuilding people. He didn't want to use magic against such criminals if he could help it—preferring mortal methods. He gripped the white mercury sword at his side, knowing to draw it would be pointless in such a small alley.

And so he ran.

And the person behind him ran, too, footsteps echoing.

He raced through the alley, throwing trash bins and paper

piles to the side to distract his stalker. They were fast, and good—he could hear them leaping over the debris easily, redoubling their pace.

But he was better.

He called his crow form and flung himself over the wall to his left, white feathers whirling in his wake as his feet touched ground and his cloak streamed behind him. His human legs pumped again, ducking around a butcher's blood run and through a stretch of low, drying herbs on twine. He was losing them—he was sure of it. Their footsteps were fading.

And then he swung himself around a corner and, without his perfect mental map of the old Vetris, into an unfortunate dead end. He pulled his sword out and whirled to face his stalker, but the dead end was still too small for the blade to be swung properly.

"*Tsk, tsk.* Should've brought a dagger, Your Highness."

His mind stuttered, his ears pricking at the voice.

Surely not.

There was no way—now, of all times? *Here?* Following him like she had that first time they met? She wouldn't—this was surely a hallucination as it had been all other times, as it had been in the times in his bed, alone, in the quiet moments of a bath, a meal, where he had wished she was here, her voice playing in his head—

They appeared from the shadows, a cloaked figure.

"Enough games!" he snarled. "Who are you?"

The figure paused and then pulled her hood down.

Golden hair, spilling over shoulders. Blue-gray eyes, like autumn sky. A smirk, that beautiful smirk, pulling at her rosebud lips.

He wanted to doubt. But he couldn't. Not with that smirk.

It was her.

• • •

If one were to cross the bridge high between Hordon's Grocer and Willowtree Housing at this moment, one would see two figures in the dead end below, one black of hair, the other gold, embracing as if the world were ending, and their murmurs to each other faint.

"How—how did you survive?" the dark-haired one asked.

"I remembered," the golden-haired one replied.

"Remembered what?"

A smile, and then, "That you love me."

In the grand scheme of things, trying to eat while crying is never a good idea. But that doesn't stop Fione and me from doing it the moment I walk in on dinner and we see each other. It doesn't stop her from holding up her son, Zeran—a dark-haired little bundle of joy that does me the honor of spraying spittle all over my face. It doesn't stop Varia from nodding at me with a faint smile. It doesn't stop Fione from pulling me through the palace and into Malachite's disbelieving arms, into Y'shennria's, into Crav's and Peligli's, who are now human and living at her orphanage. Reginall, their tutor, takes my hands gently and weeps when I show him the flower-like scar over my heart. A heart that's in my chest now. Nightsinger is the Windonhigh ambassador, Fione and I bursting into her office and her mane of tawny hair spiraling as she turns, streaking behind her like a banner as she runs to embrace me. Yorl stands no chance, either, his peppermint cordial flying everywhere as he races into my arms, asking streams and streams of curious polymath questions.

It only stops when Fione insists we share in her frankly terrible stew without a care in the world.

Chaos is, thankfully, only ever sometimes chaos. There are promises to meet again, plans and tea dates and sparring sessions and tutor visits to the orphanage, and then, finally, silence.

A silence in which only Lucien and I reside.

He leads me to the balcony of his apartment in the palace, the marble of it still dusted with sand from the construction.

In Lucien d'Malvane's outstretched hand is a bag that reads Heart.

"I never told you, did I?" He smiles down at me with velvet affection. "Why I stitched that word."

"I assumed it was because you were running low on creative juice." I smirk.

"Not quite." He takes my hand and presses the bag into it. "My heart. You're my heart, more than the one in my chest."

The swell of tears in my eyes starts again, but this is too happy a moment for them to fall. They hang there, bright and sparkling in the twilight, as my smirk melts to a smile.

"Has anyone ever told you you're rather corny, Your Highness?"

His kiss comes suddenly, like a shooting star, burning sweet on my lips and buzzing in my stomach—he remembers. He remembers our silly little promise, his joking threat to kiss me whenever I called him that. Even now. Even three years later. Maybe he thought about it every day. Three whole years. He's been waiting for three years, and all of it pours out of him and into me: the longing, the joy, the dreams, all the nights and days we missed, and all the nights and days we'll have together from now on.

"No." His dark gaze glitters back at me when he pulls away. "Most probably because I've never been in love with anyone but you."

A laugh bursts out of me, and it feels like all three years of being apart vanish with that one joyous sound.

"Stop, please. Any more and I'll be forced to throw you in jail."

"Dungeon-jail," he corrects.

"I did call it that, didn't I?"

"What feels like ages ago," he agrees, lacing his wooden hand in my free one.

There's a sunset quiet, the balcony of the former palace overlooking the busy construction below, the children—Crav and Peligli and Perriot included—running after one another in the grass, Varia and Fione sitting together under a tree napping on each other's shoulders with Zeran in their lap, Malachite arguing pettily with Yorl as they oversee the metallic matronics moving some wood and stone to and fro, Nightsinger gracefully leading a stream of new ambassadors from the Star Continent on a tour around the grounds.

"What will you do now, Zera Y'shennria?" Lucien asks, voice dour and serious so that for a moment, I see the old him. The young him, the first time I walked into the throne room on that fateful Spring Welcoming day.

I look down at the empty bag where my heart used to be and put my hand to my chest. Every memory is back where it belongs. Every part of me is me again. My parents, my hunger, my journey—all of it is here, with me. I listen to the beating of my heart. Every time is new, every time feels like the first, and I grin mischievously.

"Live."

THE BEGINNING

ACKNOWLEDGMENTS

At the end of all things comes the beginning of the rest of forever.

Things are hard, aren't they? Writing is hard, and living is hard, too. I wrote this series because a monster of a girl inside me wanted out and wanted to be loved. And now you've seen her, and heard her, and from the bottom of my heart, I thank you.

Sometimes, it is enough just to be seen and heard.

For my mother, Deb, and my father, Michael, thank you for the chance to be here, now, writing.

For my friends—Sarah H, GW, Ana, thank you. I'm a loner by nature (XD), but you make things bearable.

For the history books, I'm writing this deep, deep in the bowels of a pandemic. This book was put together in the middle of a pandemic, and that is something remarkable. A terribly huge thank-you to Entangled, to Stacy and Lydia and Curtis and Heather and Bree and everyone who's had a hand in making this book come to life, thank you. A special thank-you to Yin Yuming, the wonderful cover artist for Book One and Two. You brought Zera to true life.

To the reader—thank you. Every word was made for you. Every word, I hope, gives you the strength to carry on. You are free now. I love you.

Zera will always be here when you need her. When you need to fight. When you need to laugh.

We're on to the next journey, aren't we?

TURN THE PAGE FOR A SNEAK PEEK OF
THE EPIC, NEW FANTASY SERIES

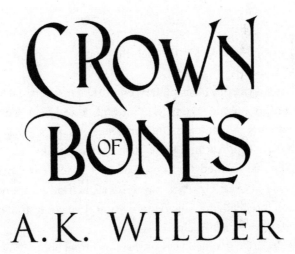

A.K. WILDER

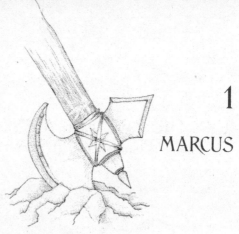

1

MARCUS

Morning light blasts through the woods, making me squint. "There! To the south."

I urge Echo, my black palfrey, on to greater speed, the hunting dogs falling behind. We gallop hard, neck and neck with True, my brother's mount, careening around giant oaks and jumping over fallen logs. Autumn leaves scatter in our wake.

"They're headed for the meadow," Petén calls over the pounding hooves. His dark hair streams behind him, revealing his high forehead, an Adicio family trait. I've got it, too, but not quite as pronounced as his.

We're alike in other ways—same tall, broad build, brown eyes, and olive skin, though my hair is the color of brass, not black. Also, Petén's nineteen, two years older than me, and non-savant—he can't raise a phantom. It's a blow to him, because I am savant and therefore Heir to the Throne of Baiseen, a fact that turns everything between us sour.

"Head them off." I signal toward the upcoming sidetrack.

"So you can beat me there and win all the praise?"

I laugh at that. Father's not going to hand out praise for anything I do, even catching Aturnian spies, if that's what the trespassers really are. Besides, palace guards are coming from the south and will likely reach them first, so I don't know what Petén's talking about. He's right, though—I wouldn't mind being the one to stop them, just in case Father is watching. "Race you.

Loser takes the sidetrack!"

He nods, and our mounts tear up the path for a short, breakneck sprint. Echo wins by half a length, and I stand up in my stirrups, victorious, waving Petén off to the right. On I gallop, a downhill run toward the meadow. When I reach the open grass, there's a clear shot at the three men who race on foot.

"Halt in the name of the Magistrate!" I fit an arrow to my bow and fire it over their heads, a warning shot. I wouldn't actually shoot anyone in the back, but they don't know that.

"Halt in the name of Baiseen!" Petén yells, bursting into the meadow from the north.

The hunted men veer to the left and keep running. Petén lets loose his arrow, and it lands just short of them, another warning.

I'm close enough to pick off all three. "Halt!" I shout, hoping they do this time.

They don't.

My brother and I barrel down on them, and in moments, we've corralled the men, trotting our horses in a tight circle, arrows aimed at the captives in the center. The dogs catch up and bark savagely, ready to attack.

"Stay," I command the two wolfhounds, and they obey, crouching in the grass, tongues hanging out to the side as they lick their chops and growl.

"Drop your weapons," Petén says just as Rowten and his contingent of palace guards, three men and two women, gallop into the field from the other end. Chills rush through me as Father appears behind them, riding his dark-red hunter. The captives unbuckle their sword belts and raise their hands as the guards join us, further hemming them in.

"Why are you here?" Father asks as he rocks back in the saddle. He turns to Petén. "Search their gear, if you are sober enough for the job." To me, he says, "If any move, kill them."

Sweat breaks out on my brow, and a tremor runs down my

arms. My brother's not all that sober. In fact, he usually isn't. If he provokes them...

But Petén swings out of the saddle without falling on his face, and I keep my arrow aimed at each man in turn while he goes through their packs. They have a distance viewer and a map of Baiseen marking where our troops are quartered, the watchtowers, and the Sanctuary with numbers in the margin.

"Scouting our defenses?" Father asks. "Who sent you?"

Officially, we're not at war with the neighboring realms of Aturnia and Sierrak to the north or Gollnar to the northwest. But that doesn't mean one of their red-robe masters isn't behind this. Tann or even Atikis. Relations are strained to near breaking if the long council meeting I sat through yesterday was any indication, and Father suspects breaches on the border. Like this one.

The captives remain silent, which doesn't help their case.

"Answer." I try to sound authoritative. "Or do you not know who questions you? Bow to Jacas Adicio"—I nod to my father—"orange-robe savant to the wolf phantom, Magistrate of all Palrio, and lord of the Throne of Baiseen."

The middle one lifts his head. He's not dressed in the robes of a savant or an Aturnian scout. He wears traveler's garb: leggings, tunic, riding coat, and high boots without a hint of mud. Their horses can't be far away. "We're lost, Your Magistrate, sir. Meaning no harm or trespass. If you just set us straight, we'll be on our way."

It's a fair attempt at diplomacy, but unfortunately for this poor clod, his accent betrays him.

"All the way from Aturnia? You are *indeed* lost." My father turns to me. "Did you track them down, Marcus?"

My chest swells as I start to answer. "It was—"

"I led the chase," Petén cuts in as if I wasn't going to give him half the credit. Which I was...probably.

"Fine," Father says, though he doesn't seem particularly

pleased. I can't remember the last time he was anything but frustrated with either of us. But then, it's no secret he's not been the same since my eldest brother was deemed marred. Losing his first son changed Father irrevocably.

While I blink sweat out of my eyes, the nearest captive makes to drop to one knee.

"Savant!" I shout.

"Shoot!" my father roars in command.

He means me.

I have the shot, ready and aimed, and I should have taken it by now. But the man is ten feet away. If I hit him at this range, with an arrow made to drop an elk, it'll stream his guts all over the meadow.

As I hesitate, my father is out of his saddle in an instant and touching down to one knee. The second he does, the ground explodes, a rain of dirt and rock showering us. The horses' heads fly up, ears pinning back, but they hold position as Father's phantom lunges out of the earth. The size of a dire wolf, it opens its mouth, lips pulling back in a snarl. Still not clear of the ground, it begins to *"call,"* a haunting, guttural sound that can draw weapons from a warrior, water from a sponge, flesh from bone. Before the phantom lands, the men's chests crack open in a spray of blood. Three hearts, still beating, tear out of their torsos and shoot straight into the phantom's mouth. It clamps its jaws and, not bothering to chew, swallows them whole.

Entranced by the brutality, my fingers spasm, and the arrow flies from the bow. Its distinct red fletches whistle as it arcs high and wide over one of the guard's heads, a woman who gives me an unpleasant look. The arrow lands, skipping through the grass to land harmlessly a distance away.

No one speaks as the horses settle and Rowten signals for the dogs to be leashed. I breathe heavily, staring at the corpses, blood welling in the cavities that were, moments ago, the bodies of three living men. Aturnian spies, most likely, but living men just the same.

But what if I got it wrong? What if the man had simply gone weak in the knees and wasn't dropping to raise his phantom at all? What if he really was non-savant, lost, virtually harmless to us? I cried out the warning that led to these deaths. What does that say about me?

"Peace be their paths," Rowten says, and we all echo the traditional saying used when someone dies. The path to An'awntia is the spiritual road everyone treads, though us savants are supposedly much further along.

I'm not so sure in my case.

When I look to Petén, I find him staring at the bodies as well, until he turns away and throws up in the grass. Somehow that makes me feel better, though I don't think it has the same effect on our father, judging by his expression.

Father examines the dead men's weapons. "Aturnian," he says and lowers gracefully to one knee, his phantom melting away as he brings it back in. It's a relief. Phantoms don't usually scare me, not those of our realm, but this one's different, more powerful, and so much better controlled than most. Merciless. If Father had continued training at the Sanctuary, he'd be a red-robe by now, and not very many savants ever reach that high level. I shudder at the thought.

Before mounting up, he turns to Rowten. "Take the dogs and find their horses. Then call for the knacker to deal with this mess." In an easy motion, he's back on the hunter, shaking his head as he turns to me. "You raise a *warrior* phantom, Marcus. When will you start acting like it?"

Heat rushes to my face, and Petén, wiping his mouth on his sleeve, chuckles. Any warmth I felt for my brother moments ago vanishes.

"Ride with me, both of you," Father commands.

The road home is short and agonizing as we flank Father, one on either side.

"Petén, if I catch the reek of alcohol on your breath again, I'll take away your hunting privileges for so long, you'll forget how to ride."

"Yes, Father," he says quietly. "Sorry."

My lips curl until Father turns to me.

"Marcus," he says, his voice a newly sharpened knife. "You know war is inevitable—if not now then certainly by the time you are meant to take the throne. Baiseen needs your *warrior!*"

A subtle reminder of my failings. "Yes, Father."

"If you can't master your phantom soon, you'll lose your vote at the Summit as well as your right to succeed me." His eyes narrow. "You know this?"

"I do."

"Then why are you acting so bones-be-cursed *weak*?"

I couldn't choke out an answer even if I had one. Even Petén looks away. My eyes drop to Echo's mane as it ripples down her neck. When I look up, Father's face turns to stone. He cracks his reins over the hunter's rump and gallops away.

Petén and I trot the horses back toward the palace, cresting a gentle rise to come out on the hill overlooking the expanse of Baiseen. The view takes in the high stone walls and gardens of the palace, the watchtowers and bright-green training field in the center of the Sanctuary, all the way down the terraced, tree-lined streets to the harbor and the white-capped emerald sea beyond. It's beautiful, but no matter where I look, those three dead men seep back into my mind.

"If they were spies, then war's coming sooner than we thought." I ease Echo to a halt. "But if they weren't, we'll have to—"

"We?" Petén cuts me off. "Keeping the peace when Father tempts war is your problem, little brother, not mine." He chuckles. "If you make it to Aku in time, that is." His face cracks wide with a smile. "This year's your last chance, isn't it?"

I open my mouth to answer, but he's already pushing past me, loping the rest of the way down to the stables.

Yes, it's my last chance, the last training season on Aku before I turn eighteen. That's when our High Savant, head of the Sanctuary, will hand me over to the black-robes if I haven't held my phantom to form. It would mean no initiate journey. No chance to gain the rank of yellow-robe or higher. No future voice at the council. No Heir to the Throne of Baiseen.

No trained *warrior* to help protect my realm.

The weight on my shoulders grows heavier. I know my father. He'll not let this incident with the spies go, and his actions may finally bring the northern realms down upon us. My thoughts lift back to those three nameless men. When I close my eyes, I can still see their shocked faces, hear bones cracking as their chests split open, smell the blood spattering the ground.

War draws near. And if our enemies are infiltrating our lands, I may already be too late.

Let's be friends!

@EntangledTeen

@EntangledTeen

@EntangledTeen

bit.ly/TeenNewsletter

entangled teen

an imprint of Entangled Publishing LLC